DEEP
THROAT
DIVA

Dear Reader:

All that I can say is that you need to fasten your seatbelt for this one. Cairo has spun a tale that will make even the prissiest woman on earth become fascinated with performing oral sex on her man. The sex scenes in this book are scorchers. Better have a cold drink nearby to cool you off; real talk.

There is more to the book than that, though. It is a delightful read that delves deep into the psyche of a woman who fulfills her desires in a most unique way and also justifies her actions by considering herself to remain true to her real love. Hmm, this should spark a lot of conversation. It is rumored that a lot of younger people, especially, consider themselves to be abstaining from sex if they only engage in oral pleasure. Personally, I believe that sex is sex and any type of intimate contact outside of the confines of a committed relationship is cheating. But not the sister in this book. She sees nothing wrong with her actions...at first.

I am not going to give this story away. The title pretty much says it all but be prepared for a lot of twists and turns in the storyline; surprise elements that only a talented voice such as Cairo could come up with. You will not be able to put this book down once you start it. You will want to know how it turns out and the ending will leave you speechless.

As always, thanks for the continuous support of Cairo, myself, and the other Strebor authors. We strive to bring you a diversified lineup of titles and the feedback has been outstanding. If you would like to visit me on the web, please check out my main website at www.eroticanoir.com or join my online social network at www.planetzane.org where all of the Zaniacs mix and mingle.

Blessings,

Zane

Zane
Publisher
Strebor Books International
www.simonandschuster.com/streborbooks

ALSO BY CAIRO

Daddy Long Stroke

The Manhandler

The Kat Trap

ZANE PRESENTS

DEEP THROAT DIVA

A NOVEL BY

CAIRO

SBI

STREBOR BOOKS

NEW YORK LONDON TORONTO SYDNEY

Strebor Books
P.O. Box 6505
Largo, MD 20792
http://www.streborbooks.com

ISBN 978-1-59309-301-3
ISBN 978-1-4391-8405-9 (ebook)
LCCN 2010940495

First Strebor Books trade paperback edition March 2011

Cover design: www.mariondesigns.com
Cover photograph: © Keith Saunders/Marion Designs

10 9 8 7 6 5 4 3

Manufactured in the United States of America

For information regarding special discounts for bulk purchases,
please contact Simon & Schuster Special Sales at 1-866-506-1949
or business@simonandschuster.com

The Simon & Schuster Speakers Bureau can bring authors to your live event.
For more information or to book an event, contact the Simon & Schuster Speakers
Bureau at 1-866-248-3049 or visit our website at www.simonspeakers.com.

THIS BOOK IS DEDICATED TO
the Queen of seduction, *Allison Hobbs*,
for being a supporter, colleague, and true friend.
I have nothin' but deep admiration, respect and love for you!

ACKNOWLEDGEMENTS

To the sexually liberated and open-minded: Thanks for embracin' the sexual revolution with me, responsibly and respectfully. Continue to let ya freak flags fly!

To my publicist—and pimptress (inside joke), Yona Deshommes at Simon & Schuster: Thanks for doing what you do best. Keep crackin' that whip!

To the growing number of readers, and fans, who continue to support my work, spread the word, and email me your comments: Thank you, thank you, thank you! I 'preciate the luv!

A special shout out to Jennifer Moore in Lewisville Texas: Thanks for being...you!

To everyone who has visited my website and blog (and who keep returning for more of the Cairo juice): From China to Egypt—and all over the US, the stats are lookin' real crazy. Thanks!

And, last but not least, to the naysayers: Understand this. Not only do I write to challenge peeps to take an honest look at their own sexual behaviors and choices, I write to entertain, to entice, and...yes, to make peeps horny. Raw, graphic, and in ya face. So if my style of writing isn't for you, it's okay. I don't take it personal. I 'preciate all of the constructive (and destructive) criticism, none-theless. So, thank you!

One luv~

Cairo

2005

"Aye, yo, you need to let me know now if you're gonna ride this shit out with me 'cause I ain't beat to be up in this muhfucka stressin' 'bout dumb shit, feel me?"

"I'm not going anywhere. I'm with you, baby."

"Aiight, that's what it is. I'ma need you to hold it down out there. Keep that shit tight, ya heard? Don't have me snappin' out 'cause you done got caught up in some bullshit."

"Whatever."

"Whatever, nothin', yo. I'm tellin' you now, Pasha, don't have me fuck sumthin' up. I didn't ice ya hand up for nothin', yo."

"Jasper, please, I'm not beat for another nigga. Four years ain't shit. I keep telling you that."

"Yeah, and? I'm gonna keep sayin' the shit 'cause I know how hot in the ass broads are when a nigga gets behind the wall. They be on some ole other shit."

"Well, I'm not them."

"Oh, so you not hot in the ass?"

"Yeah, for you. But not for any other nigga."

"You better not be either, yo, word up. Let me find out you done had another muhfucka hittin' that shit and I'ma bust yo' ass."

"Nigga, please. The only thing you're gonna be bustin' is a bunch of nuts in them hands."

"Yeah, aiight. I gotta buncha nuts for ya ass, ya heard? Talk slick if you want, but I'm tellin' you, yo."

"I heard you. And I'm telling you. I'm all yours in mind, body and soul. This pussy and my heart are for you and you only. And I got it on lock until you get home."

"You better."

"I promise, baby. I do."

ONE

You ready to cum? Imagine this: A pretty bitch down on her knees with a pair of soft, full lips wrapped around the head of your dick. A hot, wet tongue twirling all over it, then gliding up and down your shaft, wetting it up real slippery-like, then lapping at your balls; lightly licking your asshole. Mmmm, I'm using my tongue in places that will get you dizzy, urging you to give me your hot, creamy nut. Mmmmm, baby…you think you ready? If so, sit back, lie back, relax and let the Deep Throat Diva rock your cock, gargle your balls, and suck you straight to heaven.

I reread the ad, make sure it conveys exactly what I want, need, it to say, then press the PUBLISH tab. "There," I say aloud, glancing around my bedroom, then looking down at my left hand. "Let's see how many responses I get, this time."

Ummm, wait…before I say anything else. I already know some of you uptight bitches are shaking your heads and rolling your eyes. What I'm about to tell ya'll is going to make some of you disgusted, and that's fine by me. It is what it is. There's also going to be a bunch of you closeted, freaky bitches who are going to turn your noses up and twist up your lips, but secretly race to get home 'cause you're as nasty as I am. Hell, some of you are probably down on your knees as I speak, or maybe finishing up pulling a dick from out of your throat, or removing strands of pubic hair from in between your teeth. And that's fine by me as well. Do you, boo. But, let me say this: Don't any of you self-righteous hoes judge me.

So here goes. See. I have a man—dark chocolate, dreamy-eyed, sculpted and every woman's dream—who's been incarcerated for four years, and he's releasing from prison in less than nine months. And, *yes*, I'm excited and nervous and almost scared to death—you'll realize why in a minute. Annnywaaaay, not only is he a sexy-ass motherfucker, he knows how to grind, and stack paper. And he is a splendid lover. My God! His dick and tongue game can make a woman forget her name. And all the chicks who know him either want him, or want him back. And they'll do anything they can to try to disrupt my flow. Hating-ass hoes!

Nevertheless, he's coming home to *me*. The collect calls, the long drives, the endless nights of sexless sleep have taken a toll on me, and will all be over very soon. Between the letters, visits and keeping money on his books, I've been holding him down, faithfully. And I've kept my promise to him to not fuck any other niggas. I've kept this pussy tight for him. And it's been hard, *really* hard—no, no, hard isn't an accurate description of the agony I've had to bear from not being fucked for over four years. It's been excruciating!

But I love Jasper, so I've made the sacrifice. For him, for us! Still, I have missed him immensely. And I need him so bad. My pussy needs him, aches for the width of his nine-inch, veiny dick thrusting in and out of it. It misses the long, deep strokes of his thick tongue caressing my clit and its lower lips. I miss lying in his arms, being held and caressed. But I have held out; denied any other niggas the privilege—*and* pleasure—of fucking this sweet, wet hole.

The problem is: Though I haven't been riding down on anything stiff, I've been doing a little anonymous dick sucking on the side from time-to-time—and, every now and then, getting my pussy ate—to take the edge off. Okay, okay, I'm lying. I've been sucking a lot of dick. But it wasn't supposed to be this way. I wasn't supposed to become hooked on the shit as if it were crack. But, I have. And I am.

Truth be told, it started out as inquisitiveness. I was bored. I was lonely. I was fucking horny and tired of sucking and fucking dildos, pretending they were Jasper's dick. So I went on Nastyfreaks4u.com, a new website that's been around for about two years or so. About eighteen months ago, I had overheard one of the regulars who gets her hair done down at my salon talking about a site where men and women post amateur sex videos, similar to that on Xtube, and also place sex ads. So, out of curiosity, I went onto their site and browsed around on it for almost a week before deciding to become a member and place my very own personal ad. I honestly wasn't expecting anything to come of it. And a part of me had hoped nothing would. But, lo and behold, my email became flooded with requests. And I responded back. I told myself that I'd do it one time, only. But once turned into twice, then twice became three more times, and now—a year-and-a-half later, I'm logged on *again*—still telling myself that *this* time will be the last time.

I stare at my ring finger. Take in the sparkling four-carat engagement ring. It's a nagging reminder of what I have; of what I could potentially end up losing. My reputation for one—as a successful, no-nonsense hairstylist and business owner of one the most upscale hair salons in the tri-state area; winner of two Bronner Brothers hair show competitions; numerous features in *Hype Hair* magazine, one of the leading hairstyle magazines for African-American women; and winner of the 2008 Global Salon Business Award, a prestigious award presented every two years to recognize excellence in the industry—could be tarnished. Everything I've worked so hard to achieve could be ruined in the blink of an eye.

My man, for another, could…will, walk out of my life. After he beats my ass, or worse—kills me. And I wouldn't blame him, not one damn bit. I know better than anyone that as passionate a lover as Jasper is, he can be just as ruthless if crossed. He has no problem punching a nigga's lights out, smacking up a chick—or breaking her jaw, so I already recognize what the outcome will be if he ever finds out about my indiscretions. Yet, I still choose to dance with deception, regardless of the outcome.

As hypocritical and deceitful as I've been, I can't ever forget it was Jasper who helped me get to where I am today. He's been the biggest part of my success, and I love him for that. Nappy No More wouldn't exist if it weren't for him believing in me, in my visions, and investing thousands of dollars into my salon eight years ago. Granted, I've paid him back and then some. And, yes, it's true. I put up with all the shit that comes with loving a man who's been caught up in the game. From his hustling and incarcerations to his fucking around on me in the early part of our relationship, I stood by him; loved him, no matter what. And I know more than anyone else that I've benefited from it. So as far as I'm concerned, I owe him. He's put all of his trust in me, has given me his heart, and has always been damn good to me. And, yes, *this* is how I've been showing my gratitude—by creeping on the internet.

He won't find out, I think, sighing as I remove my diamond ring from my hand, placing it in my jewelry case and then locking it in the safe with the rest of my valuables. Jasper gave me this engagement ring and proposed to me a month before he got sentenced while he was still out on bail. He wanted me to marry him before he got locked up, but I want to wait until he gets released. Having a half-assed wedding was not an option. But, there'll be no wedding if I don't get my mind right and stop this shit, soon! *I'll stop all this craziness once he gets home.* This is what I tell myself, this is what I want to believe. The fucked-up thing is that as hard as I have tried to get my urges under control, there are times when my "habit" overwhelms me; when it creeps up on me and lures me into its clutches and I have to sneak out and end up right back on my knees sucking down another nigga's dick.

See. Being a seasoned dick sucker, I can swallow any length or width without gagging, or puking. I relax, breathe through my nose, extend my tongue all the way out, and then swallow one inch at a time until I have the dick all the way down in my throat. Then I start swallowing while I give a nigga a nice, slow dick massage. The shit is bananas! And it drives a nigga crazy.

I sigh, remembering a time when I once was so obsessed with being a good dick sucker that I used to practice sucking on a dildo. I had bought myself a nice black, seven-inch dildo at an adult bookstore when I was barely twenty. At first, it was a little uncomfortable. My eyes would water and I'd gag as the head hit the back of my throat. But, I didn't give up. I was determined to become a dick-swallowing pro. Diligently, I kept practicing every night before I went to bed until I was finally able to deep throat that rubber cock balls deep. Then I purchased an eight-inch, and practiced religiously until I was also able to swallow it. Before long, I was able to move up to a nine-inch, then ten. And once I had them mastered, it was then, that I knew for certain I was ready to move on to the real thing. I've been sucking dick ever since.

The only difference is, back then I only sucked my boyfriends, men I loved; men who I wanted to be with. But now...now, I'm sucking a bunch of faceless, nameless men; men who I care nothing about. Men I have no emotional connection to. And that within itself makes what I'm doing that more dirty. I realize this. Still—as filthy and as raunchy and trifling as it is, it excites me. It entices me. And it keeps me wanting more.

As crazy as this will sound, when I'm down on my knees, or leaned over in a nigga's lap with a mouthful of dick while he's driving—it's not him I'm sucking; it's not his balls I'm wetting. It's Jasper's dick. It's Jasper's balls. It's Jasper's moans that I hear. It's Jasper's hands that I feel wrapped in my hair, holding the back of my neck. It's Jasper stretching my neck. Not any other nigga. I close my eyes, and pretend. I make believe them other niggas don't exist.

The *dinging* alerts me that I have new messages. I sit back in front of my screen, take a deep breath. Eight emails. I click on the first one:

Great ad! Good-looking married man here: 42, 5'9", 7 cut, medium thick. Looking for a discreet, kinky woman who likes to eat and play with nice, big sweaty balls, lick in my musty crotch, and chew on my foreskin while I kick back. Can't host.

I frown, disgusted. *What the fuck?!* I think, clicking DELETE.

I continue to the second email:

Hey baby, looking for a generous woman who likes to suck and get fucked in the back of her throat. I'm seven-inches cut, and I like the feel of a tight-ass throat gripping my dick when I nut. I'm 5'9, about 168 lbs, average build, dark-skinned. I'm a dominate brotha so I would like to meet a submissive woman. I'm disease free and HIV negative. Hope you are too. Hit me back.

Generous? Submissive? "Nigga, puhleeze," I sigh aloud, rolling my eyes. *Delete.*

I open the next three, and want to vomit. They are mostly crude, or ridiculous; particularly this one:

Hi. I'm a clean, cool, horny, married Italian guy. I'm also well hung 'n thick. I'd love to put on my wife's g-string, maybe even her thigh-

highs, and let you suck me off through her panties, then pull out my thick, hot cock and give me good oral. I'm 6'2", 180 lbs, good shape. Don't worry. I'm a straight man, but behind closed doors I love wearing my wife's panties and getting oral. I hope this interests you.

I suck my teeth. "No, motherfucker, it doesn't!" *Delete.* What the fuck I look like, sucking a nigga who wears women's panties? *Straight man, my ass!* Bitch, *you a Miss Honey!* I think, opening up the sixth email.

Yo, lookin' for a bitch who enjoys suckin' all kinds of cock. Hood nigga here, lookin' to tear a throat up. Not beat to hear whinin' 'bout achin' jaws and not wantin' a muhfucka to nut in her mouth. I'm lookin' to unzip, fuck a throat, then nut 'n bounce. If u wit' it, holla back.

Delete.

Ugh! The one downside of putting out sex ads on the internet, you never know what you're going to get. It's hit or miss. Sometimes you luck up and get exactly what you're looking for. But most times you get shit even a dog wouldn't want. Truth be told, there's a bunch of nasty-ass kooks online. And judging by these emails, I'm already convinced tonight's going to be a bust. Try to convince myself that it's a sign that it's not meant to be, not tonight anyway; maybe not ever again.

My computer *dings* again. I have three new emails. My mind tells me to delete them without opening them; to log off and shut down my PC. But, of course, I don't. I open the first email:

5'11", 255 lbs, trim beard, stache, stocky build, moderately hairy, and aggressive. Always in need to have my dick sucked to the extreme! I love a woman who is into my cum. Show it to me in your mouth and all over your tongue, then go back down on my dick and try to suck out another load.

That's right up my alley, I think, deleting the note, *but not with you. Your ass is too damn fat!* I move onto the next email:

6'3", 190 lbs, 6" cut. Black hair, brown eyes. Here's a pic of my dick.

If you like, hit me back. Before I even open his attachment, I'm already shaking my head, thinking, "no thank you" because of his stats. Don't get me wrong. I'm by no means a size whore, but let's face it…a nigga standing at six-three with only a six-inch dick. Hmmph. He better have a ripped body, a thick dick, and be extra damn fine! I click on the attachment, anyway. When it opens, I blink, blink again. Bring my face closer to the screen and squint. I sigh. His dick is as thin as a No. 2 pencil. Poor thing! I feel myself getting depressed for him. *Delete!* I click on the third email:

Do u really suck a good dick? If so, come over and wrap your lips around my 8-inch dick until I bust off on your face or down in your throat. 29, 6'1, decent build here. Horny as fuck for some mind-blowing head.

I smile. Maybe there's hope after all, I think, responding back. I type: *No, baby, I'm not a good dick sucker. I'm a great one! Send me a pic of your body and dick so that I know your stats are what you say they are. And if I like what I see, maybe you can find out for yourself.* Two minutes later, he replies back with an attachment. I open it, letting out a sigh of relief as I type. *Beautiful cock! Now when, where, and how can I get at it?*

I know, I know, aside from being risky and dangerous, I am aware that what I am doing is dead wrong. No, it's fucked up! However, I can't help myself. Okay, damn…maybe I can. But the selfish bitch in me doesn't want to. I mean, I do try. I'll go two or three days, even a week—sometimes, two—and I'll think I'm good; that I've kicked this nasty habit. It's like the minute the clock strikes midnight—the bewitching hour, I become possessed. I turn into a filthy cumslut. In a local park, dark alley, parking lot, public restroom, deserted street in the back of a truck—I want to drop down low and lick, taste, swallow, a thick, creamy nut. Either sucked out or jacked out; drink it from a used condom or a shot glass—I want it to coat my tonsils, and slide down into my throat. Not that I've gone to those extremes. Well, not to *all* those extras. But, I've come close enough.

And tonight is no different. Here it is almost one A.M. and I should have my ass in bed. Instead, once again, I'm looking to give some good-ass, sloppy, wet head; lick and suck on some balls; deep throat some dick, gag on it. And maybe swallow a nut. Yes, tonight I'm looking for someone who knows how to throat fuck a greedy, dick-sucking bitch like me. I'm looking for someone who knows how to fuck my mouth as if they were fucking my pussy, deep-stroking that pipe down into my gullet until my eyes start to water.

Ding! He replies back: *You can get this cock, now! No games, no BS, just a hot nut going down in your throat. I'm at the Sheraton in Edison. Room 238.*

I respond, practically drooling: *I'm on my way. Be there in 30 mins.*

I get up from my computer desk, slip out of my silk robe, tossing it over onto my American Drew California-king sleigh bed. Standing naked in front of my full-length mirror, I like...no, love, what I see: full, luscious lips; perky, C-cup tits; small, tight waist; firm, plump ass; and smooth, shapely legs. I slip into a hot pink Juicy Couture tracksuit, then grab my black and pink Air Max's. I pin my hair up, before placing a black Juicy fitted on my head, pulling it down over my face and flipping up the hood of my jacket. I grab my bag and keys, then head down the stairs and out the door to suck down on some cock. I glance at my watch. It's 2:24 a.m. *Hope this nigga's dick is worth the trip.*

TWO

"Girrrrrrrrrrl," Felecia draws out while popping her chewing gum as soon as I step through the salon's door, "ya man has been blowin' up this line all mornin' tryna get you. He's called ten times in the last forty minutes." She pops her gum again. *Click-clack, click-clack.*

Felecia is my first cousin, and salon manager. And, although she's one of the most efficient and dependable women I know, she can also be a bit extra at times. But she means well and she always has my back. Besides, she's my eyes and ears. She keeps up with all the street news, and shop gossip. And trust me. If there's any dirt to be dished, she's going to be the one to serve it up. With her ear to the ground and her BlackBerry Curve attached to her hip, she doesn't miss a beat when it comes to the goings-on in the hood, or on Facebook, Twitter, MySpace, and BlackPlanet.

"What'd you tell him?"

"I told him you didn't have any appointments scheduled until noon so you probably wouldn't be in until about eleven-thirty or so."

"Thanks," I say, wondering why the hell he didn't call me at the house. I glance around the salon, taking in the happenings. For a Wednesday it's surprisingly packed. Most often, Wednesdays tend to be one of our slowest days for some reason, but not today. I count sixteen clients seated in the reception area; another seven customers are at nail booths getting their nails hooked up by nail technicians. And six clients are sitting under dryers.

I spot my twelve o'clock, Janelle, lounging in one of our lush spa chairs that has an electric-heated massager with brown leather cushioning and whirlpool footbath. She has her shoulder-length hair pinned up in a clip. Janelle's been one of my most loyal and faithful customers for the last nine years. And it's taken me almost eight of those years to get her hair together. Because, baby, let me tell you. Girlfriend's hair was tore up the first time she sat down in my chair. It was all broken off and uneven, and her edges were a hot, scattered, raggedy mess. I had to basically give her a close cropped boy cut and start from scratch. She hemmed and hawed and talked shit but when she started seeing results, she shut her trap and let me do what I know best—*hair*. Now girlfriend's mane is to die for. And she comes in faithfully every two weeks to keep it tight, along with her feet and hands. Then every two months she comes in for a waxing. I smile, watching Alicia and Anna—two of my best mani-and-pedicurists, tend to her. Alicia is filing her nails while Anna scrubs her feet.

I watch as another customer takes a seat in one of the other nine spa chairs to get her toes done. Two more customers follow behind Shuwanda—another stylist—to the waxing room, used for those more personal areas, like cleavages, snatches, pits, asses, backs and legs. Women's eyebrows, mustaches, and beards are usually done at one of our stylists' stations.

One of the things I love about my salon is that we offer one-stop services. From a wrap and a weave to twists and locks to braids and a rinse and set; from manicures and pedicures to facials, threading and waxing, Nappy No More is here to offer you the very best salon experience. Aside from me, two of my nail technicians and four stylists also have an aesthetician license to do facials and waxing.

"How many appointments do I have for today?" I ask, glancing over at Felecia.

She flips through the schedule book, counts. "Looks like five. Oh, and Greta called. She wanted to know if you could squeeze her in sometime tomorrow. I told her you were booked solid, but she said it was an emergency; something about having a date tomorrow night."

I shake my head, chuckling. *That girl is a damn mess*, I think, grabbing the mail. Greta is another longtime client, close friend, and social butterfly extraordinaire, whose hair I've been doing since high school. This girl, love her dearly, has more dates than an almanac. Every time you turn around she's going out on some kind of date. I think for a moment. *Let me see. Wanda, she wants an updo; Bianca, wants her ends trimmed; Mona, is getting a hot oil treatment. Lynn, needs a color treatment; Cynthia, wants her blunt bob with graduated layers; Knowing Greta she'll want a Doobie Wrap, which won't take me too long.* I decide to tell Felecia to squeeze her in between Bianca and Mona. "And tell her I said to bring me lunch."

"Will do. Oh, and one more thing. Erica called. She wants to know if you can see her Friday; apparently she wasn't happy with her new stylist and wants to come back to you."

I frown, rolling my eyes. When someone decides to go to another hair salon because they're not happy here for whatever reason, that's their prerogative. And I'm okay with that because I want all of our clientele to be completely satisfied. But, when you bounce talking shit about how you'll never set foot back up these doors, that's a no-no. You keep your ass right where you are! "Mmmph. So they done jacked up her scalp and now she wants me to fix it."

"Basically," Felecia says, shrugging her shoulders.

"Wrong answer. Tell that nappy-headed bitch I don't need her business."

She laughs, snapping her fingers. "Well allriiiight." *Click-clack, click-clack.* "I knew you were gonna say that." The phone rings;

she answers on the first ring. "Nappy No More. How can I help you?" She pauses, mouths, "It's Jasper." I tell her to transfer the call to my office, walking off.

Janelle sees me as I head toward my office and throws her free hand up and waves. I wave back, glancing at the clock. It's only eleven, so she still has time before she gets in my chair. I say hello to a few of the customers sitting underneath dryers.

I toss the mail up on my desk, then unlock my bottom desk drawer and place my bag inside before locking it back. As soon as my private line rings, I pick up. "Hey."

"Aye, yo, where you been? I've been calling you all mornin'."

"What do you mean, where I've been? I've been home. Why didn't you call there?"

"I did and the shit kept going into voice mail. I called last night up 'til count, then called you this morning and the same shit. Where the fuck was you at?"

"Nigga, I just told you I was home."

"Then why you ain't pick up the damn phone, yo?" *Shit,* I think, shaking my head. *I forgot to turn the ringers back on.* He's already tight—about what I have no idea, so I already know if I tell him that shit, he's going to snap.

I decide to tell him a half-truth. "I didn't hear the phone. When I got home last night, I was exhausted. The only thing I wanted to do was crawl into bed and pass out."

"Yeah, aiight. And I called you this mornin', too, yo. So where were you?"

"I already told you."

"I'm tellin' you, Pasha. Don't be on no bullshit, yo."

"I'm not on anything. But I *would* like to be up on that pretty-ass dick," I say, lowering my voice and trying to change the subject. "I'm so fucking horny."

He calms down. Usually this is all it takes to get him to shut the fuck up. I swear, I love this man, but he can make shit so damn difficult. You'd think he'd be more mellow now that his time behind the wall is short, but noooooooooo. He seems to be getting moodier, and more agitated.

"Oh, word? I'm horny, too." He sighs, pausing. "Man, I'm tired of this shit. I'm ready to come the fuck home, yo. This prison shit is for the birds, word up. I need some muhfuckin' pussy. I need my dick sucked. And I wanna eat some ass, bad."

"I know. I'm ready for you to come home, too. How you think I feel? I need some dick, bad. I'm tired of playing in my pussy. I miss that big dick, baby."

"Fuck! You got my shit bricked. I can't wait to get home and bust that hole wide open. You better not be out there giving my pussy out, yo."

I suck my teeth. "Not this shit again."

"'Not this shit again', my ass, yo. I don't know where the fuck you was last night, or this morning."

"Fuck, nigga," I snap, switching the phone from one ear to the other. "I told you, I was home. I didn't hear the damn phone because I was fucking drained. And this morning I went to the gym for an hour, from there I went to Wegmans, and then had to go to the cleaners to drop clothes off. By the time I got home, it was already going on ten, so I only had time jump in the shower and get dressed, then race out the door."

"Yeah, aiight. Why you ain't say all that shit in the first place? Let me find out some other shit, aiight?"

I sigh. "There is no other shit to find out, fool."

"I'm tellin' you, Pasha, don't have me fuck nothin' up, yo."

"What. Ever."

He lowers his voice, going from one extreme to the other. "Yo, what kinda panties you got on? We got time to get it in before your appointment?"

I glance at my watch. It's almost quarter to twelve. If I go in on him now, I should be able to get him off in like ten minutes, maybe fifteen. But that'll be pushing it. I am a stickler about not having my clients wait. If I give them an appointment time, then that's what it is, unless it's an emergency situation. Otherwise, I think it's poor business practice to have someone sitting around waiting for you when they've made an appointment.

"Hold on," I tell him, placing the receiver down on the desk, then getting up to lock the door. I return to the phone and sit back behind the desk. "I have on a purple thong."

"Damn, yo...I wish I could smell them shits; you know, suck on 'em while I beat this dick."

I smile. *He's such a nasty ass.* "Ooh, baby, I wish you were here so I could suck all over your dick. Spit all over it, and gulp it down. Aaaah...baby, I miss that dick. I can't wait to feel it deep in my hot pussy..."

"Yeah, baby, talk that nasty shit, yo..."

"You want me to straddle your face, and lower this wet pussy down on your mouth, so you can suck my clit and tongue fuck me while I swallow your fat, black cock?"

"Aaah, shit yeah..."

I glance at my watch. *Five minutes to go. I have to speed this up.* I speak in a low throaty whisper, careful that no one walking past my office door can hear me. But if I were home, I'd be panting and moaning loud as hell. I keep my eye on my watch. Count the seconds, then the minutes. "Oh, baby, you got my hole so slippery..."

"Yeah, you like how this dick feels?"

"Oh, yes...fuck me! Uh...fuck me! Uhhh...aaah shit...you making me cum, baby..."

"Yeah, take this dick, baby...bounce that ass up on it..."

"Fuck me! Harder…faster…deeper…uh, ooooh…you got my pussy so wide open…"

"Yeah, that's my pussy…I'ma tear that shit up…"

"Fuck your pussy, nigga…Uhhh, uhhhh…oh, yes…like that…"

"Oh, shit I'm gettin' ready to bust…Oh, fuck…"

"Give me that nut, baby…bust that nut deep in my pussy…"

"Uh, uh, uh…aaaaah, shiiiiiiit, yo." He lets out a deep breath. "Whew. I needed that nut."

"Me, too," I lie. Truth is I wasn't even touching myself. Most times I don't, especially when I'm here at the office. I need, want, the real thing. The only thing this phone shit does is make me hornier, more frustrated and more eager to go out and suck another damn dick. Especially since the nigga I sucked last night, well early this morning, nutted in seven goddamn minutes, literally. Hmmph. He had a nice juicy eight-incher, too. And I was greedily sucking the shit out of it before he cracked his nut all quick and whatnot. I tried to give him the benefit of the doubt since he told me my throat game was like no other he'd ever experienced. So I sucked him another round. Unfortunately, the nigga still busted off quicker than I liked. But he was able to hold out for a whopping fifteen minutes before his knees started buckling. So, basically, I spent more time on gas and travel time than on sucking dick. What a waste! "Look, baby, I gotta go. It's almost twelve."

"Aiight, do you. I'ma hit you up later tonight, aiight?"

"Okay, cool."

"And make sure you answer the damn phone."

"I will," I say, rushing him off the line. "Talk to you tonight." We say our "I love yous", then hang up. I get up and go into my private bathroom to use the toilet, then freshen up a bit. My mind should be on all these heads I have to do today, but the only thing on my brain at this very moment is getting home tonight and posting another ad.

THREE

Mmmm, daddy…feed me your thick, throbbing dick. Your balls swollen and heavy with cum. Sit back and get a slow, hot, wet and nasty, toe-curling slob job you'll always remember. Spread my lips. Move in deep. Feel my lips surround your cock as my wet tongue licks you; as the warm fleshiness of my mouth engulfs you. Go deeper. Feel my throat hold the bulbous head of your dick. Oh, yes, daddy, take my mouth; own it, fuck it as if you were fucking my pussy. You ready to get sucked? If so, PLEASE provide me with your accurate stats: age, ht/wt, race, etc.

I couldn't wait until I finished up my last head tonight and was able to jet up out of my shop so I could post this ad. Talking to Jasper earlier had me so worked up that it was hard for me to concentrate. All afternoon my pussy tingled, thinking about potential prospects for tonight. And I'm hoping there will be a much better selection of men to choose from than there's been for the last few days. I may be horny for cock, but I will never, ever, be desperate for it. Sucking bottom-of-the-barrel niggas is a no-no!

Tonight, I have decided to widen my search. Although I predominately suck black dick, there have been a few occasions where I have broadened my options and been open to other ethnicities, particularly Italian and Hispanic men. Provided they look good and their dicks aren't all pink or red-looking, like a half-cooked sausage. Yuck! Pale-skinned men do nothing for me. When I'm sucking a dick, I don't want it so bright and light that it's almost glowing in the dark. I also tend to seek out married men, for the obvious reason. I don't want any damn drama. And they aren't looking to leave their wives; just looking to get what they aren't getting at home, most times—a good dick sucking.

Ding. I have one email. I open it:

Hello. You sound like my kind of woman. MBM, 5'10", 175 lbs; well-endowed. Home alone and need my dick sucked exactly like what you describe in your post. My wife's away, can host.

Hmmph. When a man says he's "well-endowed" that shit tells me nothing about the type of cock he *really* has. So if he wants me to wet his dick, he is going to have to be a bit more descriptive, along with sending me a pic. Interestingly with this email, I know I shouldn't be too keen on going over to his home to suck him off. However, the thought of his wife walking in on us and trying to attack me, or him, fascinates and excites me. The idea of sucking a man's dick in his home while his wife's away and the thrill of getting caught entices me to disrespect her space. I type:

Hey there. Thanks for the response. How old are you? Is your dick thick and cut? I'm not in the mood for any little dick tonight, so please, let's not waste time. Send a pic of the goods. Thanks!

I have two more emails. I smile, opening up the first one. *Hey, nice post! 31, 6'2", 205 lbs, nice build, blk man. Looking to get this thick seven-and-a-half sucked tonight. Do have wifey so must be discreet.*

I reply: *Baby, discreet is my middle name. Is your dick cut?* I open the next email:

Black male, 39, available all day and night, would love for you suck this dick. I'm also looking to fuck a tight, wet pussy. I live alone and can host. Please be able to take a good, long 20 to 30 minute dicking. I like to get nasty and fuck hard.

Well, good for you. But you won't be fucking me. I shake my head. This fucker done banged his head thinking twenty minutes is a good, long "dicking." Hell, I'm just warming up around that time. Give me a break! That's a tease for me. I can already tell that the minute I clamped my mouth around his cock, and started gulping him down, this fool would nut in less than fifteen minutes. Baby, please! The last thing I'm interested in is a repeat of last night's quick-draw cum action. I delete his email. One, for not following instructions to provide his full stats; and, two, for being stupid enough to think a twenty- to thirty-minute dicking is something spectacular.

Mr. Seven-And-A-Half sends me another email: *Yeah, I'm cut. Do you swallow?*

I purse my lips, typing: *Good! And to answer your ? Not tonight, daddy! It's a suck and spit session.*

Yes, I will shamefully admit that I do love to swallow a hot nut, or two, from time to time. Or have it splatter on my face. However, swallowing or letting someone bust in my mouth isn't something I do all the time, or with everyone. But on occasion I will suck the snot out of a dick, then either swallow or spit it out. Most times I let them nut on my face, then smear it all over my lips, or I take off my shirt and let them shoot their cream all over my beautiful tits. It all depends on my mood at that very moment. The hornier I am—the nastier he talks, the more likely I'm going to get freakier with it. Nevertheless, I set the stage. I set the rules. And I decide whether or not to suck a dick raw or to wrap it up. Rubberized—dry, flavored, or otherwise—fellatio is always on my terms.

And on those days I'm using condoms, I typically use an ultra thin condom, like the Trojan 2Go condom—I like these particularly because they come in a pocket-sized card instead of a regular wrapper—or the TROJAN THINTENSITY condom. I also like using the Durex Rainbow colored condoms from time to time. And when it comes to using flavored condoms, my favorites are the banana- and strawberry-flavored ones by Trustex. I don't particularly care for the grape, chocolate, cola or vanilla ones. But I do like the idea that they're all colored according to flavor. And the best part is—they're sugar-free! So I don't have to feel guilty sucking down extra pounds.

Then there are times when I want to give a man a tingly feeling while I'm sucking his dick without the actual, flavored taste in my mouth. That's when I use a MAXPRO mint condom. It's a condom that has a mint lubricant that gives a man a tingly sensation. And what I like most about these condoms is that they come in a sleek, metal case. I use my mouth to roll this bad boy down on a dick, then suck away, giving him a sensationally mind-blowing orgasm. Mmmph!

I receive another email from Mr. Well Endowed. *I'm 8 inches, uncut.*

Oh, okay. Thanks, but no thanks. Only sucking cut dick. I delete his email, getting up from my computer. It's already going on ten o'clock and I was hoping to have something lined up by eleven so that I can dip out, drop down low, then be back home and in my bed by midnight. But judging by the way things are looking, it doesn't seem like that's going to be the case.

I head downstairs to the kitchen to get a bottle of Dasani water. For some reason I'm feeling dehydrated. I take a few gulps, then set the bottle down on the counter as my iPhone rings. I glance at the screen, rolling my eyes. It's Jasper's cousin, Stax—well, Monty. Stax is his nickname 'cause he's six-feet-six and chiseled down. And word has it he's walking with a third leg and a set of balls the size of two juicy plums. Every chick down at the shop has been drooling over him for years, except for me. Personally, as fine as he is, I've never looked at him sexually. He's cool as hell, but the way he leers at me whenever he comes around tells me he's definitely been looking at me *that* way. Not that he's ever said anything out of pocket 'cause he's always been gentlemanly and respectful around me. It's just a vibe he gives off. So to avoid any potential situation that could become awkward, I try to keep my distance from him. Besides, Jasper would break his fucking jaw if he ever found out he was checking for me, cousin or not.

"Hey, Stax," I answer, sitting at the kitchen table.

"What's good wit' you, ma?"

"Nothing much; chilling. How've you been?"

"I'm chillin', baby girl. You know how I do."

"I heard that. So, what's up?"

"You goin' down to see Jasp this weekend?"

"Yeah, on Sunday. Why?"

"That's wassup. I was hopin' to hop a ride wit' you. My whip is in the shop 'til Monday, but I wanna get down there to see my fam, feel me? It's been a minute since I've seen 'im, so I wanna go down and holla at the kid. I spoke to 'im earlier today and told him I was gonna holla at you to see if it was aiight. He said it wouldn't be a problem, but you know I wanted to make sure wit' you, first, feel me? I got you on all the gas and tolls."

I take a long swig of water, then swallow hard. Now why the fuck can't he ride down with one of his boys, or his brother, instead of trying to ride with me? The last thing I want to do is be on a two-and-a-half-hour road trip with Stax. My God, that's five hours up and back. I mean, damn…what the hell are we supposed to talk about all that time cooped up in a car together? When I take that long ass ride down to Bridgeton in Cumberland County to see Jasper, I like to take it alone. I hook up my iPod, play my beats, and ride that stretch of road like there's no tomorrow. And if I feel like stopping into AC on my way back to do a little gambling, meeting up with some dick that I've set up the night before, or do nothing at all except bring my black ass home—I can. *It's only a damn ride, Pasha; get over yourself. You're bugging about nothing.*

"That's fine," I finally say, reluctantly.

"That's wassup. Which visit you goin' to?"

Now he should know there's no way I'd ever go on the first visit. Registration is from eight to ten in the morning which means I'd have to be up and out of the house by six. Not hardly. This diva needs as much sleep as possible. "The second one," I tell him, getting up from the table, tossing my empty bottle of water into the trash, then turning out the light. I check to make sure the front door is locked, already knowing it is, before setting the alarm, then heading back upstairs to check for any new emails. "Since registration starts at twelve, I'd like to be on the road no later than nine-thirty."

"Oh, aiight. That's cool."

I sit in front of my computer. I have six new emails. "Okay, I'll be at your place around nine-fifteen."

"Aiight, see you then."

"Good night," I say before disconnecting the call, then eagerly clicking open the first email. It's from Mr. Seven-And-A-Half. *That's cool. I still want you to come wrap your soft lips around this dick. And show me how good you can suck it. U still down?* There's an attachment. I smile, opening it. My mouth instantly waters. It's dark brown and shaped like a miniature baseball bat. Of course, I won't respond one way or the other until I open up all the other emails.

36, 5'6", 155 lbs, brown hair/eyes, light-skinned. 5.5 inches cut. Wrong answer! I delete, clicking open the next email. *You sound like a sexy chick. I'm 24, 6'2", athletic build, black, thick, cut 7.5 dick looking to chill with a cool-ass chick and be sucked. Hit me back.* I decide to save this one for those nights I'm in the mood for some young cock, then go to the third email. *6'2, 240 lbs, mod. Hairy, 5" cut. Would love a deep, wet BJ from you.*

*C'mon now…*five *inches? Umm, what the fuck am I supposed to do with that? Pick my teeth with it?* I let out a disgusted sigh, clicking DELETE. I open the next email. *29, 165 lbs, 5'11" and horny with a full ten days' worth of cum. I want to unload in a hot, hungry mouth.* I delete, deciding to quit while I'm ahead and reply back to Mr. Seven-And-A-Half.

I type back: *Beautiful cock, baby. Do u nut fast?* He must have been sitting at the computer, waiting, 'cause I'm surprised when he hits me right back. *Depends. I haven't bust in four days so I'm sure if you are as good as you say you are, I probably will. But I get hard again real quick and can last much longer the next round.*

Isn't that something, I think, grinning, *a man anticipating a second round. I like him already.* We go back and forth for about three more emails before deciding to meet at twelve-thirty at the parking garage in downtown Elizabeth on the third level. He has a tinted SUV so I'm going to climb up in his truck, then suck him down.

It's already going on eleven-thirty. I hop in the shower to do a quick rinse, then brush my teeth and tongue, followed by a Listerine swish and gargle before putting on a pair of Baby Phat jeans and an orange hooded pullover. I try to be as inconspicuous as possible, careful not to wear anything too flashy or over the top. I pull my orange fitted down over my eyes, grab my keys, then head down the stairs and out the door.

"Damn, ma, you fine as hell," Mr. Seven-And-A-Half says when I open the door of his burgundy Lexus GX470 and climb in.

I smile, licking my bottom lip. "And you're not so bad looking yourself," I tell him, downplaying his looks. But the nigga is extra F-I-N-E. He's the color of milk chocolate and has the nerve to have hazel eyes. "Let me feel that dick," I say, reaching over and grabbing at his sweats. I rub his crotch, and feel his dick stiffen. He leans his seat all the way back, putting his right arm up over the back of the passenger headrest. "I'm gonna suck this real good for you."

"Oh yeah," he says in a low, husky voice. "Show me."

I tell him to lift up his shirt. He does, revealing a wave of tight, rippled abs with a patch of hair around his navel. I lick his stomach, groping his growing hard-on before sticking my hand down in the waistband of his sweats, then fishing out his dick. He doesn't have on any underwear, and I'm impressed with what I feel. It's hot and heavy and thicker than it looked in his picture.

"I hope it tastes as good as it looks," I say, running my tongue up and down the backside of it, cupping his heavy balls, then slowly swirling my tongue around the head and over the slit.

He lets out a low moan.

I lap it nice and slow. Suck it lovingly; kiss it soothingly before opening my mouth, unlatching my jaws, and taking him all the way into my hot, hungry mouth. The head of his dick hits the back of my throat. I swallow. Let him block my airway and feel the snugness of my throat while licking his balls. My eyes water but there's no gagging going on. I bob my head up and down as he thrusts his hips upward. Spit dribbles down around his balls. I pull his dick from out of my throat, then start sucking and jerking him off simultaneously.

He moans again, starts shifting in his seat. "Aaah, shiiit…uh…

damn, ma…ohhh, fuck…Gotdamn, baby…you know howta suck some dick…. Uh…fuck…you 'bout to make me nut…"

I pick up speed, sucking and slurping and making popping sounds with my mouth. Loving the way his rock-hard cock feels in my hands, in my mouth, down in my throat. I suck him as if my life depends on it for survival. Lick him as if he's a dripping ice cream cone. Pop him as if he's the sweet sticky treat inside of a Charms lollipop. I alternate from throating him to sucking him to jerking and sucking him to licking him to throating him all over again until he hums and moans and chants and grabs the back of my head, palming it like a basketball, bouncing it up and down on his shaft.

"…I'm…uh…gettin'…oh, shiiiiit…ready…mmm, fuck…to…yeah, baby…uhhhh…"

I pull up off his dick and rapidly start jerking him off, twirling my hand over the head of his spit-covered cock. "Let me see you bust this fat dick…you liked that deep throat?"

"Aaaah, shit…oh…fuck yeah…" I start sucking on his balls, wetting them up, pulling them into my mouth one at a time, until I have them both in my mouth. A few minutes later, Mr. Seven-And-A-Half's left leg starts to shake. He lets out a loud grunt and then shoots his nut up at the roof of the truck. "Whew, gotdaaaaaaaamn, ma, that was the best fuckin' head I've had, word up. You got that shit on lock, baby."

I smile as I pull out two mango-scented Pleasure Wipes from my bag, handing him one, then using the other to wipe my mouth. "Glad you enjoyed it," I say, opening the door.

He catches his breath, looks at me glassy eyed. "Enjoyed it?" he repeats, sluggishly. I stifle a snicker. Yeah, I practically sucked the life out of him. "Nah, I loved that shit, ma. If my girl sucked my dick the way you just did, I'd never leave the fuckin' house."

"Well, I'm sure she can try to match my skills. But know this, there's only one Deep Throat Diva, baby. And I'm it."

He grins, fixing himself. "That you are," he says, eyeing me. "Baby, you're a champion dick sucker and sexy as fuck. You can definitely make a cat fall for a fine-ass beauty like you."

"Although I couldn't blame him," I say, grinning, "I would strongly advise against it."

"Yeah, I feel you. You got a man?"

I laugh. "All you need to know is: I have a long throat."

"Yo, you got a number I can hit you up on?"

"Have a good night, Mister Seven-And-A-Half."

He laughs, shaking his head. "You, too, ma. I'ma holla."

I close the door, walking off toward my car with the taste of his cock on my breath, smiling. I wait for him to pull off, then back out of my space, screeching off. *I need to hurry and get home to play in my sopping wet pussy.*

FOUR

"Good morning. Nappy No More. Pasha speaking." I glance at the wall clock. It's 8:36 a.m. I wait for the recording to finish, then press ONE.

"Hey, baby," Jasper says. "How you?"

"Hey. I'm good, and you?"

"Chillin', chillin'. Happy to hear my baby's voice."

I smile. He sounds like he's in a good mood—for the moment, that is. No telling how long it will last, though. "It's always good to hear yours, too."

"It better be," he teases, "wit' ya, apple head. Or you know there's gonna be repercussions like a muhfucka, right?"

I laugh. "Yeah, yeah, okay. I see someone's been reading the dictionary this morning. What, that's your new word for the day—repercussions?""

"Oh, you got jokes? You think there won't be?"

I decide to appease him. 'Cause bottom line, I know there will be. "Baby, I know it's gonna be whatever you say."

"And don't forget it, either. So what you'd do last night?"

"Oh, nothing much; I laid around with a wet pussy waiting for you to call; that's all."

"Damn, baby. Sorry 'bout that. I got caught up talkin' to Stax last night. Did he hit you up?"

"Yeah, he did."

"Cool. So he's ridin' down with you on Sunday?"

Without thinking, I suck my teeth. "Yeah," I say, flatly.

"Why you say it like that?"

"Like what?"

"Like you ain't really beat."

"I'm not. I mean. Stax is cool and all, but I don't feel like being in a car with him for two hours. That's a bit much. I don't know why he can't rent a car, or get a ride down there on Saturday with one of your boys. Hell, he should wait until his car gets fixed."

"Yo, hol' up. You actin' like you got some kinda beef wit' the nigga."

"I don't have beef with him."

"Then why you trippin'?"

"I'm not tripping."

"Then chill. You talkin' like it's some regular-type shit. Scoop my fam up, and be done with it, aiight?" He sighs, pausing. "Damn. It ain't that serious."

"I know it's not. I already told you, I'm picking him up. I was only telling you how I felt about it. Sunday is our only time together, and I don't wanna sit there and share it with him, or anyone else?"

He laughs. "Awwww, let me find out, my baby, wants me all to herself. You want big daddy all to yourself, baby?"

No, what I want is an empty *passenger seat.* "You already know," I say, glancing back up at the clock. It's five minutes to nine. The shop'll be open in another hour or so. I flip through the appointment book. I have four clients scheduled today, and will probably end up with a walk-in or two before I bounce out of here tonight.

"I feel you, sexy. Don't sweat that shit, though. I'ma be home in a minute, feel me? Then it's on. We nonstop fuckin'—*hard*, ya heard?"

"Mmm-hmm," I moan, pressing my thighs together, remembering how good Jasper used to use his lips, his mouth, his tongue, his fingers, his deliciously thick dick—to work my pussy over until it ached and throbbed and erupted. I open my mouth to tell him how much I need to feel him inside of me, but the call is abruptly disconnected.

He'll call back, I think, watching Felecia at the door, trying to maneuver carrying a Dunkin' Donuts bag and her morning dose of Hazelnut coffee while digging into her Michael Kors python-trimmed leather hobo bag for the door keys. I walk over and open it for her.

"Thanks," she says, walking in, then shutting the door with the back of her foot. "You're here awful early this morning."

"Yeah, I have a nine-thirty."

"Oh, I thought your first appointment wasn't until noon."

"It was," I tell her, walking over to my workstation, "but Bianca called last night and asked if she could come in this morning."

"Oh, okay. She hasn't been in here in a while."

"Yeah, and I'm sure her ends are a hot-ass mess, too. She keeps cancelling her appointments."

"I guess that baby's been keeping her busy."

"I guess so," I say, glancing up at the wall clock. It's 8:55 a.m. "I know one thing. I hope she doesn't come waltzing up in here all late and wrong. I coulda stayed in bed a little longer." I yawn, covering my mouth. "Oooh, 'scuse me."

"Sounds like someone had a late night."

I shake my head. "Not hardly," I lie. "For some reason I couldn't get to sleep last night. And when I finally did, it was time to get up again."

She opens up her bag and starts digging inside. She pulls out a bottle. "Here, I have some NoDoz if you need them."

I chuckle. "Thanks, but no thanks. I'll be alright."

"Okay," she says. "Girl, I almost forgot. Did you hear about what happened to Cassandra?"

I make a face, confused. "Cassandra? Cassandra who?"

She sucks her teeth, sitting her coffee down on the counter. "You know Cassandra. Cassandra Simms." I shake my head, still clueless. "Uh, hello...Big Booty."

"Oh, why the hell didn't you say that? I only know that ho by her street name."

When Cassandra was in middle school, all the high school niggas started calling her *Big Booty* 'cause she had a tiny waist, peach-sized titties and this humongous, bubblicious ass that bounced and shook when she walked. Niggas would be sniffing behind her, drooling and whatnot, all mesmerized by the size of her ass. And she'd have them eating out of the palm of her hand—and crack of her ass—for a ride in it. And not a damn thing's changed. Her body is still tight, and that ass of hers is still bouncing and shaking niggas out of their minds. The only thing is the bitch is mildly retarded. Well, I don't know that for a fact, if she is or not. But she definitely seems a bit special. I do know, growing up, she spent a lot more time on her back and in the back seats of cars than she did in those remedial classrooms she was supposed to be in. And now all she has to show for her big, juicy ass is nine brats, six baby-daddies, an EBT card, and Section 8 housing. Oh, but she keeps her and her kids laced in all the fly shit, keeps her hair and nails done like clockwork, and is driving a new GTS Cadillac SUV. But has no savings. What a trifling mess!

"No, what happened to her? Don't tell me she's pregnant, *again*." It was more of a statement than a question.

She laughs. "No, her hot ass ain't pregnant, again. But she's laid up in the hospital."

"What happened?"

"She was fucking some young, hood nigga from around her neighborhood, and his girl done went to her house to confront her, then ended up slicin' the side of her face wit' a razor."

"What, are you fucking serious?" I ask, shocked. Not at the fact that Big Booty got her face slashed—although that's fucked up, but the idea that bitches are still pulling out razors and slicin' faces is too extra for me.

"Chile, that ain't the half of it. Her three oldest kids jumped on the chick and beat her ass into the ground. They kicked and stomped her all up in her face and whatnot and now her head's the size of a pumpkin."

I give her an incredulous look. "OhmyGod, are you serious?"

"Baaaaby, serious as a damn heart attack; they dragged her ass something terrible.

"Big Booty had to get ninety-seven stitches to her face, her kids got arrested, and the girl's in the hospital with a concussion, broken nose, and fractured eye sockets."

"Wow," I say, shaking my head. "I hope that dick was worth it. Is she still messing with those credit cards?"

"Yeah; and she done got buck wild wit' 'em, too. I think she's addicted to the shit."

I shake my head. Her ghetto ass's been fucking with stolen credit cards for almost four years, thanks to some scam artist-slash-hood-nigga she used to fuck with. He showed her how to make a buncha purchases, then sell the shit on the streets. Then when his ass got knocked on burglary and theft charges, she started going to his connect to make moves on her own. Unfortunately, the nigga wanted some pussy and head from her ass, so she eventually started sucking and fucking him to ensure the cards kept coming in.

I look over at the door as it opens. Bianca walks in. She looks fabulous. "Girl, motherhood must be all that," I say as she removes her coat. She's stylishly dressed in a pair of tight-fitting jeans that leave nothing for the imagination. She has them tucked into a banging pair of chocolate knee-high boots. And she has a cute, form-fitting brown and beige sweater that hugs her full breasts, and narrow waist. There's not one ounce of baby fat on her. You'd never know she recently gave birth. "You look good, boo."

She laughs, walking over toward me. "Thanks," she says as she sits in the styling chair. "I never thought I'd be the one saying this, but motherhood is all that and some." Her eyes light up as she speaks. "My son is my pride and joy. I am so in love with him."

"Oh, I can tell. Girl, I'm happy for you. And your baby daddy?" I ask, teasing.

She blushes. "He's a great father, and a wonderful man."

"Ohhhhhkaaaay, so does this wonderful man have a name?" I ask, tying my apron on, then wrapping the shampoo cape around her neck.

"Garrett," she tells me, smiling. She lifts her left hand and flashes me her ring finger. She's wearing a glittering two-and-a-half carat princess cut engagement ring set in 18k white gold.

I gasp, clutching my chest. "OhmyGod, girl, your ring is gorgeous."

To be honest, I'm still shocked over the fact that her ass had a baby, and now to learn she's engaged. Talk about surprises. Not that we've ever been close friends, but when you're someone's hairstylist for as long as I've been hers, you start to develop a certain rapport. And, although Bianca has always been a very private woman, we've had conversations over the years about men and relationships and whatnot. And she's shared some things to me about her personal life. Not much, though. But there were two things she was clear on: One, she had no use for men, or a serious relationship with one; and, two, she had no interest in having children.

"My how fast things have changed," I say, leaning her back at the sink. I turn the water on, make sure it's the right temperature, and then begin wetting her hair. "What ever happened to your 'I'm Done with All Men' speech?" I ask as I'm shampooing her hair.

"Girl, life happened," she says, smiling. "A handsomely stubborn man came into my life and refused to be pushed aside, or dismissed. And, in the end, he won me over."

I smile, genuinely happy for her. She tells me how the pregnancy was unexpected and how she had thought about having an abortion, but couldn't go through with it. About how she thought about not telling him about the baby and raising it on her own, but felt that keeping it from him wouldn't have been fair to him because he had the right to know.

"Sounds like you did the right thing," I tell her, wrapping a towel around her head, then sitting her up in her seat.

She nods. "Yes, I did. I can honestly say I have no regrets."

I smile, understanding all too well her comment.

As I'm giving her a deep moisturizing conditioning, Shuwanda walks through the door. She speaks—actually mumbles—as she heads toward her workstation. And as usual she looks pissed off about something. But what do I care about her moody ass. She brings in a lot of money so she can mope around here every-damn-day if she wants, as long as she keeps her appointment book full. I don't bother to ask what's wrong 'cause: One, she's the type of chick who likes attention; two, I'm not in the mood to know; three, everything is always a damn crisis for her; and four, if I ask her what's wrong, she's going to say "nothing" any-damn-way. So why even bother. *That bitch is real pitiful*, I think, combing out Bianca's hair. It has gotten thick and is now almost past her shoulders since she's had the baby. But her ends are a hot mess! Just like I said they'd be. Lucky for her, there's not a lot of damage.

I part Bianca's hair into thin sections, then run it through my middle and ring finger. "Girl, you haven't been in here in months, and these ends are showing it," I say, pulling out my scissors.

"I know, girl."

I add, "You should really have your ends trimmed every eight weeks or so."

She winces at the thought, like so many other chicks who come into my shop. But they realize I know my shit when it comes to hair. I'm not like some stylists who are "scissor happy." If I tell you I'm going to trim your hair, that's exactly what I do. One-quarter to a half-inch; that's it. You will leave this chair with a *trim*, not a haircut, unless that's what you specifically ask for.

"So when's the big day?" I ask Bianca.

"We haven't actually set a date, yet. But if Garrett had his way we'd be married—*yesterday*."

I laugh. "He sounds like Jasper. Every time we talk, he's asking"— I dip into a deep voice, mimicking him—"'when we doin' this, yo?'"

She laughs. "Speaking of that fiiiine-ass man of yours," Bianca says, "he should be coming home soon, right?"

Everyone knows Jasper's locked up, so it's no secret that I've been more or less a prisoner's wife for the last four years. I nod. "Girrrrl, not soon enough. This shit has been hectic."

"I'm sure it has," she says, lowering her voice. "Personally, I don't know how you've done it. Lord knows I don't think I could have been as devoted and committed as you've been."

"Chile, it requires a whole lot of patience and a drawer full of double-A batteries."

She chuckles. "Good thing it's almost over."

"You got that right."

Shuwanda butts in. "Girlfriend's good 'cause I couldn't do it either. Melvin knows if his ass gets knocked, someone else is gonna eventually be taking his spot. This kitty needs to be stroked every two to three days; otherwise it starts clawin' my insides out. So ain't no way I'd ever be able to go *four* years, hell four weeks, without sex."

Bitch, every other week someone else is taking his spot. I keep my mouth shut.

"I'm with you on that," Bianca says, shaking her head. "It'd drive me crazy."

The door opens and in comes this very attractive, brown-skinned female I've never seen before. Behind her is this deliciously, tall, dark nigga with a neatly trimmed beard and dreads. He takes a seat while the chick is at the receptionist desk talking to Felecia. I cut my eye back over at the dude.

For a brief moment, he looks vaguely familiar to me. *Damn, I know I've seen him somewhere*, I think, taking another section of Bianca's hair and running it through my fingers. I snip the ends; *then, again, maybe not.* I erase the thought from my head as she walks over to him, then kisses him lightly on the lips. Clearly marking her territory and letting the rest of the bitches in the room know—he's taken. Shuwanda waves her over.

"New customer?" I ask her, knowingly.

She nods. "Yeah, we met a few weeks back. Her daughter goes to my son's school."

Very good, I think, smiling. *Keep them dollars coming in.* She smiles and says hello to everyone. Shuwanda introduces her as Robyn. I give her a warm welcome; introduce myself as the owner, then bring my attention back to Bianca. She quickly changes the subject, asking if we've set a wedding date, yet. I tell her no.

Robyn asks, "How long have you been engaged?"

"Almost four years," I tell her. I can almost see her thinking how crazy that is. "I know. It's been an extra long engagement."

"Oh, I totally understand. James and I have been engaged for almost three years. But we *finally* set a date."

"Good for you," I say. "Is that him sitting over there?"

She nods, beaming.

Shuwanda lowers her voice and says, "Giiiirrl, he's fine."

"Thanks," she says, smiling. "I really have to admit, I got me a damn good man."

Alicia walks by, ear hustling as usual. She stops, puts one hand on her wide hip, and says, "Chile, and a good man is hard to come by; especially one that doesn't come with a bunch of unnecessary baggage and bullshit. Or one who wants to cheat on you or beat you."

Shuwanda adds, "Or wants you to be his momma."

"Or is too damn emotionally needy," Alicia adds.

"Welllllllll," I say, raising my hand in the air. "Sounds like ya'll trying to get service started up in here. 'Cause you preaching."

Robyn's smile widens as she retrieves her phone and begins to text. "Thank God, I don't have to deal with any of that. I am truly blessed."

"Amen to that," Bianca cosigns.

A few minutes later, I peep her "blessing" getting up and walking over toward us. Everyone practically stops what they're doing, drooling as he makes his way over. My eyes are fixed on him as well, but I quickly shift them when he locks his eyes on mine. He speaks to everyone, and we all speak back.

Robyn digs in her bag and pulls out a set of keys. "By the time you get back, I should be almost done."

"Aiight, I'll be back in an hour. Ya'll ladies take care." He glances over at me on the sly.

I blink, blink again. Hearing his voice; watching his swagger, it hits me. *OhmyGod, I had this nigga's dick in the back of my throat.*

FIVE

After all this time, besides not having steady access to Jasper's dick, or being able to lay in his arms at night, I don't know what I hate more about going to see him in prison—the drive or the painstaking process. When Jasper was at Rahway State...uh, I mean East Jersey State Prison, it wasn't bad—the drive that is. Hell, we could fuck if we wanted. Not that we did 'cause there was no way I was going to play myself like that out in the open. But the opportunity to get at his dick was always there. But standing in a pen like cattle with a bunch of trifling-ass, ghetto bitches was a hot mess! And then these bitches wanna fight and argue about who cut the line, and who was standing where first. Oh, and let me not even get started on how them coons carried on once they got inside the visiting area. From hogging up the microwaves and talking shit about it—'cause you could get food out of the vending machines and heat it up—to sucking and fucking, they carried on. Straight niggerish!

Now, hold up. I'm not saying every chick who was out there to see their loved one was ghetto...but, baaaby, trust me. Most of them hoes were. Not to mention the fucking retarded-ass CO's who I believe are hired to make the whole experience as miserable and as uncomfortable as they possibly can so you'll get so pissed off that you don't wanna come back. Miserable bastards! Still, being able to see Jasper whenever I wanted—at least three, sometimes four, times a week between window and contact visits— made all the extra shit I had to go through bearable.

But, now...mmmph, forget it. The drive alone is enough to make me sick! Jasper claims the only reason he put in for the transfer from Rahway to way down here in this Godforsaken hick town was to get into a halfway house faster. He completed some kind of TC—therapeutic community—drug program, and his application to a halfway house has finally been approved. Now he's waiting to leave. And the good thing is he'll be closer to home. But, shit! In the meantime I still have to take this treacherous drive! Truth be told, I wish he would have kept his ass at Rahway. Oh, well.

I cut my eye over at Stax as I slow down and prepare to stop at a light. He's laid all the way back in his seat knocked the hell out, lightly snoring. And that's fine by me. I let my eyes roam all over his thick, muscular body longer than I should. I take in the sparkle of his diamond-crusted Rolex and pinky ring, then shift my eyes back on the road when the light turns green, making a left turn onto route 49. As soon as I turn right onto Burlington Road, he wakes up.

"Damn, ma, you aiight?"

I glance over at him. "Yeah, I'm fine. How'd you sleep?"

"Like a newborn baby," he says, smiling while adjusting his seat upward.

"A newborn?" I repeat, laughing. "More like a wild boar."

He laughs with me. "Sorry 'bout that, ma. I didn't mean to crash out on you like that. I planned on keeping you company."

"The way you were snoring," I tease, "I knew you had to be tired. So, trust me. It's quite alright. Besides, I'm used to taking this ride by myself." I can feel him staring at me. I glance over, arching my brow. "What? Why are you looking at me like that?"

He shakes his head, smiling. "Nah, I was just thinkin'."

"About?"

"How beautiful you are." I blush, shifting in my seat; visibly uncomfortable by his remark. He notices this and says, "No disrespect meant, ma. I'm sayin'. You mad cool, that's all. And you got flava that I'm sure got the nigga's sweatin' you, hard."

I force a smile. "I don't know about all that. But thanks for the compliment."

"You're a good woman, Pash." This is the only nigga outside of Jasper who I actually let call me that. Anyone else, I've always checked. But him…I don't know, I guess it's the way he says it in that Ja-Rule-sounding voice of his. "I hope Jasp knows how lucky he is."

I feel guilt rising up in me. I swallow it back, hard. "Umm, why you say that?"

"C'mon, ma, you been ridin' this bid out wit' my fam hard. And I haven't heard shit 'bout you creepin' on him. That's wassup."

Because I do my dirt discreetly. "And you won't," I say without blinking an eye.

"So you've never stepped out on him?" he asks, eyeing me as if he's not convinced.

I slowly shake my head. Rationalize in my head, lie in my heart, that what I'm doing isn't really cheating. That it's only a means to an end. Just until my baby gets home. I glance over at him. "Nope." I say, looking him dead in the eyes.

He seems surprised. "Not *ever?*"

I'm kind of surprised myself that he's sitting here asking me this shit. All the years I've known Stax, and all the times I've seen him since Jasper's been locked up, he's never come out his face to ask me about cheating. But today he is. Hmmm. *I wonder if Jasper put his ass up to this?* If you ask me, this whole ride thing is suspect. Yeah, the more I sit here thinking about it, the more I'm thinking Jasper's behind this little inquisition. I'm telling you, niggas are dumb as hell. Does this fool actually think I'd ever tell him the damn truth, knowing he'd go back and tell Jasper? Puhleeze!

"I have no desire to fuck another man," I tell him, bluntly. *Just suck his damn dick!* Well, at least there is some truth to that.

"That's wassup, ma. Not too many females out here gonna hold their man down behind the wall without having another muhfucka knockin' their guts around, feel me?"

"Well, you make sure you tell him what I said, and remind him of how lucky he is."

He grins. "Oh, I got you, ma. Jasp doesn't even know I'm kickin' this to you, though." I roll my eyes up in my head, disbelievingly. He laughs. "Nah, real talk. I was only askin'."

"Hmmm…why, are you taking a poll or something?"

He keeps laughing. "Nah, not at all. I'm sayin'…I admire you for holdin' it down. That's all."

"Thanks. But don't think this prison shit has been easy on me," I confess, quickly glancing over at him. "Doing a bid with a man comes with its challenges, trust me."

"Oh, I know it's not easy—for you or anyone else. But, look at you. You holdin' shit down. And Jasp doesn't haveta worry about you playin' him. Hell, my baby mother was shittin' on me the whole time I was locked up. And I was lucky if I got a visit once a month, if that. I couldn't really hate on her, though, 'cause when I was on the bricks I was doin' me, feel me? And she put up wit' alotta shit."

I nod, turning into the prison entrance, then driving around until I find a parking space. "I hear you. So, how ya'll doing anyway?"

"We good," he says, opening and closing his legs, then pressing his hand down into his lap. I cut my eye over at him, glancing down in his lap, then quickly shift my eyes back on the road in front of me. For a brief second, I could swear I saw a lump forming in his pants. "You know, we have our ups and downs, but it's all good."

When I finally find a parking space, I pull in, then shut the engine off, looking over at Stax. "Out of curiosity, why'd you come home to her, knowing what she was doing?"

"On some real shit," he says, pulling his bottom lip in. "She's my son's mother."

I never really noticed how his brown eyes sparkle when the light hits them until now. Damn. It's a good thing that: one, I'm not sexually attracted to him; two, I have healthy boundaries and don't believe in fucking my man's family or friends; and, three, I promised Jasper I wouldn't give up any of this pussy while he was locked up. Otherwise I'd probably have dropped down on his dick at least once by now.

I twist my lips, raising my eyebrow. "That's the only reason?"

"Nah," he says, pausing. "I had no other place to go."

"And now?"

"'Cause she's pregnant again," he says, opening his door. I open mine as well, but don't get out of the car until after I check my face and whatnot in the mirror. I put on a fresh coat of lipstick, then pull the key out of the ignition. I remove my ID and money from my wallet, then pop the trunk to put my handbag inside. I get out of the car, then make sure my prison garb—a simple, ankle-length, long-sleeved black dress and a cute pair of four-inch, black Prada heels—is on point. Yes, I'm going to a prison, but I still have to keep it sexy. However, I try not to wear anything that is too revealing or provocative—no cleavage, nothing form-fitting. No open-toed shoes. Or anything that is beige, tan, or orange (because the inmates wear those colors) to keep the CO's from turning me away, like I've seen them do to other chicks. And just in case there's a hating-ass female officer on duty, I keep a change of clothes in the trunk for backup.

"By the way, congratulations," I finally say, grabbing my clear plastic purse with my tokens for the vending machines out of the trunk, then shutting it and activating the car alarm.

"For what?"

"For having another baby," I say, tilting my head.

"Yeah, thanks."

"Wow, you don't sound too happy about it."

He stuffs his hands in his front pockets. "I'm not. But, hey, what am I gonna do? She wanted another baby."

Hmmph, why the hell females wanna keep having babies is beyond me. This'll be her third child. One with some dude she was fucking with way before Stax, and now two with him. Two damn baby daddies. I catch myself from rolling my eyes up in my head. I shake my head. Poor thing!

SIX

After we sign in, we go through security. Now this is the shit I really hate—the fucking pat-downs! The security here has been tighter over the last several months. Jasper was telling me how there's been a lot of drugs being smuggled up in here, and how the CO's have been running down on them with the dogs and whatnot. Still, what this ho is doing doesn't feel right. Hell, it isn't right! It feels more like a grab-down the way this mannish, manhandling bitch is grabbing at my goddamn titties! I know the frisks are to make sure no one's bringing in contraband—like so many dumb-ass bitches do, but this he-man bitch right here is taking it a bit too far if you ask me. It's almost like the freaky bitch is trying to get her rocks off. I want to scream on her black ass. But I keep my mouth shut 'cause I'm not trying to have her cancel my visit. Like she did a few weeks ago to this chick—who, by the way, takes two buses and a train, then walks from the train station to get here—because she said something slick to her about the way she was grabbing her up. I felt so bad for her.

Anyway, after the frisking, we finally get to the visiting area and find a table facing the door that the inmates come out of so that Jasper can see us as soon as he walks out. I scan the room, looking at all these Bama-fied bitches in their late wears, some of them carrying snotty-nosed babies, dragging loud-ass toddlers, or both. There's a sprinkle of decent-looking chicks with some cute kids here. And you can tell they have good home training. Then there are the mules, the bitches smuggling in the damn drugs, stuffing them in their pussies, all in the name of love—and in the promise of a life with their men beyond these walls. Promises that'll be broken the minute the nigga touches down.

The more I look around the room, the more disgusted I feel myself becoming. I am so sick of this shit! Some of these chicks look so comfortable and happy and excited being here. And here I am, sitting here—in my designer wear and bling—feeling so out of place. This whole prison shit is depressing.

"Yo, I'ma hit the bathroom," Stax says, snapping me out of my thoughts. "You want something outta the vending machine while I'm up?"

I shake my head. "No, I'm good. Thanks." I watch him walk toward the men's room, then glance down at my watch. We've been here for almost ten minutes already. Five minutes later, the first batch of inmates are coming out. I keep my eye on the door, waiting. Then scan the room, turning my lips up as two female CO's walk in. Jasper had pointed them out a few months ago, telling me how they were both fucking inmates here. Hmmph. Nasty bitches! How the hell you gonna be fucking on the job? Yeah, I'm doing what I'm doing, but I'm not jeopardizing my damn career and livelihood behind it. I've heard over the years how some chicks have gotten caught up in a bunch of bullshit over some jailhouse cock.

Ten minutes later, another batch is coming through the door. Jasper is the fourth one to enter. Even in his prison-issued khakis, he's still a sexy motherfucker! He quickly scans the room looking for me. I smile, standing up. His face lights up as he smiles back at me. I admire him as he makes his way over to me. His swagger is so damn thuggish and sexy. I feel my pussy clenching and unclenching as I stare at the imprint of his dick.

"Damn, baby, you look good as hell," he says, sweeping me up in his arms before quickly kissing me on the lips, then sliding his tongue in my mouth. His kiss is deep and passionate, and in that brief moment, filled with an overwhelming love. We don't linger too long 'cause the CO's will get on their bullshit. He takes a seat next to me.

"Yo, where's Stax?" he asks, looking around the visiting area. I tell him he went to the bathroom. "Oh, aiight. So how you?"

"I'm good. And you?"

"Better now," he says, wrapping an arm around me, pulling me into him. He kisses me on the side of the head. "I miss you, girl."

"I was just here last week," I say playfully. I peep Stax over by the vending machine talking to some chick. From where I'm sitting she looks like she might be a pretty chick. I point over in his direction. "There he is over there."

"Yeah, I see him," he says, looking over there, then bringing his attention back to me. "Aye, yo, don't start ya bullshit, ya heard?"

I frown. "What in the world are you talking about?"

"Don't think I didn't peep that slick lil' comment you made. So what if you were here last week? What that gotta do with me missin' you?" He stares at me hard, searching my eyes for something—lies, maybe.

"Nothing," I tell him, staring back at him, smiling. "I miss you, too."

"Oh, aiight. You better. Damn, you smell good. What's that you have on?" I tell him it's Euphoria by Calvin Klein. "Oh, word? That shit's makin' my dick hard."

I smile. "Nigga, your dick stays hard."

"Damn straight, baby; rock-solid. You keep a nigga horny wit' ya sexy ass." He leans over on me and whispers. "Put ya hand under the table, and play wit' my dick."

I suck my teeth, rolling my eyes. Then quickly search the area to see where all the CO's are. They all seem preoccupied so I slide my hand over into his lap and rub the bulge that's pressed against the inner part of his thigh. The mouth of my pussy instantly starts to pucker. I feel my juices slowly stirring inside of me.

"You like that shit, don't you?" he asks in a low voice. I nod, keeping my eyes locked on all the CO's. He brushes his lips to my ear and whispers, "I wish I could fuck you right here on this table. I want some pussy so bad."

His warm breath causes my skin to tingle. And for a split second I almost forget where I am and close my eyes, imagining myself spread out on the table, ass up, being deliciously fucked deep from the back. "My pussy's getting wet," I tell him; glad I wore a panty liner, otherwise I'd end up having a bad case of sticky drawers. I remove my hand when a young girl and an elderly woman walk toward us and sit at a table next to us. "Party's over."

He sucks his teeth. "Yeah, and my muhfuckin' dick's ready to bust out these fuckin' pants. You got my balls bubblin' 'n shit." I laugh. "Shit ain't funny. But it's all good. I'ma beat that ass up as soon as I get to the halfway house. The minute I get a furlough, it's on, baby."

"I can't wait. When are you supposed to be leaving?"

"I'm just waiting, baby. It should be any minute." *Yeah, okay,* I think, glancing around the visiting area. He's talking prison lingo 'cause, in my mind, "any minute" is literally that. But in prison, the shit could mean weeks…shit, months! I want to ask him to be a little more specific, but decide against it.

Out of nowhere he tells me he wants to set a wedding date. Tells me he's tired of waiting. That he wants to wife me—*now*. I tell him we should wait until he's done with the halfway house. He's not trying to hear it.

He shoots me a look. "Yeah, well, I don't wanna wait that long. I wanna marry ya fine ass today, aiight?"

I smile. "I know you do. And I feel the same way. But I don't want to half step either. When I go down that aisle with you, it will be the first and only time for me, so I want it to be right. It has to be fly and fabulous."

"I hear you, baby. You'll have it no other way, but I don't need all that fancy shit. We can shoot down to city hall..."

I roll my eyes, sucking my teeth. "Ooooh goodie," I say sarcastically, "then head on over to Red Lobster or Cracker Barrel for the reception."

He laughs. "Whatever, man. Set the damn date already. And stop draggin' ya damn heels."

"I'm not," I say as Stax comes back over to the table with a handful of junk food and two orange sodas. Jasper gets up as he places his chips and whatnot on table.

"Yo, son, what's good wit' you?" They embrace.

"Shit. Wassup wit' you?"

"I'm in prison, nigga." Jasper laughs. "What the fuck ya dumbass think is up with me? I'm jailin', nigga. I swear...ya moms musta dropped you on that big-ass dome of yours when you were a baby."

They both laugh, sitting down. "Yo, fuck you, biscuit head."

"Nigga, I know you ain't talkin' with that Herman the Munster forehead of yours."

They bullshit back and forth for a while before Jasper asks him who was the chick he was talking to. "Oh, that's Peanut's sister." I see Jasper make a face like he's trying to picture her in his mind.

"Oh, word? Which one?"

"The youngest one." I'm not sure who they're talking about. Nor do I care. So I get up and excuse myself. Tell him I'm going to the bathroom. I walk off, but the whole time I'm walking, I can feel Jasper watching me. I bet if I turn around right now, he'll be eyeing me like a hawk. This nigga doesn't miss a beat.

And he's going to be up on any other nigga trying to check for me on the sly. I smile, shaking my head.

When I finish using the bathroom and start walking back toward the table, I can see Jasper has his forearms resting up on the table and he's leaning forward as if he and Stax are in a deep conversation. When he sees me walking toward them, he sits back in his chair and smiles. And that gesture alone leads me to believe they were either talking about me, or discussing some shit they don't want me to know. The question is: about what?

I take my seat next to Jasper and he immediately wraps his arm around my waist and kisses me again. "What's that for?" I ask, almost paranoid.

"Oh, so now I need a reason to kiss you?"

"Not at all," I say, forcing a smile. This time I kiss him lightly on the lips.

He smiles at me, then looks at Stax. "Yo, man, I love this damn girl right here, you feel me?"

Stax grins, rubbing his chin. "That's wassup. It's the kinda love a nigga kills for." I shift my eyes from Stax, who sneaks a look at me. There's something in the way he says this that makes me uncomfortable.

Jasper gives him some dap. "No doubt. You already know, son."

They shift the conversation to their family, with Stax giving him the goings-on with everyone. I tune the discussion out, sweeping my eyes around the room. I fix my gaze over at a chick sitting at the table on the right side of us with her hands under the table, rapidly jerking off her man. I smirk, wondering what she'll do with his nut once he busts in her hand. Will she discreetly lick her palm and fingers? Or will she waste all that cream and wipe it off in a napkin? I imagine myself under the table, lapping at his balls while she's jacking him off. The thought causes my mouth to water.

"Aye, yo, what you over there thinkin' 'bout?" Jasper asks, bumping his shoulder into me. "You look deep in thought."

"You," I tell him, turning my attention to him.

He grins. "Yeah, you better be."

I start to say something slick, but don't. Instead, I shake my head, smiling. And for the rest of the visit we talk about the salon, the halfway house and the wedding. When the CO's announce that the visit is over, we get up and say our goodbyes. Jasper kisses me deeply, then squeezes my ass on the sly. Then he and Stax hug and give each other dap.

"Yo, man, keep an eye on her," he says to Stax.

Stax laughs. "I got you, son."

"Oh, please," I say, rolling my eyes. "Both of you can go to hell." They laugh. Jasper grabs me by the waist and kisses me again.

"I love you, girl."

"I love you, too."

He gives Stax another hug, then gives me another long, deep kiss before walking off to go back to his life behind the wall.

SEVEN

Flashback. Friday, October, 6, 2000. Shyne's "Bad Boyz" was the song blaring through the speakers. I was in the middle of the dance floor in my own zone. Eyes closed, hips gyrating, hands and fingers running through my shoulder-length hair. I was a bad bitch wrapped in a pair of skin-tight jeans, a beige poncho and a sexy pair of six-inch Manolo Blahniks on my feet. All eyes on were on me. Several niggas kept trying to get their mack on while dancing with me, but I wasn't interested. The only thing I wanted to do was mix, mingle, and shake. Not get caught up in some nigga's dream of getting between my thighs. I hated it when motherfuckers disrupted my groove by trying to have a conversation with me while I'm on the dance floor, yelling in my goddamn ear over the music. It was a major turn off, and grounds for walking off and leaving a nigga standing in the middle of the floor, looking like a fool.

And this particular night was no different when I clicked on my spiked heels and attempted to strut off the dance floor to get away from this annoying peanut head dude who kept trying to spit whack game in my ear. He reminded me of a damn beetle in his Emporio Armani glasses.

I was disgusted and ready to go. And was kicking myself for allowing Mona—a girlfriend of mine, to drag me out that night. The only reason I decided to go is because she had bugged the shit out of me for almost three weeks until I finally agreed. It was a birthday party her family was throwing for one of her cousins. And she had insisted I go. She had this grand idea about fixing me up with one of her cousins who had recently moved down to Jersey from New Haven, Connecticut.

"Pasha, I'm going to keep bugging you until you say yes," she stated, sucking her teeth. "You *need* to meet my cousin, girl. So you might as well get your mind right and figure out what the hell you're going to wear."

I huffed, eyeing her suspiciously. "Bitch, why are you so interested in *me* meeting him?" I finally asked, exasperated.

"'Cause he's a real good dude," she smirked, pausing. Then she added, "And he's your type."

"And what's my type, Miss Know It All?"

She snickered. "Dark, chiseled, and hood."

I grinned, feigning insult. "Fuck you. If he's such a good dude, then why isn't he already dealing with someone?"

She clucked her teeth. "He *was* dealing with someone. But the bitch is a bird. She doesn't want anything outta life. And he does. All she wants to do is drink and smoke and hang out with her girls. And he wasn't havin' it. So he gave her ass the boot. Now he's lookin' for somebody he can chill wit'. He asked me if I had any single friends who were about somethin'. And I immediately thought about you."

"Mmm-hmm, why?"

"'Cause you're exactly what he's lookin' for."

"Oh, yeah? And what's that?"

"Bitch, you fly—which is why I hangout wit' ya stuck-up ass..." She laughed. "...You're sexy, you have a fat ass, and I know underneath all them designer clothes is an undercover freak."

I laughed with her. "OhmyGod, you're so damn stupid. Let me find out you like it both ways," I joked.

"Bitch, please," she said, cracking up, "wrong answer. That was his request—a fine, fly bitch with a fat ass who wants somethin' more outta life than runnin' the streets. And that's *you*."

"Hmmph. And he wants all that wrapped up in a freak?"

She chuckled. "Well, no. I mean, maybe."

I raised my brow. "Bitch, which is it?"

"Neither." She smirked. "I added the last part as a bonus 'cause I know how nasty he is. And you know how nasty you like it."

I shot her a look and gave her the finger. "And that makes *me* a freak? Whatever, ho."

She laughed.

"Ohhhkaaay. So what's his name?"

"Don't worry 'bout all that. Make sure you bring ya ass to the party, and you'll find out everything you need to know then."

"I'll think about it," I finally told her, sucking my teeth. But, in truth, there wasn't anything that needed to be thought about. It wasn't like I had a social life or anything. I hadn't been fucking anyone since my breakup with Glenn—the man who I invested close to three years of my life in. To only find out that the nigga had a wife stationed over in Kuwait. While she was overseas risking her life to serve and protect our country, his black ass was here serving me his thick, pulsing cock. But, trust. The minute I found out, along with getting his face slapped, I abruptly ended it with his lying ass, then sealed my pussy up. I had officially banned myself from men. So meeting someone who might eventually turn out to be another lying ass, no-count nigga was the last thing on my mind. And it definitely wasn't something I was looking forward to.

So when I turned on my seven-hundred-dollar heels to strut toward the bar, and over to where Mona was—perched up on a barstool with a frosty drink in her hand, like I wanted to be—I was slightly annoyed when some nigga grabbed me gently by the forearm, pulling me back to the floor. "Dance with me," he said over the music. There was something in the way he pulled me that made my pussy muscles shiver. It was strong, yet firm and gentle. In that brief moment, electricity shot through my arm. Not too mention he was fine; no, fine isn't the right word. He was D-I-V-I-N-E. Still, his touch was unwanted and unacceptable.

I frowned; stared him down, yanking my arm out of his grasp. "No thanks."

"C'mon, pretty baby, one dance." He pulled in his bottom lip, real sexy-like, then added, "Please."

I sighed. "One dance," I flatly stated. He flashed me a crooked smile, taking me by the hand. Surprisingly, I didn't pull back. I allowed him to lead the way. Erick Sermon's "Music," featuring Marvin Gaye, started playing. And we started dancing. I checked out dude's two-step, peeped his swagger. There was a street edge to him; a rugged sexiness that was beginning to make me dizzy. A few times he flashed me a smile, moved into my space, brushed his body against mine, then pulled away; almost teasing me. And I allowed it. We both seemed to be quietly enjoying the other. He focused on me. I kept my eyes on him. And the few times I'd closed my eyes and gave into the music, I'd open them to see him gazing at me, smiling.

I hated to admit it, but I was starting to have a good time. We partied, hard. And by the time "Ante Up" by MOP finished playing, I was drenched. I politely leaned in and told him I'd had enough when the DJ slid on Ludacris's "Area Codes."

"So how 'bout you hit me wit' ya area code?" he asked, following behind me as I walked toward the bar. By this time the dance floor was packed, and we had to maneuver our way over to the other side of the room.

I smiled, shaking my head. "It was only a dance."

"Try four dances," he stated, grinning.

"Okay, four. And I enjoyed them. But I'm not interested in anything else."

"Oh, what...you got a man?"

I shook my head. "No."

"Oh, aiight. Then what's the problem wit' you hookin' a nigga up wit' them digits? You'se a real, sexy-ass dime I'd like to spend some time wit'."

"Thanks, but no thanks. I *said*, I'm not interested."

"Oh, aiight, I got you, ma. I ain't the type of cat to sweat no broad. So I'm out. You enjoy the rest of ya night, pretty baby." And with that said, the nigga bounced on me. I stood there, thinking: *Bitch, you dumb as hell. You shoulda took his number.* I watched his fine ass get lost in the throes of bodies bouncing and swaying to the music before walking off toward the ladies room. On my way to take a damn piss, I must have gotten stopped at least six times by some dudes trying to get in my ear before I finally made it inside the bathroom.

When I finally made it over to Mona, she was still posted up at the same spot wit' a bunch of niggas swarming around her, laughing and whatnot. She was clearly lit up and feeling good.

"Girl, where the hell you been?" she screamed over the noise. "My cousin was just here and I wanted to introduce you to him."

"I was on the floor dancing," I said, fanning myself to cool off.

"Yeah, I saw you out there dancin' with some square-type nigga. I was over here laughin' my ass off, but then it got packed out there and I lost my view of the sideshow."

I flicked my hand at her. "Chile, please. That bottom-of-the-barrel nigga was getting on my last damn nerve."

She laughed. "When you didn't come back right away, I thought dude mighta kidnapped you or somethin'."

"Oh, please. Not hardly. But I did end up getting held hostage on the dance floor by this fiiiine-ass nigga."

"Oh, for real?" she asked, grabbing her drink from off the bar.

I watched her as she took a sip of her drink. I swallowed, realizing how dry my throat was. "What's that you're drinking?"

"You already know, Thug Passion, baby." I frowned as she glided her lips down onto the straw, taking a slow sip. I wasn't really in the mood for Hennessy and Red Alize, but I gladly accepted the concoction when she handed it to me to taste until I was able to get the bartender's attention to order my own drink. I took a long, deep sip. "Girl, slow down. That shit'll get you right. Have you stumblin' home."

I laughed, standing in front of her, with my back toward the dance floor. "Yeah, you're right, I better go easy. Let me flag down this waiter," I told her, handing her glass back to her, "so I can get me a damn drink."

"Girrrrrrl, all these niggas up in here, you don't need to be buyin' no damn drink. Let one of them standin' 'round gawkin' at that juicy ass of yours buy it."

I rolled my eyes, sucking my teeth. When the bartender finally got over to me and I leaned up on the bar to place my order, someone stepped up in back of me, then pressed up against me. I craned my neck to see who the hell was all up on my ass trying to be on some slick shit. It was the sexy, chocolate nigga from the dance floor.

He gave me a crooked grin. "I got you, ma. It's the least I can do." I grin back at him. "What's your pleasure?"

"Surprise me," I told him, stepping aside so he can place the order. He leaned in and said something to the bartender while I glanced back at Mona, who was looking at me with raised brows, holding her drink in her hand. I turned from the bar. "That's the nigga I was dancing with," I stated.

She smirked. "*That's* the fine-ass nigga you were talkin' 'bout?" I nod. "Now ain't that somethin'."

Just as I was about to say something else to her, he turned toward me and handed me my drink. It was in a hurricane glass garnished with a pineapple slice and two cherries. "Here you go, beautiful." He flashed me another smile.

"Thanks," I said, taking the drink. I sipped it, licking my lips. "What is it?"

He leaned in; lips flushed to my ear, and said, "Tap That Ass." I almost choked. "Yo, you aiight, ma?" I nodded, taking another slow sip. "That's wassup." I asked him what was in it, and he told me it was a mixture of Hennessy, Red and Yellow Alize, a splash of cranberry juice topped with soda water.

"It's good," I finally stated. "Thanks."

"So, I see you've met my cousin," Mona said to me, grinning.

"Excuse me?" I asked, not sure I had heard her correctly. "Which cousin?"

"The one you weren't beat to meet," she snapped, laughing.

He laughed with her. "Oh, word? It was like that?"

"Yep," Mona said, still laughing. "I had to practically twist her damn arm to come out. And look. She ended up meeting you, anyway."

"Yeah, we've met already," he said, grinning at me. "But not officially."

"Jasper, this is my girl, Pasha. Pasha, meet my sexy-ass cousin, Jasper."

He extended his warm hand and took mine in his, then pulled me into him and kissed me on the cheek. I almost fainted.

He stepped back. "So…you still not interested?" he asked, eyeing me up and down, slowly licking his bottom lip, then pulling it in.

I eyed him back real sexy-like. "Maybe, maybe not," I stated, slyly.

He stepped back into my space, stared deep into my eyes. "Check this out, baby. Just like that drink you sippin' on, I'ma be tappin' that ass, all in due time. So I hope you ready for a real nigga like me. Enjoy the rest of ya drink. I'll be back later to get ya digits."

He leaned over, said something to Mona—who started laughing, then walked off, leaving me standing at the bar with my drink in my hand—dumbfounded. And that's how it all began.

Crazy thing, that night my feet ached, my shins ached, and my toes were on fire, but none of that shit mattered. I had snagged the finest, sexiest nigga in the room.

EIGHT

"What's good, baby?" Jasper says into the phone. He is extremely animated, and excited, for…I glance over at the digital clock…7:43 A.M. *In the goddamn morning!* I scream in my head. I stretch and yawn. "Get that sexy ass up! Daddy's on his way home to drill another hole in that ass."

"Say what?" I ask, wiping sleep out of the insides of my eyes.

"Yo, you heard me. I said Daddy's on his way home to beat that pussy up, so get ready."

I've heard him correctly, but it takes me a minute to finally feel the weight of his words. My eyes widen as I snap up in bed. "OhmyGod, when?"

"I'm outta this muhfucka tomorrow, baby."

"Where are they sending you?" I ask, feeling my nerves unraveling. This is the moment I've been longing for. Four long years, I've waited. And now, it's finally coming to an end. I want my man home; need him here, but…for some reason, I am not as excited as I had thought I'd be. Not as prepared as I should be. He tells me he's being sent to Talbot Hall—an assessment center in Kearney, New Jersey. That he will be there for about sixty days or so before he makes it to a halfway house.

"Then you know what it is. Once I'm done wit' all that assessment center bullshit, it's on and poppin'. Ya heard?"

"I can't wait," I say, sitting on the edge of the bed. I pull the carpet beneath my feet with my toes. *OhmymotherfuckingGaaaaawd, Jasper's coming home.*

"Listen, baby, I'ma need you to hit the mall and pick up a few things, then drop them off to me tomorrow, like 'round six or seven, aiight?" Before I can respond, he starts firing off a list of things he wants and needs. Five shirts, five pants, a sweat suit, six pairs of boxers, six white tees, a pair of Timbs, two pair of Nikes...

"Aye, yo, hit me wit' some Polo and MEK joints, like in a thirty-four waist. But nothin' too over the top, feel me?"

"I got you. You want the straight-legged or boot cut?"

"Whatever. You know how I do it."

"Alright. What about the sneakers? You want two pair of Air Force Ones in different colors?"

"Nah, hit me wit' some Air Max joints, and a pair of AF Ones."

"What color you want them in?" I ask, deciding to finally get out of bed.

"I don't care. Whatever color you want. Somethin' hot, though."

I laugh. "Neeeegro, who in the hell you trying to get fly for?"

"Aye, don't try 'n play me, yo. You know how I get down."

"I can't say that I do," I tell him.

"Yeah, aiight," he says, laughing. "You already know what it is."

"It's been a long while since I've seen your work," I tease. "You'll have to refresh my memory, Daaaaddy."

"Yeah, I'ma refresh ya memory aiight. As soon as I run this tongue up against that sweet clit, then push this dick up in you, you'll remember all you need to know."

I laugh. "You do that, and I'm gonna end up doing more than remembering. You're gonna have me cumming, too."

"That's what I'm talkin' 'bout, baby. I want you to cream that good shit all over my tongue and dick. Make that shit drip down 'round my balls..."

I feel the restless cock 'n cum beast stirring up inside of me. My mind starts to slowly drift off. Go to a place I have no place going;

especially when I have a man who is that much closer to coming home. But something takes a hold of me and drags me into the dark corners of my warped imagination.

I'm in an apartment building, sitting in an empty room in front of a wooden door with a large hole cut in the middle of it—a glory hole. I have already sucked off eight niggas and their cream is all over my mouth and my face. And there's a line behind the other side of the door of horny men with their dicks hanging out of their pants waiting to get throated. And I greedily suck them all. Then, when I am done, I slowly open the door, and walk out—purposely leaving wads of cum dripping from my face and lips so I can see the looks on all of their faces as I walk out. They stare at me; some in amazement, some in disbelief, others in disgust. Probably thinking how much of a cum slut I am. But I don't care. Sucking cock is what I love to do. I smile at them, licking my sticky lips and popping my hips toward the door. Then I hop in my car, and drive off, glancing in the rearview mirror, admiring the glaze of cum still covering my face.

"...I'm ready to fuck, baby. You feel me?"

"Hunh?" I ask, snapping back to the conversation.

"Aye, yo, what the fuck is you doin'?"

I quickly blink the images out of my head. "Nothing," I say, trying to remember the last thing I heard him say before my mind started wandering.

"Nothin' hell, yo. A muhfucka's talkin' to yo' ass and you somewhere the fuck else."

"I am not," I lie. "I heard what you said."

"Then why the hell you 'hunh' me for if you heard me?"

"Why are you yelling in my ear?"

"'Cause I wanna know what the fuck got you so distracted that you can't hear when a muhfucka's talkin' to you."

I sigh. "You know what, Jasper? You really know how to fuck up a bitch's wet dream. I was listening to you and playing in my pussy at the same time. I got caught up imagining all the nasty things you say you're gonna do to me when you get home, baby. That's all." I sigh. "Damn, why you always gotta start tripping and shit? You act so damn paranoid."

"Yeah, whatever, yo," he says, not sounding convinced. But he lets it go, this time. "Listen, I gotta bounce. The phone is 'bout to cut off on us, anyway. But I'ma hit you up later tonight. Make sure you pick up those things I need."

"I got you. I'll have everything ready tomorrow."

"Yeah, make sure you handle that."

"Shut up. I told you I'll have it."

"Cool. And don't forget, deodorant. Arrid Extra Dry."

"Alright," I say, walking over to the window, then peering out of the side of the curtain. It's kind of cloudy out, and looks like it's about to rain.

"Aye, yo, you know I love you, right?"

"I know you do, baby. I love you, too."

"Let me find out you out there on some extra shit, Pasha."

I suck my teeth, sighing. "Jasper, c'mon…not this shit, again."

"I'm tellin' you, yo. If I hear any crazy shit, I'ma bust ya ass." And with that said the line goes dead.

I stand in the middle of the room for a minute, looking around, taking everything in. Ever since Jasper's been locked up, this bedroom—the bed, the master bathroom, the three closets—have been mine! Not to mention my freedom to come and go and do whatever I like, want, without him physically being able to keep tabs on me. I'm going to have to get used to sharing my space with him, have to get into the habit of letting him know what's on my daily agenda—again. I swallow back my nerves. The truth is: those things aren't a major issue. But what really has me nervous is…well, what happens if I can't give up this internet?

I take in a deep breath, hold it into my lungs, then slowly blow it out. *Jasper's coming home.* I shut my eyes tight, try to block out the throbbing headache that's barging its way to the front of my head. *Jasper's coming home*, I repeat in my head, replaying the night he proposed to me. The night he beat this pussy down so bad it wept more than I did. I had taken his dick down into my throat and sucked him so hard and deep until my neck cramped.

"I love you, girl," Jasper said, kissing me on the side of the head, pulling me into his sweaty arms. I lay my head on his chest, twirled my fingers through his wet chest hairs, then lightly circled his left nipple. He squirmed, grabbing my hand. "Yo, you know that shit tickles…"

"Yeah, and by the look of things," I said, grinning, reaching for his growing dick. It was still sticky and wet from my juices. "I see that shit turns you on, too." I squeezed it, then rolled up on top of him, kissed him on his forehead, then his nose, then lips. I left a trail of kisses down the center of his chest before dipping down low and taking him into my mouth. I inhaled his musky scent and felt my pussy begin to tingle and twitch. I sucked him until he became stiffer than a steel rod, pushing past my tonsils. I sucked and gargled and gulped my man down until his toes opened and closed and he started grabbing and clutching the sheets, moaning out my name. And, then, just as he was about to splatter his nut, I abruptly stopped. Pulled my mouth up off his dick, then looked up at him and grinned.

"Yo, baby, what you doin' to me? You got my head all fucked up. Why you fuckin' wit' me? You got my dick all bricked up 'n shit." I licked his balls, then pulled them into my mouth. "Aaah, shit…you fuckin' wit' me, baby…"

I crawled up on him, then reached up underneath me and guided his pulsing dick into the back of my pussy. I leaned into his ear and whispered, "I'ma fuck this dick all night, nigga."

Jasper stared into my eyes. "And I'ma fuck this good pussy right back, baby." As I galloped up and down on his dick, he rapidly matched my rhythm, thrusting upward into my smoldering hole. We fucked until my pussy cried out in aching pleasure. Fucked until Jasper's black dick turned purple.

"Damn, girl," he said, breathing all heavy and whatnot, "I'ma hate leavin' ya fine ass, and all this good lovin'."

"I'ma hate it, too, baby. But it'll all be here waiting on you when you get home."

"Yo, it better be," he said, getting out of bed. I watched his bare, muscular ass as he walked over to his closet, then walked in.

"What are you doing in there?" I asked, hearing him fumbling around with shoe boxes. He walked back into the room with his right hand behind him with a big-ass grin on his face. "Why you smiling?" I asked.

"You'll find out in a minute," he said, slowly walking over toward the bed. "Lay back and spread open ya legs, then bend ya knees up for me." I did what he asked, anticipated what was to come next. And Jasper delivered well. He kissed my clit, flicked his tongue against the opening of my hot slit, then dipped his tongue in. I opened my thighs wider, reached for his head, and pushed him further into my zone. He sucked all over the front of my pussy, then lapped around both sides of my pussy lips before opening his mouth wide and feasting on my entire hole. He had my head thrashing and my hips bucking and my teeth gritting as I held back screams. He tongue fucked my pussy until I finally screamed out. When he was done he crawled up on top of me, then kissed me, offering me his tongue soaked in my juices. I sucked on his chin, his mouth, then gasped when he stuck his dick back inside of me. He told me to close my eyes, then he took my left hand into his and kissed on it; sucked on my fingers, then slid something on my ring finger.

He stopped and told me to open my eyes. I gasped. Even with the flickering candles that had practically burned down, it sparkled. My eyes widened, my heart raced. "OhmyGod," I exclaimed, "is that what I think it is?"

He put his finger up to my lips. "Don't speak, aiight?" I nodded my head, fighting back tears. "I done a lotta dirt out here, fuckin' wit' a buncha broads, bringin' drama into our relationship and shit, but I'm done wit' that bullshit. And I'm not just shootin' a buncha shit 'cause a muhfucka's 'bout to do time. I'm speakin' from the heart, yo," I opened my mouth to say something, but he stopped me, again. "Listen, yo. I gotta get all this shit out now so let me finish." He kissed me softly on the lips. "I love the hell outta you, baby. You my heart, girl. And I wanna give you the world. I've never loved anyone as much as I love you. That's some real shit. I wanna build a life wit' you, grow old wit' you, and have a buncha mini-mes and mini yous. When I step up in that courtroom, you already know what it is. I'ma be down for a minute, baby. But I'm comin' home to you. And I wanna know you gonna be here when I get out. Are you gonna be here for me, yo?"

"Yes," I whispered, choking back tears.

He looked me in the eyes, stared deeply into them, and said, "I want you to be my wife, yo." He paused, staring at me long and hard. "Pasha Nivea Allen, will you marry me?" OhmyGod, my man actually had tears in his eyes!

I nodded my head, letting my own tears stream down my face. One, because I saw his love for me in his eyes in a way I hadn't seen before; two, because I couldn't believe that he was actually proposing to me; and, three, because I knew that in a matter of weeks it was going to be the last time he'd be fucking me. "Yes, baby," I answered, feeling overwhelmed with joy.

We kissed, then he took my face into his hands.

"I'm givin' you my heart, Pasha. Whatever you do, don't play me, yo."

"I promise, baby," I said, inviting him back into the wet space between my legs. I gasped as he filled me up, "I won't."

NINE

Beautiful black diva with a hot, wet mouth seeks sweet, black dick down in her neck. Deep...Deeper...Oh, yes...listen to the gurgling sounds that escape from the back of my throat as you thrust your powerful dick down into my throat, watching my neck expand to receive every inch of your pounding. If you like what you've read, and you're ready to nut, reply back with complete stats: age, ht/wt, dick size. No fat men, no smelly men, no hanging bellies, no STDs; just long, hard, freshly-washed dicks!

I proofread what I've written, shaking my head. I chuckle to myself at the last line. It's almost amusing and downright disturbing that grown-ass niggas have to be gently reminded (and told) to wash their damn asses before trying to serve up the dick to someone. I mean, really! Now don't get it twisted, I don't mind a little bit of man-musk funk every now and again; especially when it's a natural odor that emits from moving around throughout the day. But, damnit...there's a big difference between crusty-haven't-washed-ya-ass-in-a-week funk to just-washed-this-morning-but-got-sweaty funk. Of course, a lot of these nasty-ass niggas wouldn't understand that. Trifling!

I press the PUBLISH AD button, then click on the AOL icon. As soon as I type in my password, I am instantly greeted with the "you've got mail" voice. I click on my inbox, scanning my emails. My eyes scan through my messages. Mr. Seven-And-A-Half has sent me an email. I click it open. *Hey beautiful. Would love another round of that bomb-ass head game of yours. Let me know what's good.*

I smile.

Now this might sound crazy to some of you...hell, to most of you, but I rarely suck off the same cock more than once unless it's an exceptionally delicious piece of dick. Otherwise, I won't waste my time, energy, or spit. Now, wait one minute. I already know bouncing from dick to dick is potentially more risky than if I were to find one or two steady streams of nut to suck until Jasper gets home. But, in my mind, that would open the door for more drama than necessary. The last thing I need, or want, is a no-string situation turning into a nigga getting attached. But every so often, I come across a nigga whose dick deserves a sec-ond—sometimes a third, and fourth—round of this deep throat action. And Mr. Seven-And-A-Half is it. I type back. *I'm ready when u r*

My brow furrows when I peep an email with the address: mydikneedsUrtongue2@gmail.com. The subject heading reads: U GOT ME FEENIN'! I click it open, then read its contents. *Hey baby. Watz good withchu? I wanna feel ur tongue on my dick, again. Let's meet up.*

I type. *Who are u?* Then go down to the next message.

I click it open. *You sound hot, baby. I love head, but my girl will only suck it a little. And she's not very good at it. I am looking for a long, hot, wet, tight BJ to completion, while you play with your clit. Or if you prefer, I'll eat ur pussy. YOU MUST HAVE a FACE pic to send, or I won't meet. Yours gets mine. I am 5'10 180 muscular build, tattooed, mod hairy. A real man. 7 cut & thick. I am drug & disease free. I can only travel within 10 minutes of Livingston because I will have to sneak out while gf's sleeping. I haven't jerked off or had sex in over 2 weeks, so it should be a big load. U down?*

I reply. *Sorry, boo. I don't send face pics. It's too bad ur girl isn't putting in any throat work. Hope u find someone who will. Good luck 2 u!*

The next email reads: *I'm what you're looking for, beautiful. Well endowed man here. 35, blk, 5'9, 180lbs, brown eyes, powerful 9" very thick and cut, large head and full balls. Would love for you to come to my office so I can stretch your neck with all of this dick.*

I type. *Please send a cock pic. Thanks!*

Next email: *Hey there, beautiful. Bi-racial cat here: 44, 6'3 about 225 lbs, 36" waist, shaved balls. Married and love to get sucked. I'm also into some kink, like lightly twisting my balls, nipple clamps, etc. Can host in my backyard in a camper. Very discreet here; not looking for drama. I'm available after 11 tonight when wife goes to bed. If interested, let me know.*

Kink? Mmmph…definitely not interested. I delete, shaking my head. All I'm looking for is a hard dick to suck. What the fuck is wrong with some of these niggas? Either they can't read, or they're plain stuck on stupid. In either case, it gets on my damn nerves!

Over the last year, since I've been posting these sex ads, I've come across a dozen or so men who have wanted something extra along with getting piped out. Like the nigga who could only get off if he got on all fours and had his dick sucked from the back. I sucked him off once. And probably would have sucked him off again had he not come out his face and asked me to lick his asshole, too. I was goddamn through! I couldn't even finish the nigga off once he made that request, which pissed me the fuck off because he had one of those cucumber-thick, foot-long dongs that made my mouth water. It was a beautiful, mouthwatering piece of man meat.

Then there was another nigga I met online who wanted to smell my panties while I sucked him off. I really didn't mind that part too much. What bothered me was him wanting me to push a dildo up in his ass. A finger, I can get with. But a motherfucker requesting an ass-fucking while I'm sucking on his dick…hmmph, now that's a bit too extra for me. However, truth be told, I did it. I punched his asshole up real good with that dildo, and sucked him off so good he almost forgot his wife's name. Still, I was looking at his ass real sideways. Not that I'm one to be judging anyone. Annnyway…

I click onto the next email. It's from MydickneedsUrtongue2. *U sucked me off about three months ago. I haven't had my dick sucked like that since. Wanted to get at u again but got locked up. But I'm home now and ready for another round, tonight or sometime this weekend. U really know how to handle a dick. The whole time I was in the county, that's all I kept thinking about.*

The county? Nigga, please! I still have no clue who this man is. Not that his email gave me any real hints. Still, I have no interest in playing the guessing game with him. Obviously, this nigga has no clue how many dicks I've swallowed, especially in the last three months. Hell, at least ten or eleven. I type. *Glad I was able to leave a lasting impression on you and your cock. But, that was a one-time slurp session, baby. Good luck 2u!*

The next email reads: *Hey baby. I had a bad day. Would love to release some stress tonight down in your throat. 6ft1, 195 lbs, gl blk dude, 37.*

I click on the next email: *5 foot 9, two hundred fifty lbs, slightly hairy with 4 inch erect, very thin, uncut cock. Hope you're okay with it.* I roll my eyes. No piggy dick, I'm not! *Delete!*

Another email with an attachment comes in from MydickneedsUrtongue 2. I open the attachment. It's a picture of his long, veiny dick. Unfortunately, it still doesn't tell me shit about who the hell it's attached to. Nor does it change my mind about wetting it. I reply back: *Thanks for the pic! I'm sure there are a ton of women who'd love to wet that up for you, but I'm gonna pass. Thanks though.*

The next email is from Mister Seven-And-A-Half. *Hey, baby. I can sneak out for a bit tonight. What about u?*

I reply back. *Tonight is perfect!* Two minutes later, an IM screen pops up. It's Mr. Seven-And-A-Half.

THICKSEVEN-AND-A-HALF4U: Wassup?

DEEPTHROATDIVA: Me sucking on that fat-ass dick. That's what's up

THICKSEVEN-AND-A-HALF4U: lmbao. I need that, bad! This dick's hard as shit now thinkin bout it

DEEPTHROATDIVA: Mmmm. And my mouth is wet. I'm here drooling

THICKSEVEN-AND-A-HALF4U: Yo, I'm sayin, ma. What's good? U wanna do this?

DEEPTHROATDIVA: Absolutely. But I should warn u. I'm really hungry tonight, so I hope u can bust more than 1 round

THICKSEVEN-AND-A-HALF4U: No doubt. I got u. Can we meet somewhere else besides in my truck? I wanna stretch out naked so you can get all up on these balls 2

DEEPTHROATDIVA: Where?

THICKSEVEN-AND-A-HALF4U: The Hilton in Elizabeth?

DEEPTHROATDIVA: on Spring St?

THICKSEVEN-AND-A-HALF4U: Yeah. 9 good?

DEEPTHROATDIVA: It's perfect!

THICKSEVEN-AND-A-HALF4U: Aiight, bet. I'll meet u in the pkg lot. And we can go from there

DEEPTHROATDIVA: C u then

As I'm preparing to exit out of the IM box, another IM screen pops up. *What in the hell?*

MYDICKNEEDSURTONGUE2: Hello

DEEPTHROATDIVA: Uh, hello 2 u

MYDICKNEEDSURTONGE2: U still sucking dick?

DEEPTHROATDIVA: Listen, I'm not sure who u r, but I said no thank you

MYDICKNEEDSURTONGUE2: So u sayin, no I can't have that tongue game?

DEEPTHROATDIVA: Exactly

MYDICKNEEDSURTONGUE2: Oh, so u 2 good 4 a nigga like me. Is that it?

DEEPTHROATDIVA: It has nothing 2 do w/being 2 good. I'm not interested. That's all

MYDICKNEEDSURTONGUE2: U not interested? How u know?

DEEPTHROATDIVA: Obviously I sucked u b/4, right?

MYDICKNEEDSURTONGUE2: No doubt!

DEEPTHROATDIVA: So if I'm not offering up another dose, then that must mean: a). I wasn't impressed; or b): I'm not interested. U decide

MYDICKNEEDSURTONGUE2: Yo, u think u can get all up in a nigga's head, then dismiss me? That's peace. Stuck up bitch!!!!!

Bitch?! I frown. OhmyGod, did this nigga threaten me? Well, maybe he didn't straight out threaten me, but it damn sure reads like a threat. See, now this motherfucker is taking it a bit too far now. "What a fucking whack job!" I say out loud. I'm tempted to curse his ass out, but decide getting into an internet squabble with some invisible nigga behind a screen isn't worth the typing, nor the energy. I block him from my list, then click out of the IM screen instead. Then I sign out of AOL. There's no need to continue going through emails, or dealing with IM's when I've already made my plans for the night.

I get up from the computer, take off my robe, and toss it over onto the bed. I switch my ass into my bathroom to shower, thinking about all the little nasty dick sucking tricks I'm going to do on Mister Seven-And-A-Half tonight. The idea of having him buck-naked, spread out in the middle of a bed, is turning me on. *Hmmm*, I think, stepping into the shower. *It's been awhile since I've been eaten. If I get horny enough I may have to lower my pussy down on his face.* I trim my cat hairs, then give it the extra attention it needs by placing the showerhead between my legs and letting the stream of water beat up against my clit until I release a stream of hot juices.

Forty minutes later, I am pulling up into the hotel's parking lot. I slowly drive around until I spot his truck. He flashes his lights, and I pull into the parking space next to his. I take a deep breath. Tell myself that after tonight, I am shutting down my NastyFreaks4u page. With Jasper closer to coming home I can't take any chances. "This is the last cock I suck," I repeat in my head, commit it to memory. However, the scary thing is. Those same words aren't committed to my heart.

"Damn you sexy as fuck," he says, grinning the minute I step out of my car.

I smile, looking him up and down. Under the lights, this tall, sexy nigga looks finer than he did the first night I sucked him. "Thanks. You're not so bad looking yourself."

He grins wider. Tells me he already has the room for us, and hands me the room key. Tells me the room is on the third floor, and to go in before him. He'll follow behind. I walk off popping my hips just enough to let him know what I've been blessed with underneath the garments.

Once inside the room, I quickly slip out of my clothes, then slip the hotel's white complimentary robe over my crotchless, fishnet teddy. Five minutes later, Mister Seven-And-A-Half slides his room key in the door, then walks in.

The minute he shuts the door, I pounce on him, pushing him

up against the door. I unbuckle his jeans, pull down his zipper, then slide my hand into the opening of his pants, stroking his dick over his boxers. He moans. "Damn, girl…I can't wait to feel them lips on this dick. I've been thinkin' 'bout them big, pretty lips all week."

I look up at him and grin, squeezing his dick while slow stroking him. "Oh, yeah? And what have you been thinking about?"—I drop down to my knees, yanking his pants and underwear down in one swift motion—"This?" I ask, licking the tip of his dick.

"Oh, yeah, baby…"

"Or this?" I slowly suck on his balls, then pull them into my mouth; one at a time. I get them nice and wet with my spit.

He moans, again. "Aaah, shit, yeah. Damn, baby."

My mind is made up. Tonight I'm going to make sweet love to this motherfucker's cock. I grab it at the base with both of my hands, then gently stroke it while bobbing my neck back 'n forth along the length of his thick shaft. I start making loud slurping sounds with my mouth, then gurgle as the tip of his dick pushes past my tonsils. As he moans, I increase the suction on his cock, wrapping my hands along the back of his muscular thighs, then grip his calves, giving him my infamous no-hands-all-neck-and-throat action, ramming his dick in and out of my throat, which immediately causes his knees to buckle.

I slow down the pace, lick the underside of his dick, flick my tongue across his balls, then pucker my mouth around the head, twirling my tongue around it. I suck him in slow motion, moaning. My pussy is starting to overheat. It needs, aches, for attention. I want this nigga to tongue fuck me.

"Aaaaaaaaaaaaahhhhh, fuck! Shit! Goddamn, baby!" he cries out.

I pull back, close my eyes, and let him bust off. His nut hits my face, hard and hot, and has my creamy cunt dripping. I open my eyes and look up at him as I smear his gooey nut all over my lips.

I stand up with his nut dangling from my eyes and nose and make my way into the bathroom. I run warm water on a washcloth, then begin wiping my mouth and face.

"Whew, baby! You got the head game on lock. I want some more of that shit."

I stick my head out of the bathroom door. "Oh, so you think you can handle another round?"

"Hell fuckin' yeah," he says enthusiastically, walking up on me. He's removed his jeans and boxers and is standing here with only a white wife beater on. He steps into the bathroom, turns on the water, and grabs a rag to wash himself off. But I stop him.

"Oh, no, Daddy…Leave that sticky cream for me. I'll take care of you."

"Oh, daaaamn. It's like that?" I smile at him, nodding my head, then slowly lick my lips. "You sexy as hell, baby," he says to me, taking his dick in his hand and lightly rubbing it.

"What time do you have to be home?" I ask, keeping my eyes locked on his cock, then slowly bringing them up to meet his eyes.

"I can hang for about two hours or so. Is that cool?"

I smile again. "Oh, it's more than cool. Why don't you and that fat dick go lie on the bed and wait for me." He happily does what he's told. And two minutes later, I step back into the room, sauntering over toward the bed, removing the bathrobe and letting it fall to the floor.

He lifts up on his forearms, takes in my body. "Daaaaaamn, baby…you can really make a nigga forget he got a girl."

"Well, tonight," I say, climbing up on the bed, shifting my body in the opposite direction of his, then straddling his face, "act like you don't and eat my pussy while I suck this fat-ass dick. And if you can make my toes curl, I'm going to suck you until you nut down in my throat."

"Ah, shit, baby...you ain't said nothin' but a word. Give me that pussy and let me show you what a nigga like me can do."

And with that said, I lower my hips down on his face, then let out a moan as he begins lightly licking my juicy pussy. I lean forward and take his throbbing cock deep into my mouth and suck him, forgetting he has a girl. Forgetting I have a man. Forgetting the promise I made to myself earlier. And erasing any thoughts of ending these dick sucking adventures I've gotten myself so deep into anytime soon.

TEN

"Nappy No More. How can I help you?" Felecia says, answering the phone. She looks over at me and mouths it's Jasper. I tell her to give me a minute to get to my office and then to transfer the call. I strut to my office, closing the door behind me, then pick up the phone.

"Hey, baby," I say, sitting on the edge of my desk.

"How you, beautiful? What you been doing with ya sexy-ass self?"

"Thinking about you," I tell him, closing my eyes to shut off the images from the other night. I press my thighs tightly together.

"Yo, thanks for droppin' off those things. I 'preciate that. You got ya man lookin' right, baby."

"And so you should. Did you put me on the visiting list yet?"

"Nah," he says coolly."

"Why not?" I ask with attitude. Maybe it's not warranted because of the shit I'm doing behind his back, but that doesn't change the fact that he's my man and I want to be able to see him.

"I'm only gonna be here for thirty, maybe forty-five, days at the most. Once they finish all these bullshit-ass assessments, I'ma be shipped outta this muhfucka, feel me?"

"Mmmph, if you say so."

"Yo, c'mon, baby."

"'Cmon' nothing. All of a sudden you getting brand new, acting like you don't want visits."

He laughs. "Aye, yo, knock it off. It's not that."

"Then what is it?"

"I'm sayin', baby. You already know what it is. You the only one I'm tryna see, real talk. You should know that shit. How the fuck you think I made it the last four years? You've been ridin' this shit out wit' a muhfucka faithfully. And that shit says a lot. Those visits kept me sane, baby. They got me through all this shit, feel me? But I'm tired of 'em. I wanna hold you in my arms. Tongue ya sexy ass down, and not have a muhfucka cock-blockin' me. This shit is almost over, baby. And the next time I see you I want it to be you picking me up at the halfway house so we can slide off and get our fuck on. Period. Thirty days, baby; that's all. Then it's on. It'll go by fast, feel me?"

"Yeah, I guess you're right," I finally agree half-heartedly.

All of a sudden my mind starts racing, thinking up crazy shit. Like maybe he's trying to get brand new 'cause he has some side bitch on his team. I know how niggas do once they've finished a bid. They'll have one chick riding out his whole sentence with him, gassing her ass up to think he's coming home to her. So she plays her position to only find out that her ass's been played; that the joke's been on her all the time. Because the nigga's got another plan and her ass isn't a part of it. I feel myself about to go off, feeling the green-eyed monster rearing its ugly head. But I'm smart and sane enough to know that all the messy shit I'm conjuring up is all in my head because of my own guilty conscience. I take a deep breath.

"You know I love you, right?"

Ohhhhkay, where is this going? I wonder, sitting further back on my desk. I nod as if he can see me through the phone. "Yeah," I reply, pausing. "I know that. And I love you, too."

"Yo, no secrets, aiight?"

"I wasn't aware we were keeping any," I say coolly. I silently hold my breath, anticipating the direction this conversation is headed.

"For better or for worse…we in this, right?"

I know this man loves the hell out of me. "Jasper, do you even have to ask?" I ask indignantly. "Of course we are. We've been through too much not to be."

"No doubt," he says, pausing. "Yo, so keep it gee, baby. Am I comin' home to a tight pussy, or am I gonna haveta snap out?"

"Excuuuse me?" I say crossly, trying to act like I didn't hear what he's asked. "What did you ask me?"

"I wanna know if you let any muhfuckas run up in that good shit while I been behind the wall?"

I roll my eyes up in my head, sucking my teeth. Prepare myself for the staged theatrics I'm about to go into. "OhmyGod, I can't believe you asked me some shit like that. How many times do we have to keep going over this? You keep asking me the same shit, and I keep giving you the same answers. Yes, it's tight. No, I'm not getting fucked. I've been waiting for you. Damn. Why is that so hard for you to believe?"

"'Cause I know how chicks do, that's why."

"And I know how niggas do. And I know how you used to do, but you don't constantly hear me bringing the shit up. Damn."

"Aye, yo, why you gettin' all defensive 'n shit? I'm only askin' a simple question."

"I'm not getting defensive," I snap.

"Sounds like it to me."

"Well, I'm not," I huff. "But what I'm getting is sick of you asking me the same shit over and over, like you doubt me or something. What if I started asking how many bitches you've been writing and calling? Or how many bitches have been coming to see you on the days I don't?"

"You can ask me that shit all you want. And I'ma keep the shit one hunnid."

"Oh, like you used to when you were out here fucking around on me?"

"Yo, hol' up. You not 'bout to flip this shit on me. I fucked up when I was out on the bricks, but that shit's in the past, yo. I deaded all that lyin' and cheatin' shit the last time you caught me out there."

For some reason my mind drifts back to the last time I caught Jasper's ass cheating. I was on South Orange Avenue on my way to Livingston Mall, stopped at the traffic light, when I spotted a black Range Rover stopped at the other side of the light facing me. At first I didn't pay it much attention because there was a chick behind the wheel, but then I glanced at the license plate as it was making a left turn onto South Munn Avenue and realized that the SUV this chick was driving was definitely Jasper's. I snatched up my cell and started to call his ass, but quickly dismissed the idea and decided to follow her to wherever she was going instead. Ironically, as I'm following his truck, he called me.

"Hello," I answered, trying my damndest not to start interrogating him.

"Hey, baby," he coolly replied, "where you at? I called the shop but Felecia said you left already."

"Yeah," I told him, keeping a nice distance between me and the truck. Even though I was ready to go off, I kept my tone even; kept my eye on the truck as it stopped at a home in the Vailsburg section of Newark. "I'm on my way to Livingston Mall. Why?"

"Just askin'. What time you gonna be home?"

I glanced at the clock. It was two-thirty in the afternoon. I decided to tell him I wouldn't be home until after seven. I stopped a few houses down, turned off the engine, and watched this chick get out of *my* man's ride—like she owned the shit! She opened

the backseat and pulled out several bags. The bitch had been shopping, probably spending his money. "Why? As a matter of fact,
where are *you*?"

"Oh, uh…I'm in Maplewood wit' Stax."

"Oh, tell him I said hey. What, ya'll getting into? Visiting your
grandmother?"

"Yeah, she got us painting and moving shit for her."

"Awww, how cute," I told him. "That's real nice of ya'll. Are
you riding with Stax?"

"Nah, I'm driving," he lied.

"So what time are you gonna be home?"

"Uh, I'm not sure; late most likely."

"What's late?"

"Like 'round midnight or so."

I peeped the house the broad went into, waited a few minutes,
then got out of my car. I popped open my truck, pulled out my
ice-pick, then started walking toward his truck. Yes, in broad
motherfucking daylight, I dropped down low and punched up his
tires.

"What are you driving?"

"My truck, why?"

"Oh really? That's amazing."

"Why you say that?"

"'Cause motherfucker, I'm standing outside looking at the shit
as we speak." I rattled off the license plate number.

"Say whaaat?"

"You heard me the first time, nigga. I *said*, how the fuck you
driving your truck when I'm outside looking at it? I just finished
ice-picking two of your motherfucking tires so you had better
hurry up and get your black ass out here right now before I stab
up the other two."

"What the fuck? Say what?!"

I started counting, "Ten, nine, eight…bring your motherfucking ass…seven, six, five…out of that goddamn house…four, three, two…NOW! Or I'm gonna start busting out your motherfucking windows, nigga…one."

I saw someone looking out an upstairs window, then heard him say, "Oh, shit." Then I heard scrambling around; someone running down stairs, then the front door flung open. And out came Jasper's ass, pulling his shirt over his head. His jeans were unbuttoned and his Timbs were unlaced. Clear signs that the nigga had been undressed. His eyes were wide as saucers when he looked down and saw his truck slumped over on one side.

"Motherfucker, you better explain what the fuck you're doing over here when you're supposed to be in Maplewood with Stax. And what the fuck was that chick doing driving your truck?"

"Damn, Pasha…what the fuck, yo?"

"Ain't no Pasha 'what the fuck' nothing, nigga. I wanna know what the fuck you doing over here and why the fuck you have some bitch driving your shit."

"I ain't have no bitch driving my shit. Yo, you buggin' for real. Why you flatten my tires?"

"Nigga, you're a motherfucking liar. I know what the fuck I saw. So don't try 'n switch it up on me. I asked you a motherfucking question, but since you can't seem to give me a straight answer, I'll go to the source." I started walking toward the house. Jasper ran up on me, snatching me by the arm.

"Aye, yo, you buggin'. It's not what you think for real, yo."

"Oh, really? Nigga, I followed some bitch driving your motherfucking truck, you give me some bullshit-ass story about being with Stax in Maplewood, then come running out of another ho's house trying to put your goddamn clothes back on. Nigga, the only one bugging is you!" He tried to calm me, but I wasn't having it.

"Tell that bitch to bring her ass outside, now." She must have been listening at the window because when the door opened she stepped out onto the porch. "Bitch," I yelled, "how long you been fucking my man?"

Before she was able to open her mouth to respond, Jasper ordered her back into the house. And like an obedient, dick-whipped bitch she went back in. And that only pissed me off more, causing me to smack his face and punch him in the chest for not allowing her to speak.

Anyway, come to find out, he'd been fucking the chick for close to six months and lacing her with wears and money and shit. So, basically, his ass was not only creeping, but in a whole 'nother relationship. Trust and believe, I boxed and bagged all of his shit and dumped it off on that bitch's porch. Then I went to Home Depot and bought new door locks, changed the code to the alarm system, and blocked his numbers from my cell. He begged and pleaded and made promises to cut all of his extracurricular hoes off. But I wasn't trying to hear it. I was through! And when I got tired of him coming here to the shop, I took out a restraining order on him. Of course that shit only lasted for three months before I went back to court to have it dismissed and he was right back where he belonged—in my bed and in between these legs.

"...the only person I've been fuckin' wit' is you," he says, bringing my attention back to the conversation. "And that's what it is. You're all I need and want. So don't try 'n flip this shit on me. This is 'bout you, baby. And me comin' home findin' out you was lettin' some other muhfucka bang ya back in. So you already know if you ain't tight I'ma fuck you up. You do know that, right?"

"Nigga," I huff, "don't be threatening me."

"Yeah, aiight. You already know what it is."

I glance up at the wall clock. It's 12:38 p.m. My next appointment isn't until two. I sigh. "Well, it's apparent you don't trust me, so I gotta wonder why we're even together."

"Yo, save that reverse psychology shit for them clown-ass muh-fuckas. What the fuck you mean you gotta wonder why we're together? Don't start no dumb shit, yo. We're together 'cause that's how it's fuckin' supposed to be. You ain't goin' nowhere, and neither the fuck am I."

"Hmmph."

"Oh, you goin' somewhere?"

"I didn't say that."

"That's what the fuck I thought. So what the fuck is you gruntin' for?"

I'm trying to understand how the hell we've gone from having a nice, easy-going conversation to this shit. I swear I think this nigga's bipolar.

"Look," I tell him, having enough of this. "I gotta go. I have an appointment coming in."

He laughs. "Oh, now you got an appointment 'n shit. It's all good, though. I gotta get ready for this bullshit-ass group, any-way. So I'ma let ya sexy ass off the hook for now, baby."

"Jasper, kiss my ass, okay?"

"Yeah, aiight," he says, laughing. "I'ma be doin' more than that in a minute. Believe that. And you better remember what I said, yo: Don't fuckin' play me."

It's close to six o'clock and I'm so ready to get the hell home. Today, for some reason, has been a day from hell. It has been one thing after another. And just when I don't think it can get any worse, it does. "Pasha, you have a call on line three," Felecia says into the phone's intercom system.

"Okay, thanks," I tell her, pressing the third blinking light, then picking up. "Hello? This is Pasha speaking."

"Those sexy-ass lips of yours were all I thought about when I was in county. I beat my dick every night, thinking 'bout you suckin' my joint again," the voice on the other end says. His voice is deep, and unfamiliar.

"Who is this?" I calmly ask.

"The nigga you dissed a few days ago," he snaps. "I bet you didn't think I was gonna figure out who you were, did you, you dick-sucking bitch? I almost didn't think I would either—until now."

I hang up, feeling my nerves starting to unravel. Less than a minute later, another call is being transferred to me. I pick up. "Hello? This is Pasha."

"Bitch, I'ma keep calling you so don't fuckin' hang up on me."

"And I'ma call the fucking cops," I warn.

He laughs. "Yeah, right. And tell 'em what, bitch? How you tried to suck the skin off my dick? Go right ahead."

I take a deep sigh. He's right. There's no way I want that to come out. OhmyGod, I'd be the laughingstock of the town. These bitches here would have a field day with that kind of dirt on me. "Look. Why are you calling me?"

"To hear that sexy-ass voice of yours. After you told me you weren't beat to suck my dick again and blocked my emails, you had me feelin' some kinda way. I told you my dick needed your tongue, too…" His email flashes in my mind. OhmyFuckingGod, how did this nut find me? He continues speaking as if he read my thoughts.

"…But as luck would have it. I found you without having to look very hard. All this time, you've been right under my nose. Nappy No More, I like. It has a nice ring to it."

"Look, what do you want from me?"

"Don't play stupid. Why else would I be calling ya smutty ass? I want your lips wrapped around my dick again," he tells me. "Seeing your pretty face in the paper on Sunday got my dick on brick…"

I frown. Try to figure out what this fool on the other end of the phone is talking about seeing my face in the paper. Then it dawns on me. *Oh, shit!* I think, gasping. He's talking about the photo of me in the local news section of *The Star Ledger*. The one taken of me at Nana's church's Community Day a few weeks ago. I was so caught up in the moment, overwhelmed by the number of women who had turned out, that I didn't have a chance to think about what those photos could potentially do to me. Now I wish I could rewind back to that day. I would have told them no fucking pictures.

"...You got me wanting to bust a few rounds of nut down in that nasty-ass throat of yours. That shit feels just like a wet, gushy pussy."

"Excuse me?" I ask, feeling the hairs on the back of my neck raise. "Who the fuck did you say are?"

"I didn't. But don't worry ya pretty lil' head 'bout that. You'll find out soon enough, trick. All you need to know right now is I'ma 'bout to be your worst fuckin' nightmare. Check your mail, baby. And if you don't do what I want, there'll be more where that came from."

"Listen..." the line goes dead. I try to star-sixty-nine the call, but it's from a blocked number. I glance over at the stack of mail sitting on my desk, then start frantically sifting through it. When I come across a manila envelope with my name typed on it without a return address, I immediately know it's from him. My stomach knots as I reach for my letter opener. I swallow hard, then slice open the back of the envelope. I pull out its contents. *Oh...my...fucking...God!* I hear myself scream in my head as I gasp, cupping a hand up over my mouth. My heart has dropped into my lap. I can literally feel the color draining from my face. I sit, staring at the sheet of paper, gripping it in my hand—

mortified. It's a color copy of the photo from the newspaper neatly cut out, and taped in the center of white copier paper. The newspaper caption reads: BUSINESS OWNER, PASHA ALLEN, STYLIST AND OWNER OF NAPPY NO MORE HAIR SALON IN ORANGE, NEW JERSEY, GIVES BACK TO THE COMMUNITY. Underneath that, in cut-out lettering, glued to the white copier paper. Reads: PASHA ALLEN (AKA DEEP THROAT DIVA) IS THE COMMUNITY DICK WASHER. DICK SUCKING BITCH!

ELEVEN

It's seven o'clock in the evening. I am wrapped in a chenille throw curled up on my sofa, with a glass of Chardonnay and my leg tucked beneath me, reading—well, trying to read—*Stealing Candy* by Allison Hobbs about teen girls being forced into prostitution by a malicious pimp. The book doesn't hit the stores until July, which is another four months from now, but one of my clients at the salon belongs to a book club and was able to get a review copy for it. She raved about it and told me I should read it. So when she brought it into the salon with her the other day, I decided I would. Besides, I love all of Allison's books. Many of her characters I can relate to on some level. They're all nasty, uninhibited, and freaky as hell.

But two hours have passed and I am still only on the second page of chapter three. As interesting and disturbing as this book is, I am unable to stay focused tonight. The words are colliding into one big, blurry ball. I put the book down and toss off the throw, downing the last bit of my wine. I reach for the remote to the stereo, press play for the CD player. I wait for Fantasia's latest single, "Bittersweet," to start playing. She doesn't even have an album out yet, but I'm glad to have this song in my collection. Someone came into the shop selling a compilation of songs on CD for five dollars. I don't normally buy bootleg shit, but there were a few songs on the disc I wanted to hear and I couldn't wait until the album's release.

I lean my head back on the sofa, closing my eyes as Fantasia's voice comes through the speakers and fills the room.

I decide I need something else besides sitting up in this house to occupy me. I have to get up out of here before I drive myself crazy, letting some psycho motherfucker rent space in my head. You always see on TV and on the internet shit about someone being harassed by some kook who has made them the object of their desires. But, geesh...all I did was top the nigga off one time, and he's coming at me all nutty and whatnot. Shit! And I don't even remember what the nigga looks like. I can only imagine what he'd do if I had given him some pussy.

Although it's been two weeks since that disturbing phone call from that nut, I am still trying to block out the echoing in my head. *Have you opened your mail today? Bitch, since you won't suck my dick, I'm gonna make ya life a living hell...*

The fact that I haven't heard from him should make me feel relieved but somehow it doesn't. Still, it doesn't keep me from wanting to suck down on some dick tonight. And it doesn't prevent me from thinking irrationally, knowing damn well I have no business still thinking about cock and cum. But I am!

"I'm not going to let this nigga control me," I say aloud as I attempt to convince myself that I have nothing more to be concerned about. I get up and make my way upstairs to my laptop. I turn it on, then wait for it to boot up.

As soon as I click into my browser to pull up the Nastyfreaks4u website, my cell rings. I get up and walk over to my nightstand to retrieve it. I glance at the screen. It's Felecia.

"Hey, girl, what's up?" I ask, sitting on the edge of the bed. I glance down at my toes, and notice chipped polish on my left pinkie toe. I frown, inspecting all of them. *Oh, hell no,* I think, getting up to get my nail polisher remover, *this is not acceptable.*

"Nothing much. You feel like going into the city for drinks later tonight?"

"Where?" I ask, contemplating if I should go onto the NastyFreaks4u website or not. I know, I know. I'm still playing with fire. I try to let this shit go, but something keeps enticing me. "Bitch, don't," the voice in my head warns. I take a deep breath, deciding to log onto AOL to check my email messages instead; it's been a few days since I've last checked them.

"The Katra Lounge," she says.

"Where's that?" I ask, waiting for the page to open. The place she's talking about sounds vaguely familiar.

"In SoHo."

"Oh yeah; that's right. I heard that was a nice spot." A slight smile forms my lips when I am alerted that I have new messages.

"It's a bangin' spot."

I laugh. "I already know what that means. They have good drinks."

She laughs with me. "Yep."

She goes onto rave about how delicious the mojitos with champagne in them are and how great the martinis are; how delicious the appetizers are. "Girl, it has a real sexy atmosphere. Only problem it gets extremely crowded. Oh, and the drinks are sooooo overpriced. Other than that, it's a cute setup." Overpriced drinks; extremely crowded. Those two things are enough to turn me off from going.

"Well, let me sleep on it," I say, stopping her before she goes into a full review of the place. "Call me in an hour or so and I'll let you know. I need to take a quick nap."

"Alright. Talk to you later." We hang up. Needless to say, a nap is the last thing on my mind. I open my first email. *Hey there. Are u still looking to suck dick? 6'1, black hair, dark brown eyes,*

African American male with a really big and thick dick that loves to be sucked. I'm 185 pounds all cut and toned muscle. Located in New Brunswick. Can travel to you, or meet up somewhere. I reply back: Hello. Let me be the judge. Send me a pic of that really big dick. Let's see if it's fact or fiction.

27 6ft 190 brown hair blue eyes 6.5" cut gfs out for 2 hrs looking to travel close to Clark

Hey baby. 6'4" 215 lbs Buzzed Short Hair Goatee Hazel Eyes here; Looking for now. Can't host gotta travel 2 u

hello. I work in edison. lookin 4 when i get out. my quit time varies. u sound nice. i really need a sloppy wet bj. i get a lil dirty at work so either i shower with you or if u like a lil sweat on ur meat then u can clean me off with ur tongue. no games, no bs here. just sloppy, wet dick sucking. please be close to edison. and able to come to me. will be checking my emails from my phone throughout the day.

I roll my eyes, wondering what the hell this idiot looks like. *Who in the hell sends an email in all lowercase letters,* I think, turning my nose up. *His retarded ass is probably some dusty, fat-ass.* I delete.

Somehow I find myself sitting here musing over how I've gotten myself so wrapped up in all of this online bullshit. I never, *ever,* thought or considered that I would become addicted to sucking dick. I don't want to admit that I am, but it is the only thing that can possibly explain why the fuck I'm sitting here in front of this computer, reading emails from motherfuckers looking to get topped off, in the first place. It's the only logical explanation that makes sense. 'Cause only someone addicted to this shit—or maybe the idea of getting caught—would be crazy enough to keep doing the shit, especially when it seems like shit is starting to close in on them. I want to believe I'm a sane, rational, open-minded woman. Hell, maybe, I'm too damn open-minded. Or, perhaps, too damn stupid to see how what I am doing can potentially blow up in my face. I'm still kicking myself for allowing that photographer to snap my picture and have my face plastered all over the front page of the *Star Ledger* Community section. Everything would be fine, if I would have been on my P's & Q's instead of sleeping on the potential consequences. How the hell was I supposed to know I'd have some psycho on my heels sweating me for a dick suck? Yeah, my head game is tight. And, yes, I can curl a nigga's toes and make his knees buckle. Yes, I can suck and swallow a dick down to the base, then extend my tongue out to lap his balls. Plus, in some instances, pull his balls into my mouth as well. All that still doesn't warrant a begging-ass motherfucker trying to work my nerves about it.

Okay, call me what you want. Bottom line, I'm a skilled, dick-sucking bitch. And if I were able to give instruction on the art of dick sucking, giving head, fellatio, throating, etc., I'd give this advice: First, I'd tell them that dick sucking is a craft that needs to be perfected. That like eating pussy, it's an art. That there is definitely a science behind successfully sucking a nigga's dick without scraping or cutting it with your teeth, or throwing your last meal up in his lap, and all over his dick, fucking up his sheets, drawers, and/or pants, which will surely piss him off, and have him throw you out of his house or car. Or flat out curse you out, if he doesn't punch a bitch in her skull first.

Secondly, I'd show them how to tease him with touch. Licking and kissing and nibbling—as well as running her fingertips, along the inside of his inner thighs, along the sides of his dick, over the head, then around the backside of the head—which is the most sensitive part of a nigga's cock.

Next, I'd show them how to use their tongues to explore the dick. In slow, wide strokes, and with lots of spit, wet every inch of his dick up, licking that shit like it's her favorite ice cream cone or—if she's lactose intolerant—Popsicle. Hell, a lollipop. Whatever works, damn it! Just lick the shit like it's dipped in something you love.

Then I'd tell them to—if he's not already bricked up—to begin their dick sucking experience by putting his semi-hard cock in their mouths, guiding their lips over the tip of his cock, making sure their lips cover their teeth. The last thing any man wants is a bitch snagging up his dick skin with her teeth. I'd let them know that, in my experience, sucking on a soft or semi-hard cock helps her get comfortable with his dick; especially when he's swinging a Mandingo cock.

Then I'd show them how to breathe through their noses while swallowing the dick—slowly, one inch at a time, and using their hand to control how much of the dick gets pushed down into their throats, to keep the nigga from choking the shit out of her with it.

Then I'd encourage them to alternate between sucking and licking the dick, to lapping and sucking on their balls and jerking them off, never neglecting the dick or balls. If she's sucking the dick, she should be caressing or massaging the nigga's balls. If she's sucking his balls, then she should be stroking his dick. And if any of the students had rough hands, I'd give out coupons for a paraffin wax so they could have them soft as cotton. And I'd encourage them to keep their lips moisturized, glossy and wet. No man wants a bitch with rough, cracked hands and/or lips stroking up and wetting up his dick.

I'd continue by letting them know that great dick sucking involves knowing how to use their hands and mouth, simultaneously and alternately. Hand and mouth coordination is a must to ensure bringing and taking a nigga over the edge. You want him opening and closing his toes, clutching the sheets, thrashing his head, bucking his hips, and moaning and groaning, slurring your name out in pure ecstasy.

Then I'd close with the following remarks: I'd tell them to not suck the dick like it's a tedious, laborious job. To suck it like it's their passion. Slob it like they love it, damn it! Trust me. I'd tell them men love for women to adore the dick. No matter how big, or small, if she's going to suck the dick, then, goddamn it, be the best damn dick sucker she can be. Then I'd pause for effect, let all that I've shared sink in, then say, "To swallow, or not to swallow? That is the question."

I'd tell them if they're going to swallow, then work that nut up out of him and gulp that creamy shit down with a smile on their faces, slathering it all over their lips, back onto his dick, then licking it clean. But if they're not going to swallow, then I'd suggest that they should let the nigga know, out of courtesy, what they intend to do with the nut. Spit, swallow, or face bust, or a combination of the three. It is totally up to them. However, most men love to see a chick swallow him, and some are okay with her not doing it. So if she's not going to drink his milk, then she should remove her mouth when he's about to nut and replace her mouth with her hands to continue stroking him until he cracks and pops that nut out.

Then I'd probably run off and chase down the nearest dick to suck off since I'd be so damn worked up over all that demonstration. 'Cause the truth is I love sucking dick! Always have. Always will. Which is why I'm great...no, exceptional, at it. Sucking on the head of a nigga's dick; twirling my tongue all over it, licking and lapping its slit—slick with his sweet precum, turns me the fuck on. I can't deny it. There's something about slobbering all over a dick, gliding my lips and mouth up and down its length that makes my pussy soooo wet. I don't know. It's almost as if I was born with two clits—one between my legs, and the other stuck somewhere between my tonsils and the little thingy that hangs in the back of my throat. Shit, that actually might be my clit, now that I think about it. The minute a dick pushes past that point, everything in me starts to tingle and I start creaming in my panties. I find that my orgasms intensify when my pussy is being eaten while I'm sucking a nigga off. The beautiful thing about dick sucking is that you can swab a nigga down slow and seductive, making love to the dick. Or you can throat him real fast and nasty, necking him with a bunch of spit and shit-talking. Either way, there's a nice delicious, hot, creamy treat waiting to erupt.

TWELVE

"Girl, the key to sucking a man's dick is seducing him mentally first, then sucking him like you love him. Fuck his mind, make love to his dick. Stroke his ego, and worship the dick! That should be every woman's strategy...You want it so that every time he sees you or hears your voice, he'll think about how good you sucked down on his cock. In the still of the night when he's lying in bed, alone—or with his woman next to him, his dick will brick up thinking about your head game..."

I'm not sure what made me think of this conversation. It was one of those rare off-the-record moments Bianca and I were having behind closed doors in my office a few years ago. And it has always stuck in the back of my mind because it is something I wholeheartedly agree with. Interestingly, when I asked her how she knew so much about dick sucking, she laughed, lowered her voice, and said: "Girlfriend, who isn't sucking dick in the twenty-first century? And if it's her man, she needs to be swallowing every drop of that dick milk. It does the body and face good!"

I laugh, replaying the conversation in my head. *That damn Bianca is a mess*, I think, opening another email. *And that's exactly why we clicked.* I read, sighing.

Hello. R U still looking to suck cock? Would like some head. I like my balls licked and cock sucked nice and slow. Into face-fucking pretty chicks. DDF here expect the same. Hit me up if u still looking.

There's no stat info, no pic, nothing that would make me want to reply back. I delete, and move onto the next. *Wassup deep throat diva? How u? Itz been a minute since we chatted. Been thinkin bout u and that long, wet tongue wrapped around this dick. U still putting in that throat work? A nigga could definitely use some right now. Holla back. 973-333-5555.*

I have no idea who this nigga is. I stare at the screen, trying to figure out who it might be. The email address, Thugdick09@gmail.com, doesn't ring a bell. I go into my folders. Search through the emails I've saved of niggas who sent pics of their dicks, torsos, or full bodies. There's no one with that email saved in the folder so I delete.

My cell rings. The special ring tone lets me know it's Jasper calling. I sigh. Not sure if it's out of relief or regret. I mean, a part of me is relieved that he is saving me from myself. Then there's that part of me that wants to ignore the call. That feels like he is disrupting my secret moment. Damn him! I glance at the time on the laptop, getting up to retrieve my phone from off the bed. *I can't believe it's almost nine o'clock.* "Hey," I say, walking back over to the laptop and sitting down.

"Yo, what's good wit' ya sexy-ass?"

I smile. "You," I say, deleting the remaining twenty-eight emails.

"It better be." I suck my teeth, sighing. He laughs. "What you up to?"

"Nothing." I fake a yawn. "Resting; that's about it. Did you *work* today?" For the last few weeks, he's been on the books down at his boys detail shop, doing everything *except* detailing. These niggas always got some kind of scheme going on. I told Jasper when his ass gets got that I'm not trying to hear shit about it. He told me to stop wishing bad luck on him; that he's got this. So, I'm leaving it alone.

"Yo, don't start ya shit, Pasha."

"How am I starting shit?" I ask, coyly. "I only asked you a question."

"Yeah, aiiight. Play stupid, yo."

I don't know why I feel like fucking with him when I hate it when he does the shit to me. Oh, well. "How is asking you if you went to work playing stupid? Help me understand that. All I want to know is how my man's day was."

He sucks his teeth. "Whatever, yo. Yeah, I *worked*, smart-ass."

"And did you have a good day?"

"Yo what the fuck, man?" he huffs, sounding agitated. "Yeah, I had a good day. Damn."

"That's good," I say sarcastically, opening a new email. Still nothing worthy of a response. I delete it, then get up from the computer and lay across the bed.

No response.

"Why are you getting all quiet on me?"

"Yo, you always gotta try 'n be on some extra shit."

"How you figure?"

"Nothing," he snaps. Felecia is calling in. I tell him to hold on, then click over.

"Hey, girl, I gotta call you back. I'm on the phone with Jasper."

"Oh, aiight. Tell him I said hey. You still up for drinks?"

"Yeah," I tell her, deciding going out is probably the best thing for me to keep me from going out on the prowl tonight. "Let's meet in an hour." We hang up. I click back over. "Okay, I'm back."

"Yo, who the fuck you clickin' over for?" I tell him it was Felecia. Tell him she wants to go out for drinks. "On a Wednesday night? Where at?" I tell him where. He grunts. In my mind's eye, I can see his jaws tightening. "What, ya'll goin' to meet up wit' some niggas?"

I suck my teeth. "What kinda shit is that? Nigga, please. Meeting up with a nigga is the last thing on my mind." Oh, okay, I'm lying. Well, partially. Shit, I'm not interested in meeting up with a nigga at a damn bar. Meeting his ass in a dark alley, an empty parking garage, or even a park, perhaps, might work. But not in a public social setting. "Besides," I continue, "I got a man, and so does Felecia."

"And? What's that got ta do wit' shit?"

"I guess nothing. If you don't know, then neither do I."

"Yeah, okay. Keep it up, aiight. You gonna have me go in ya mouth, word up."

I laugh. "Yeah, right. The only thing you gonna have go in my mouth is that black dick, and that thick creamy nut, nigga."

"Aye, yo," he says, lowering his voice. I knew saying that shit would calm him down, for the moment at least. Anything that has to do with me fucking or sucking him does the trick all— well, *most*—of the time. "Go 'head wit' that 'fore you have me sneakin' outta this muhfucka to beat that back up." I open my mouth to say something, but he tells me he has to go, then abruptly hangs up. I yawn, feeling my eyes getting heavy. I glance at the clock on the nightstand. 9:47 P.M. *I'm gonna close my eyes for a quick minute, take me a disco nap, then hop in the shower and be ready to meet up with Felecia*, I think, sinking into the plushness of my bed. *All I need is a few, quick zees.*

I hear the doorbell, but think I am dreaming. It isn't until I hear heavy banging and my cell phone ringing at the same time that I realize it's real; that I am not stuck in LaLa Land. I jolt up in bed, glancing at the clock. 11:18 P.M. I reach for my cell. Look at the screen and answer, getting off the bed to see who is banging on my door like they've lost their fucking mind. I can't believe

I fell asleep on top of the covers, with my clothes still on, like that. "Hurry up and come open the door," Jasper says the minute I pick up.

"Open the door? That's you downstairs banging like that?"

"Yeah, who else you think it's gonna be?"

I frown. "Nigga, how the hell I know? Why you think I didn't get up to answer it?"

"Yeah, aiight. Well, hurry up and get down here." Just like that, he hangs up. What the hell is he doing here when I told him I was going out with Felecia? *Shit, I forgot to call her.* I check my cell. Notice she sent me a text. I reply back to her as I make my way to the door. I unlock and open it.

"What in the world are you doing here this time of night?" I ask, swinging the door open. I step back as he hurriedly walks in. "Who's that outside?"

The minute I shut the door, he starts removing all of his clothes. "Yo, I only got thirty minutes, so we don't have time for a buncha chit-chat." He tells me he slid one of the night counselors a hundred-dollars to let him slip out. He tells me he has to be back in by twelve-thirty. That the nigga outside is one of his man's.

"Are you crazy? Nigga, you trying to get your ass locked back up." It's a comment, more of a statement, than a question.

"No, I'm tryna get some pussy and you wasting time wit' a buncha questions. Take them fuckin' clothes off," he says, pressing me up against the door. "You already know what it is."

"Nigga, you're crazy."

"Yeah, for ya sexy-ass. Now take these muhfuckas off 'fore I tear 'em off of you." He starts pulling at my shirt, and tugging at my jeans. He unbuttons them, then gets down on his knees and yanks my pants down around my ankles. I step out of them, kicking them out of the way. He pulls my panties over to the side and begins licking and kissing on my pussy. I let out a soft moan, grabbing his head. I throw one leg up over his shoulder, giving him full access to my slippery slit.

Within moments of his tongue-assault on my clit and slit, I pump my hips and fuck his face, mouth, and tongue until I feel my first wave of orgasms washing over me. Jasper quickly stands up with his lips glazed with cum and begins kissing me. I reach down and start grabbing at his hard dick, sucking my juices from his lips and tongue. He quickly lifts me up by the hips, then reaches up under me and slaps his dick up against the back of my pussy before pushing the head in. Neither of us says a word as his cock and my cunt make music. Smacking and sloshing in between low, deep moans and guttural grunts and groans are the only sounds heard. I have my fingers interlocked behind his neck, leaning back, bouncing up and down on his dick as we stare into each other's eyes.

I can read his thoughts through his eyes, and he is reading mine through mine. We are both in love; both horny; both in desperate need of release. I blink a few times, hoping he doesn't look too deep into my eyes and uncover my deceit.

"Aaaah, shiiiiit...aaaaah, fuuuck, baby...you got my dick so... aaaaah, wet ..."

"Oooh, yes...you make my pussy scream, Daddy...Oh, your dick is so good . . ."

"Yeah, wet that dick up, baby...let me get all up in that good pussy...goddamn, fuck!"

Ten strokes later we are both nutting; him deep inside of my smoldering hole. And me all over his pulsing cock. My juices, along with his, shimmy down the sides of his dick, then drip to his balls. "Damn, that shit was good," he says, lightly kissing me on the lips. I continue pumping my hips on his dick until it goes limp and slips out of me. He puts me down. "I gotta bounce, baby."

"I know," I say, watching him put back on his clothes. He snatches up my panties and stuffs them in his front pocket. "I'ma need these for later tonight."

I laugh. "You so fucking nasty," I state, glad he's not taking a pair of my expensive underwear this time.

He kisses me on the lips, grabbing my ass. "I wish I could bust another 'round up in you. I'ma hit you up in the morning."

I smile. "Okay. Get back safe."

"No doubt," he says, kissing me. I part my lips and his tongue slips in, swirling around mine. "Damn, I gotta get the fuck on," he states, pulling back. "I love the hell outta you, girl."

"I know you do. I love you, too."

I step behind the door as he opens it, then I shut and lock it behind him. I peek out of the window and watch him as he hops back in the car. It's not until the lights flash on, the car backs out, and they head down the road that it dawns on me that this nigga can come through on some drive-by shit anytime he feels like it.

I climb the stairs to my bedroom, go into the bathroom, turn on the faucet and then wet a washcloth with soap and warm water. I wash the cum off that's gliding down my legs, brush my teeth, then head back to bed. Exhausted and exhilarated. *Damn, I really needed a dose of that good dick.* I smile, pulling the sheets up over my sticky body and closing my eyes.

THIRTEEN

It's been extra crazy here today. The salon has been packed since ten o'clock this morning with every stylist, nail technician, esthetician, pedicurist, and masseuse hopping around here trying to keep things moving, and keep customers from sitting up on top of each other. Though I'm not complaining, it's been a damn zoo!

Today is the third day we've been running our "Nappy on the Go" special—a mani/pedi, full-body massage, facial, and hair—for two-hundred-and-fifty dollars. Something we like to do from time to time for clients who might like to do a little extra-pampering, but have limited funds due to the economy, plus it's good for business.

Interestingly, most of the chicks coming in this afternoon for pedis are requesting the Bavarian Chocolate and the Chocolate Chip Cookie pedis we're now offering. The Bavarian pedi starts off with a warm cocoa bath, followed by a cocoa and brown sugar scrub, followed by a chocolate syrup mask. The Chocolate Chip Cookie pedi starts with a vanilla soak, followed by a sugar and honey scrub with a chocolate mask and vanilla lotion rub. Chile, it'll have your man wanting to lick the balls of your feet, and suck your damn toes off.

And all manis this week include a warm oiled stone massage and paraffin wax to deep moisturize those overworked hands, keeping them baby soft.

A few clients have also come in requesting our exclusive back facials to get those backs and shoulders ready for those strapless evenings. Mmmmph, there's nothing worse than seeing a woman with her back out and it's covered with pimples, blackheads, and blemishes. That's a no-no. Definitely not a good look, boo! So, for a limited time, you can get all of these wonderful services that would normally cost close to a grand or more for a damn steal. Even the requests for Brazilian, chin, and lip waxes are crazy today, since we're offering a two for one package. You can get your pubes and underarms, or chin and lip, or chest and legs, or any other combination, for the price of one.

Annnnyway, so here I am—on my feet, finishing up my girl Greta's doobie when I see Big Booty sauntering through the salon's door, like she's ghetto-fabulous. There's so much chitter-chatter and laughter going on that I can barely hear myself think. Let alone try to keep up with all the conversations going on around the room. Greta is finishing up telling me about her latest date. A retired army captain she met at a meet-and-greet social mixer in Newark last month who happens to be fifteen years older than her. "He's a little older than what I'm used to, but—"

"Change is good," I state, cutting in. "Besides, fifty isn't *that* old."

"Mmmph, it's old enough. I mean, I'm thirty-five."

"Okay, and?"

She shakes her head. "It's gonna take me some time to handle that whole 'age is just a number' thing."

"Well, do you like him?"

"It's too early to tell. We've been out on three dates so far, and each time he's been very respectful."

"Well, that's a start," I offer, knowing that the only reason she's been on three dates with him is because they haven't fucked, yet. Greta believes in fucking her dates on the first night to see if she wants to invest any more of her time with them.

"The start of what?" she asks, handing me the mirror. "This looks good." She swings her hair from side to side, admiring how silky it is.

"The start of something new," I state, unsnapping the cape from around her neck. "I mean...hell, the fact that you've been out on three dates with him says a lot since we both know that most men don't make it past the second date with you."

She laughs, getting up. "Girl, you know that's right. That's because once I've tasted the goods, I don't normally want a second helping of what they're offering. And the only reason I haven't sampled the Captain yet is because he's being so damn gentlemanly. But the minute he makes a move on me, I'm gonna eat him alive. I hope he keeps a hard dick. I'd hate to have to toss him out of my bed."

I laugh. "Girl, get the hell out of here. You better worry about not killing him in the process."

She taps the tip of her index finger on her chin. "Mmm, maybe I should marry him first."

I continue laughing. "Girl, you're too much."

She shrugs, handing me a twenty-dollar tip. "I'm keeping it real."

"I know you are. That's what so damn funny."

"I'll keep you posted," she says, walking off. "See you in two weeks."

I shake my head, watching her walk off toward Felecia to pay her bill. I see Janelle is finished getting her pedicure right on time and wave her over.

"Girl, ya'll are doin' the damn thang up in here," she says, sitting down in the chair. I got the Chocolate Mint-pie pedi and it was heavenly. Where in the world did you come up with the idea to give names of desserts for different types of pedicures?"

The Chocolate Mint-pie pedi starts off with your feet being pre-soaked in a coconut milk and mint mixture; then we add chocolate coffee to the mixture, letting your feet soak for ten minutes, then comes the chocolate scrub and feet massage. Once the scrub and massage are over, then comes a warm chocolate paraffin wrap brushed onto the feet. Finally, we apply the chocolate mint therapy lotion.

An hour later, your feet are relaxed, soft as silk, and you walk out feeling like you're in seventh heaven. What most people don't know is that not only does the chocolate aroma calm the senses; the chocolate contains ingredients that can hydrate and moisturize the skin. I learned this from checking the going-ons in white-owned salons. Most black-owned salons aren't up on this, and they damn sure aren't offering it.

"Girl, you know I like to stay on top of shit, keep customers talking and wanting to come back. You gotta know when to step outside the box."

I tell her about the eyelash and eyebrow clinic that Nappy No More is about to undertake, where we'll be offering eyelash extensions and eyebrow-shaping and powders. We'll also be providing eyelash dyeing for women who don't want to keep using mascara, and eyelash perming for those who have straight lashes. It'll be a forty-five minute procedure and the results will last for about six weeks or so. "I'm telling you, we are catering to the woman on the go who wants one-stop, customized salon care for her hair, face, body and feet."

"I know that's right," she says as I snap the cape around her neck. "I'm impressed. Umm, speaking of stepping outside of the box, I want a whole new look; something real drastic, yet sassy for the spring."

"What do you have in mind?" She tells me to do whatever I want. I smile, and decide to give her a retro bob cut. I see Big Booty still at the counter talking to Felecia, either catching up on—or dishing out—the latest gossip, then she speaks to a few clients sitting in the waiting area before she makes her way over to my workstation. Over all the chemicals floating through the air in here, I can practically smell her signature perfume—Juicy by Juicy Couture before she approaches me. This is the first time anyone has seen her since she got sliced in the face. She lifts her up her designer shades, tossing her shoulder-length weave to the side. "Miss Pasha, girl, can you fit me in today? I see you kinda busy up in here. How many heads you got?"

Shit, I can't ever remember her damn real name. "Hey, girl," I say, mindful not to call her by her street name. "I have two or three, but I'm sure I can fit you in."

"Perfect" she says, running her hand along the nape of her neck. "I need to get this kitchen handled. These peas are poppin' for real."

I laugh, eyeing her white Louis bag and admiring her wears. "You better go, girl," I say, waving a finger in the air. "You look good. And that bag is hot."

Shuwanda comments on the bag as well. "Yeah, girl, that's shit's fiyah for sure!"

"Thanks," she says, letting her bag rest in the crook of her arm. "It was a treat to me after that ho cut me." Her weave piece covers the right side of her face. She pulls it back to show us her scar. "Yeah, the bitch got me good. But she got even better."

"Did she get charged?" Shuwanda wants to know.

"That bitch sure did, and she got stomped, too. Shit, we all got charged. That ho was snappin' over some damn dick, comin' up to my door tryna bring da noise." She rolls her eyes, sucking her teeth. "Bitch, puhleeze. And the nigga was still tryna come through for some'a this goodie-goodie, okay."

"And I know you sent his ass on his merry way," I say, eyeing her as I turn on the water. When it's the right temp, I lean Janelle back in the sink and begin washing her hair.

She bucks her eyes. "The hell if I did. I dug into that nigga's pockets for all of my pain 'n sufferin' first. Then I pulled a nut outta him."

Shuwanda chuckles. "Ooh, girl, you messy. But I love it!" It figures she would, since the two of them are cut from the same cloth.

"Messy, hell," Big Booty replies. "If that nigga don't respect his relationship, then why should I? The only fool in the room is that dumb-ass ho thinkin' she got shit on lock."

"I know that's right," Shuwanda agrees, encouraging Big Booty to stand here and keep the shit going. "I feel the same way. Cheatin'-ass niggas ain't shit. So do you, boo. I saw what you posted on Facebook. Girl, it was hilarious. You called her out."

"Sure did. Then had Marquelle post her beatdown on YouTube, okay? Fuck wit' me if you want."

I shake my head. Marquelle is her fifteen-year-old son who drinks and smokes around her—and from what I hear, with her. She stands here giving us all blow by blow details of how her and this girl fought. Come to find out the girl she and her kids beat down is only twenty-two. This bitch should be ashamed of herself. I keep my thoughts to myself.

An hour and a half later, Janelle gets out of the styling chair, looking like a new woman. "Girl," she says, checking out her new do in the hand mirror. She smiles at her reflection. "I love it." She glances down at her past—long, thick hair, then back up at the new her in the mirror. "This is exactly what I needed."

I smile, sweeping her hair into a dustpan. *I need to start making wigs*, I think, dumping it into the trash. *I'd make a killing.* The wheels in my head start to churn as an idea for developing my own line of wigs comes into view.

Janelle hands me a ten-dollar tip, then makes her way over to the register to pay Felecia. I call Big Booty over. She struts over, swinging her hips. I peep a few customers cutting their eyes at her never-ending ass. She sits in the chair.

"Miss Pasha, girl, I appreciate you squeezing me in. I'm going to see Ledisi in the city at B.B. King's tomorrow night and I gotta be right."

"Oh, I love her," I say, snapping the cape around her neck. "I saw her last year in Atlanta, and she threw down. She gives a great show."

"Girl, yes," she agrees. She tells me this will be her second time seeing her. Tells me one of the young niggas she's got pushing her back in got her tickets to see Maxwell and Jill Scott at Madison Square Garden in June.

"I'd love to see Jill in concert again. But I can do without Maxwell. He doesn't do it for me."

"Chile, please...Maxwell can get it."

Who can't, I think as I begin removing the loose stitching from her tracks. Her iPhone starts buzzing with text messages. She busies herself reading and responding back, which shuts her up for a while. And that's fine by me. Twenty minutes into removing Big Booty's weave, an unfamiliar man's voice slices into my space.

"'Scuse me, ma."

I look up from Big Booty's head. Standing in front of me is a thug-type nigga with dreads and big, round brown eyes. He looks to be in his early twenties. His facial features kind of remind me of a browner version of Hill Harper. Yes, he's a cutie. "Yes, can I help you?"

"Yeah, my man said if I came through you'd hit me off with one of ya deep throat specials."

I think I hear him correct, but need to make sure. He repeats himself and I feel myself getting lightheaded as I notice all eyes are on me, glued to the scene that is about to unfold before them. Seems like everything in the shop freezes. All I hear are gasps and the air being sucked in all around me. I can tell they are all standing and watching with baited breath to see how I react. This sonofabitch has come up in my fucking shop and called me out in front of everyone. I am about to pass out. I am through! Now I will have to bring it to him, and bring it hard! Or every bitch up in here will think this nigga is speaking truths.

"Say whaaaaat?!" I snap, flipping into bitch mode, slamming my hand up on my hip. Although I'm curious to know who the fuck his man is, asking would make me look suspect, like there might be some truth to what he's dishing. I'm shaking inside; the last thing I'm about to do is validate shit he's saying. "Mother-fucker, do I know you?"

"Nah, but you know my man," this cocky-ass nigga says, smirking.

"Nigga, you got the wrong motherfucking one," I snap, "coming up in my motherfucking shop with that disrespectful ass shit. What you better do is bounce before you get bounced."

I can't believe this nigga has me coming out of script like this. When I opened my salon, I made it my business to always talk and act and dress professional. To always carry myself with grace and class. But, right now, baaaaby, I feel the hood in me coming out. I am so goddamn pissed and embarrassed that I could take these scissors in my hand and stab him in his motherfucking eyeball.

"Yo, ma, I'm only tellin' you what my man said. He said you sucked him off while he drove his whip down twenty-two in Hillside. Said you sucked him so good he forgot where he was driving to. I'm sayin', can I get my dick sucked or what?"

I catch Shuwanda clutching her imaginary pearls, with her lips curled up in a wicked smile as if she's enjoying the show. And knowing this bitch...she is! That in itself sets me off even more.

"Nigga, get the fuck up outta my shop before I have the cops up on ya ass. I don't know who the fuck sent you here, but you go back and tell that nigga I said to kiss my black ass. I don't play that shit . . ."

"Oh, hell naw," Felecia says, storming up over to where we're at with a can of mace in one hand and the aluminum bat she keeps behind the counter. "You fuckin' tryna get ya head taken off, muhfucka! I will knock ya shit straight out the park real quick, nigga."

The nigga doesn't blink. He glances at her over his shoulder and calmly says, "Yo, ma, no disrespect to you, but you need to stay in ya lane. I ain't talkin' to you, boo. I'm talkin' to ya peeps." Then he turns his attention back to me. "So what's good? Can you hook a nigga up wit' some of that deep throat or what?"

I swear this day has turned into a fucking nightmare! This nigga picked one of the busiest days of the week to call me out and drag me for filth! Do you hear me!

"Well, muthafucka, I'm talkin' to you," Felecia snaps, rolling her neck and swinging the bat. "So anything you sayin' to her, you sayin' to me. Now get. The. Fuck. Out!"

I glare at the nigga, hearing him in my head say something real slick and me and Felecia jumping on his ass. In my mind's eye, I snatch the hot curling iron off its plate and slap him across his face with it and—as if on cue—Felecia bangs him in the back of the head with the bat. He yelps. And from that point on, it is on and popping. Felecia and I start beating this nigga down like we used to when a nigga would come out of his face all sideways when we were younger.

I see this nigga hitting the floor before he can swing off. And Felecia fucking him up with the bat so bad that all he can do is ball up and try to cover up his head and face with his hands and arms to keep her from smashing his brains out. And I am stomping and kicking him, yelling for someone to call the police. I see cell phones out and the shit being recorded and this whole fiasco on the internet.

Luckily, it doesn't unfold the way I play it out in my head. Instead, this disrespectful bastard grins and starts backing out toward the door. "Aiight, ma. You got that. I'ma bounce. But I still wanna feel them pretty-ass lips on my dick."

To save face, I go in on him, throwing a can of hairspray at him. He ducks. And it hits the wall. "Get the fuck outta here. You wish a bitch like me would suck down on ya nasty-ass dick. Coming up in here tryna disrespect me. You couldn't handle a bitch like me, let alone afford one like me."

"Yeah, nigga," Felecia warns, gripping the bat tighter. "Get the fuck out before you get beat the fuck up."

I can't believe this shit. First, the nigga sends me a crazy ass email wanting his dick sucked. Then he calls me at my shop and sends me an envelope calling me out. Now this shit—sending another motherfucker up in here to put *me* on blast like this. The shit is surreal.

"Yeah, yeah, yeah," he says, grabbing the crotch of his jeans. "Suck my dick." I forget I have Big Booty in the chair, forget I have a salon packed with clients, forget I am in slippers, and start chasing behind him as he races out the door.

I yell at him. "You pussy-ass bitch, you better run. If you ever step foot up in my motherfucking shop again, I'ma bust a round of lead in ya ass, then call the motherfucking cops on ya bum ass."

He turns around when he's halfway down the block and yells out, "Suck my dick, bitch!" He laughs, running off.

That nigga has completely disrupted my day. Got my nerves all rattled. All I want to do is run to my car and speed off. The last thing I want to do is go back in and look into questioning eyes. But I do. I pull in a deep breath. Walk back into the salon. It's so quiet I can hear my heart pounding. I hold my head up and sashay back over to my workstation, like nothing ever happened, slowly exhaling.

Big Booty says, "Miss Pasha, girl, don't let that nigga shit on ya day. I don't know who the fuck he was but when I find out, I'ma have my goons take it to his head for you."

"Girl, please. It's not that serious."

I peep Shuwanda eyeing me with her lips all tooted up. She grunts. "Mmmph, you good 'cause I would have fucked him up for coming at me like that; especially when he's coming at me about some shit that *ain't* true. Then again, I'd still fuck him up even if it was; just for calling me out like that."

"That nigga adds no value to my life," I state, meeting her stare, "so he can say whatever the hell he wants. But I do know that if he ever comes back into this shop, he won't be leaving the same way he walked in."

"I know that's right," Big Booty says. "That nigga had me wantin' to go in my bag on his ass."

"Well, I'm glad you didn't," I say, removing the remaining tracks of hair, then combing out her own hair. It's a woolly mess. "You have enough shit to deal with."

"Still," Shuwanda adds, "why would a muhfucka walk up in here and say some shit like that?"

Bitch, because the shit's true. I shrug. "Who knows why crazy-ass niggas do what they do."

"'Cause half of 'em have more dick than brains," Felecia says, walking over.

"Then what about the niggas with more brains than dick?" someone asks.

"Oh, them niggas are dickless brainiacs."

Everyone laughs. Then a discussion about nutty ass niggas being stuck on stupid starts and the shop comes back to life, filling up with incessant chatter and laughter. I go through the rest of the day acting as if nothing that nigga said rattled my nerves, but his voice and his words ring in my head. *Bitch, suck my dick!*

FOURTEEN

"So, how'd you like the lil' delivery boy I sent you the other day?"

Hearing his voice makes my skin crawl, and makes me want to scream. It's like listening to someone drag their jagged fingernails across a chalkboard. "Motherfucker, why are you still fucking with me?" I hiss through clenched teeth. I swear I want to snap on this crazy-ass nigga so fucking bad, but my office door is open.

He laughs. "You sound distressed."

"No, nigga," I correct. "I'm pissed. I'm tryna be nice about this, but the shit's getting real played."

"Well, check this out. I'll stop the shit now. You ready to suck this dick?"

Click. I hang up on him, knowing in a matter of seconds he'll be calling back. I quickly get up to close my office door. And as if on cue, a call is being transferred to me as I return to my seat. I take in a deep breath, then exhale. "Hello, Pasha speaking."

"Bitch, I see you one of them hard-headed hoes. Hanging up on me ain't gonna change shit. I thought I told you this already. All you gotta do is suck this dick and swallow my nut and I'm gonna dead it. But if you keep actin' all stank 'n shit, it's only gonna get worse. The more you say no, the more I'm gonna do to you. I don't give a fuck how long it takes, I'ma fuck wit' you until you either suck this dick, or take your slutty ass outta ya misery and off ya'self."

I shudder. "And how do I know that for sure? That'll you'll leave me the fuck alone?" I ask, contemplating giving in. I want this shit to be done and over with already. I don't know how much more of this can go on before someone starts putting two and two together, and comes up with the final answer—that I sucked this nigga off, and have been wetting up a string of other niggas as well.

He laughs. "You don't."

I huff. "Exactly. So, kiss my motherfucking ass!" I slam the receiver down, getting up from behind my desk and walking out into the shop. I walk over to Felecia and tell her to take messages for all of my calls for the rest of the day.

She lifts her eyes up from *The New York Daily News*, with a questioning gaze. "Oh, okay. Speaking of calls, who's that nigga who keeps calling here for you? The nigga sounds like a real nut."

He is. I'm standing here, hoping I can come up with a convincing enough lie to keep her from asking more questions. "Girl, he's some nigga bugging me about a job here. And he won't take no for an answer. He read that article they did on us in the *Star Ledger* and now has it in his head to work with us."

"Doing what?" she asks, pursing her lips. I can tell her wheels are spinning.

"He's a barber." *Bitch, you couldn't come up with something better that that?*

She taps her lip with her index finger. "Interesting."

Fuck. "Why you say that?"

"Uh, hello...for starters, a barber means tapping into them niggas' pockets. And if he can style, too...Mmmph. Chile, we..."

Oh, hell no. I already see where she's trying to go with this. Even if the nigga could cut hair, which I doubt, I wish the hell I would let that crazy motherfucker up in here.

"No, thank you," I flatly state, stopping her in her tracks.

"Damn, you didn't even let me finish and you already shutting me down."

I laugh. "'Cause, boo, I already know what you're gonna tell me. That having a barber on board would be great for business and would bring in a new set of clientele. And I agree. Don't think I haven't considered that. But it *won't* be him. My gut tells me he'd be more of a liability than an asset here. And *that* is the last thing we need around here."

"Well, alrighty then. Say no more. The next time he calls, I'll tell 'im to drop dead."

Wouldn't that be a blessing! "Sounds damn good to me," I say, walking back to my office.

The rest of the day flies by without incident. And I am relieved. I still don't know what the hell I am going to do about that nut harassing me for head. But what I do know is I need to do something 'cause sitting around doing nothing isn't cutting it. If for nothing else, I need to figure out my next course of action before this nigga does something else. In my heart, I realize it's only a matter of time. Am I scared? No, not really. Should I be? Probably. This nigga, whoever the fuck he is, has become a painful thorn in my side. And I want it removed, before it does more damage than it already has. This walking on eggshells bullshit waiting to see what happens next is starting to drive a bitch batty. Yet, I keep my game face, pretending I'm not fazed by anything. *I refuse to give that nigga any power over me*, I think, gathering my things to leave for the day.

Three weeks pass, and like clockwork, I arrive at the shop before Felecia—purposefully. So far the nigga has been letting me breathe. There've been no harassing phone calls, no mail, no messenger boys coming into the salon with disrespectful requests; nothing. I would like to think he's given up; that he's found himself a new victim to torment. Somehow, I know that's wishful thinking.

I sit in my car, waiting for the rain to stop. It's been pouring down off and on since late last night, so a lot of the side streets are flooded. I watch the heavy droplets pound against my windshield, thinking about being somewhere laid out naked in front of a fireplace being fucked long, slow and deep until my pussy walls shake. I think about Jasper. The idea of him being so close to coming home excites me on some level but makes me extremely nervous on another. And rightfully so. I'm cheating and lying to him, doing the same shit he used to do to me. No matter how I try to justify it, the fact is I am still a fucked-up bitch for doing what I've been doing behind his back.

I sigh, glancing at my engagement ring. I love Jasper, I swear I do. With everything that is in me. I have a lot to lose, if I don't get shit under control. I gotta do something about this nigga who's been harassing me. Ways of disposing of the nigga begin to take up space in my head. I imagine myself agreeing to spin his top, luring him to a dark, secluded park where I throat his dick. I drop to my knees, holding a blade behind my back, grabbing him by the base of his dick with my free hand. Slowly, I begin licking and kissing and nibbling all over it, encircling the tip of his dick with my lips and applying light suction over it before inching all of his cock into my mouth and down into my throat. He holds the sides of my head with both hands as if he's holding a basketball, pounding himself in and out of my wet throat, balls deep. Then in one swift motion, I thrust my knife upward into his balls, twisting and pushing until he collapses.

In another scenario, he is reclined back in his car seat and my face is in his lap. I have his semi-erect cock in my hand, licking his balls while stroking it. The minute he closes his eyes, I reach in my pocket and pull out a scalpel blade, swiftly slicing off his motherfucking dick, then shoving it down into his screaming mouth.

A tapping sound forces me out of my killing trance. It's Felecia peering into the passenger side window. I crack the window, realizing it's stopped raining. "Girl, you must be deep in thought. Didn't you hear me tapping on the window?"

I shake my head. "Chile, I have so much on my mind right now. I didn't hear shit."

"Well, what in the hell you sitting out here for?" I tell her I was waiting for the rain to stop. "Well, as you can see, it's stopped. So hurry up and come in before it starts coming down again. Geesh, you act like you gonna melt or something."

"Whatever," I say, rolling the window up on her. I turn off the ignition, removing the key, then gathering my things to go inside. Felecia is already through the door when I finally get out of the car. She leaves the door open for me.

Once inside, she and I chat for a bit, about nothing in particular, mostly about the appointments for the day. She doesn't have any gossip for me today. And honestly, I'm kind of glad she doesn't. As I make my way to my office, we make plans to sneak out of work early tomorrow to catch happy hour down at P.F. Chang's.

"And I wanna be outta here by two-thirty. So that means no appointments after twelve."

I laugh. "It figures your drunk-ass would want to be the first one there."

She laughs with me. "Yep…damn straight. I wanna be pressed to the barstool by three-fifteen so I can get my three hour's worth of drink on." I shake my head, preparing to walk off when she stops me in my tracks. "Umm, by the way...I meant to tell you Cassandra wants you to give her a call. I ran into her last night in Wal-mart with three of her bad-ass kids."

"Oh, okay. Does she need a hair appointment?"

"No, she said something about tracking down that roach-ass nigga who came through here tryna call you out a couple of weeks ago."

OhmyGod, please don't tell me she told Felecia more than this. "Oh, really," I say, trying not to sound anxious. "Did she say anything else?"

She shakes her head. "Nope; just for you to call her when you can. Hopefully, she got the rundown on that muthafucka so we can find out who the hell put him up to that shit. I shoulda knocked all of his fronts out, coming in here with that bullshit."

I roll my eyes, waving her on. "Girl, let it go. His ass ain't even worth it. We have no time getting caught up in some ignorant ass nigga's shit. As long as he doesn't bring his ass up in here with that shit again, I could not care less who sent him here. Fuck 'im."

She tilts her head; eyes me, furrowing her brows. "So let me get this straight. You mean to tell me you're not the least bit curious about who put that nigga up to it?"

"Exactly."

"Hmmph, you're good. 'Cause I'd wanna know."

"Then what?" I ask, trying to keep the edge out of my voice. But the truth is this conversation is not only making me uncomfortable, it's starting to give me a pounding headache.

"Then I would have that nigga handled."

"Well, I don't have time for that."

"No, but that's what you have a man for—to step to that nigga for comin' outta pocket."

"Wrong answer," I say, putting a hand up on my hip. "Jasper

does not need to be getting caught up in no dumb shit. There was no harm done, so he's not to hear anything about it," I warn, pausing. I eye her for effect. "Agreed?"

She puts her hand up in mock surrender. "I'm just sayin'. He—"

I put my hand up to stop her. "Not. A. Word."

Alright," she says, shaking her head. "Not a word. Still, I think he should know."

I sigh. "Sweetie, this is not about what you think; it's about what I need you to do—to have my back. So, let it go."

"Okay," she says, dusting her hands off, "done."

I smile. "Thank you. Let me know when my appointment gets here," I tell her, walking back to my office. I try to keep my steps slow and steady. One foot in front of the other, seemingly unnerved. But the truth is I am a fucking wreck!

I shut the door behind me, racing to the bathroom to splash cold water on my face. *I need an apple martini—no, scratch that...a damn bottle of tequila*, I think, opening my medicine cabinet and grabbing my bottle of extra-strength Excedrin. I pop two in my mouth. Swallow, hard. Then make my way over to my desk, plopping down in my chair. I pull out my cell, scroll through my address book, then dial.

"Hey, Miss Pasha, girl."

"Hey, girl," I say, mindful to not call her Big Booty since I can't ever remember her name. "Felecia told me you wanted me to call you." I hold my breath.

"Yeah, I wanted to let you know that I ain't forget about tracking that nigga down for you."

"Oh, girl, don't even worry about that. Like I told Felecia, let that shit go. The nigga can't block my flow. I'm still standing, still making moves, so fuck his bitch-ass."

"Oh, I know that's right. But, still…that disrespectful nigga needs to be handled for how he came at you. I got my goonies on alert. And when we figure out who the fuck he is, and where he rest at, he's gonna get got."

"Listen, chile. Don't. Just leave it alone, please. I don't want you or anyone else getting caught up in shit that ain't that serious. I appreciate you having my back, though. But *please*, drop it…"

"Are you sure?" she asks.

"Yes, very. It's done and over with."

"Well, okay, then. It's dropped—for now. But, if the nigga comes through again…"

"Then his ass is gonna get lit the fuck up," I finish for her.

"That's right. We gonna pop that ass like a firecracker. Oh, wait…Day'Asia, get yo' sneaky ass back up them goddamn steps fo' I beat the dust off ya black ass," she snaps in my ear, talking to her fourteen-year-old daughter who is almost as wild as she is. "I don't give a shit what that nigga said, I *said* take yo' ass…Bitch, did you hear what I said…girl, I gotta go, this little nappy-headed heifer tryna raise up on me like her pussy's bigger than mine…"

"Go…" the line went dead. I sigh, looking up from my desk. Felecia is standing in the doorway, leaning up against the frame with her arms folded.

She tilts her head. "Is there something going on?"

"Not at all," I say, matching her stare. "Why you ask that?"

She shrugs. "I don't know; something doesn't seem right. Too much strange shit's been poppin' off all at once. That one nigga callin' here back to back, then another nigga comin' up in here wit' dumb shit…" she pauses. Takes me in for a few seconds, then adds, "But I tell you what. I'ma leave it alone." She turns on her heels and walks off toward the front of the shop, leaving me sitting here feeling like the walls are closing in on me.

FIFTEEN

The minute I log online, IM screens start popping up. Some of the screen names I'm familiar with; some I'm not. Most of them I ignore. Others I give very brief replies to, then click out of. I grin, shaking my head, when a screen comes up for Mr. Seven-And-A-Half.

THICKSEVEN-AND-A-HALF4U: Hey, Beautiful. How u?
DEEPTHROATDIVA: Hey 2 u 2. I'm doing well, thanks. And u?
THICKSEVEN-AND-A-HALF4U: Horny
DEEPTHROATDIVA: LMBAO. Why I think u stay horny?
THICKSEVEN-AND-A-HALF4U: LOL. No doubt
DEEPTHROATDIVA: where's wifey?
THICKSEVEN-AND-A-HALF4U: OOT
DEEPTHROATDIVA: OOT? What's that?
THICKSEVEN-AND-A-HALF4U: Out of town
DEEPTHROATDIVA: Oh
THICKSEVEN-AND-A-HALF4U: U busy?
DEEPTHROATDIVA: not really. Why?
THICKSEVEN-AND-A-HALF4U: I wanna c u. U down?
DEEPTHROATDIVA: I am. But

I take a deep sigh. Try to decide if seeing him is really a good idea. I swear this nigga is fine as hell, but damn it…I've sucked him twice, already. So technically, I could go another round with him since three rounds is my max. Lord knows his dick is… tasty! No, fucking delicious is more like it. Mmmph. And those heavy-ass balls of his are delightful. Another round for the road won't hurt. Will it? *Bitch, leave this shit alone. Tell him no.*

THICKSEVEN-AND-A-HALF4U: But?

DEEPTHROATDIVA: I don't want u getting strung out

THICKSEVEN-AND-A-HALF4U: 2 late! ☺

DEEPTHROATDIVA: Poor u! Let me find out u a nut on the loose

THICKSEVEN-AND-A-HALF4U: LOL. Never that, baby. Ur screen name gets my dick hard

DEEPTHROATDIVA: So u want me 2 suck that shit for u?

THICKSEVEN-AND-A-HALF4U: All night!

Instead of taking heed to the voice in my head, telling me to dead this—*now*, I start to rationalize my thinking. If I throat him this last time, I can get this out of my system—now, instead of posting another ad.

Besides, this nigga does have some good dick. And that nut…oh Lord…yes, I let him bust in my mouth, and I swallowed him. And it was good to the last damn drop! It had been so long since I actually ate a nut out of a dick. But he had earned that extra treat. The way he ate my pussy the last time I was with him, he was the first nigga I actually contemplated giving some pussy to. Thank God I'm grounded. Otherwise I would have been bouncing up and down on his cock with no thought or regard for Jasper or my promise to him. I know in my heart what I need to do, what I'm supposed to do. But the freak in me overturns any rational decision of doing what's right. I take in a deep breath as I type.

DEEPTHROATDIVA: When and where?

THICKSEVEN-AND-A-HALF4U: Same spot. 8?

DEEPTHROATDIVA: Cool. C U then!

THICKSEVEN-AND-A-HALF4U: Bet

I close out the screen, then begin opening emails. There are several emails from niggas responding to last week's ad posting. Most of them I delete. A few I read. *Hello. I can definitely use some nice slow, wet head. I'm actually looking for someone to cum over and lick my girlfriend's pussy juice off my cock. I fucked her this morning and still smell of her, and assume taste of her, too. 6 feet, 180, and seven cut here. I can host.*

I frown. What the fuck?! *Delete.*

I move on to the next email. *You: Just what I need! Me: 5ft10in 32years old brown hair/blue eyes, 180 lbs white guy with a lady back home but a hard dick here in need of some no-strings dick sucking. Always wanted to try a sexy, black woman.*

I delete as I glance at the clock over on the nightstand. It reads: 6:23 P.M. I make a mental note to log off in another ten minutes so I can get ready to wet down Mr. Seven-And-A-Half's dick. I decide to open two more emails, then delete the other eight.

Hello. Can you handle a cock over 8 inches? It's pretty thick, too. Nice guy with a big cock looking for head. And if we click, I'll eat your pussy and ass, or fuck you good. Prefer sweet, wet, hairy pussy.

I sigh, realizing stupid is what stupid does. And a lot of these motherfuckers are about as stupid as they come. I type: *Hello, 8 inches? Baby, that's a snack for a deep throat diva like me. What are your stats? Pic of the cock, please.*

I open the next email. *Hello. Are you still looking for a dick to suck? I'm always looking for a warm, wet mouth. Would love to get sucked off tonight and feed you a sweet load of cum. Mutual oral is cool,*

*too. Love eating black pussy. 42, five-nine, one-ninety; 7 cut med-thick
and meaty full balls that like to get worked over. Let me know if you're
still looking and interested. Thanks!*

I delete, then log off. I remove my clothes, tossing them on the
bed before walking into the bathroom to take a quick shower. I
quickly shower, wrap myself in a plush towel, then oil my body
with Vaseline Cocoa Butter. I stand in front of my mirror, gliding my hands over my body. My skin is smooth and silky. I allow
my hands to wander over my firm breasts, over my flat stomach,
then back up to my breasts, lightly pinching my nipples. They
are the size of gumdrops; erect and eager for a tongue swirling
over them, hungry for a mouth to devour them.

I slip into a faded denim skirt, then put on a denim jacket over
a tangerine camisole. I fasten the last four buttons on the jacket,
leaving the first two undone—showing off my ample cleavage. I
slide my feet into a pair of orange Gucci stilettos, grab my hobo
bag and keys, then head downstairs for the door. Just as I'm
about to turn the knob to walk out, the house phone rings.
Instead of ignoring it, I turn around and head to the kitchen to
check the wall phone's caller ID to see who's calling. As luck
would have it, it's Jasper.

"Hellllllooo," I answer, trying to sound half asleep.

"Yo, baby," he says over the noise in the background. "Sounds
like you were sleepin'."

"I was," I lie, sitting my bag on top of the counter.

"What you doin' home so early, anyway?"

"I wasn't feeling well."

"Damn, what's wrong?"

"Cramps," I say, shocked at how quickly the lies roll off my
tongue. In all the years Jasper and I have been together, I've never
felt the need to lie to him about anything—until now. I glance at

my watch. It's already a quarter to eight. "And I have a terrible headache."

"Damn, baby. What'd you eat today?"

"I had a tuna salad earlier." He asks if I think that might have made me sick. I tell him no. Tell him my period is about to come on. That I feel achy all over.

"See, baby, that's why I gotta hurry up and get the fuck home. You need Daddy there to take care of you."

"Awwww, I know. I wish you were here now. I need my back rubbed."

"Baby, ya man's 'bout to rub a whole lot more than that."

"I can't wait." I let out a low groan, glancing at my watch. *I need to get going.*

"Listen, baby…I'ma let you get back to sleep, aiight?"

"Okay. Are you okay?"

"Oh, no doubt. I'm good, baby—real good. I'ma go on back and beat this hard-ass dick."

"You so nasty," I say, chuckling.

"Yeah, I'm nasty for you. I want some pussy."

"And this pussy wants you," I say, moaning. Talking to Jasper, hearing his voice, has only escalated my horniness, and has made me that more eager to rush over to the Marriott to get this pussy sucked and licked on—and, yes, gobble down on some cock.

"Getting home to you, and getting up in that pussy—making love to my baby—is all I think about, feel me? You got ya man sprung."

OhmyGod, what he says pulls at my heart.

"Jasper, baby, you coming home is all I think about as well. It's almost over."

"No doubt, baby. Look, go on back to sleep. Feel better. I'll hit you up in the mornin', aiight?"

"Okay, thanks. I love you."

"I love you, too—for *life*." On that note, we hang up, and I quickly grab my shit and race for the door. *For life*, I repeat in my head. At the rate I'm going, I won't have much life in me left if I don't stop this madness. And stop it soon! But knowing this doesn't keep me from cranking up my engine and peeling out of my driveway, heading toward some hard cock.

By the time I pull up into the hotel parking lot, it's already eight-thirty. I see Mister Seven's truck as he flashes his lights. I pull up beside him and park. We both get out of our rides at the same time.

"Hey, what's good, beautiful? For a minute there, I thought you was gonna stand a brotha up."

"Never that," I say without thinking. "Umm…I meant…definitely not. I got caught up in something that I had to handle first."

"Oh, I feel you," he says, handing me the room key. "Everything aiight?"

I nod. "Couldn't be better. I hope you have a lot of energy stored up 'cause I am horny as hell tonight," I warn him.

"No doubt, baby. This dick is fully loaded and ready for you."

I smile. "See you upstairs." I walk off, popping my hips toward the hotel entrance.

As before, the minute he steps into the room, I attack him. Tugging at his belt, then yanking his jeans down to his ankles. I massage his meaty dick over his white Calvin Klein boxer briefs. Suck him over the fabric until he thickens.

He grabs me by the head. "Damn, baby. You know how to make this dick feel good. You don't even have my dick in your mouth yet and you already got me wanting to bust. Shit, girl. You can get a nigga in trouble."

I remove my mouth from his growing bulge, replacing it with

my hand. I knead his dick in his underwear, glancing up at him, grinning and eyeing him all sexy-like. "Baby, I'm not here to get you in trouble. I'm here to make you feel good, and get that nut out of this fat-ass dick."

"You got me hornier than a muhfucka. I wanna put this dick up in you tonight. You gonna let a nigga make love to you?"

I keep my hand locked on his cock, stroking him as I stand up. I gaze into his eyes. "I can't. But we can sixty-nine all night and you can fuck my throat as deep as you want."

He stares at me. I can tell this nigga digs me. And truth be told, I don't blame him. But it's not me—the woman, he is feeling. It's this throat and tongue he's enthralled with. He pulls me into him, grabs and squeezes my ass, then catches me totally off guard by leaning down and kissing me. At first a quick peck, then it becomes a lingering kiss with all lips, then evolves into a passionate tongue-probing kiss. And the fucked-up thing is, I don't resist, don't pull away, don't do shit to keep this from turning into more than what it's supposed to. Kissing has always been off limits. It's too personal, for me. Well, okay, it isn't any more personal than sucking a nigga's dick, and then swallowing his load.

I finally pull back, placing my hand up against his hard chest. "We better stop before this ends up somewhere else. So let's stick to the script and let me suck on this dick. That's what you're here for, right?"

"Most definitely, baby. But, I can't get ya sexy ass out of my head. I'll be with my girl 'n shit, got my dick all up in her and you start popping up in my head. Those lips, the way your twirl your tongue around my dick, the way you suck my balls—I can see all that shit. I close my eyes, fucking my girl, and see you down on your knees handling this dick."

It's never my intention to have any of these niggas I suck get caught up, which is why I only suck them a limited number of times, but there's something different about this nigga here that has me thinking that…just maybe, I could become his personal dick sucker with no strings attached. OhmyGod, what the fuck am I thinking? My man is too close to coming home for me to be thinking about some crazy ass shit like this.

I drop back down on my knees, pulling his dick and balls out over the waistband of his underwear. I kiss the head of it, then tenderly lap at his balls before taking him into my warm mouth, sucking him like a lollipop. Inch by inch, I swallow him down into my throat until I have every inch of him down.

Less than a minute later, his nut gushes out, splattering all over my face and down on my hands. I continue stroking him until the last drop of his nut oozes out. I run my fingertip over the slit of his dick, smearing his nut into his skin, then take him back into my mouth and suck him all over again. He moans, clearly at the brink of losing his mind. I got the nigga on the verge of collapsing. He knows I know this, so he snatches me up and carries me over to the bed on wobbly legs, trying to buy himself some time to recover.

I grin. "I see this wet throat got you stumbling."

"Oh, you think that shit's funny, huh?"

"Yep," I tease, licking my lips.

"Oh, aiight, get ya laugh on, baby. The tables are about to turn. So let's see how funny you think shit is now." He tells me to lift my hips. I do. He removes my skirt, tossing it into the corner of the room. I get ready to remove my laced Vickies, but he stops me. Tells me he wants to eat my pussy over them, first. And I am more than fine with him wetting my pussy up over my panties. He buries his head in between my thighs, starts licking the center of my pussy, then begins sucking it until the thin fabric of my panties are drenched. I let out a moan, palming his head with one hand and pinching my right nipple over my shirt with the other. I wrap my leg around the back of his neck, pulling him deeper into me.

"Yeah, that's right, tease my pussy, nigga. Wet my panties up…" The nigga doesn't even have his tongue in me yet, but the way he's working me over has my insides already shaking. I know a lot of it has to do with hearing Jasper's voice earlier, and me missing his dick inside of me. Then there's that other part of me…that side of me that knows I'm playing with fire, taking risks, playing a dangerous, deadly game. And it is this knowing that ignites the flames between my thighs. "Rip my panties off," I demand in a low, husky moan. He grabs them with his teeth, then tears them apart, exposing my engorged clit and dewy lips. "Suck my pussy, nigga…"

I reach for him, direct him to shift his body, to lower his dick down into my mouth so I can take him into my throat. He does and we get into a wet, sweaty, nasty groove of moaning and groaning and sucking and slurping each other. I run a finger along the crack of his ass, gulping his cock down into my neck. Before long he is deep-stroking my neck while eating me out. The loud slurping sound he is making is music to my ears and makes me hornier than I already am. I lift my legs up, roll my hips up from off the bed, then wrap them around his back, offering him access to my asshole as well.

We are both trying to outsuck and face-fuck the other. We are both frantic, trying to outplease the other. It has become a race to see who can make who nut first. In the end, I win—as I always do, bringing him to the finish line in multiple waves of ecstasy. His body shudders as I continue nursing on his dick. I let his baby batter slide down in my throat, then pull his dick out of my neck and begin sucking on the head while rapidly jerking his shaft. He has another nut ready to erupt and I am determined to coax it up. After tonight's rendezvous, this nigga will never forget being with the Deep Throat Diva. And no matter whoever else he gets to suck his dick outside of "wifey," none of them hoes will ever compare to me.

A few minutes later, I start creaming on his tongue. Not long afterward he lets out another loud moan and nuts in my mouth again. I swallow him. Then he shifts his body around and collapses beside me, breathing heavy.

"Whew," he says, catching his breath. "I ain't gonna front. I ain't tryna leave my girl, but I damn sure don't wanna stop this shit, either."

"Trust me, boo. I'm not asking you to leave her, either. Nor do I want you to. And I'm not going to front. I enjoy sucking your dick. And you're the first nigga in a long-ass time who I've let bust in my mouth and I swallow that shit."

"Word?" he asks, seemingly surprised.

I nod. "I'm a dick sucker, baby. But I'm not a messy one. Most niggas get the latex treatment, so consider yourself one of the lucky few."

"That's wassup. So, what's really good with you? You single? Gotta a man? The last time we kicked it, you was actin' all secretive 'n shit. Dig, I'm discreet, too. I'm not tryna disrupt my home situation. And I'm definitely not lookin' to disrupt your groove either. But I dig you. And I wanna know more about you. This shit we got goin' is a no-strings arrangement between us, and I'm good wit' that. Just two peeps freakin' it on the low."

"Good," I say. "And that's how it should remain. But, after tonight, this is it for us. I have to chill out."

"Oh, word? I guess that answers my question. I can dig it."

For some reason I decide to keep it real with him. I break down my situation and tell him all about Jasper without telling him who he exactly is. Explain to him how I got caught up in this internet shit. When I am finished, he stares at me, stunned. "Damn, so how many dicks have you sucked off since you started going online, if you don't mind me asking?"

Shit. The truth is I don't exactly know how many niggas I've topped off. But I can guesstimate. And in my approximation, I count at least—including him—thirty-seven dicks…in two years. As embarrassing as this is, I tell him. And it feels like a ton of bricks have been lifted up off my shoulders. I am relieved to have someone to share my dirty little deeds with. Besides, I don't see him as a threat. He has as much to lose as I do, if not more.

I watch him intently as I tell him this, gauging his reaction. There is none. But I can tell he's thinking—something. "Go 'head. Say it."

"What?"

"What you're thinking. How trifling I am."

He strokes my cheek, then kisses me on the forehead. "Nah, actually that's not what I was thinking at all."

"What were you thinking, then?"

"I was thinking, what ya man will do if he ever finds out."

I inhale a deep breath. Hold it in my lungs as if it were going to be my last, then slowly exhale. I close my eyes for a few seconds, then open them. "Kill me," I whisper.

SIXTEEN

Seven A.M., Monday morning, I am at the shop handling some last-minute things before the place starts buzzing with people. And as usual, Felecia is here in diva style, done up in all of her finery: white gold tennis bracelets, two carat diamond earrings, and a diamond choker. She's wearing a sexy black and white BCBG Max Azria tunic dress and a bad-ass pair of four-inch black L.A.M.B. leather and suede strappy booties with twisting straps. Then to top it off she has on a damn multi-toned color bob style wig with a sweeping bang. I glance over at her sixteen-hundred dollar Ferragamo satchel she has propped up on the counter, shaking my head. This bitch is worse than me when it comes to handbags and wears. I swear she has enough clothes and accessories to open up her own boutique. Not that I have room to talk.

"I see you serving up another new look."

"Oh, please," she says, waving me on, "I just rolled outta bed and threw this on."

I laugh. "Yeah, right. And you popped the tags, when? This morning?" She laughs, knowing I'm right. That's the one thing we definitely have in common—our love for high-end fashion. The only difference—well, two differences—I'm not into all the different wigs and hairpieces, and I can now afford to buy my own shit. She, on the other hand, has a different type and style of wig for every day of the week and she still relies on her man, Andre, to keep her laced. I'm not hating, though. I was that same chick once.

The conversation shifts into her filling me in on all the things she forgot to mention last night when we spoke on the phone. She feeds me drops of new gossip. And for some reason, I cling onto every morsel. Like Alicia getting pissy drunk over the weekend and sucking off some stripper nigga's dick in front of everyone at some chick's bachelorette party. The image flashes through my mind and I feel myself becoming turned on. Then pictures of that nigga who walked up in here looking for me to suck his dick flash through my head and my mood shifts, but I don't let on. *My man said if I came through you'd hit me off with one of ya deep throat specials…Suck my dick, bitch!*

I buck my eyes, shaking his words out of my head. "You have got to be kidding me," I say, feigning disgust. But I know more than anyone that I am no better, or no different, than she is. At the end of the day, we're both two dick-sucking whores.

"Now you know I don't kid when it comes to the street news. And baby, Miss Hotbox was in rare form, I hear."

"Well, how'd you hear about it?" She tells me Shuwanda was there, too. That they had gone to the party together. "Hmmph," I grunt, knowing how Shuwanda's messy ass moves. If she sees it, she's telling it. "Say no more."

She flips through the appointment book. "Alicia is my girl and all. But she really played herself. And I gotta say if what she did is true, I'ma be looking at her real sideways from now on."

"Why?" I ask, twisting my face up. I'm surprised she would say something like that. Since she claims to be so nonjudgmental, believing people should be able to live and be who they are.

"Because…one, she has a man; two, she's sucking off a nigga she doesn't even know—a stripper at a party, no less; and three, it's just straight nasty."

"What? Sucking dick?" I ask, trying to play stupid.

She looks over at me, sucks her teeth. "No, sucking dick isn't nasty. Topping off a nigga you don't know is. Then to have a man on top of that…" she shakes her head, frowning. "…what kind of bitch would suck some nigga's dick off, then roll up on her man like shit's all good?" *A bitch like me*, I think, shifting my eyes. "Chile, that's grounds for an immediate beat down."

"I guess."

She slaps the leather book shut, putting a hand on her hip. "You guess? Bitch, what kind of mess is that? Wait. Please tell me you don't think that shit isn't trifling?"

Now, I'm standing here trying to act as if I'm equally turned off by the whole random dick-sucking thing, but who am I to pass judgment on Alicia, or anyone else when I'm just as messy—or worse?

Felecia and I are very close and there's typically no topic of discussion off limits between us, with the exception of my extra-curricular oral activities. That's a subject she and I will never have, especially now. It's bad enough she recently asked me—again, which I found quite strange—if I've ever cheated on Jasper since he's been locked up. And of course, as I did the first time she asked me this—I looked her dead in the eyes and told her a bold-faced lie. "Nope. I have no reason to."

"Girl, good for you," she said, sipping on her third Agave Margarita. We were at P.F. Chang's for their happy hour, eating and drinking. "I don't know how you do it. Personally, I'd be pulling my damn hair out if I had to go without sex. I'm sorry, I love Andre. But if his ass ever got locked up I'd have to have me some dick on-call until he got out. Fuck that. I'm not about to deprive myself of some cock just because a muhfucka can't keep his ass out on the streets to handle his business in the sheets."

I chuckled, licking the salt from around the rim of my Margarita glass, then taking a slow, deliberate sip. It was also my third drink, and I was starting to feel the effects of it. "Well, I'm not saying it's been easy because it hasn't. But with the help of a whole lot of batteries and a collection of toys, I get by."

"Hmmph," she grunted, scooping out another helping of brown rice, then arranging several shrimp over it. She puts a forkful of food in her mouth, then points her fork at me as she chews. "Girl, if the shoe were on the other foot, do you actually think Jasper would be so quick to keep his dick in his pants?"

"Of course not," I say, grabbing a shrimp from her dish, then popping it in my mouth. "He'd probably be slamming his dick into something the same night."

"So if you know that, why wouldn't you want to get a little side action until he comes home?"

Truth be told, I wasn't sure if she was asking me this to bait me—call it paranoid if you want, but I knew better than to give her anything other than my scripted truth. "Because it wouldn't be worth it. I don't need the headache."

She stared at me, took another sip of her drink. "So, tell me this. Did Jasper tell you that you better not fuck around on him, or was he open-minded enough to realize that you're a woman with needs and that if you're going to do it, then do it discreetly and responsibly?"

I gave her a crazy-ass look, raising my eyebrow. "Girl, what you think?"

She laughed. "I know; stupid question. He probably said,"— she deepened her voice—"'Pasha, let me find out you giving up my pussy, and I'ma beat the dog shit outta you.'"

I crack up. "Exaaaaactly "

She sucked her teeth. "Niggas kill me. They can fuck and do whatever they want, but the minute they think we're letting someone else get what they think belongs to them, it becomes a damn problem."

"You ain't never lied. You know how these niggas are."

"Yep," she said, eyeing me. "And Jasper's the type of crazy-ass nigga who'd be more than happy to go back to prison if he ever found out some extra shit about you."

I started choking on my drink. "OhmyGod, girl, don't say no shit like that."

"Well, it's the truth."

I sighed, shaking my head. "And you're probably right. Hopefully," I slipped, hoping she didn't catch it, "That'll never happen."

"*Hopefully*? Bitch, whaddaya mean 'hopefully'? I thought you said you've never cheated on him."

"I haven't," I quickly stated. "I was only saying. You know what I meant."

She eyed me, then grunted. "Mmmph, let me find out…"

"Bitch, please. There's nothing to find out. This pussy is sealed tighter than a fortress."

She laughed, taking another sip of her drink. "Girl, you don't have to convince me. I believe you. The question is: does ya man?"

"Want another round of drinks?" I asked, avoiding the question.

"I sure do," she said, gulping down the rest of her Margarita. And for the remainder of the evening we ate, drank and laughed until it was closing time.

I bring my attention back to Felecia. "Girl, please. It doesn't matter what I think, or you for that matter. Alicia's a grown woman, making whatever choices she makes by her own free will. What she's done or is doing has nothing to do with me."

"Whatever. The shit's still nasty to me." She stuffs her bag into her drawer, then locks it. "Annnnnway, I meant to ask you. When's the last time you went on Facebook?"

"It's been months, why?"

"Girrrrrlfriend, you are missing out on the dirt. That chick who cut up Big Booty has been reading her for filth on Facebook, posting all kinds of messy shit about her on her wall. Somebody musta tagged Big Booty, and that shit got her cranked up. She turned around and posted all types of shit about what chick's man used to do to her in bed, challenging her position as his woman and whatnot. And she even got the video of that chick getting stomped down by her kids posted on YouTube."

"Are you serious?"

"Baaaaaaby, as a heart attack. They've been going at it hard for the last two days."

I roll my eyes, disgusted. I mean, really…grown-assed women carrying on like dick-whipped school girls is beyond my reach. Whatever beef the two of them have, they need to handle that shit like adults instead of airing out each other's personal business on some public site for all to see. I have two Facebook pages; one for me, and the other for the salon. And I rarely go on either. I think the last time I actually logged onto my personal page was about two months ago. That's how far removed I am from it all. And, when I did go on it, half of the people who had requested me as a friend, I declined. And any notes I had, if they didn't pertain to making money, I ignored.

"If you ask me," I state, pulling open my BlackBerry and scrolling through my messages, "they both sound like two stupid bitches. Hmmph, I'm glad I don't waste my time on that shit. Only sick bitches and niggas air out their personal business online."

And only a sick bitch posts sex ads online, then goes off and has random sex with them. But that hasn't stopped you. Now has it?

"Well, girl, as true as that may be. I looooove it!" she says, getting up from her seat. She glances at her profile in the mirror hanging on the wall behind the counter. "It keeps me in the loop with all the minute-to-minute details of the latest hood gossip. Them messy bitches make my day, boo."

"Hmmph. Well, you can have it. And while you're at it, how 'bout you make yourself useful and maintain the salon's page, too, 'cause you know I can't be so bothered with that mess."

"I got you," she says glancing at her watch, walking toward the front door. She opens the miniblinds, lets the morning light in. "Just give me the password and I'm on it." Her iPhone buzzes. She walks back over to the counter and picks it up, then scrolls through it. "Hmmph. Alicia just texted me. She's not coming in today."

"I shouldn't be surprised. Does she have any appointments scheduled for today?"

"Two. But they're not until later this afternoon. I'll call them to see if they want to reschedule or see someone else."

"Okay, well let me let you do your thing," I say, walking toward my office. "I'm gonna check the emails, then try to go through some of that mail that's been sitting on my desk for the last few days before my appointment gets here."

"Okey-dokey," she says, watering the tropical plants situated around the shop.

I leave her to her task, going into my office. My cell rings. I pull it out of my bag, then glance at the screen, smiling. It's my seventy-year-old grandmother who we lovingly call Nana. But for me, she's more than *Nana*. She's the woman who loved and nurtured me when my own mother couldn't. Then she became the woman who would raise me after my father was murdered.

Quiet as it's kept, because Nana refuses to admit it despite what everyone else in the family, and in the streets, has said about my father— he was a menace. Ralphie Allen, aka The Boogey Man—

was a ruthless drug dealer and street bully who muscled up lower-level drug dealers, shaking them for their paper and product. And for the most part, he had niggas shook at some of his crazy antics, like tossing gasoline on someone for not coming up off their money and drugs, then setting them on fire, or biting off someone's ear for ear-hustling in on a conversation he was having. He had gotten his street name because he was as black as night with dark piercing eyes and a menacing presence. He'd always do his dirt late at night, swooping down on his unsuspecting targets, beating, maiming and robbing them—in no particular order, instilling fear in them. Whomever he thought was caking up that week, could and would get it. So, niggas in the streets stayed strapped and ready; most of the time looking over their shoulders, knowing that The Boogey Man was somewhere lurking in the shadows. Unfortunately for him, he strong-armed the wrong niggas and ended up getting gunned down. My father died of multiple gunshot wounds to the head and chest. I was eleven.

Then, in 1999, my mother was murdered in a car-jacking incident where three men approached her at gunpoint for her '98 Porsche 911 GT1. When the police finally recovered the car—four days later, her body was found tied up in the trunk. The autopsy showed she had been killed by two bullets to the head. I was twenty.

With no questions asked, Nana opened her heart and doors to both me and Felecia, losing both of her own children—my father, and Felecia's mother—to drugs in one way or another. In many ways, Nana tried to shelter us and kept us in church, hoping to keep Felecia and me from becoming wayward, like our parents. Though she was strict, she was extremely fair. And, for the most part, she did a damn good job raising us.

"Hi, Nana," I say. "How are you? Is everything okay?"

"Hey, baby," she says in her soothing voice. "I'm fine. My knees hurt and I can't get around like I want some days, but I'm favored and blessed. You know God is good."

"Yes, Nana, I know," I respond, hoping she doesn't get into one of her mini-sermons about sinning and thieving hearts and us living on earth in our last days and needing to get closer to God. I love my grandmother dearly. But sometimes...never mind. "I'm glad you're doing okay."

"Yes, baby. God has kept me wrapped in His grace and mercy. And He's been good to you, too."

"Yes, He has, Nana," I say, bracing myself for what's coming next.

"And you need to give Him some praise."

"I know, Nana. I do."

"I raised you and Felecia to be good servants of the Lord, but neither one of you have taken heed to His call. I haven't seen either of you at service in months."

"Nana, things have been busy at the shop and then I'm back and forth to see Jas—"

"Mmm-hmm. And the devil's a liar. So you can keep dancing with him if you want, but he brings you nothing good. I'm gonna keep praying for you and Felecia. That's all I can do. I'ma leave it in God's hands. The two of you seem to have gotten so high and mighty these days."

"Nana," I say, offended, "why would you say something like that? That's not true."

She smacks her lips. "Hmmph. When's the last time you came to fellowship in the house of the Lord?"

I roll my eyes up in my head. Felecia sticks her head in the door. I mouth to her that it's Nana and she snickers. I shoot her an evil eye, giving her the finger. She decides to come in, plopping her ass down on the orange leather sofa. "Nana, Felecia is sitting right here. Would you like to speak to her?"

"Now don't go trying to brush me off; I already spoke to her. And don't try and change the subject, either. Felecia did the same thing this morning when I called her and asked her about coming out for Women's Day. It's the least you can do. I don't ask much from you girls."

I sigh. "You're right, Nana."

"I expect to see both of you there, for *both* services. It's the second Sunday of the month. You hear? No excuses."

"Yes, Nana."

"Good. And you and Felecia can ride together and pick me up."

OhmyGod, Nana is gonna drag the shit out of us, I think, shaking my head. The thought of sitting up in church—no disrespect— all morning and afternoon makes me nauseous. "I'll have to check my schedule," I tell her, then add, "I'm supposed to be going out of town that weekend so I'll have to let you know. But Felecia will be around."

"Bitch," Felecia hisses. I smile.

"Pasha, I raised you better. After all I've done—putting you through school and paying for braces and dermatologists so you can walk around with that gorgeous smile and beautiful skin— the least you can do is make time for your aging grandmother. Nothing on earth lasts forever. You never know when my time is going to come and I'll be called home to glory by my Lord and Savior to step foot through the pearly gates of Heaven."

I hate when she starts talking like this. Her way of guilting me. I glare at Felecia as she chuckles, already knowing Nana's work. "Nana, I have to go. My first appointment is here."

"Uh-huh. Go on. Rush me off the phone, like I don't know any better."

"I'm not rushing you, Nana. I love talking to you. It's just that I'm at the shop right now and it gets busy here."

"Hmmph. Well, go on then. Oh, before I forget."

"What's that?"

"The Missionaries would love for you to be a part of next year's Community Day. Since this year's was such a huge turnout. You and the other girls over at the salon really made a difference giving back to the needy. You know doing the Lord's work and giving back to the community is what keeps joy in my heart, and should keep joy in yours."

Yeah, and giving back helped a motherfucking nut track me down, too. Donating time and staff to do hair and nails to the homeless and needy at Nana's church's annual Community Day is how I ended up having my face plastered all in the newspaper. At the time when I agreed, I thought it would be great publicity for the salon; not knowing it would have major consequences for me.

"Glad I could help out, Nana," I say, half-heartedly. We say our goodbyes, then hang up. Felecia stares at me, grinning. I suck my teeth. "Bitch, what the hell you grinning for?"

"Temper, temper," she teases. Her cell rings. She pulls it from her waist, glances at the screen, then shakes her head. "It's Nana calling back."

I snicker. No matter how many times Nana calls one of us, or no matter how annoying she can be at times, neither of us would ever ignore her calls. She answers, glaring at me. "Hey, Nana.... Yes, I know...Pasha reminded me...I'll have to check my schedule...No, Nana...that's not true...Okay, Nana...I know. I will... I promise...Nana, can I call you back? It's getting busy here... Okay, Nana...I'll stop by tomorrow to see you...I love you... okay, bye..."

As soon as she disconnects the call, I tease her. "What a punk.

What happened to 'I'm not going to that shit' spiel? You are so full of shit."

"*Whaaat*ever," she snaps, laughing. "You know damn well I have a hard time saying no to Nana. So kiss my natural fat ass."

I laugh with her. "No thank you, boo. I'll save the ass kissing for you." I mock her. 'Okaaay, Nana. Yes, Naaaaana'. Girl, you crack me the hell up."

She sucks her teeth. "Unlike you, Nana always makes me feel guilty."

I roll my eyes, getting up from my desk. "Whatever. You need to get over it."

"Mmm-hmm, I'll be sure to let her know that the next time I speak to her."

I laugh. "Well, whatever you do. You make sure you don't tell her it came from me."

"Unh-huh, punk…just what I thought."

SEVENTEEN

The following morning, I am literally surprised to see Alicia sitting in a chair in front of my desk, scowling when I come out of my private bathroom.

"Oh, hey girl," I say, walking back over to my desk. I glance up at the wall clock. It's ten A.M. "I see you made it in today."

"Girl, I'm going through it right now. Sorry 'bout yesterday. I had to take a day off to get my mind right."

"No worries," I say, taking a seat behind my desk. "Is everything okay?"

She sighs. "It will be. You need to have a chat with Shuwanda, though, before I do. Because trust me. This time it ain't gonna be cute."

I feign ignorance. "What are you talking about? What happened now?"

"That ghetto bitch doesn't know when to keep her fucking trap shut. I thought she and I were cool. But obviously we're not. This is the second time she went back and told one of her clients some shit about *me*. She's always running her damn mouth, but the bitch forgets to tell what she does."

I will myself from rolling my eyes. If you know you hang with a bitch who can't keep shit on the low, then stop hanging with her. If you choose to keep doing shit with her or around her, then your dumb ass deserves to get what you get. These two tricks go out drinking, then end up in some kind of situation that generally involves some stray nigga they done picked up from the bar and freaked together. And the fucked-up thing, both of these hoes have men. Not that I'm in a position to judge. But damn... at least be discreet about it.

She tells me practically the same thing Felecia did. The only thing that's off is the fact that it wasn't a bachelorette party after all, it was some erotic book release party a friend of Shuwanda's was having at the Diva Lounge in Montclair. Afterwards, they went to a private after-party that consisted of strippers—four males, and two females—where Alicia got real freaky with hers and dropped down, dug her hand down into one of the stripper's jockstraps, and started sucking him off in front of everyone. Somehow the shit ended up posted on Facebook. And are you ready for the kicker? Drum roll, please...her man done found out! And he doesn't even have a Facebook page, but the niggas in his clique do. So of course they put him on. And this is what the world has come to: Evil social networking tactics!

I'm not sure what to think, or feel, or even say to her for that matter. The only thing that comes out of my mouth is, "Damn girl. That's fucked up."

"Shit. Tell me about it," she says, holding her head in her hands. "Chauncey been blowing my cell up for the last two days snapping on me, talking all crazy. I'm glad he's out of town, though. At least that'll give him some time to cool down."

"Well, that's good. How long is he gonna be gone?"

"Until Thursday night, I think." She pauses, picking at her cuticles. "I swear, if I see that bitch today, I'm gonna light into her ass."

I frown, trying to understand why she's blaming Shuwanda for something she did to herself. "Umm, Sweetie," I say, raising my eyebrow. "I don't think so. You're going through it, but when you piped that nigga off in front of everyone you brought that shit on yourself, boo. However, lucky for you, she's off today."

"Hmmph. Good for her."

"Listen, Alicia," I warn. "Any beef you have with Shuwanda you need to handle outside of here. Do not bring that ghetto shit up in this shop. How I see it, if you can't handle your liquor, then you shouldn't be tossing them—"

Felecia walks in, interrupting us. "Umm, Alicia, there's a situation out front brewing and you need to come handle it, *now*. Ya man is here, and he is snapping the fuck out."

Alicia looks at me, shocked and scared shitless, knowing it's about to be problems. I stare back at her, giving her one of those bitch-don't-look-at-me looks. Soon as she's about to open her mouth to say something to Felecia, a deep male voice booms in back of her, startling all three of us. It's Chauncey. This is my fourth time seeing him since she's been with him. He's a tall, strapping Mandingo-type nigga: six-feet-six inches of dark, chiseled man meat; with deep waves and a mustache and goatee. Why the hell Alicia would do anything to get on this nigga's bad side is way beyond me. Then again, who am I to talk?

"Yo," he says, brushing past Felecia to step up in the room, "we need to talk, now. So get ya fuckin' ass up and let's go."

Alicia's eyes pop open, clearly embarrassed by what's about to go down. "Baby, can this wait 'til my break?"

"Bitch," he snaps, walking up on her, "fuck outta here with that! Fuck a break! Ya ass been breakin' every since I've been gone. A muhfucka can't even roll out wit'out you gettin' caught up in some dumb shit. I been calling ya skeezin' ass all muthafuckin' mornin'. And I came by ya muthafuckin' crib and ya punk-ass didn't come to the door, or answer ya phone. What the fuck is you doin' all up on Facebook 'n shit on ya muthafuckin' knees in front of some nigga?"

Alicia, poor thing...she looks like a deer caught in headlights. She looks scared as shit right now. "Baby, I..."

"Bitch, don't fuckin' baby me. I wanna know what the fuck you was doin', yo. Was you suckin' some nigga's dick the other night?" When she doesn't respond fast enough, the nigga starts sceaming. "Bitch, did you have a nigga's muthafuckin' dick hangin' out ya mouth? And don't muthafuckin' lie to me."

OhmymotherfuckingGod, this nigga looks one pill from crazy, I think, shifting in my seat. The look in his eyes tells me he's about to go postal. And depending on how she answers—shiiit, on second thought, there's really no answer she can give that's going to make an ounce of sense. He's going to beat her ass. Images of Jasper choking and beating the shit out of me come into full view. It'd be an ass whipping well-deserved, and I know it. Still, I quickly blink the images away, pulling out my cell. I dial 9-1-1.

Before I can open my mouth to tell the dispatcher what's the emergency, he yanks Alicia by the back of her weave and in a flash my office becomes this nigga's personal boxing ring as he starts beating her down right in front of us.

"Bitch, you try 'n play me, yo?" She tries to fight him off of her, but he is punching her all upside her face and head like she's a nigga on the streets. She's screaming and fighting him back, begging for him to stop. Felecia's screaming at him to stop. Customers and other stylists are running back here to see what all the commotion is about. There are even a few bitches with their cell phones open snapping pictures. This nigga is whooping her ass like he doesn't have a care in the world. I can't believe this shit!

"Felecia, get them out of here," I snap. She pushes the spectators back, shutting the door in their faces. I yell into the phone at the dispatcher and give her the details, then—when the dumb bitch starts asking me a bunch of extras—I start screaming at her to get the police here before this loon kills her. The last thing I want is a body in my shop. And the way he is punching her up, it's bound to happen.

By the time the police arrive, my office is all tossed up. There's blood everywhere. Alicia gets taken out on a stretcher, and he is escorted out in handcuffs. The way he beat her down, I feel so bad for her. I truly do. What happened to her could ultimately happen to me if I'm not careful. Still in all, empathetic or not, the bitch is fired!

At a quarter-to-three, Mona, Jasper's cousin, waltzes into the shop—*late* and wrong for her appointment. And after this morning's episode with Alicia getting her ass stomped out in here, then having to clean shit up, the last thing I want to do is be on my feet any longer than I have to. The only thing I want to do is take my ass home, run a nice hot bath, and soak. Lucky for her, she's my last appointment for the day. Still, I cut my eye at her as she plops down into my chair, letting her know my dismay.

"Girl, I'm so sorry. I had to go over to the school to pick up Mario's ass from school. That fool done got suspended for a week."

I grunt, placing a cape around her neck, then fastening it. Mario is her fourteen-year-old, fine as hell, spoiled ass son who she's been having some behavioral problems with over the last few months or so. He's been talking slick to her and not following curfew. What he needs, if you ask me, is a foot in his ass. But she doesn't believe in hands-on disciplining a.k.a. beating that ass. And neither does his father, so…there you have it. "Mmmph, what did he do this time?"

She shifts in her seat. "Are you ready for this?" She pauses, waiting for a response.

"Girl, will you tell the damn story," I say, swinging her around in the chair to face the mirror. I'm glad she's already washed and conditioned her hair. That saves me some time.

She continues as I run a comb through her hair. "This little nigga got caught in the girl's bathroom with some fast-assed thirteen-year-old with his pants dropped around his ankles."

"You have got to be kidding me. Were they fucking?"

"No, chile. That little bitch was down on her knees sucking his dick."

My mouth drops open. When I tell you I'm done, I mean it. I...am...motherfucking through! Do you hear me? First, Alicia; now this. And we won't even go into the all the dick-sucking I've been doing. For some reason, it seems like lately I'm being surrounded by incidences that involve swabbing a nigga's dick. Anyway, she goes on to say how dick sucking has become the new trend in middle and high schools. How these kids think sucking the skin off of a raw dick is safer than fucking. "OhmyGod," I gasp, feigning shock. "I don't believe it."

"Hmmph, believe it. I heard she was sucking his dick a mile a minute. Had his ass shaking and moaning so damn loud that neither one of them heard the security guard walk in."

I try not to laugh at the visual in my mind's eye. I don't even want the image of her son getting his top spun in my head. But it slowly starts to take up space in my mind's eye. The slutty part of me wants to know if the little tramp swallowed. Did she gulp down his gooey cream? Ugh...I know, I know—it's fucked up. I swallow back my seedy thoughts, moisten my throat, then say, "Girl, you know these kids today are too damn grown, and fast. I hope she got suspended, too."

"Yeah, she did—for three damn days."

"What, that's it? And Mario got suspended for five, why?"

"They say 'cause he skipped a class and was in an unauthorized area, so he got two additional days."

"That shit doesn't make any sense," I state, clipping her ends. "If I were that girl's parents, I'd beat her little ass every damn day until her ass went back to school. DYFS would be locking me up by the time I finished with her."

"Oh, don't think her mother didn't come down there and fuck her up. The principal had to pull her up off of her. Chile, what in the hell does a thirteen-year-old know about sucking a damn dick?"

"Apparently a lot," I answer.

"Hmmph. When I was that age I was still playing with Barbie dolls."

I shoot her a look, smirking. "Bitch, you *know* I know you. You were playing with many things, but a damn blonde-haired, blue-eyed doll wasn't one of them."

She sucks her teeth, laughing. "Oh, shut up. What...ever! The point is I didn't suck my first dick until I was almost seventeen. And this little hussy was down on her knees sucking my son's like it was dipped in chocolate."

She rambles on about how she beat his ass, then told him he was going to be on punishment for a whole month. Personally, I think she's being a bit extra with it. Please, who you know going to turn down getting head, especially a teen boy? Shit, I don't know many horny-ass niggas that would. With his golden brown skin, sandy-colored hair and athletic build, Mario has had the girls ogling him since he was in second grade. Even teachers have told Mona that her son was going to be a heartbreaker. So it's not surprising they'd start throwing him the pussy and throat.

"Girl, let him be," I say, chuckling as I flat-iron her hair. "He only did what any teenaged boy with raging hormones woulda done. And you know like I do it was that nasty-assed girl who lured his horny ass into that bathroom."

She laughs. "Girl, you sound like Avery now. You shoulda heard him on the phone when I was telling him about it. I told him I wanted him to get with that ass, and he had the nerve to tell me to stop cock-blocking and let him get his. Girl, I screamed on his ass. I bet you he changed his tune then. This nigga gonna say he'll talk to him and tell him next time to wait until he gets out of school to get his nut off."

I shake my head, laughing. That is so Avery. In high school, his nasty ass was always somewhere humping his dick into someone. He had pussy being tossed at him left and right, too. And he probably still does. But, knowing Mona, she's keeping him on a very short leash. "Like father like son," I say, twirling her around in the chair, then handing her a mirror. I've given her a simple layered cut with a tapered nape, then added a few curls to give it body.

"Annnnnnyway, have you and Jasper set a date yet?" She checks out her do, shaking her head, her tresses swing loosely about. "Oh, yes, this is it, girl."

"No, that's something we are still working on," I tell her, smiling. "He wants to get married now while he's still in the halfway house. And I want to wait."

"He called over to Momma's the other night and spoke to Sparks..." Sparks is her younger brother. He's one of them rugged, pretty-boy types that all the chicks swoon over. Come to think of it, Mario actually looks more like Sparks than he does his own father. Sparks' sexy-ass definitely could have spit him out as his own. "...You know he asked him to be in the wedding."

"No, I didn't know that. But I'm not surprised. I figured he would."

"Oh, and trust," she says, putting the mirror down and giving me an accusing eye, "I just know you got me in the wedding since I'm the one who hooked ya ass up with him. Miss I Ain't Beat To Meet No One."

I laugh. "Girl, that goes without saying. If it weren't for you, there's no telling who I might have ended up with. My man's definitely a keeper." I finish up the final touches on her hair, then remove the cape.

She gets out of the chair, staring at herself in the mirror. "Girl, as always you hooked a sista up right. I'll see you in two weeks," she tells me as she's walking toward the counter to pay Felecia.

"Hmmph. And make sure you have your ass here on time," I warn.

She laughs, waving me on. "Yeah, yeah, yeah. Love you, too."

EIGHTEEN

"Yo, you comin' through today?" Jasper asks, sounding like he's been up and about for hours. I slept like shit last night. Tossed and turned practically the whole fucking night. Even though it's been two days since that phone call incident, the nigga's voice has stayed locked in my head, haunting me. *I'ma 'bout to be your worse fucking nightmare.* I really don't want to invest too much energy into worrying about whether or not I should take his threats serious. But, then again, I don't want to take the shit he said to me lightly either. *I'm not gonna think about it, or let this shit worry me,* I think as I yawn and stretch, glancing over at the clock. 6:52 A.M. *In the goddamn morning! Oh my fucking God, this nigga is crazy!* It feels like I just shut my eyes. "I got a four hour pass to look for a job today."

Jasper has been at the halfway house in Newark for the last three weeks and this is his first opportunity to the leave the building. He tells me that normally it takes longer to get out, but he has this counselor chick who's been looking out for him.

I purse my lips. "Mmm-hmm. And what does this bitch look like?" I ask, hoping like hell this ho is keeping her professional boundaries in check and this nigga isn't trying to cross them. I heard how some of them counselors and whatnot working in the correctional system—particularly in the halfway houses—like to fuck with the inmates, so I already know what it is. I'm only hoping Jasper's ass isn't dumb enough to get caught up in it.

He sucks his teeth. "Yo, go 'head wit' that dumb shit. She's mad cool. That's it. Besides, she ain't got shit on my baby. Trust me. There's no one up in this joint I'm checkin' for. It's all you and that good pussy I'm 'bout to tear up."

"Mmmph," I grunt, stretching. "If you say so."

"Pasha, don't start ya shit, yo. You hear me, girl?

I yawn again, ignoring him. "What time can you leave?"

"I can bounce at nine. I gotta go fill out a few bullshit-ass applications to keep shit legit, then you already know what it is. I'm tryna grind up in them hips. We can slide off to the crib or get a room, feel me, baby. But I gotta be back up in this bitch by one."

"What time you want me to come get you?"

He huffs. "Yo, what the fuck is you doin'? Didn't you hear anything I just said? I told you I can bounce outta this muhfucka at nine. So you tell me. What time do *you* think I want you to come?"

"Nigga, don't start talking shit," I snap, sitting up in bed. "It's too goddamn early in the morning for you to be coming out your face all crazy. First of all, you shoulda called me last night and told me this shit. Hell, I spoke to you earlier in the day and you didn't mention shit about getting picked up. All I asked you is a simple-ass question."

"Aye, yo, knock all that shit off. Is you comin' up here or not?"

Luckily I don't have any appointments scheduled until later this afternoon. "Yeah, I'll be there. Where you want me to pick you up at?" He tells me that he's supposed to take public transportation, so he has to leave out of the building and act like he's going to the bus stop. He tells me to meet him at the gas station-slash-convenience store across the street. "Alright," I say, finally deciding to get out of bed. "See you at nine."

"Aiight, bet. Let me go hop in the shower. See you when you get here." We say our goodbyes, then disconnect.

At exactly nine I pull up into the convenience store-slash-gas station. I don't see Jasper anywhere, so I back into a parking space, then shut the engine off. As soon as he hops in the car, he leans over and kisses me on the lips. "Damn, baby, you look good," he says, buckling his seatbelt.

I smile. "You ain't looking too bad, either." He's dressed in a pair of PRPS jeans—where he got them from is beyond me 'cause they definitely weren't anything he asked me to bring him while he was at the assessment center—a blue and white striped Polo Jersey, and a crisp pair of white Air Force 1s. He has his Yankees fitted cocked to the side.

"Damn, you got my dick hard as hell; smelling all good 'n shit." He grabs at his crotch. "I can't wait to get up in that pussy."

I shake my head, starting the engine, then pulling out of the lot. I make a left, heading toward downtown. We stop at several places where Jasper goes in, then comes right back out with an application. After the fourth spot he does the same thing. Goes inside, then a few minutes later comes out with another application in his hand. I decide to ask him why he isn't filling them out there. Are you ready for his answer? This nigga tells me, "I ain't beat. I wanna hurry up and get to a room so we can fuck. I'll drop 'em back off the next time I get my pass."

I take my eyes off the road, and stare at him like he's fucking stupid. "Nigga, are you crazy? Why the hell would you do that? All it takes is ten minutes, if that, to fill out an application."

"Yeah, and?"

"Don't you need to get a job?" I ask, feeling myself getting annoyed. Shit, I have to wonder exactly where his head is. And I'm not talking about the one between them muscular thighs of his, either.

"I don't need to get the shit today," he snaps, frowning at me.

I shake my head, bringing my attention back to the road. "You know what. Do you."

He reclines his seat back. "Yo, chill, baby. I got this. Let's swing by this last spot over in Elizabeth, then hit up a motel." He rattles off where we need to go. "I'm tired of all this ridin' 'round 'n shit, anyway. It's time for you to ride up 'n down on this heavy-ass dick." He unfastens his belt, then unzips his jeans and pulls his dick out of his blue Polo boxer briefs. I glance over at it. And, between you and me, it takes every bit of my strength not to swerve off the road and fuck him down in this car.

An hour and a half later, the moment we've both been waiting for is finally here. So here we are—me and Jasper—in a hotel room on Route 9; not too far from Aviation Plaza in Linden. Jasper is out of his clothes lying in the middle of the bed playing with his already hard dick. His long dick looks…bigger, thicker and wider, than I remember.

The curtains are drawn and I have candles lit around the tiny room. I'm trying to get the mood right. Make shit sexy, for the both of us. I'm standing here in the middle of the floor wearing a Frederick's of Hollywood black, strappy lace teddy and a pair of red, four-inch stiletto mules, slowly gyrating my hips to Pleasure P's "Lick, Lick, Lick."

As I'm dancing, I peep my reflection in the mirror and smile. My body is banging. My small waist and abs are toned. My ass is big and bouncy; yet firm. Titties are full melons of joy. Even with clothes on, I have always been able to make a nigga's neck snap trying to take it all in. Hell, I've seen a few niggas' dicks sprout out in their pants without ever taking off my clothes. So, I already know what this little dance tease is doing to my man.

"Damn, girl, you rollin' them hips," he says, stroking his erection. "Turn 'round; let me see that ass bounce. I give him what he wants. Popping and dropping it down low for him, then making this ass clap. It's crazy, though. All the years I've been with Jasper, I've always felt like I've known him. But today's different. It feels like it's the first time I'm being with him. And in some ways it is. As familiar as I am with him, he almost feels like a stranger to me. Despite all the visits and phone calls, four years is a long time to be apart from someone.

Now, after all this time, here my man is…in the flesh, hard, hot and horny.

I taunt him and myself, running my hands all over my body, allowing them to linger between my legs. I suck on my fingers, pinch on my nipples, then continue winding my hips. By the time the song finishes, the lyrics and watching Jasper play with his dick have me on fire. Whatever inhibitions or reservations I might have had earlier are long gone. The only thing on my mind now is getting my pussy stroked, deep and hard.

I slowly make my way over to the bed, standing at the foot of it. "C'mon, girl," Jasper says, groaning. His cock is on rock and leaking with excitement. I lick my lips, getting up on the bed, then crawling my way between his legs. I take his dick in my hands, stroke it, then lick the slit. His precum is sticky and sweet. I moan. He moans. I lick his dick again. He moans again. "You like how I lick your dick?"

He gazes down at me. "Uhhh, yeah, baby…" I lick him again, then put my mouth over the head and lightly suck on it. I close my eyes and imagine that it's a thick, long, chocolate candy bar. "Aaah, shit. Right there…Aaah, shit. Suck that dick. You like that shit don't you?" I moan, continue my slurp session. "Aaah, fuck, baby…you miss Daddy's dick? Damn, baby…aaah, shit!"

I pull his dick from out of my throat, tell him I can't talk with my mouth full, then go back to wetting him up. I lift up his dick, slowly lap at his balls, then pull them into my mouth one at a time.

"Yeah, that's it...Bury that pretty face with them balls..." Then, without thought, I fuck his head up, and mine, and do something I've never done to him before—I lick his ass. He flinches, then relaxes. I'm jerking him off with soft, gentle strokes while rimming him. "Oh, shit, damn..." I continue working him over until he starts grabbing at the sheets, then yelps. "Aaah... aaaah...aaaah...I'm 'bout to spit, baby. Stop...oh, shit...stop..."

I don't. I keep on going, stroking and licking him faster until he shoots a thick stream of cum up in the air. His nut shoots over his head and hits the wall, underneath his chin and all over his chest. I'm so turned on by the amount of cum that has erupted from his dick that I greedily start licking it all up off of him, climbing up on him. We kiss passionately. Tell each other how much we've missed the other. Then he reaches up underneath me and slowly works his still hard dick in my sopping wet hole. It takes a minute and some extra maneuvering for it to finally get all in.

I moan as it stretches me. I forgot how good his big dick felt inside of me. He strokes me slowly and, after ten deep strokes, I feel an orgasm churning inside of me. "Oh, yes. Ooooh...oh, fuck...Oh, Jasper...uhhhh..." My pussy coats his dick with a bunch of cream as he continues thrusting his hips up into me. I gallop up and down on him, matching his rhythm.

I press my titties up in his face, offer him a nipple and he opens his mouth and suckles on it. In between his sucking, his says, "Damn, baby, I've missed this good-ass pussy." I pull in my bottom lip and moan. And in one swift motion, Jasper lifts me up and flips me onto my back. He gazes at me, strokes my face; grinds himself into me. "I've missed the hell outta you, girl."

"I've missed you, too."

He kisses my face, my neck, then sucks all over my titties, alternately twirling his tongue around my nipples before lightly grazing them with his teeth. He slowly pulls his dick out of my dripping pussy and starts kissing down the center of my chest. Licks all over my stomach, then dips his tongue into my belly button. I spread my legs wider. Allow him to kiss the inside of my thighs, my knees, the back of my calves, then the balls of my feet. He licks them, then sucks one toe, then two toes, at a time. I moan. He reverses his kisses, going from my toes, to the balls of my feet, the back of my calves, then back to the insides of my thighs; he fingers me, causing my pussy to yelp and weep and beg for his lips, his mouth, his tongue, on my clit. And he delivers, knowing what I need, without missing a beat. "Oh, shit…yeah motherfucker! Eat Mommy's pussy, baby…"

I grab him by the head with both hands, grip it like a basketball and grind against his tongue. He laps, and sucks, and gobbles up my pussy until I am nutting in his mouth. He swallows all of my juices. I can't lie. Jasper has my head spinning. I'm spent, panting and clutching my chest, trying to catch my breath. But he's not done. This nigga must be on Viagra or some shit 'cause he's still hard and ready to fuck. He pulls me down to the edge of the bed. He squats, slipping his arms under my hips, then scoops me up. We kiss as he slides himself into my pussy. He squeezes my ass as I ride down on his dick. I clutch his dick with my pussy; milk him, and talk real dirty in his ear and it doesn't take him long to bust his nut deep inside of me, filling me up with four years of locked away passion.

He holds me tight, shoving his tongue into my mouth. We kiss for a few seconds longer, before he puts me down. "Gotdamn," he groans, licking his lips as he grabs a chunk of my ass, "you got some good-ass pussy, baby. And that shit's nice 'n tight."

I smirk. "Yeah, nigga, just like I told you it would be."

He slaps me on the ass. "Yeah, it betta had been."

I suck my teeth. "Whatever, nigga." I head toward the bathroom. He follows behind me.

"Aye, yo, when we doin' this shit?"

"When we doing what?" I ask, feigning ignorance as I turn on the shower. But I know what that what is—getting married.

"Tying the knot," he says, pulling me into him. I lean back on his chest and crane my neck to look at him. He lightly kisses me on the lips. "I wanna wife you up, baby."

I smile. "And I wanna be your wife; especially after the way you fucked me down today with that big-ass dick."

He grins. "Yeah, aiight. So answer the question, then."

"You set the date," I tell him as I step out of his embrace, then step into the shower. He gets in behind me.

"Next Saturday," he says.

I laugh. "You have got to be kidding me. That's too soon, silly. I need to find a dress."

He twists his lips. "All them damn clothes you got, and you mean to tell me you don't have something you can rock? Give me a break."

I look him in the eyes. Step up into his space. "Jasper, when I marry you it's going to be my one and only marriage. So when I come down that aisle or staircase or sandy beach, I'm gonna be the baddest bitch you've ever seen for a bride."

He smiles, reaching for my nipples. He kneads them between his fingers. "Oh, yeah. Well, check this out. You already the baddest bitch, baby. And that's why a nigga's tryna snatch you up on some official shit."

I grab his hard dick, stroke it. "Mmmph," I say licking my lips. "I've missed the hell out of that dick."

"Oh, word? Is that all you missed."

I reach up on my tippy-toes and kiss him on the lips, slipping my tongue into his mouth. We kiss for a few moments, before I pull away. "And those sexy lips."

He grins, reaching for the soap and washcloth and washing himself off. "I can tell."

As soon as we finish our shower—after another round of intense fucking, we dress, then head out the door, leaving behind the scent of sweet, sweaty sexing.

I drop Jasper off where I picked him up from earlier. He tells me he'll call me later on, then says, "Saturday, October ninth. Two P.M."

"October ninth? What's happening then?"

"I'm marryin' ya fine-ass. That's seven months away. It's Columbus Day weekend and gives you more than enough time to do whatever the fuck you need to do." I smile, but inside I'm wondering when he came up with that date and how the hell I'm going to find a place in such short notice. I can tell his mind is made up. "I don't wanna hear no bullshit, yo. That's what it is, ya dig?"

"So is this you putting your foot down?"

"Damn straight."

"Well, alright then, big daddy. Whatever you want."

He leans over and kisses me, then gets out of the car. "It better be. Where you going from here?"

"The shop," I tell him.

"Yeah, aiight. Make sure you take ya ass straight there, too."

I roll my eyes. "Whatever."

"Yeah, aiight. You heard what Daddy said. Take ya ass straight to work, yo. You hear me?"

"Bye, Jasper. Call me later."

"No doubt, baby." I watch him as he walks across the street like he's been riding up and down on buses all day, looking for work. As I'm pulling off, I smile, replaying our encounter back at the motel in my head. My pussy is well-fucked, my throat well-coated, and my heart overflowing with love. *Damn, life can't get any sweeter than this*, I think, making my way to the salon.

NINETEEN

When I walk through the salon's door, there's a lot of lively chatter going on. Shuwanda's new client Robyn is sitting in the waiting area with her man—the nigga whose dick I'd wet a while back. She's leaning up on him, flipping through a magazine, while he's on his iPhone. She speaks when she sees me over at the counter with Felecia. Her man eyes her, then quickly shoots a look over at me before going back to doing whatever it was he was preoccupied with. I feel a level of discomfort, seeing him sitting up in here for the second time.

"We set the date," I say to Felecia, sharing the news about my upcoming nuptials.

"Girl," she squeals, "it's about damn time. Congratulations."

"Thanks," I say.

She gets on the intercom and announces, "Alright ya'll…listen up. It's official. We have a wedding to plan. Pasha and Jasper are finally jumping the broom. Columbus Day weekend it's gonna be on and poppin'." Everyone claps and cheers, and gives their congratulations. I blush, visibly embarrassed by the unwanted attention.

I tell all the well-wishers thanks, then shift my attention back to Felecia. "Do I have any cancellations?"

"Nope. So far, looks like everyone's gonna show. Umm, did Alicia call you?" she asks as she hands me the mail.

"No, she hasn't. Why?"

"Chile, don't quote me or anything. But I think she's gonna ask you if she can have her job back."

Now, between you and me, I really like Alicia. And maybe if she was paying rent like everyone else up in here I might be a bit more open to reconsider my decision to let her go. But since she's working off commission, and had the nerve to call out because she got messy, then comes up in here the next day and gets tossed around in my office, there's no room for a change of heart. Not only did she cost me paper, the bitch came up in here bringing drama to my place of business. Whether intentional or not, I don't give a goddamn. There's nothing to discuss. It's nothing personal. She has three small kids to feed, but that's not my problem. This is a business. And I'm about the business of running a classy, upscale salon. And fighting up in my shop isn't it. It's bad enough a motherfucker came up in here and tried to bring it to me. But, this…unh, not acceptable!

"Well, I don't know why she'd do that. She can't be that crazy to part her lips to even come at me with that nonsense. After that shit that went down up in here there's no way she'll ever step foot through these doors again." I feel like a two-faced, hypocrite. And I should. Still, it's my shop; my rules. So, it is what it is.

"I hear that. Oh, before I forget. Your three o'clock is gonna be fifteen minutes late. Gina called to cancel her hair appointment for tomorrow. She said she'll call back later to reschedule. And Bianca wants to know if you can squeeze her in for next Tuesday."

"I'll call her," I say, gathering my things to head to my office. As Robyn gets up to walk over to Shuwanda's workstation, out of the corner of my eye, I glance over at her man, wondering if he's even recognized who I am. I'm hoping he hasn't. But judging by the way he's checking me on the sly, I can tell he's trying to figure it out.

"By the way," Felecia says, "a package came for you. I put it on your desk."

"Okay, thanks." As I'm about to walk off, I realize that I left my phone in my car. I sit my things back up on the counter, then head for the door. "I gotta go back outside. I left my phone in the car."

As I'm walking out the door, I see this thug-type nigga standing across the street, looking over in the direction of the salon not too far from where my car is, like he was standing there waiting for someone, or something. I can't really make out who he is since he has a brown hoodie pulled up over his head—which I think is odd since it's almost seventy degrees today. Anyway, the nigga looks like he's up to no good. However, I don't put too much attention into it.

As soon as I step to the curb waiting for cars to go by, I glance over my shoulder and see Robyn's man coming outside as well. He speaks. "How long you been working here?"

"Since it opened," I answer, eyeing him. I glance back across the street. The hooded man is standing in the same spot, staring.

"It's a nice spot."

"Yeah, it is," I say, moving a strand of hair from my face as I take him in. I can't deny he's a handsome nigga. He has a chiseled face with deep, piercing brown eyes, full lips, and a dimpled chin. His hair is cut close and his neatly trimmed goatee makes him look sexier than he already is. He's wearing a brown, short-sleeved POLO button-up, beige khakis and a pair of brown designer loafers. For some reason, he reminds me of a computer geek.

He looks back toward the shop, then at me. Instinctively, we both step out of the view of the shops window in case someone was looking. "Congratulations to you," he says, giving me the onceover.

"Thanks."

He licks his lips, pulling in his bottom lip. "I was hoping you were gonna be here today."

"Why?" I ask, pretending to be clueless. "James, right?"

He nods. "Yeah. When I initially saw you the other week, you looked familiar to me, but I couldn't put my finger on where I knew you from. I went home and kept thinking about it. Then it hit me. Damn, I didn't think I was ever gonna run into you again."

I shift my weight from one foot to the other. "Umm, I'm not sure what you're talking about."

He smiles. "I'd never forget a face or set of lips like yours." I nervously shift my eyes, looking around to make sure no one else is in earshot. "Don't worry, I'm not gonna put you out like that," he says, sensing my uneasiness. "Your secret is safe with me. I just wanted to let you know, I remember who you are. Shit. I actually haven't stopped thinking about that night in the park."

I want to ask him which park he's referring to, but decide against it. The fact is it doesn't matter where I had sucked his dick. The point is I did it. He goes onto tell me how that was the best mind-blowing head he's ever experienced in his life. It's meant to be a compliment, but it has me feeling extremely uncomfortable. I swallow my nerves down, not believing how shit is unfolding right before my eyes. Of all the times I've gone out cock prowling, he's the first man who I have actually run into in public—surprisingly, my goddamn salon.

I decide to be honest with him. "I remembered you when you were here two weeks ago. I'd definitely like to keep this quiet."

He chuckles. "I'm engaged, remember? Who you think I'm gonna tell?"

I let out a sigh. "Point taken."

The cell in his hand chimes, alerting he has a text. He looks down at it. "Listen, that's her texting me."

I put a hand up, waving him on. "I gotta get my phone out of my car anyway."

He shoots his future wife a quick text back, then says, "It was nice talking to you. Maybe we can hook up one more time before we both tie the knot."

I smile. "Perhaps we shouldn't. With your wife-to-be coming into the salon now as a client, it's too close for comfort. The last thing I need in my shop is drama."

"I'm not looking for any drama either," he says, eyeing me. He smiles, glancing over his shoulder at the salon. "So this is your shop?" I nod. "Wow, impressive."

"Thanks. So you can understand how another encounter wouldn't be good for business."

He grins. "Then again, it may increase your business. Shit, she doesn't mind spending my money to come here."

I return the smile. "And I do appreciate the patronage, but that's as far as I can go with it. Besides, as you've heard, I'm about to be married."

"I understand. And so am I. But if you ever change your mind,"—he reaches into his back pocket, pulling out his wallet—"give me a call, or shoot me an email." He hands me a business card. I glance at it. He's an IT tech.

I smile. "Thanks." He smiles back, then glances down at his cell as it chimes again. It's another text from his fiancé. He walks off, texting back. And I prepare to cross the street. Dude with the hoodie is still standing by my car waiting, watching—or looking, for something. While I'm crossing the street, I see him lean down, picking up something. As I make my way toward my car, this motherfucker lifts up this big-ass cinderblock, draws his arms back, and hurls the shit at the rear window of my car. He takes off running down the street like a bat out of hell at the sound of glass shattering and my alarm blaring, yelling out, "Bitch!"

"OhmyGod!" I scream, running to my car. "Someone stop him! The motherfucker threw a brick through my window!" I quickly unlock my door, snatch my cell out of the passenger seat, then dial 9-1-1. In the meantime, I'm standing in the middle of the sidewalk, watching as this nigga disappears down the street.

"Fuck!" I yell. This is the last thing I need today.

TWENTY

Whoever came up with the saying: When it rains, it fucking (added for effect) pours never lied. 'Cause right now it feels like I'm being soaked by a monsoon. When I get to the shop this morning I am greeted with a slew of fliers taped all over the front door and window of the salon. Fliers, damnit!!! About me! Each one had a different slogan. Shit like: FOR THE BEST HEAD IN TOWN, PASHA ALLEN'S GOT THE DICK SUCKING GAME ON LOCK...FOR THAT 24 HOUR DICK WASH, COME THRU NAPPY NO MORE FOR THAT DEEP THROAT TREATMENT...PASHA ALLEN'S A DICK SUCKING SLUT...VISIT THE QUEEN OF COCK-SWABBING AT WWW.NASTYFREAKS4U.COM...PASHA ALLEN A.K.A DEEP THROAT DIVA WILL LICK YA DICK AND SWALLOW YA NUT 'CAUSE SHE'S A CUM-SLUT...

There were literally a hundred or more fliers covering the door and window. When I say my nerves were rattled, they were wrecked. Two weeks ago it was my car, now this shit! Thankfully, I still get here before anyone else. Then the nut has the audacity to call me. I'm sitting here at my desk, trying to push back a throbbing headache as I replay the conversation. "How'd you like the fliers?"

"Why are you doing this to me?" I ask, feeling exasperated. "Of all the people in the world you just have to fuck with me. Why?"

"I told you before. I want my dick sucked."

"Nigga," I snap, "you are outta ya motherfucking mind. I'm not sucking shit."

"Then I'm gonna keep fucking with you until you do."

I hang up on him. Two minutes later, the nut calls back.

"Bitch, hanging up doesn't stop me from calling. I'm gonna call ya smutty ass every day 'til you put those pretty-ass lips on this dick, again. By the way, how many nuts you swallow a day?"

I take deep breaths, counting to ten in my head to calm my nerves down. Even though my nerves are rattled, the last thing I should do is let this nigga know he is getting to me. "You're fucking crazy," I respond.

"You sucking this dick?"

"I told you…hell. Fucking. No!"

"I guess having the back window knocked out of that fancy whip of yours still isn't enough, is it ho?"

"Fuck you," I snap. Maybe talking slick isn't the smartest idea. But he is plucking my last nerve with all of this psycho shit.

He laughs. "Yeah, like how I'm gonna fuck that throat of yours. I'ma call every day. And I'ma ask you the same shit. And every time you say no, I'ma give your dumb ass something to remember me by."

"Like I said, bitch-ass, *fuck*…you."

"By the time I finish with you, slut, you gonna wish I hada fucked ya nasty, trick-ass. Get ready for ya next surprise," he warns.

"Nigga, do what the fuck you gotta do. I'm not sucking your raggedy-ass dick." This time, the nigga hangs up on me. I'm telling you this shit with this motherfucking nut is really getting out of hand. And the truth of the matter is I don't know what the fuck I'm going to do about it. I definitely can't go to the police with this. If I suck his dick, then this motherfucker will have me under his thumb. But if I don't, then the nigga's gonna keep harassing me. Either way, I'm fucked. I wish I knew someone I could call to handle this…him, for me. Some hood niggas who'd track his ass down, then stomp him the fuck out.

Anyway, here we are less than three hours later, and I have the goddamn police here at the salon, again, because someone tossed two big-ass metal pipes through the salon's window. Glass and shit is everywhere. I'm glad no one got hurt. The last thing I need is someone trying to sue me on top of everything else that's going on. Of course, no one was able to give a good description of the motherfucker who did this because he, like the nigga who smashed out my car window, had a hat pulled down over his eyes and a hoodie blocking his face. The only difference is he was short and dark-skinned.

Then, to add to my already pounding headache, I have these nosey ass police asking me a bunch of questions: Have you made any enemies recently? Have you had any disagreements with any-one? Could this have been a scorned lover? Do you know why someone would target you? My answer: No!

Now everyone here is all up in my business, asking me a ton of questions. I'm sure out of concern. But, still…it's embarrassing to say the least. First, the shit with the nigga coming to my shop, next my car window being smashed out, then the fliers. Now this shit. I'm convinced this nigga is not going to give up until he breaks me down.

To makes matters worse, my paranoia has me thinking I hear bitches snickering as I walk by. I know how messy hating ass hoes can be, especially Shuwanda, so it wouldn't surprise me if their laughter is at my expense. But come to find out Felecia tells me that while I was outside Shuwanda was in here running her mouth about Alicia giving everyone in earshot a play-by-play recap of how Alicia carried on at that party she took her to. Shuwanda was only being Shuwanda—a messy, backstabbing, two-faced bitch.

Then, coupled with everything else happening around here, Stax walks through the door with Jasper as I'm sweeping up glass. *Shit, shit, shit,* I think, trying to keep my face from cracking.

"Yo, what the fuck happen here?" Jasper asks, frowning as he points at the window. His jaw tightens as he looks around.

I stop sweeping. "Some crazy ass threw a pipe through the window," I tell him, cutting my eye over at Felecia. She lowers her head, busies herself looking through the appointment book. She keeps her mouth shut, but I know her. She wants to say something about my car. I have Jasper thinking it's in the shop for repairs because someone sideswiped me.

"Did they catch this nigga?" he asks, staring at me.

I tell him no. Look over at Stax who's standing by the counter, eyeing me on the sly while talking to Felecia. "Hey, Stax," I say to him.

He nods at me. "What's good, Pash? You aiight?"

"Yeah, I'm good."

"Oh, aiight, that's wassup. I was telling ya peoples if you need me to set up a goon squad up over here, all you gotta do is say the word."

That's the last thing I need here. I force a laugh. "Oh, no. We're fine. It was only some idiot acting a—"

"So what this nigga look like?" Jasper asks, cutting me off. A few of the stylists see Stax and Jasper and make their way to the front, smiling and grinning and shaking and popping their asses for attention. I give him what little information I know, tell him the people were coming out to replace the window, then change the subject.

"Umm, what are you doing here?" I ask, trying to mask my nervousness as I walk over and give him a quick kiss.

"I came to see my woman," he says, pulling me into him. "Why, I need a reason to come through?"

"Not at all. I'm surprised. That's all."

"Yo, let me talk to you for a minute," he says, taking me by the arm. "Yo, Stax, I'll be ready to roll in a minute."

"No doubt, playa," he says. "Do you."

Jaspers leads me to my office. All eyes are on him as we walk past the stylists' stations. A few of the girls speak. He acknowledges them with a nod. As soon as we get inside the office, he shuts the door behind us, then locks it. He's all over me.

"Yo, what's good wit' ya sexy-ass? I came through for some quick pussy."

OhmyGod, is this nigga crazy? I have glass and shit all over the place. The last thing on my mind is fucking. However, I already know if I don't give him a taste there's going to be problems. And it'll end up with him asking me a bunch of questions that I can't answer honestly. Beefing with him today is definitely not what I need.

I reluctantly give in as he pulls me into him and starts kissing me and cupping my ass with both hands. He slips his tongue into my mouth, and we go at it until we've both gotten ourselves worked up. I'm stroking his dick, squeezing the thick bulge in his sweats as he kisses my neck, then tweaks my nipples, massages my titties. Slowly my pussy starts percolating in anticipation for what's to come. I forget about the phone call earlier, the fliers, and the smashed out window. I block out the nigga's threats, blank out the nigga telling me to suck his dick. Nothing else matters, but feeling my man's dick deep inside of me. I squat down and yank his sweats down around his ankles before unleashing his beautiful black dick from out of his boxer briefs. I wrap my lips around the head of his dick, then slowly take him all the way to the back of my throat. I breathe through my nose, then swallow him past my tonsils until I have my nose buried in his pubic hairs.

He moans as I make soft humming noises while slurping him. "Oh shiiiiit..." I suck him nonstop without coming up for air, causing his knees to buckle. "Oh, fuck, baby...Gotdamn, your mouth feels like a pussy...this shit is so hot and wet..." He thrusts his hips, holding the back of my neck.

Bitch, suck my dick! You sucking this dick? Bitch, suck my dick! Suck my dick! You sucking this dick? I shut my eyes. Try to concentrate on getting Jasper off. Try to get these voices from out of my head. Spit drips down my chin as I continue rapidly bobbing my head back and forth, gulping his dick.

"Let me get in that pussy," he says, reaching for me to stand up. I pull his dick out of my throat. "Damn, girl, you got my head all fucked up. C'mon, take them drawers off." I'm glad I am wearing a skirt today, which makes it easier to remove my panties for him. He grabs them from me and sniffs them. "Yo, you got these panties nice 'n wet wit' that gushy shit, baby. Bend over ya desk and let me eat that shit from the back."

I do what I am told, forgetting that we are in my office and there are clients and staff on the other side of the door. He darts his tongue in and out of the back of my pussy, teasing my clit with his finger. He pulls open my ass cheeks and buries his face deep in the crack of my ass while he tongue drills me.

"Put your dick in me," I beg in a whisper, winding my hips. *Bitch, suck my dick!* I need him to fuck my mind clear. *You sucking this dick?* "Fuck me, baby." He gets up and slowly slides his thick shaft in me until he has every inch of himself deep inside of me. Jasper takes long, steady, purposeful strokes—making sure he hits every angle possible. He hits my G-spot, causing a wave of pleasure to wash over me. "Oooh, aaaah...oh, yes...right there, baby...mmmm...this dick feels so good..." Jasper pumps harder and harder until we both let out low, guttural moans as we climax.

Twenty minutes later, we waltz out of my office like nothing ever happened, holding hands. Stax is sitting at my workstation talking to Shuwanda, Felecia, and a few patrons. They all seem to be hanging onto his every word like a bunch of lovestruck groupies. I shake my head, grinning.

"Yo, Stax, you ready to roll out?"

"Yeah, let's roll," he says, getting up. He looks over at me, smirking. "Yo, Pash, be easy, ma."

"You, too," I say, letting go of his hand. He grabs it back, then pulls me into him, kissing me in front of everyone. He and Stax say their goodbyes. And every bitch in the shop says goodbye back, ogling them as they walk out the door.

I am relieved to see the window repair truck pulling up outside. I make my way to the front of the salon to meet them. It's then that I realize that I don't have on my panties. *Damn it*, I think, shaking my head, *Jasper's nasty ass took them with him.*

Two days later, I am picking Jasper up at the same spot for another "job search." He has me sitting out in this fucking parking lot for almost forty minutes before he finally gets to the car. "Aye, yo," he says, getting into the car and shutting the door. "Sorry you had to wait so long. Them muhfuckas up in there be on some real extra shit, word up. They had some bullshit-ass inspection, then I had to wait for my counselor to give me my pass. This bitch be on some extra shit, too. I can't wait to get the fuck up outta there."

I bite my bottom lip. Keep my mouth shut and let him rant on until I get sick of hearing it. "Where are we going?" I ask, changing the subject.

He glances at his watch. It's going on ten in the morning. "Let's go to the crib. I wanna stretch out in our bed."

"Don't you need to find a job?"

"Fuck that shit. I got my man hookin' me up wit' a connect so I'm good."

I raise my brow, cutting my eye over at him. "What kind of connect?" I ask with a tinge of skepticism in my tone.

"Him and his peoples have a detail shop on twenty-two. He's gonna put me on the payroll."

"Where's this shop at?"

"In Hillside. Why?"

Now, I'm far from naïve. I know what time it is with Jasper and his paper. But there's an idealistic part of me, hoping that he's done with the game. Unfortunately, he's not the type of nigga who'll ever be content working for minimum wage. So asking him what his intentions are is not only a moot point, it's a stupid one. Still, I ask. "And what will you be doing there?"

"Detailing," he huffs, reclining his seat all the way back. "What else you think I'ma be doing?"

I laugh, shifting my eyes back on the road ahead of me. "I don't know. You tell me."

"Aye, yo. Don't start ya shit, aiight? I got this."

"Yeah, okay, whatever you say, baby." I glance over at him, laughing and shaking my head. "You detailing cars, picture that."

He smirks. "Yeah, aiight. Get ya laugh on. But I'ma be detailin' that ass in a minute. Let's see how much laughin' you do then."

"Yeah, yeah, yeah," I tease. "Promises, promises. Don't talk about it, be about it."

"Yeah, aiight. Front if you want. You already know what it is. I'ma beat that shit down."

Against my will, my pussy twitches. I grin, pressing down on the pedal, hitting seventy, zigzagging my way through traffic to get home.

Ten minutes later, I'm pulling up into my driveway, shutting off the engine. I can tell Jasper's dick is already hard, the way he keeps fanning his legs open and shut, then grabbing at his shit. The nigga's had this pussy on his brain, and I've had his hard dick on mine, the whole ride. I already know the first nut is gonna be a quick one. But, after that, it'll be on and popping. His sexy, thuggish ass keeps me turned on. My pussy is so wet for him.

As soon as we step through the house and shut the door, we are all over each other. I'm grabbing his dick. He's palming my ass. Soon we begin kissing, and it doesn't take long before our wet tongues are doing a bump and grind of their own. Jasper's hands roam all over my body, massaging my breasts, pinching my nipples, then traveling down between my thighs. I dry hump on his hand, stroking his cock over his jeans. Before I know it, Jasper scoops me up in his arms and carries me upstairs to my…uh, I mean, our, bedroom, then lays me on the bed. He kicks off his AF Ones. Then off come his t-shirt, his jeans, and his boxers. Seeing him standing before me in his naked glory—rippled abs, chiseled chest, thick, shiny black dick—send a tingling sensation up my spine. I am instantly turned on. Already I can feel myself getting moist. This nigga is so damn fine! Next he removes my clothes, then tells me to assume the position on my knees. He wants to feed me his tongue, and his dick, doggie-style; one of my favorite positions.

I get on all fours, arch my back, then wait as he gets on his knees, pulls open my ass, then presses his face in between my cheeks. He kisses, licks, sucks and nibbles on my pussy, clit, and ass. He works me over. Takes me to the edge of an orgasm, then pulls me back. His tongue-lashing causes me to buck my hips, throw this ass up on his face. I ride his face; his tongue, as he darts his long tongue in and out of me. I am wet and ready and aching for what's to come next.

I crane my neck, look at him over my shoulder. I reach for him, urge him to replace his tongue with his dick. I'm ready to be FUCKED. "Aaaah, Jasper…oooh, baby…fuck me, baby…Give me the dick…"

"Oh, you ready for this dick, hunh? You want me to bust this nut up in ya guts, baby?"

"Yes," I pant, pumping and winding my hips. I reach back and pull open my ass. "Fuck me, baby…"

It doesn't take much urging to get him to fill my pussy up with his meat. He stands behind me, places one palm down on the small of my back, then slides himself into me. I gasp. "Oh, shiiit…uhhh…"

Jasper keeps banging my magic spot, causing wave after wave of sparks to shoot through my body. I am shaking, but he doesn't let up. He grabs me by the back of the head, pounds balls deep into me, talking mad shit that gets my snatch hotter and wetter with each stroke. "You got that bomb pussy, baby…ahh fuck, this shit is good…Uhh, fuck…mad tight pussy, baby…I own this muthafuckin' shit right here…"

"Yes…oh, yessssssss!" I moan, biting down on my hand as I am hit with another orgasm. My juices squirt out of me, splash up against his cock. Between the swishing sounds of my pussy juices and the rapid noises from his pelvis smacking into me and my ass slamming back onto his dick, I am completely lost in a trance. The pleasure Jasper is causing me is blinding. Ten minutes more and I feel the head of his dick expanding inside of me, alerting me he is about to shoot his hot load inside of me. He lets out a loud moan, gripping me extra tight around the waist as he plows his cock rapidly into me, filling me up to the rim with his cream. He pulls his dick out. I squeeze my pussy muscles to hold in his nut, then relax them to let some of it ooze out. I want so badly for him to eat the back of my pussy out with his cum dripping out, but he won't ever consider doing no nasty shit like that. I keep my thought to myself. Still, the idea turns me on.

"Wheeeeew!" he exhales, wiping sweat from his forehead with his hand. He is still on his knees as I shift my body around to face him and take his slick, sticky dick into my mouth. I suck him until his dick thickens, again. I clean his cock and balls, licking and slurping and sucking up any remnants of his nut and my juices. When I finish tongue bathing his dick and balls, I tell him to lie back on the bed, then begin giving him the Deep Throat Special. If he only knew how horny sucking a dick gets me. He'd be trying to keep a muzzle on me. I block the notion out of my mind and concentrate on giving him the blow job of his life. "Aaaah, fuck…aaaah, shiiiiiiit…goddaaaaamn, ya head game is sick…"

I glance up at him. His face is all twisted up, his bottom lip is pulled in and his eyes are shut tight. I grin, then slip his balls into my mouth one by one. I roll my tongue around them, then stop.

"Damn, baby…why you stop?"

"Get on your knees. I wanna suck your dick from the back," I tell him. He has me so fucking horny. I want to freak him in every way imaginable. He gets on his knees and I reach between his thighs and pull back his dick and balls, then begin licking the backside of his cock, the underside of the head, and his balls. He moans as my wet tongue slithers up along the crack of his ass, licking around his hole.

"Yo, what the fuck you doin' back there?" he asks, panting. I tell him to shut up, to relax, and let me have my way with him. His body tenses as I begin licking his asshole, darting my tongue in and out of it. But, slowly he begins to relax as I am stroking his cock at the same time. Five minutes later, he is bucking his hips and moaning as he shoots a thick load out. Again, I suck him clean.

We lay in silence, listening to each other's breathing. I'm not sure where his thoughts are. But mine have drifted back to the menacing phone calls, the fliers, the smashed car and shop windows, trying to figure out who this psycho on the loose is. *Them pretty-ass lips...that's all I thought about...you sucking this dick?* I have got to find that nigga and get him under control before Jasper gets home for good. *Maybe I should just go 'head and suck his damn dick and be done with it since that's all he wants*, I think, rubbing Jasper's hand. He has it resting on my stomach. I am so fucking disgusted with the idea of some loon trying to disrupt my life. If I had a gun I'd blow his fucking balls off, then shoot him in his face for wreaking havoc in my life. Fucking bastard!

"Yo, what you thinkin' 'bout?" Jasper asks, nudging me.

"You," I say, looking back at him. I flash him an award-winning smile.

He grins. "Oh, word? What you thinkin' 'bout?"

"About how much I love you, and how lucky I am to have you in my life." Shame starts to creep in and I feel myself becoming emotional as I tell him this, because it's true. I do love him with all of my heart. And I do feel blessed to have him as a part of my life. I only wish I could shake my demons. Find a way to rid myself of that motherfucker who has become a thorn in my side. My guilt begins to overwhelm me and I break down and start crying.

"Damn, baby. Why you cryin'? Wassup?"

"I-I'm...so...happy. And I love you...so much," I sob uncontrollably.

"Damn, yo," he says, pulling me closer into him. He holds me tighter. "I'm the one who's a lucky muhfucka. You my world, baby. I'm in this 'til we die, baby, real talk. And that's my word. You hear me?" I nod, feeling his dick harden. "Good. Now, let me get some more of this good pussy before we gotta bounce." He lifts my left leg up, slides himself into the back of my pussy, then fucks me in long, deep strokes until he busts another nut in me.

TWENTY-ONE

"Aye, yo, what nigga's ass you been lickin'?"

I frown, looking over at the digital clock. 12:22 A.M. *I don't believe this shit*, I think, rolling my eyes up in my head. He has a cell phone—along with practically everyone else in the building—that he keeps hidden up in the ceiling of the halfway house because it's considered contraband. Now he calls me around the damn clock, checking for me. "Jasper, what in the hell are you talking about?"

"Don't think I didn't peep how you licked my asshole while you were suckin' my nuts the last two times we were together."

"OhmyGod, nigga," I snap, sitting up in bed. "You fucking mean to tell me you're waking me up in the middle of the night to ask me about some shit I did to you almost two weeks ago? You have got to be kidding me."

"Nah, I ain't kiddin' shit. I wanna know what's really good wit' you. Since when you start lickin' assholes?"

"Nigga, what's good is: I sucked your dick. Sucked your balls, then felt the urge to lick around my man's asshole. Maybe, I wanted to try something different. Shit, you damn sure didn't seem to take issue with it while I was doing it, nigga. So what's the problem now?"

"The problem is I wanna know since when you start lickin' a muhfucka in his ass? All the years we been together you ain't never done no shit like that. Now, all of a sudden, you on some new type shit."

My mouth drops open. The nerve of this motherfucker. I literally feel myself about to blow a gasket. "New type shit?" I ask incredulously. "Are you fucking serious? Nigga, I haven't been with my man sexually in almost five years. A bitch was horny, and fucking turned on that I finally had my man stripped down in bed with his hard-ass dick hovering over my face and the only thing your ungrateful, paranoid ass is thinking about is whose asshole I've been licking. Newsflash, nigga: The only ass I've ever licked is yours. I tried something new. And guess what, motherfucker? I liked it. No, cross that. I loved it, nigga! That's why I did it twice! So get the fuck over yourself."

"Aye, yo, don't try 'n come at me all crazy 'n shit. I only asked you a simple question."

"No, nigga. It was a crazy-ass question; that's what it was."

He huffs. "Whatever, yo."

"Whatever nothing," I snap, pausing so I can get my thoughts in check before I say some shit I don't really mean. But, this nigga done got me riled up with this dumb shit. "Well, since you're into asking simple questions, answer me this, nigga: Did you like it? 'Cause the way you had your ass tooted up I'd say you were enjoying it a little too much. So maybe I should be asking *you* who you've had licking your hole while—"

"Aye, yo," he snaps back, cutting me off, "don't fuckin' play me, yo. Ain't nothin' pussy 'bout me, yo."

"How I know?" I ask, deciding to fuck with him some more.

"Yeah, aiight, Pasha. Don't get beat the fuck up, yo."

"Whatever, Jasper," I say, hanging up on him. Two minutes later, he's calling back. When I don't answer the house phone, he starts calling my cell, then house line again. "Yes?"

"Aye, yo. Why you gotta play?"

"I'm not playing. Why you always gotta start your bullshit? I mean, damn. Why can't you enjoy the moments we share without turning them into a buncha extra shit?"

"I do enjoy them," he says, lowering his voice. "You know how long I've been waiting to be with you, girl? You had a muhfucka feelin' good; too good."

"Then why you calling here with nonsense?" I ask, swinging the comforter off of me and getting out of bed. I walk over to get my laptop off of my desk, then bring it back over to the bed. I climb back in, propping two pillows up behind me. I turn it on; wait for it to boot up.

"'Cause you did some shit that fucked my head up."

"Well, did you like it?" He gets quiet. So I add, "I wanted our time to be all about you, Jasper. Don't you know how much I've missed you? I didn't wanna just suck down your dick, baby, or swallow your balls. I wanted to taste all of you. And licking your ass is something I've always wanted to do to you."

"Why you ain't say somethin' then?"

"I didn't think I needed to."

"You got me buggin', yo," he says, pausing. I can hear him breathing. He's thinking, wondering. He blows out air into the phone. "And you ain't do that shit wit' no one else?"

"No, Jasper, I haven't."

"Yeah, aiight, then," he says. I hear relief in his voice. "Go on back to sleep. I'ma hit you up later on, aiight?"

"Good night," I say, turning off the PC volume, then logging onto AOL.

"Good night? That's how you doin' it?"

"Jasper, what else you want me to say?" The mail icon says I have twelve new messages.

He huffs. "Fuck it, yo. What you gettin' ready to do?"

I open the first email. *Vgl Italian married male here who never*

*gets what he likes the most, head! I am 5'10 180 musc, tattooed with
buzz cut. 7 cut & thick here. I will have to sneak out, so you must be
within 10 minutes of south Plainfield, or be willing to come to my house,
and blow me in my detached garage. Wifey is a sound sleeper. I will be
up till around 2 am so definitely interested in a sexy, black chick with
great oral skills to give me a hot wet tight bj to completion. Willing to
eat your pussy if you want.*

"I'm going back to bed," I lie, deleting the message, then clicking down to the next email. *6'3" 220, handsome, 8 cut brown eyes.
Need a great SLOW BJ. Tonight!!! Working midnight shift. Come
thru and suck my dick in the parking lot. I'll finger your pussy for you.*

"Yo, I gotta bounce. This nosey punk-ass counselor is comin'
through doin' rounds and he be on some bitch-type shit tryna
hem muhfuckas up. I love you."

"Love you, too."

He abruptly hangs up, and I go back to reading emails. *Damn,
baby. U sound hot! 22. Italian. 6'4 195 8c. Always wanted to experience skull-fucking a sexy black chick. Hit me up. Young, horny and full
of hot cum for your throat.*

I smile, tempted to give his young ass a taste of what this deep
throat is all about. I type: *Baby, if u think you're ready for the dick
suck of ur life, then hit me back with a pic of ur sausage. I've always
heard Italians had good cock!*

After I send my reply I decide to delete the remaining emails.
However, just as I'm preparing to exit out of my account, an IM
screen pops up from mister Italian Stud Cock.

ITALIANSTUDCOCK: watz up?

DEEPTHROATDIVA: sucking a clean, fat cock

ITALIANSTUDCOCK: Then I'm ur man, baby. Got that stud cock
4 u. Thick, clean and always hard. Multiple cummer here. Shoot
big loads. U host? Travel?

DEEPTHROATDIVA: Travel

ITALIANSTUDCOCK: what r ur stats?

DEEPTHROATDIVA: 34-22-38. Soft, luscious lips, hot tongue with a long, deep throat. Can swallow a dick in one gulp

ITALIANSTUDCOCK: Damn, that sounds good. I like that!

DEEPTHROATDIVA: And it feels even better

ITALIANSTUDCOCK: Itz gettin late. Can we meet? I'm ready if u r

I glance over at the clock. It's almost one o'clock in the morning. I contemplate what I should do. The idea of tasting some young Italian dick is appealing to me. I tell him to send me a dick flick before I make my decision. In the meantime, another IM screen pops up.

THICKSEVEN-AND-A-HALF4U: wassup, ma? How u?

DEEPTHROATDIVA: hey there. I'm good, and U?

THICKSEVEN-AND-A-HALF4U: chilln-chilln. Horny as fuk 4 some of that deep throat

DEEPTHROATDIVA: is that ur way of say'n u wanna c me?

Italian Stud sends me an email with an attachment of two pics. I click it open. My mouth waters the minute his dick appears on the screen. It's a nice thick piece with a big, juicy mushroom shaped head. There's a big vein that runs across the top of it. I can't deny, it looks…delicious. And I'm tempted.

THICKSEVEN-AND-A-HALF: Maybe. But I'ma respect ya space. My dick is hard 4 more. ☺

DEEPTHROATDIVA: U betta be glad I'm on a dick-fast; otherwise U'd be in trouble. LOL

THICKSEVEN-AND-A-HALF: LOL. Me and my dick like trouble.

ITALIANSTUDCOCK: U still there?

DEEPTHROATDIVA: where u @?

ITALIANSTUDCOCK: Union. Earl Street

DEEPTHROATDIVA: do u have a safe spot we can go?

ITALIANSTUDCOCK: yeah.

DEEPTHROATDIVA: is 40 mins too late?

ITALIANSTUDCOCK: Nah. Itz good. I can meet u on the corner. I'll be in blue jeans, white tee, and white sneakers wearing a blue fitted. 908-444-1111

DEEPTHROATDIVA: k. C u then!

I write his number down, then close out the screen. Mister Thick Seven and I chat back and forth for a few more minutes before he tells me he has to go. That he has to go jack off because I got his dick rocked.

DEEPTHROATDIVA: Ooooh. *licks lips* U nasty. ☺ Imagine me on my knees with my head back and mouth open wtg 4 u to bust ur nut in my hot mouth

THICKSEVEN-AND-A-HALF: Daaaaaamn. No doubt! Gotta go, babe. TTYL

I click out of the box and shake my head, knowing damn well I have no business entertaining any of these niggas after all the shit I've been going through. *Girl, turn this shit off and take your crazy ass back to sleep*, I think, mulling over my options. Suck dick. Go to sleep. Suck dick. Go to sleep. What's a girl to do? Before I am able to make a decision one way or the other my cell rings. And in that instant my choice is already made for me. I sigh, feeling almost relieved. "Hello."

"You sleep?"

"No, Jasper," I say, leaning over the side of the bed, sitting my laptop on the floor. I slide it under the bed. I lie back against the pillows, resting my head up against the headboard. "I'm sitting up in bed."

"Oh, word? Doing what?"

"Thinking about you," I tell him.

"Oh, word? That's wassup. What you thinkin' 'bout?"

"Sucking on that dick."

"Damn, baby. I wish I was home in bed wit' you."

I let out a soft moan. "Me, too. Right now I'd be all over you."

"Yo, you feel like gettin' off?"

"Where you at?"

"In my bunk," he says in almost a whisper. "I got my locker door blocking me. I wanna bust this nut, baby."

I smile. "You got your dick out?"

"Yeah."

"Then let's do it, Daddy." I cut off my night lamp, then begin removing my panties. I toss them across the room. "I'm sticking my hand in between my thighs, rubbing my clit while I'm on my knees sucking your big-ass dick, baby...you like that?"

"Ah, shit, yeah...you gonna let me taste that pussy?"

I moan. Then for the next twenty minutes, Jasper and I go back and forth, moaning and groaning and talking nasty shit to each other until we both cum all over ourselves; me all over my fingers, him on his chest and stomach. I clutch the phone to my ear, breathing heavy into his ear.

"Damn, baby...that was good," Jasper says, catching his breath as well. "Yo, my shit is still hard. I need to be way up in that pussy, yo."

"I need you up in it, too." I glance over at the clock. 2:42 A.M. *Fuck!* I yawn, feeling sleep coming down on me. "But I need to go to sleep now. I'm exhausted."

"I feel you; me too. Good night, baby. Love you."

"I love you, too, Jasper." We hang up. I close my eyes and drift off to sleep with no other thoughts of sucking dick—*for now*.

TWENTY-TWO

The following morning, I wake up late and wrong. It's almost eight o'clock. And I have to be at the shop by ten. I have six appointments scheduled today, back to back, starting at ten. I race around the house, trying to get myself ready. I jump in the shower, wash the snatch real good, then hop out.

Thirty minutes later, I'm peeling out of my driveway. As I'm turning out of my development, my cell rings. I pull it from out of my bag, then glance at the screen. It's Mona. "Hey, girl," I say, pressing on the Bluetooth connection.

"Pasha, girl, is everything okay? I heard what happened down at the shop. Stax told Sparks. And you know how his ass can't keep shit to himself."

I laugh, knowingly. "Yeah, everything's good. Thanks. The police, of course, still haven't found the motherfucker who did me in. But it's all good."

"Hmmph, figures. Were you able to see what he looked like?"

"Not really," I tell her. "One of the customers caught a glimpse of him, but it wasn't enough for an accurate description of him." I tell her he was brown-skinned and wearing a hoodie and a pair of baggy blue jeans. "So, in a nutshell, with no fingerprints and no concrete description to go on, the police still have no leads."

She laughs. "Chile, that description fits half the nigga's in the hood."

I laugh with her. "Girl, you ain't never lied about that. I only hope they catch this kook before his nutty ass does something else." *Shit, shit, shit*, I say to myself, realizing I've said more than I should have. Mona picks up on this and doesn't miss a beat.

"Wait, what do you mean 'before he does something else'? Are you trying to tell me he's done some other shit besides smashing out the shop's window? Do you know this nigga?"

"Oh no, not at all," I quickly state, trying to clean it up. I make a left turn onto Central Avenue. "All I'm saying is, with that nigga still lurking around there's no telling who else's property he'll damage. And I don't want his ass coming back to mine."

"Mmm…yeah, you right. But, why the fuck would someone wanna smash out your window like that in broad daylight? That shit makes no sense to me."

"Me either," I say, regretting I ever answered this call.

"And the nigga didn't even try to rob ya'll." She pauses. "Mmmph. Girl, you know like I do, anyone busting out windows is usually on some personal shit."

I sigh, feeling a headache stirring. Mona has always been some-one who doesn't let too much shit get by her. If you ask me, she's too damn smart for her own damn good sometimes. "Well, shit. I don't know why. I haven't done shit to anyone."

"Girl, I'm talking about one of them stylists you got working up in there. Shit, as messy as Shuwanda is, who's to say it's not some nigga she done put on blast?"

I roll my eyes. *OhmyGod, I need to change the subject*, I think, *before she keeps dragging this shit on*. "Well, I hope not. Anyway, enough talk about that. Jasper and I set a wedding date," I tell her, stopping at a red light.

She laughs. "Is this your version? 'Cause it definitely isn't the story Jasper's telling."

"Girl, whatever," I say, laughing with her. "The point is the date is set."

"Yeah, the point is Jasper put his foot down on that ass." She continues laughing. "Whew. I sure got a kick outta that when he told me."

"Whatever."

"Well, it doesn't matter who set the date. All that matters is that it's finally happening. So congratulations. It's about damn time."

I smile. "That's more like it. Thanks."

"Now the real work begins. So, what's next?"

"Well, first I gotta work on the guest list, then find a place so I can get the invitations printed up. Then I need to find a dress…" Shit, shit, shit! I have all this stuff to do, and only five months to get it all done. "…the flowers, the cake and—"

"Girl, slow down," she says, cutting me off. She chuckles. "You don't have to do it all yourself. That's what you have me and Felecia for—your Matron and Maid of Honor."

"Now who said anything about having your ugly face all up in my wedding?" I tease, laughing.

"Shit, you're uglier than me," she says, teasing back, "but that's beside the point, Miss Celie. Jasper wouldn't know ya funky-ass if it wasn't for me so you owe me, boo."

I'm cracking up as I turn into the salon's parking lot. "Well, since you put it like that. I guess it's a done deal. Find me a florist. Then see if you can get Raven the Cake Man to do my wedding cake. I want his slamming red velvet cake. I don't have a design in mind, yet. He's usually booked months in advance, but let him know I'm willing to pay extra if he can fit me in."

She laughs. "Well, damn…shall I wash your feet while I'm at it, your highness?"

"No, that'll be all for now. I'll give Felecia her things-to-do list next." I shut off the engine, then gather my things, getting out of the car. I glance at my watch. 8:22 A.M. "Well, let me get off this phone. I'm getting ready to walk up in the shop. Call me later with an update."

"I swear, girl. If you turn into a Bridezilla I'm gonna set your dress and hair on fire. Speaking of dresses, do you have any idea what your colors are gonna be?" I tell her that since it's a fall wedding I'm going to go with an ivory gown—either Valentino or Chanel; I tell her that chocolate brown will be the color of the bridesmaids' dresses. Tell her that their floral arrangements will be pink roses, hyacinth and gloriosa lilies.

"Alright now. I like. But, remember what I said. If you turn into the Bride of Frankenstein, it's off with your damn head." We laugh, hanging up.

The minute I walk into the salon, I see Stax leaning on the counter talking to Felecia. He's wearing a grey and black Nike muscle shirt and a pair of nylon sweats. The way his muscles are bulging, I can tell he's been to the gym. Felecia stops speaking when she sees me. And it makes me suspicious. But I don't plan on letting it occupy my thoughts today. "Hey, girl," she says, grinning. The way she's cheesing definitely lets me know the two of them were talking about something. I don't know what. But whatever they were discussing, I'd bet my last hundred that it had everything to do with me.

"Hey, ya'll," I say.

"What's good, Pash?" Stax says, smiling.

"Hey, girl," Felecia says.

"Nothing much," I say before bringing my attention back to Felecia. "Any cancellations so far?"

"Not yet. So far, it looks like it's going to be another money-making day for us."

"That's what I like to hear," I say, smiling.

"I know that's right."

"Anything else going on?"

"Nope," she says, adjusting her burgundy blunt-cut wig.

"You good, Pash?" Stax asks.

"I'm doing great," I tell him. "Couldn't be better; how about you?"

"I'm good, ma. You know how I do."

"Mmm-hmm. That's why I asked."

He laughs. "Nah, it's all good."

"Okay, if you say so."

"You lookin' fly as usual," he says, running his eyes all over my body. The way he dips his voice and gazes at me when he says this causes me to nervously shift my weight from one foot to another.

I playfully roll my eyes. "Whatever. Flattery will get you nowhere. What brings you by so early in the morning?"

"I was hopin' I could holla at you for a minute."

I glance at my watch, raising my eye, then placing a hand on my hip. "At eight-thirty in the morning? Stax please. You could have called."

"I was over this way anyway. My gym's not too far from here so I decided to swing by. I saw Felecia's whip and stopped in. I know you're usually here early. Plus Jasp wanted me to come through to make sure everything was aiight here."

I suck my teeth, shaking my head. "I should have known. You can tell my husband-to-be that everything's okay here." I grab my things from off the counter. "C'mon to my office so we can talk." I glance over at Felecia, narrowing my eyes. She shakes her head, shrugging. I walk off with Stax following behind me. The whole way to the office I can practically feel his eyes on my ass. I unlock the door, then walk in. He shuts the door behind him.

I plop my things on the sofa, then take a seat at my desk. "So what's up?"

"My girl wanted me to holla at you to see if you could put her on."

I raise my brow. "Put her on how?" Braiding hair here, he tells me. "Which girl?" I tease.

He grins, playfully rolling his eyes up in his head. "Oh, you got jokes, I see. Mariah; my baby's mother. Who else?"

I shrug. "I don't know. I thought maybe you were talking about one of your jump offs."

"Nah, that's not how I do mine," he says, eyeing me.

"That's good to know. Umm, wait a minute. Isn't your girl about ready to drop soon?"

"Oh, nah," he says nonchalantly, "she lost it." He doesn't seem fazed by the loss. Then, again, I guess he wouldn't be since he wasn't beat to have another baby with her, anyway.

"I'm sorry to hear that. Is she alright?"

"Yeah, she's good." *And knowing her, she'll be trying to get pregnant again real soon.*

I've never really cared for Mariah. Not that I know her personally. I might have seen her three, maybe four, times—and have seen Stax out in public with her once or twice—since I've known him. Now I will say this about her, she's a cute chick, and she wears some of the fliest shit. Other than that, she's loud and obnoxious. And ghetto as hell when she's set off, cursing and fighting. Hell, I don't think she's ever held down a job longer than a month or two before she's knocking somebody in the head. Shit, I can see her now, smacking up Shuwanda for trying to come at her sideways. And the way Shuwanda runs her mouth, she'd definitely try her. "I don't know, Stax. Your girl is a bit on the wild side, if you know what I mean."

"Yeah, tell me about it. That's always been one of our problems, her ass not wanting to work, or keep a job when she gets it."

Although my first mind tells me to say hell fucking no, I'm a businesswoman. And the fact that Mariah can braid the fuck out of some hair would definitely be a nice touch around here. The bitch can do all types of exclusive braid designs. This could definitely be a good look for the salon; especially since I'm now looking to bring on a barber-stylist as well. Shit, niggas like to keep their heads tight, too. And if there's money to be made, I need to be getting it. "Does she have her papers?" I ask, pondering the possibilities.

"Nah, she doesn't. I keep telling her to take her ass back to school to get them shits. But she's always on some 'I ain't beat' type shit."

"Well, tell her as soon as she gets her papers straight, she can definitely come on board. I'd love to have her. But until then, sorry, I run a licensed salon, and everyone who works here must have all their credentials in order."

"I feel you," he says, fanning his legs open and shut. I try to keep myself from looking in his crotch. I've never, ever, looked at Stax sexually. But, I can't front. His body is fucking ridiculous. I had no idea he was chiseled up the way he is. OhmyGod, I'm embarrassed to say this shit. But this nigga, sitting here all buffed up and sweaty, is making me horny. "Pash, on some real shit, I wish she was more like…" His voice starts to trail off as I glance at the veins running along his forearms. Without thinking, I pick up a stack of mail that's been sitting on my desk for the last few days and start shuffling through it. "…I swear she's so unmotivated. All she wants to do is hangout with her girls 'n shit."

The minute I see the manila envelope addressed to me with no return address I know what it is and who it's from without having to open it. I slump my shoulders. Everything in my body goes numb. I will my hands steady.

"Yo, Pash, you okay? Pash?"

I bring my attention back to Stax. "Unh, what'd you say?"

"I asked if you were aiight. I was talkin' and you went some-where else on me. Is e'erything aiight?"

"Oh yeah," I say, getting up to walk toward the shredder. I decide that whatever is in this envelope I don't need to see it. Stax watches me as I stick it in the slot. When the whirring stops and it's completely shredded, I walk back over to my desk. Force a smile on my face. "I'm good. Actually, I haven't felt better."

He tightly presses his legs together, causing me to catch a quick glimpse of the thick lump in his sweats. I shift my eyes as he stands up. "Aiight, then. I guess I betta go."

OhmiGod, his dick is hard, I think, feeling myself break out in a sweat. I quickly shift my eyes, standing as well. "Thanks for stop-ping by," I say, walking around the desk.

"No doubt, ma." He gives me a hug and a kiss on the cheek, then steps back. The gesture catches me completely off guard. "Yo, Pash...on some real shit, if you ever need me, I got you, aiight?"

I tilt my head, not understanding the intent or the meaning for his statement. "Thanks, I appreciate you saying that. But why?"

He shrugs. "I don't know. You seem like you're goin' through something, that's all. You my peoples so if somebody's fuckin' with you, then they fuckin' with me. You feel me?"

I hope Felecia didn't run her mouth to him. I smile at him. "You know, Stax, I knew underneath all that muscle and attitude was a big ole loveable teddy bear."

He laughs. "Yeah, aiight, ma. Keep that shit on the low."

"I got you," I say, widening my smile.

"Aiight, I'm outta here. Remember what I said. I got you."

I nod, waving him on. "I appreciate it. Thanks for stopping by."

"No doubt." I follow him to the door, shutting it behind him. I lean up against it, wondering where the hell all that was coming from. I suddenly feel hot and dizzy at the thought of him knowing more than he should. And if he does, the idea of him getting in Jasper's ear makes me want to vomit. I head into the bathroom and turn on the faucet, staring at my reflection in the mirror. *Trifling bitch!* I hear in my head as I splash cold water on my face, then grab a hand-towel and pat dry my face and neck dry. *Oh God, I think I'm gonna be sick.* I flip up the toilet seat, grip the sides of the bowl, and toss my guts up.

TWENTY-THREE

"Aaaah, aaaah...you sucking the shit outta this dick, baby... fuck!" I am squatting down in front of Jasper—naked and horny with his dick in my mouth, slurping and gulping down every inch of him while playing with my clit. I am moaning. I'm not sure if it's sucking his dick, me playing with my clit, or a combination of the two that has me in a zone. "Fuck, yo..."

My spit rolls down his shaft. I lick it. I wash his balls, wet them up with a bunch of spit, then pop them both in my mouth. I moan. He moans, dipping at the knees.

"Mmmmm...aaah, shit...fuck...make love to that dick...Aaah, shit...let me get that throat, baby...yeah, that's it...grab them titties for me..." I'm giving Jasper all neck using my hands to play with my nipples.

"You nasty...yeah, you like that shit...damn...you takin' all that dick...oh shit, you fuckin' nasty, yo...Let me taste that sweet pussy, yo. Can I have that fat pussy, baby?"

I nod, moaning. Five minutes later, I'm gulping down his nut, then licking my lips; completely satisfied. "It's my turn," Jasper says, dropping down on his knees. He pulls my tangerine thong to the side and starts sucking on my clit. I stand, watching my man's long tongue flick in and out of his mouth, lapping at my clit. He grabs me by the ass, pulls me into his face, burying his nose into the soft curly patch of hair. I grab the back of his head and push him further into my pussy.

I start playing with my titties, then lightly pinching my nipples until my knees buckle. Before I know it, I am squirting my juices everywhere. In Jasper's mouth and all over his face. He continues lapping and slurping every bit of it up, causing me to have one orgasm after another. My legs feel like they're ready to give out any minute now. I brace myself up against the wall to keep from collapsing. Pleased with his tongue assault on my clit and pussy, Jasper stands. He has pussy juice dripping down his chin. He grins. "My baby got that good juicy shit, word up."

He leans into me, gives me his tongue. I greedily suck on it, then begin sucking on his lips and chin. He slips two fingers inside of me and starts finger-fucking me. In a matter of minutes, I am cumming again; this time all over his hand.

"Fuck me," I beg, humping on his fingers while grabbing for his dick. I jerk it. "Oooh, let me feel this big dick in me…"

He parts my legs, lifts me up, then brushes the tip of his dick against my wet slit. He sticks the head in, then quickly pulls out before I can grind down on it. "Is that what you want?" he asks, teasing me.

"Yesssss, damn it!"

He pushes his dick back in me, loosens his grip on my hips, then says, "Ride that shit then…" He braces his back up against the wall, and I do just that. I wrap my arms around his neck, lean back and wildly buck my hips, galloping up and down on his dick. He matches my rhythm with deep upward thrusts, driving his cock deeper inside me. I bounce up and down on his dick. We both let out loud groans and moans of pleasure, letting the other know we're about to cum. Jasper's dick swells inside of me and he relentlessly pounds in and out of me. "You wanna nut wit' me, baby?"

"Uhh…uhhhhh…yes, I wanna nut all over this big-ass dick…"

He slaps me on the ass as I gallop faster and faster, grabbing and milking his shaft. I am cumming. He is cumming. We both let out another round of loud moans, then he explodes inside of me. And, as my body uncontrollably shakes, I splash all over his cock, juices gushing out everywhere.

With his dick still inside of me, we both slide down to the floor, sweaty and exhausted. But the freaky beast in me wants to pull his cock out of me and begin sucking my juices off, along with the juices around his balls before it dries up. But I don't. I'm too weak to move. And so is Jasper. The only thing each of us is able to do is gaze into the other's eyes. No words are needed. We kiss, savoring the hot, sweaty fuck session.

For the rest of the day, Jasper and I fuck. Make love. Fuck some more. On the floor, in the shower, on the counter, on the dining room table, across the sofa, in the laundry room, in the bedroom, we christen every part of the house, leaving the scent of sweat and a well-fucked pussy etched in the air.

After fucking all morning and most of the afternoon, it dawns on me that we haven't eaten all day. I am downstairs in the kitchen preparing him something to eat. This is actually the first time I've cooked for Jasper since before he got locked up. As I'm slicing cucumbers and tomatoes for a garden salad, the house phone rings. I rinse my hands, then pick up the cordless on the counter. It's Nana.

"Hey, Nana," I say, placing the phone in the crook of my neck. I decide to put it on speaker instead so I can move about the kitchen more freely.

"Hey, baby doll."

I smile. "How are you?"

"I am blessed and favored. God is good."

I shake my head. "Yes, He is."

"All the time," she continues. "He keeps me wrapped in His grace and mercy."

I roll my eyes up in my head, catching Jasper standing in the doorway bare-chested with a brown towel wrapped around his waist. He grins. "I know, Nana."

"I just got off the phone with pastor. I reserved the church for the wedding."

Jasper shakes his head no, making slicing gestures across his throat with his hand to dead that idea. I wave him on. "Church? Umm, Nana...listen, Jasper and I aren't having a church cere-mony." Jasper snickers. I roll my eyes at him. I can imagine her bucking her eyes, adjusting her rimmed glasses at that. "We're planning a garden wedding."

"A garden wedding? What in the world? You young people today..."

Jasper drops his towel and starts playing with his dick. I stare at him; watch him pleasure himself, feeling myself becoming flustered. "Ummm, Nana...I have to go. Can I call you later, please?"

"Go on, baby," she says. And before she can say another word, I hang up on her. I stare at Jasper, raising my eyebrows, grinning. "Why you come down here like that?" I ask, pointing at his nakedness.

"I'm hungry," he says, licking his lips.

I walk over to the oven and open it, checking on the salmon. "Well, the fish is almost ready. You'll be able to eat in a few."

He walks up on me, grabbing me by the waist. "That's not what I'm hungry for."

I smile. "Then what you hungry for?" I ask, coyly.

He kisses me, softly at first, then more passionately. He grabs my ass over my silk robe, presses me up against his growing cock.

"You," he states, dropping to his knees. I untie my robe, slide it off my shoulders, and let it fall to the kitchen floor.

"Then eat me," I softly say, parting my legs. I toss my head back and moan the minute he mounts his mouth over my clit and greedily sucks on it until my juices splash against his tongue and all over his face.

After Jasper finishes snacking on me, then eating the lunch I've prepared for him, he goes downstairs in the basement to watch the sports channel on the Sony 52-inch flat screen that I hardly ever watch, or turn on for that matter. I leave him down there, yapping on the phone with Monty, talking sports lingo that's way over my head and of no interest to me.

I go upstairs, run myself a hot bath, then slowly slink my body down into the steamy, fragrant-filled water. I lean my head back and close my eyes, remembering when it all began.

"So dig. This sexy bitch had her hot mouth mounted 'round my dick 'n shit. Nah, son...I ain't do shit. I lay back and let her nasty-ass take control, feel me? Hell yeah, the bitch had me feelin' right. She licked 'round the head, then kissed my shit before runnin' her tongue up 'n down the right side, then the left side of it. Then my whole dick disappeared in her mouth. She downed *nine*, son, like a champ. Yo, word is bond, son. She's a dick-suckin' machine. Nonstop suckin', man. ...Yeah, man...She cupped my balls, then started squeezin' them shits. Had a muhfucka moanin' like a real bitch, son. Nah, real talk, baby boy. You know how I do it, yo. When you ever know me to front on some broad wettin' this dick? Exactly, son. So, you know what it is. Yeah, son... she knows how to yank them muhfuckas wit'out tryna rip 'em off a muhfucka, feel me. Had a nigga's toes curlin', son. Man, listen...this bitch is the truth, son....Nah, nigga...I met her online...You remember that site I was tellin' you 'bout? Word is bond, my nigga... that shit's live. Hell, yeah, son...they freakier than them bitches on MySpace and BlackPlanet put together.... Nah, she ain't ugly. The bitch is fiiyah, son. Bangin' body, the works..."

I stood in the bathroom of the seedy motel I was in, with the door cracked, listening to how the nigga I had just finishing sucking off was on his cell with one of his boys, bragging on my skills. He was sitting on the edge of the bed, still naked, with his back toward the bathroom door.

Truth be told. A part of me wanted to be pissed that he couldn't keep his trap shut. I had to remind myself that he was young— twenty-three, to be exact. However, there was this other part of me that was flattered that he couldn't wait to get on the phone to let his boys know the good dick sucking he'd been blessed with. He had been the chosen one for the night out of the twenty or so email responses I had gotten that night. And he was the youngest out of the responses. Still, I liked his stats, and he had a pretty golden brown dick that looked made for all-night sucking.

He was one of them thuggish, tree-smoking roughnecks who wore his sagging jeans practically around his knees—showing off his designer boxers and ass—instead of up on his waist where they belonged. And he wore his hair in neatly braided cornrows and had a fresh edge up and trimmed mustache. He was young and sexy with a hard, horny dick. I let him finger my pussy while I dusted him off. Then when the nigga asked to eat my pussy I knew right then that I was going to give him another round of tongue and throat. So the fact that he was on the phone excitedly sharing what I'd done to him was to be expected.

I smiled as I listened for a few seconds more before stepping back into the room. I cleared my throat so he knew I was back. He glanced over at me, quickly telling whoever he had on the line that he had to bounce.

I guess I surprised him when I walked over to him, then pushed him back on the bed and took his dick into my mouth and sucked it back to life. Slowly, I started inchin' his dick into my mouth, then down into my throat. I gurgled and gulped his dick until his toes started to open and close, then I pulled his cock from out of my mouth and spit all over it, before popping it back in my mouth and rapidly sucking it; making loud popping sounds.

"Damn...oh, fuck..." he moaned, gripping the sheets and bucking his hips while thrashing his head from side to side. If I had been a prostitute, I could have had him trick up every dime he had in his pocket on my head game. Lucky for him, I was only a chick who enjoyed sucking dick—free of charge.

As soon as he was ready to spill his nut, I pulled off his condom and began jerking his cock between my titties, flapping my tongue back and forth as the head of his dick popped in and out. He came in a loud roar, releasing a bucket of cum that coated my titties, neck and face. I looked up at him with a satisfied smile on my face. His eyes were closed and he was breathing heavy as he laid there motionless.

When he finally opened his eyes and was able to sit up, I told him that I had overheard him talking on the phone. He looked completely embarrassed. "My bad. No disrespect meant, ma. It's just that..."

I reached up and placed a finger to his lips. "You never had your dick sucked like that before," I finished for him, smiling. "No apology needed."

He grinned. "Yeah, sumthin' like that."

I climbed up on the bed and straddled him. "Well, how about whoever you were on the phone with, you call back and tell them to come over so they can watch how it's done."

He looked at me surprised. "Word?" he asked excitedly. "You want me to call my niggas and tell 'em to come through?"

"Not niggas," I corrected, stroking his sticky dick. "Nigga, as in one of your boys. But there are some ground rules. No phones, no cameras, no video recording devices. The only thing he can bring with him is a hard, clean—and I do mean, *clean*, dick. Understand?"

His face lit up like at kid at Christmas. "No doubt." I rolled off of him onto my back, playing in my pussy. "Can we fuck you?"

I smiled, shaking my head. I couldn't blame him for wanting to feel my pussy wrapped around his dick. After all, he'd already had his tongue in it. "No. There's no fucking involved. Sucking dick and eating my pussy are the only two things on the menu tonight. Make sure your boy understands the rules."

"I gotchu, ma," he said, retrieving his cell. "Aye, yo, my nig... guess what? 'Member the chick I was tellin' you 'bout?..." he lowered his voice, glancing over at me. I pretended to be too caught up in the throes of a self-induced orgasm to be paying him any attention. "...yeah, son...Yo, she wanna a threesome, my nig...Nah, she ain't fuckin'...she suckin' and gulpin, son... You wit' it? Bet..." he gave his boy the name of the motel, then told him what the ground rules were. "...aiight, no doubt. Hit me on the hip when you 'bout to get here...aiight, one!"

Forty minutes later, his boy walked through the door wearing baggy jeans, a long white tee and a pair of Timberland boots. He had a fitted Yankees cap on his head. The chitchat and banter were kept to a minimum. I told the young buck to strip down, and surprisingly his dick was already brick hard by the time he stepped out of his boxers. I summoned him over to the bed with my finger, then laid back and hung my head over the edge of the bed.

I opened my mouth, then reached up and guided his young hard dick down into my throat while his boy ate my pussy. By the time we finished, it was almost three in the morning and I had them both stumbling out of there with empty sacks.

"Hey," I hear in my head. "Pasha, yo, wake up." I open my eyes, realizing I had dozed off. Jasper is fully dressed, standing in the doorway, leaning up against the frame of the door. I blink, wiping drool from the corner of my mouth. "Yo, that musta been some kinda dreamin'," he says, frowning.

"What are you talking about?" I ask, reaching over and flipping up the lever for the drain.

"You were in here moaning."

I laugh, sucking my teeth, trying to play it off. "Boy, I was not."

"Yeah, aiight. I know what I heard," he says, stepping into the bathroom, grabbing my towel.

I ignore him. "OhmyGod, what time is it?"

"Time for you to get ya ass up outta there." I stand, letting the remnants of soapsuds glide down my body. The chill causes my nipples to harden like milk duds. Jasper inadvertently licks his lips, letting his gaze fall on my titties. "Here. Let me."

He opens the towel. And I step in.

"Damn, my baby's sexy as hell," he says, lightly drying me off. I raise my arms up over my head, smiling. "Let me find out you in here dreamin' 'bout some other nigga, aiight? And I'ma bust ya ass, yo."

I suck my teeth, rolling my eyes. "Jasper, don't start your shit. We had a good day without any incidences so, please, let's not fuck it up."

"Yeah, aiight," he says, drying my body. "You've been warned, Pash."

I stare him down, shaking my head. "Whatever. Where you going?"

"Stax is comin' through to scoop me up. I gotta make a few

runs before I head back to the halfway house." He lets out a frustrated sigh. "I can't wait for this shit to be over wit' so I can be home wit' ya sexy ass for good."

"I can't wait either," I assure him, taking my towel from him. I wrap it around my breast, then tuck the ends in, walking out into the bedroom. The room is a mess. Shit is thrown all over the place. I start picking up clothes. "Umm, what kind of runs you need to make?"

"Business," he says, grinning.

"What kind of business?"

"Yo, chill," he says, picking up my purple bikini-cut panties. I catch him sniffing them, then sticking them in his pocket. "I got this."

"Ugh, you're disgusting. What's up with you taking my under-wear with you? That's like the third pair you've taken."

"And? Was those ya last pair or somethin'?"

I roll my eyes. "No, smart-ass."

"Oh, aiight, then." I lotion my body up with Victoria Secret's peach lotion, then slip into a pair of pink thongs and a matching bra. Jasper watches me. "Yo, where you going?"

"To the mall," I tell him.

"Oh, now all of a sudden you takin' ya ass to the mall. Yeah, aiight."

"Ummm, excuse you," I say, turning around to face him, "I *thought* I was going to be laid up with my man all day until it was time for me to take him back to the halfway house, but since he's made other plans, Yes, I'm going to the mall."

He stares at me, grinning. "I'ma be home in a minute. You'll have me all to ya'self, then."

I roll my eyes. "Whatever."

He walks over and kisses me. "Yo, you know you sexy when

you pout. You makin' my dick hard." I smile against my will, rubbing it. "Yo, stop that." I grab it more aggressively, pressing my body pelvis up against him.

"Give me some more of this dick," I say as he gently sucks on my neck. He loops his two thick fingers in my underwear and begins playing in my wetness, stirring my pussy.

The doorbell rings, abruptly shutting shit down. I suck my teeth as Jasper pulls his fingers out of me. "Time's up," he says.

"Yeah, perfect timing," I say sarcastically. "You make me sick."

"Yeah, aiight. What I do?" He sticks his fingers in his mouth, sucks my juices off, licking his lips. "Damn, you taste good. I'ma hit you later, aiight?"

"Yeah, okay," I say, slipping on my robe.

"Oh, you gotta attitude now?"

"No, not at all. Do you. I'll talk to you tonight."

He gives me a peck on the lips. "Yeah, aiight. Yo, scoop me up a pair of white on white shell-toes while you at the mall."

"Nigga," I say, following him down the stairs, "you goin' out. Get your own Adidas."

He laughs. "See, there you go. Startin' ya shit, again. Go, get them shits and stop playin', aiight?"

"I'm not getting shit," I say, pouting. I cross my arms over my chest. Mad that he's bouncing three hours before he has to be back at the halfway house. *This nigga knew he had other plans and didn't say shit to me about 'em.*

He opens the door, yells out to Stax that he'll be right out. Remembers he left his cell down in the basement, then goes to retrieve it. Three minutes later, he comes back up, gives me another kiss, then heads out the door.

TWENTY-FOUR

*S*exy, *cock-loving diva, looking to discreetly deep throat a thick, cut dick tonight. Lay back, spread open your legs, and let me suck your dick until your toes curl and you shoot out a nice, hot, load of cum. And as an extra bonus: Eat my pussy, and get me extra horny and I might let you bust in my mouth, making sure to not miss a drip, drop, or spurt. Then I'll swish it around in my mouth so I can taste all of your sweet cream before swallowing some, and leaving the rest in my mouth, and on my tongue so I can paint my lips with it. If you like what you're reading, and think you can hang, send your stats. You must be ht/wt proportionate—I am not attracted to overweight men, or men who look like they're 8 months pregnant. Also, you must be clean—meaning ass, balls and cock freshly washed; be drug-free—that includes weed, poppers and pills; and, please, PLEASE be disease free.*

I reread the ad, then post it. It's been several weeks since I've been out on the prowl. And I was doing really good, staying off the site. But, tonight, temptation is much greater than rationale for me. I want dick!

"This is my last post," I say to myself, "then I'm closing this shit down." I make myself invisible on the IM radar, then begin opening emails from a few days ago.

Hey, baby. Blk man here 6'3 180 drk skinned, slim built, average brutha here with a big, thick dick that loves to be sucked. Big balls heavy with cum, too. Ready to bust! Holla back!

I type back. *Hello. Thanks 4 the reply. Nice stats. Please send me a pic of the dic. Thanks!* I open the next email. *Hey diva. Good looking here. 36, 6'4, 186 lbs, average/fit build, moderately hairy, light skinned, blk hair, brn eyes, 7.5c. THICK. Drug/disease free. Married so looking to stay that way. 420 friendly, though. Love getting my dick sucked by a cock loving chick.*

Hey, baby. If you wanna milk my cock with your hot throat and swallow my meat whole; If you wanna feel a white, thick, 8" cock slide in and out your mouth, down in your throat, explode all over your tongue, then I'm your man. 37, 5'9, 168 lbs, toned, gym body. Love sexy blk women.

Mister six-foot-three sends me another email, this time with an attachment. When it opens, I smile. It's long, thick and dark-chocolate. And reminds me of an oversized Snickers bar loaded with delicious, chewy nuts; instantly, my mouth waters. My choice has been made. I'm sucking this nigga's dick. I reply back. *I wanna wrap my lips around the head of your cock and milk the nut out of that sweet, black dick. Looking 4 now. Can u come out & play?*

I delete the rest of the emails, deciding if I can't suck his, then I'm not sucking on anyone else's tonight. Instead, I'll take my ass to bed and call it a night. I glance at the time at the bottom, right corner of my laptop. 9:15 P.M.

I sit in front of the computer screen, waiting to hear back from him, like a junkie needing a fix. Four minutes later, there it is. The email I've been waiting for: darkstallion69@ymail.com. I open it. *Hell yeah, I can cum out. I can't host, but we can get a room in the area*

I reply back. *When?*

Two minutes later, he replies. *Tonight!* It takes two additional emails for us to coordinate the when, where and how of the night. I am meeting him in forty minutes at the Hilton on JFK Parkway in Short Hills.

I log off the computer, jump in the shower, hurriedly put on a pair of Baby Phat jeans and matching tee over a black, lace teddy, then race out the door, hoping this nigga I'm sneaking off to meet has some damn good dick.

For some reason this…the drive, the feelings—everything about this ride over to the hotel feels strange. Okay, wrong. Still, I continue on my way. Continue pushing back the lies; continue pushing back the illusions; continue pushing back everything I have in Jasper—his love, in particular; continue pushing and pushing and pushing the nagging, aching feeling that I need to turn around and take my black ass home. But I don't and I can't. My lust won't let me.

I pull into the parking lot, push back my guilt and drive around until I spot Mister Dark Stallion's white Ford Explorer. He flashes his lights as instructed and I flash mine back, then park a few spaces from him. I check myself in the rearview mirror, applying a fresh coat of lip gloss, then get out of my car. We go through the formalities of greeting and sizing each other up. We both smile. He's tall, dark and sexy; has a baldhead, smooth-shaven face, and a dimpled chin. I can tell underneath his Polo warm-up he has a nice body. I glance down at his Nike-clad feet. Take in his big feet, then glance at his thick hands. He soaks in my smooth, cocoa-brown skin, dreamy eyes, and luscious lips. His eyes wander along the dangerous curves of my body as I slowly turn around so he can get a full view of all of my *ass*ets. He tells me that he got here twenty minutes ago, and has already checked in. I smile as he gives me the room number. As always, I will go in first. Take the elevator to the fourth floor to the room, then wait for him to come in.

Five minutes later, he walks in. I am undressed and on my knees in the middle of the room in my negligee, waiting. I summon him with my index finger to come to me. Tell him to not speak. He grins. I stick two fingers in my mouth. Suck on them as he walks over to me. I reach up and start rubbing and massaging his cock over his sweat pants. My pussy leaks with excitement as his dick thickens. I pull him into me by the back of his legs, rub my face in his crotch area until he is completely hard. "I can't wait to taste this big, black dick," I tell him, reaching up and yanking his pants down. He removes his nylon jacket and t-shirt. I pull down his boxers and dick springs upward, almost hitting me in the eye. I smile at its length and thickness, licking my lips. I take it in my hand, looking up at him as I lick over the head, then slowly swirl my tongue around it. I do that a few times, then pucker my lips over it, gently sucking the tip of his dick, until he starts moaning and shaking. I replace my mouth with my hand and jerk his dick in upward strokes while licking and sucking on his balls.

"Aaaaah, damn, baby...you good..."

"I'm only getting started," I state, getting up and pulling him by the shaft of his dick toward the bed. I push him back on it, then pull out a cherry-flavored condom that I stuck in the top part of my teddy. I tear the wrapper with my teeth, then lean in and roll it down onto his dick with my mouth. Once I have the condom down to the base, I push his dick deep into the back of my throat, then swallow him down, reaching between my legs and playing with my clit. I neck his dick, rapidly bobbing my head until he starts bouncing his legs.

"Fuck...aaaah, shiiiiiiiit...where the hell you been all my life, baby?" I pull his dick out and start slapping and smacking it against my lips and tongue, before shoving it back into my mouth. "You 'bout to make me nut...aaah, shiiit, baby..."

I continue sucking and slurping and gulping him down, cupping his balls. He lets out a loud moan. I pull his dick out of my mouth, yank off the condom, then rapidly stroke his dick until he shoots out a load of hot, foaming cum. He falls back on the bed to catch his breath, staring up at the ceiling—clearly dazed. I get up off my knees, wishing I could have swallowed down his thick nut.

"My turn," I tell him, climbing up over his face, lowering my hips down to his mouth. My wet lips tingle in anticipation. "Eat my pussy, big daddy..."

"Damn," he says, grabbing me by the hips, "you gotta pretty pussy." He takes his tongue and laps around the outer edge of my wet lips, then pulls my lips back and starts licking my center. I grind my hips down on his mouth, rocking back and forth on his tongue. I fuck his face until my juices squirt out all over his face. "Aaaah, fuck, baby...you gotta wet, juicy pussy, baby," he grunts as he slurps and licks. I squirt again. I finish cumming and roll off of him. Then look at him. He looks sexy as hell with his mouth and chin glazed with my juices. I lean over and start sucking his chin, then his lips, cleaning my stickiness off of him.

I roll back over onto my back. "Damn, baby," he says, shaking his head. "Mmmph...you're incredible. I don't know where you learned to suck dick like that, but you need to insure that mouth and tongue of yours. They're dangerous." I smile. He faces me. Tells me how wicked my head game is. Asks me if I'm involved with anyone; tells me he's married with two children. That his is name is Wil; that he'd like to see me again.

"Well, Wil," I say, tracing his lips with my fingertip, "No, I'm not married, yet—engaged. My name is Deep Throat, and no, I don't have children."

He laughs. "Oh, okay, Deep Throat, I got you; no real names."

"Exactly." He asks if we can meet up again. I tell him not at this time. Shit, I know. I should have said not at all. Oh, well.

"You like fucking?"

"My pussy's off limits to dick," I tell him. "Mouth and tongue are the only things allowed near it."

He laughs again. "I understand. Well, can I at least get another round of head for the road?"

I smile. "Baby," I tell him, getting up to get another condom. "As good as your dick is, how 'bout I give you two rounds?"

"Aaaah, I love the sound of that." He lays back, spreads his toned legs apart, and waits for me to get back between his thighs. I roll another condom down onto his dick, then suck the life out of him. Two hours later, I walk out of the hotel room with a well-licked pussy; and he walks out five minutes after me, well-sucked and drained to the last drop.

TWENTY-FIVE

itch, I think, glancing at the clock in my dashboard. 1:18 a.m., *either your ass is stupid, crazy, or fucking obsessed with dick. With a nut on the loose, you had no business taking your ass out. You need to stop this shit, now!* I sigh, pulling down my visor. I look at myself in the mirror, shaking my head.

"This dick sucking shit has really gotten out of hand," I admit to myself, removing my key from out of the ignition. I grab my wallet and cell from off the passenger seat, get out of the car, then activate the car alarm. The minute I get up to my door and prepare to stick my key into the door, someone jumps out from behind the bushes that are situated next to the door and grabs me. I scream, but a gloved hand quickly covers my mouth.

"Shut the fuck up, you dick-suckin' bitch. Or I'll break your muthafuckin' eye sockets." The minute I hear his menacing voice, I literally piss on myself. It's him. I thought he had gotten over the idea of me sucking him off. Thought he had gotten bored with harassing me and moved on to someone else. But, obviously he hasn't. Now I wish I would have taken his warning serious. "Yeah, I bet you thought I was long gone, didn't you? I wanted you to think that, ho. But I've been following your every move, slut. Now open ya fuckin' door so I can get your tongue back up on this dick."

OhmyGod! My heart literally sinks when I hear this. The crazy shit is a part of me would rather this be a random assault instead of some psycho nigga who I've sucked off. How the fuck will I ever be able explain myself out of this shit?

I'm not listed in the phonebook. My phone numbers are restricted. And I don't use my home address for anything. All of my mail goes to a P.O. Box. So tracking where I live isn't an easy feat. But with the internet, nothing is impossible.

On top of that, anytime I've ever gone out on the prowl, I have always made it my business to be very careful about not pulling off until after they have, waiting at least ten to fifteen minutes. Then I don't drive directly home. I circle the area, first, to make sure I'm not being followed before I head home. But this nigga right here had to have followed me from the salon. The one place I never thought I'd have to be careful.

"Hurry up, bitch!" he snaps, pushing me up against the door as I fumble with my keys. He keeps his hand covered over my mouth. My mind is made up. There's no way I'm letting this nut-ass nigga into my home. I throw my keys across the yard, then slam the heel of my shoe into his shin as I attempt to bite his hand and fight him off of me. But he's much stronger than I expected and his leather glove is too thick. He slaps me upside the head. And in that split second, I think I hear birds chirping.

In all of my life, I have never been hit by a man so this stuns the shit out of me. I wildly kick him in his shins and stomp on his feet until he loosens his grip on me. As soon as he does, I spin around and attempt to dig my nails into his face but he's wearing a ski mask. He wrestles me down to the ground, grabbing me by the neck. I claw at him until my nails connect with skin, then I dig my nails into his flesh, digging in deep and drawing blood.

He punches me. "Aaah, fuck! Stupid bitch!"

I start screaming, kicking, punching and clawing at him. "Aaaaaaah… HELP! HE'S KILLING ME!" I knee him in his balls, causing him to yelp. Thank God a car is pulling up into my neighbor's driveway. This nigga lets me go. He gets up and starts running down the street. He yells, "This shit ain't over, bitch!" Clint, my next door neighbor, jumps out his car and comes running over to me.

"Pasha, you okay?" I rapidly shake my head, holding my neck. "Call the police. I'll be right back." He runs off, trying to catch whoever it was trying to do me in, but the nut's already ghost. Clint walks back over to me. "Did you call the police?"

I shake my head. "No."

He gives me a puzzled look. "Why not? What if he comes back for you?"

"I don't think he will," I say, picking up my wallet, then searching the area for my keys. "I want to get in the house and take a long, hot shower."

He reaches for me. "Pasha, whoever that cat was he looked like he was really trying to hurt you. You really should call the police."

I look up at him. "I know. I will. I promise; just not tonight. I'll go down in the morning and file a report. Right now, I need to find my damn keys so I can get in the house." He helps me look for them. I have to admit. He's a sexy-looking nigga. He's about six feet tall with what appears to be an athletic build; has cocoa-brown skin and soft curly hair with a neatly trimmed goatee and mustache framed around succulent, pussy eating lips. Not that I'd ever want to fuck or suck him. But he definitely has it going on. He tells me he doesn't think I should be in the house alone. Tells me I can stay at his place for the night if I'd like. I smile at him, genuinely touched by his offer. "Thanks, but I'll be fine. I'll call someone to come over and stay with me." He pulls my keys from out of the bushes, then hands them to me. I thank him. He insists on walking me into the house and checking to make sure all of my windows are secured and that no one is in the house, even though my alarm is activated. I let him. This is the first time he and I have said more than a hello or goodbye to each other. And it's definitely the first time he's been inside of my home. But under the circumstances I think it's warranted.

"Nice place," he says when he's finished checking things out. "I checked everything out for you and nothing looks out of the ordinary. You should be safe."

"Thanks. I really appreciate it."

"What's your number?" he asks me. He catches the look I'm giving him, then quickly adds, "I want to call you so you can have my number locked in your cell in case something else pops off."

"Oh, okay. Thanks." I give him my number, then watch him call my cell. When it starts ringing, he disconnects the call.

"I don't care what time of the day or night it is, if something sounds or looks out of pocket, you call me, aiight?"

I nod, feeling somewhat relieved, following him to the door. "Thanks, again," I tell him.

"Anytime. Lock up. And set your alarms. Remember, call me if you need me."

I force a smile. "I will." I close the door behind him, locking it. Then press my back up against it and slide down to the floor. I lightly bang the back of my head up against the door. "Shit, shit, shit!" *What the fuck have I gotten myself into?* I shut my eyes, then open them slowly, trying to blink tonight's events out of my mind. But they are etched in my brain; the sound of his voice still echoing in my head. *You dick suckin' bitch… This shit ain't over, bitch!* Before I know it, tears begin to well up in my eyes. And I let them fall unchecked until I am sobbing uncontrollably.

Who ever heard of a nigga stalking a bitch for not sucking his dick? I get a flashback of all the niggas I've topped off and all the times I've heard them beg for another round of this throat. And then I remember all the times I said I was going to stop this shit before Jasper gets home. Now look at me. Sitting on a floor with my legs pulled up to my chest and my arms wrapped around my knees, crying hysterically. I wipe my face with the back of my hands and try to pull myself together so I can think long enough to figure out who that nut was. I try to match his voice to a face, or a place where I might have wet his dick. There are way too many to consider. I pull in a frustrated breath.

At some point, I make my way upstairs, remove my clothes and get into the shower. The palms of my hands are scraped up and raw from falling on the concrete. I stand under the water for almost twenty minutes, trying to clear my head and make sense out of why someone would want to hurt me. Yet, no matter how hard I rack my brain, I can't come up with a logical explanation. *So you not gonna suck my dick again?* This shit can't be happening to me. My body aches, but the steam and heavy beating of the water against my skin slowly relaxes me. I lather up my mesh sponge with Cinnamon and Buns body wash, then scrub my body, inhaling the soothing, tantalizing scent of the soap.

When I am done, I dry myself off, then oil my body before slipping into a pair of red laced brief panties and a white T-shirt with the words DIVA printed in red letters across the chest. I put my robe on, slip my cell down into my pocket, grab my cordless phone, then head downstairs. I go through the house, closing the blinds and shutting all the curtains. I call Felecia and tell her what happened. We hang up with her saying she'd be right over. I go into the kitchen, fix myself a cup of green tea, then saunter into the living room and turn on the stereo. I press the remote for CD, then wait for Sade to play. I curl up on the sofa, blow the steam from my cup then take a sip.

"OhmyGod, girl," Felecia says, rushing through the front door the minute I open it. It's almost three in the morning. "I got here as soon as I could. What the hell happened?"

"I was attacked." Although I calmly state this, I feel myself becoming unnerved as I give her the lowdown as I close the door and lock it behind her. I am feeling paranoid. I wish I could pretend that this shit didn't happen. But I can't. His voice still haunts me. *Bitch, I will break your muthafuckin' eye sockets.*

"My God!" she exclaims, dropping her bag on the floor. "These niggas are off the motherfuckin' chain. But I'm so glad that psycho motherfucker didn't hurt you. Thank God your neighbor pulled up when he did."

"Yeah, I am, too. There's no telling what he might have done to me had Clint not pulled up when he did." I shudder. Without thinking, I touch the right side of my face where he punched me.

"Your face is swelling up. You need to put some ice on it to keep it from getting any worse." She gets up and heads into the kitchen.

"It's not as bad as it looks," I say, following behind her. She goes into the pantry and pulls out a large Ziploc bag, then fills it up with ice. I pull out a stool and sit at the counter. She hands me the ice. "Thanks."

"Have the police caught this fucker, yet?"

I take a deep breath, brace myself for the series of questions she's going to start firing at me. I shake my head. "No. I haven't called them."

She gives me an incredulous look. "You haven't called them? What do you mean? Why not? Girl, what if that crazy nigga decides to come back? What if this nigga is stalking you?"

"I'm going to stop by the station in the morning on my way to the shop," I lie. Truth of the matter is I don't want them sniffing around. The less I have to talk about this, the better. The last thing I want to do is keep rehashing what happened. "I don't think he'll come back here tonight or any other time. I'm sure it was a random attack." *You dick-sucking bitch!* I shake the voice from my head. "But, trust and believe. In case he does, I'll be ready for him." I decide to apply for a gun permit, then purchase me some heat. In the meantime, I am going to start carrying me a can of mace and a blade.

"Girl, Jasper is going to blow a gasket when he—"

Oh, no. She is out of her fucking mind if she thinks I'm telling Jasper anything. I quickly cut her off. "He's not going to know about this." Before she can open her mouth to say something else, I continue talking. "And you are not going to open your mouth and tell him." I pause, drill my stare into her eyes to let her know I mean business; that she is not to cross the line. "Right now, the only thing I want him to be concentrating on is doing what he needs to do to get out of that halfway house. I don't need him stressing out over this. If I tell him what happened, you know like I know he'll be ready to call in his goon squad and wreck shop. I don't need him getting caught up in any extra shit that's going to get him hemmed up."

She tilts her head, chews on her bottom lip. She nods her head, knowingly. "Yeah, I guess you're right," she says thoughtfully. "But you definitely need to make sure you file a police report, first thing this morning. Do you have any idea who it was?"

I shake my head. "No."

"That shit's crazy," she huffs. "I don't think you should be staying here alone. I'm gonna stay here with you for a while; at least for a few days. I don't want this nigga thinkin' shit's all sweet. We family, boo. And that muthafucka done fucked with the wrong one."

I smile, reaching for her hand. I squeeze it. "I'll be fine. There's no need for you to disrupt your life for me."

She rolls her eyes, waving me on. "Oh, girl, puhleeze. We're like sisters. You ain't disruptin' nothin'. I can stay as long as you need me to."

As much as I appreciate her gesture, there's no way in hell I could have her, or anyone else, staying here watching me like a hawk. "Thanks. But, it's really not necessary. You being here is more than enough. It means everything to me."

A tear slides down my face. I wipe it as quickly as it falls.

She gets up and hugs me. "We're all we have, Pasha. If something were to ever happen to you, it'd kill me, girl." We hug and rock for a few minutes, before she sits back down.

She sighs. "I still can't wrap my mind around this."

I blink back more tears. "Me either," I say, holding my cup in both hands. Its warmth calms my nerves as I gulp down the last bit of my tea.

"Chile, the last thing we need is another nut on the loose."

"Yeah, you're right about that."

I get up and refill the tea kettle with water then turn on the stove. I offer her a cup of tea. "No, that's alright. But what the hell you got to eat up in here? You got a bitch up outta bed all early and shit, the least you can do is feed me."

"I got you," I tell her, walking over to the 'fridge. I open it, peering in. "Let's see. There's eggs, turkey sausage, four slices of pizza and—"

"Where's the pizza from?"

"Papa John's; vegetable."

"With extra cheese?"

"Yep. Six cheese with mushrooms."

"Hook a sista up, then." I ask her how many slices she wants, pulling them out of the 'fridge. "All of 'em," she says, laughing. "Andre broke me off some of that good stuff before you called. And the shit always has me starving afterward."

I feign disgust, laughing as I place all four slices on a plate, then stick it in the microwave. I set it for two minutes. The tea kettle starts to whistle. I turn off the stove. I place another teabag into my cup, pour water in, then let it steep for awhile. When I bring her plate over to her, she thanks me.

"No problem," I tell her, pouring two teaspoons of honey into my tea. I grab the cup, then walk over to the table and sit across from her. Felecia takes a big bite into the first slice. I watch as grease spurts out and coats her lips. She licks them.

"Damn, this pizza is good as hell." I agree, watching her finish her slice in three huge bites. There's a minute or two of silence between us as she chews and I sip my tea. She slices into the quiet with her question. "Umm, what time did you say that shit happened?"

"About one," I say, shifting my eyes as I take another sip from my cup.

She studies me. "One?" she asks, frowning. She eyes me accusingly. Or at least that's how her gaze feels to me. "Girl, please tell me what the hell you were doing out at that time of night."

The lie forms my lips before I can even think. "I had to run out to the store." She tilts her head, squints at me. Before her wheels start spinning in the wrong—well, right—direction, I add, "My period came on three days early and I needed some more pads."

"Hmmph," she grunts, pausing. "I hate when that shit happens," is all she says, taking a bite into her second slice of pizza. She keeps her eyes on her plate, slowly chewing. I can tell her mental wheels are spinning. Can tell she's conjuring up images in her head. She slowly lifts her eyes from her plate, rests them on me.

She squints. I brace myself for what's about to come out of her mouth. "Wait a minute. First, the nigga in the shop, then your car window gets smashed out, then the shop's window gets knocked out; and, now this. Something's not adding up here." I avert my eyes from hers, shifting in my seat. She catches my nervousness. "Does this nigga know you or something?"

"No," I boldly state. "I don't know who that crazy mother-fucker was."

She tilts her head, unbelievingly. "Are you sure?"

I look her dead in the eyes. I don't flinch. "Yes. I'm sure. Like I said, I don't know who the fuck he is."

She leans up in her seat, resting her forearms on the table. "And there's nothing else going on that you're not telling me?"

I bite my lower lip. Pull in a deep breath as I shake my head. "No, like what?"

"Like, uh, maybe you fucked the nigga and he done went cuckoo for the cootie."

"Well, it's obvious the nigga's a kook. But trust me. It has nothing to do with getting the pussy. I haven't fucked one nigga since Jasper's been locked up. So that's definitely not the issue."

"My God," she says, flopping back in her seat, "then this makes the shit even crazier."

"You're telling me." I lift my cup to my lips, take another slow, deliberate sip, then silently exhale, thinking: *How the fuck am I going to avoid Jasper until my face heals?*

TWENTY-SIX

"Hey, baby, I have to go outta town for a few days."

"Outta town? For what?"

I didn't get any sleep, stressing myself over how I was going to keep Jasper from seeing my face so I wouldn't have to explain—or lie, I should say—to him about what happened. It wasn't until Felecia left here about an hour ago that a plan hatched in my head. I immediately called Felecia to get her on board with my scheme.

"Bitch, you're crazy. I can't rush off to L.A.," she huffed. "Who's gonna look after the shop?"

"Nakea will," I told her as I looked online for airline tickets. "I already woke her ass up and told her I needed her to handle things down at the salon for a few days." Nakea is one of our cousins from Philly who owns The Pussy Palace—an upscale erotic sex toy store. She also owns a condo in the Tribeca section of Manhattan where she stays three days out of the week.

"A few days? What's 'a few days?'"

"We'll be back on Sunday."

She grunted. "Mmmmph. And what did you have to do for Nakea to agree to all this?"

"Nothing," I stated.

"Lies!" she snapped. "I love her to death. But 'Kea is about making paper and she ain't doing shit unless it's gonna benefit her. So spill it."

"I agreed to host a sex toy party at the salon."

"And?"

I laughed. "And I guaranteed her at least a thousand dollar in sales; even if I have to buy everything myself."

She laughed. "I knew it."

"Now I need you to go with me; it's the only way Jasper will believe me. Don't make me beg your ass."

"Bitch, you make me sick," she huffed. "I wanna window seat and a raise. And Saturdays off."

I laugh. "Done," I told her, knowing she was going to have my back. "And for an extra bonus, I'll buy you a few pieces on Rodeo Drive."

She laughed. "Well, in that case. Book my damn flight." I joined in her laughter, relieved that she would be my alibi.

"Felecia and I are going to look at wedding dresses."

"Wedding dresses? Where?"

"L.A.," I tell him, holding my breath. In my mind's eye I can see him through the phone frowning.

"What the hell you goin' way out there to look at dresses for when the city's right across the bridge? You can get all the hottest shit right there in Manhattan."

He's right. And I know exactly where I'm going—Madison Avenue to one of the boutiques. "Yeah, true. But I wanna go look. Besides, I want some real exclusive shit."

"Yeah, aiight. Don't let me find out you out there on some ole other shit, yo."

I suck my teeth. "Jasper, don't start your shit."

"Yeah, aiight. When you gonna be back?"

"Sunday," I tell him as I'm texting Felecia with the flight info. I tell her to call all of my appointments I have booked for the next few days and offer them to reschedule for when I get back, or to see one of the other stylists—on the house, of course since it is last minute. Then I tell her to only pack an overnight bag. That we'll shop when we get to L.A.

"And what time you gettin' in?" I tell him we land at two in the afternoon. "I'ma be at the crib at three, waiting on you."

"Nigga, you ain't slick," I say, laughing.

"Yo, what you mean?"

"Jasper, please. Why you gonna be at the house waiting on me on a Sunday?"

"'Cause I ain't gonna see ya ass, that's why."

"Yeah, right," I continue, still laughing. "The only reason you're coming through is to make sure I don't loan out any of this pussy while I'm gone."

"Yeah, whatever, yo. You already know what it is."

Yeah, I know what it is. It's him being jealous. And not being able to keep tabs on me. Being in prison has really done a number on him. He's so damn paranoid about everything. Still, I decide to stroke the green-eyed monster, soothe its raging spirit.

"Yeah, I'm gonna be extremely horny when I get back so having your hard dick in bed waiting for me will be exactly what I need. So make sure you take your vitamins, big boy, 'cause you're gonna need all of your strength to feed this pussy, nigga." Telling him this seems to relax him—for the moment, anyway.

He laughs. "Yeah, aiight."

He tells me he'll have to be back at the halfway house by nine, so we'll only have a few hours to spend. Tells me to make sure I bring my ass straight home from the airport. It dawns on me that Jasper doesn't have keys to the house, or the code to the alarm. I tell him the code and where the spare key'll be. The minute I do, I want to kick myself. Something inside of me says giving him easy access to getting in and out of here may be a bit more than I'm ready for.

Girl, get over yourself. He's going to be home soon so you might as

well get used to the idea of him coming in and out of here. Besides, bitch,
his name is on the deed, too.

I glance at the time, realizing I need to get off this phone so I
can get showered, packed and to the airport. "Baby, I gotta hop
in the shower. Call me later. Love you."

"Yeah, aiight," he says, sounding annoyed. "I gotta bounce, anyway. But know this, I'ma be home in a minute. And it's gonna be
a wrap."

"Umm, what's gonna be wrapped?"

"You hoppin' on planes 'n shit whenever you feel like it."

I laugh. "Whatever, Jasper. You like to hear yourself talk, baby."

"Yeah, aiight. Laugh if you want. But when I start shuttin' shit
down, don't say I didn't warn ya ass. Go on and have ya little fun,
baby. Daddy's gonna be home in a minute." Before I can open
my mouth to say something slick, he disconnects. Of course I
don't put any energy into it since I'm pressed for time. I hop in
the shower, throw a few items into my Louis carry-on, then take
it downstairs and set it by the door. I go back upstairs, lotion my
body up, then slip into a cute brown Emilio Pucci Jersey wrap
dress. I walk into my shoe closet, pulling down boxes of designer
shoes until I find the right pair to set off my outfit. I decide on a
red pair of six-inch Gucci stilettos. I give myself the once-over in
my full-length mirror, admiring myself. I put on a pair of brown
Versace shades. Despite my swollen eye and the bruise on the
side of my face, I'm still looking good. But—*this* time, am I
scared? Hell, motherfucking yeah!

If that motherfucker was crazy enough to hide out in bushes for
me, he's crazy enough to come back. And next time, most likely
try to kill me. So, hell fucking yeah, I'm scared—shitless!

Between you and me, I'm glad to be getting out of town for a
few days. The change of scenery will do me some good. Hope-

fully, help me clear my head. The last time I was out to in LA was almost two years ago for a hair and fashion show. I smile at the idea of being out in Tinseltown to shop and chill for a bit. Oh, and *look* for a wedding dress.

Once I get to Newark Airport, I park in short-term parking, then hop the shuttle to Terminal A. I text Felecia to let her know where I am, and she texts back, telling me she just got dropped off and will meet me outside the door for Continental. We get our tickets, go through security, then make it to the gate and board without any problems.

"What did you tell Jasper when you told him you were going to LA?" she asks, snapping her seatbelt in.

"I told him we were going to look at wedding dresses. And we are."

She looks at my bruised face. "Well, let's hope your face is healed by the time we have to come back."

"Well, if it's not," I say, cutting my eye at her, "you can come back without me. I'll stay a few extra days."

"And tell Jasper what?"

"That I decided to look at some commercial property while I was out there looking for my dress. Bottom line, I'm not coming back to Jersey until my face is back to normal. The last thing I need is Jasper asking me a bunch of questions." She opens her mouth to say something. I put my hand up, stopping her. "Don't. He's not to hear a word about any of this."

"Alright already. Geesh. Trust me. He won't hear it from me."

I take a deep breath, placing my head back on the headrest. "Good. Now let's enjoy our flight."

"Jasper, baby?" I call out, walking through the door, dropping my bags in the middle of the foyer. Jasper's Timbs are beside the sofa. When he doesn't respond, I think he's upstairs laying in bed with a hard dick in his hand, waiting on me to pounce on it. I start stripping off my clothes, going up the stairs to be fucked down by my man. By the time I reach the top of the stairs, I am only in my panties. I walk into the bedroom, look over at the bed. It is empty; still made. I look into the bathroom. Empty. I walk back downstairs. "Jasper, baby, where are you here?" Walk into the kitchen. Empty. Head downstairs to the basement. "Jasper?" He's sitting on the sofa with his white-socked feet propped up on the table. "Jasper, baby, what are you doing down here?" Silence. He doesn't turn to look at me; doesn't acknowledge my presence. He stares straight ahead. "Jasper?" I call out to him, walking over to him. "What's wrong?" I sit beside him. Reach out to touch him.

He glares at me, smacking my hand out of the way. "Don't fuckin' touch me, yo?"

I blink, blink again. Shocked at what he says to me, at him knocking my arm out of the way. "Excuse me? What in the hell's wrong with you?"

"What the fuck's been goin' on around here, yo? Who's this muthafucka who attacked you in the yard?" Before I can play stupid and ask him what he's talking about, he tells me that my nosey-ass neighbor saw him outside as he was coming in and asked him if I ever called the police; if they ever found the nigga who attacked me. Tells him how he had to fight the nigga off of me and tried to chase him down, but he had gotten away. Jasper tells me he played it off like he already knew about the shit and told him no; that the police were still looking for the nigga.

My chest tightens and I feel myself getting dizzy as the color drains from my face. Alicia getting her ass beat in my shop immediately flashes through mind. I've seen Jasper heated many times, but I've never seen him in that I'm-about-to-black-the-fuck-out mode until now. And it's scaring me. I stand, shocked and at a loss for words.

"I-I-uh…"

"Yo, don't come at me wit' all that fuckin' stutterin' bullshit, yo. I wanna know who the fuck put his muthafuckin' hands on you and why the fuck you ain't tell me about the shit?"

I scoot back from him, slowly stand up. "Jasper, just calm down for a minute, baby—"

He jumps up from his seat, and yanks me be the arm. "Don't fuckin' 'baby' me, yo. I wanna know what the fuck's been goin' on, yo. So you better start talkin' now before I break ya goddamn jaw, yo."

His grip on my arm is so tight it feels like he's about to rip it out of its socket. "Owwww, Jasper, you're hurting me."

"Bitch!" he shouts in my face. "I don't give a fuck about hurting you. You cheating on me, yo?"

"No!" I shout back, hurt and shocked that he has called me out of my name. In all the years we've been together, he has never, ever, called *me* a bitch. As deserving as it might be, it cuts through me. Tears well up in my eyes.

"Then who the fuck is that nigga?"

"I don't know." And on cue, the waterworks begin and I start fast-talking as if my life depended on it. Shit, it does! "I swear to you, Jasper, I don't know who he was or what he looked like. He had on a black mask. I was putting my key in the door and out of nowhere he jumped out of the bushes and grabbed me. He was trying to get me into the house, but I threw the house keys so he couldn't. I started…yelling and screaming and fighting him. But he was too strong. He-he beat me, Jasper," I sob uncontrollably. He loosens his grip. The fire in his eyes slowly starts to extinguish.

"I wanted to tell you, Jasper. But I was scared. I know you. And

I know you woulda tried to track him down. I didn't want you getting caught up in anything. I just want you home. I'm tired of being here by myself." He lets go of my arm. I grab it, rubbing the spot where his hand was. "If Clint didn't come home when he did, I don't know what woulda happened to me."

"Did you call the police?"

I nod. "Yes," I lie, knowing if I tell him I hadn't he would want to know why not. And there's no answer I could give him that would make sense. "But they haven't found him, yet. He wore gloves so there are no fingerprints anywhere."

"Is this the same muhfucka who smashed out the shop's window?"

"I don't know. I don't think so. One of the clients said he was a shorter, stocky dude. This one was over six feet, and built more like a basketball player."

"This shit ain't makin' no muthafuckin' sense. All of a sudden you got muhfuckas smashin' in windows and tryna snatch you up 'n shit."

"I think it's two separate situations; completely unrelated. Niggas wilding out doing dumb shit, that's all. You know these niggas are crazy now."

"Well, if you know that, then where the fuck was you comin' from at one in the goddam mornin', yo?" I open my mouth to speak, but he cuts in, narrowing his eyes at me. "Before you open ya muthafuckin' mouth to say some dumb shit, yo, you better think about what the fuck you gonna say 'cause I'ma fuck you up if you don't."

"I had cramps really bad and had to go out to the store to pick up a bottle of Excedrin and some tampons 'cause I was all out." The way he's looking at me I can tell he's trying to figure out if he should believe the lies that have fallen out of my mouth or not. My tears continue to fall rapidly and unchecked. They're more real now than they were earlier. Fear and guilt fuel them. "Jasper, have I ever given you reason to doubt anything I've said to you? Have I ever played you?"

He narrows his eyes again. His jaw relaxes. "Nah, yo."

"Then why would I start now? We have too much invested for me to go there with you."

"That don't mean shit, yo. There's a first time for e'erything."

"I have done nothing but love you, Jasper. I'm not trying to lose what we have, baby."

"And you don't know who that nigga was?"

"No, I already told you that."

"I know what the fuck you told me," he snaps. "And I'm asking you again. Did you know the nigga?"

I shake my head. "No, Jasper, I don't know who he is."

"Have you been fuckin'?"

"No, Jasper. I told you. This pussy is yours, and only yours. Always has been, always will be."

"It better be, Pasha. I don't want no other muhfucka puttin' his hands on you. If I find out who that nigga is I'ma snap his mutha-fuckin' neck, word up. And if I find out you been playin' me, yo; that you had another nigga's dick up in you, I'ma beat the dog shit outta ya ass, you dig?"

I nod my head, wiping my face with both of my hands. He cuts his eyes down at my hard nipples. I know better than anyone how easily I turn him on; even when he's pissed off. As nervous and scared as he has me right now, there's one thing I know for certain, Jasper loves me, but he loves this tight, wet pussy even more. And if I wasn't sure before, I am now. This nigga means every word he says.

He pulls his shirt off, unbuckles his jeans, then steps out of them. His angry dick is already getting hard. He grabs at it, stretches it out. "Take them fuckin' drawers off, yo. And bend over." I don't ask questions, don't blink; just do as I am told.

I walk over to the edge of the sofa, then lean over the arm of it. Jasper walks up behind me. I flinch glancing over my shoulder, hoping he's not going to beat me upside the head while he's fucking me. I can't front. This nigga has me shook right now. I close my eyes, relieved when he gets down on his knees, pulls open my ass and eats my pussy from the back, getting me slippery and wet. With each tongue stroke I become more relaxed. I let out soft moans, winding my hips to match his rhythm. He squeezes my ass with both his hands, jiggles it, slaps it, then stands up and straddles me from behind, pushing his dick deep in me. He stretches me. Lets my muscles grab his cock. Then violently rams himself deeper into me. I dig my nails into the leather. Bite down on the arm. Try to hold back screams. His aggressive thrusts make it very clear that he intends to fuck the shit out of me.

"Uhhh, uhhhhh…oooooh…" He pounds the inside of my walls with one powerful thrust after another, hitting my spot. My stomach tightens with each rapid stroke. "Aaaaaaah…oooooohh-hhhh…"

He slaps my ass, hard; makes it sting and burn. He slaps it again. He grunts, groans, slams his hips into my ass, causing my whole body to jerk forward. Sweat drips off his body onto my back. "I love the fuck outta you, Pasha…"

"Uhhh, aaaah…uhhh…oooh…I love…you…too…"

"This pussy's so good," he grunts, pounding his dick into me like a runaway train. "I'm warning you. Don't…"—he slams his dick in, pulls out—"make…"—slams it back in—"me…kill…"—pulls his dick out, slams it back in—"you…"

I let out a loud scream as one nut after another erupts and coats his cock. He is fucking me mercilessly. I look over my shoulder. Plead with my eyes for him to keep beating my walls. To fuck me, hard; fuck me, deep. He grabs me by the shoulders, forcefully pulls me back into him and beats my pussy until it screams. Two minutes later, Jasper's grunting and groaning and moaning, dumping a load of anger and doubt deep inside of me.

TWENTY-SEVEN

Two months later, there is no more mention about the nigga who attacked me. There are no harassing phone calls to the salon. No mail; nothing. It's like the nigga just vanished. Still, I am too leery to become overly excited. Until he's picked up or bodied, and I know he's off the streets; that he's behind bars or buried, nothing is over. Nevertheless, I am thankful for the peace, no matter how short-lived it may be.

Jasper is home from the halfway house. I am still surprised at how fast he made it home. Only thing, he's been released on parole for the next year. Of course he hates the shit. And bitches about it every chance he gets. "These cracker muhfuckas are always lookin' for ways to keep a nigga down. They wanna see a muhfucka fail wit' all this dumb shit they got me doin'?"

"Like what?" I asked him the last time he complained.

"Like this fuckin' curfew, yo. What the fuck I look like bein' in the muthafuckin' house at nine o'clock? I'ma grown-ass man, yo. This nigga talkin' 'bout if I'm one minute late he's gonna violate me. What kinda shit is that? Shit, I coulda took my ass on ISP if I wanted to have a muhfucka breathin' down my back e'ery fuckin' day. That muhfucka needs some pussy in his life, yo. Maybe then, the nigga wouldn't have so much free time ridin' my nuts 'n shit."

I am always so tempted to remind him that he got himself caught up in this shit so stop fucking complaining about shit he can't control. Instead I keep my mouth shut. Let him vent. "A muhfucka can't even get his drink or smoke on fuckin' wit' these crooked-ass muhfuckas."

I had to smile, shaking my head. I realized it wasn't the fact that he was on parole that was his issue. He was pissed that he didn't have his parole officer in his back pocket, like he's had everyone else his whole bid; from CO's to counselors.

Anyway, aside from his "detailing job" five days a week and checking in weekly with his parole officer, Jasper's been pretty much hanging around the house. And for the most part, it's fine 'cause I'm down at the salon the majority of the day. The week-ends haven't been so bad. Most times he's out with Stax doin' whatever they do. Or he has everyone chilling here. The only problem: I can't get away with shit. If I sneeze wrong, he's on it. This fool watches me like a damn hawk. He won't let me out of his sight. And when he does, he's calling every ten to fifteen minutes checking on me. Even when we're in bed, I can feel him watching me. A few times I woke up with him standing over me watching me sleep. Ever since he found out about that incident with that nigga, he's become excessively possessive and protective over me. It's not all the time. Mostly when something snaps in his brain and has him thinking crazy shit, like I'm out doing some sneaky shit, which I'm not. Hell, I'm too damn paranoid to.

"Yo, wake ya sexy ass up," he says, shaking me. I don't budge. "Pasha? Get ya ass up, yo."

I groan, stretching. "Fifteen more minutes."

"Don't you have to go into the salon today?"

"No," I mumble. He asks why not. I tell him, "I have a doctor's appointment this morning." He wants to know what kind of appointment. "For a checkup." I decide this nigga isn't going to let me get any sleep so I might as well get up. I pull the covers back and get out of bed.

"What kinda check-up?"

"I have a GYN appointment," I tell him, bending over to look in one of the bottom drawers for my pink camisole. He gets out of bed and walks up behind me, pressing his nude body into mine. He grinds his dick into me. I straighten my body, sucking my teeth. "Will you quit it, nasty?"

"What you need a GYN appointment for?"

"To make sure shit's right," I tell him. But the truth is I think I might be pregnant. I took a home pregnancy test last month, and it came back negative. Then I took another one two weeks ago, and that one was positive. I've been feeling feel strange lately. Hard to describe it, like something is fluttering in my stomach. So I decided to make an appointment.

"Yo, the only pussy checker you need is me. As long as that shit stays tight, it's right."

"Whatever," I snap, rolling my eyes. "You get on my fucking nerves with that stupid shit."

He laughs. "Yeah, you know what it is."

"Yeah, what I know is your black ass ain't getting any more of this pussy, so laugh at that." I turn on the balls of my feet and head into the bathroom, popping my hips; pissed the hell off that he still makes snide remarks; subtle comments about me cheating. And I'm not. Okay, I was. But that's beside the point. I'm not *now*, and that's what matters. I know what you're going to ask. Nooooo, I haven't shut down my NastyFreaks4u page, yet. I haven't had time to. And I haven't logged into my Deep Throat Diva email account either. So, that should say something. Jasper follows behind me.

"Say, what?"

"You heard me," I say, turning on the water to brush my teeth. I place my toothbrush under the water, then squeeze out a glob of Crest. I brush my teeth. Then spit and rinse.

"You buggin' for real now. You know damn well I'm gettin' up in that ass, so you need to cancel that dumb shit you talkin', ya heard?"

"Whatever," I say, shutting off the water.

He grabs me by the arm as I attempt to brush past him. He pulls me into him. "C'mon, baby. You know I was only fuckin' wit' you."

I mush him in his face as he tries to kiss me. "Nigga, please."

"C'mon, don't start ya shit, yo. You got my dick all hard 'n shit."

He presses himself into me. "That's too bad," I say, trying to ignore his growing dick. He interlocks his fingers into mine. Kisses me on the forehead, then slowly moves down to my nose, my lips, then nibbles on my neck. I don't stop him, quickly forgetting my weak attempt at being mad at him. Before I know it, I have his hard dick in my hand, jerking it as we kiss. He slips his hand in between my thighs, plays with my clit, then dips two fingers into my sticky honey.

In no time, I am down on my knees, doing what I love most—sucking his dick. This is the only time—besides when I'm riding his dick—that Jasper submits. That he lets me have control.

I take him into my mouth and suck him, lovingly. Suck him with everything that is in me. He moans, grabs the back of my head, rocks on the back of his heels, trying to brace himself as I spit shine his nozzle.

I pull his dick from out of my neck, then begin twirling my tongue around the head of his dick, lapping at the precum. I lick the slit of his dick, then cup my lips around the head again, popping his dick with my lips and mouth. I take the shaft of his dick back in my mouth, then swallow him again. He lets out another moan of pleasure. I glance up at him and see that his eyes are shut, tight. The minute I tickle his balls with my tongue, Jasper's leg starts to shake.

Two minutes later, I can feel the head of his dick swelling inside of my throat. I rapidly bob my head back and forth on his cock until he empties his balls down in my throat. I gulp his cream down, then pull his dick out of my mouth and suck and lick it clean, getting the last remaining drops of his creamy milk. I stand up, licking my lips. He kisses me, looking dazed, sliding his tongue back into my mouth. Jasper's an undercover freak. Not too many niggas would tongue down their girl while she still has his nut on her tongue. But Jasper isn't ever bothered by it. It seems to turn him on more. And that within itself turns me on even more.

When I am done, Jasper staggers back over to the bed and collapses. I turn on the shower and step in. By the time I get out, and walk back into the room, Jasper is sprawled out in the middle of the bed, snoring. I smile, getting dressed, then making my way to my doctor's appointment to confirm what I already know in my heart.

Two weeks later, Jasper and I are in Philadelphia having an early dinner at Warmdaddy's—a Rhythm & Blues soul food spot on Columbus Boulevard. I haven't been to Philly in years, so when Jasper said he wanted to take a drive down here I was pleasantly surprised; particularly since he wanted to go to Penn's Landing, the waterfront area of Center City. The weather was beautiful today so it was perfect for a stroll along the river, holding hands, talking and laughing. Something we haven't done in years. It felt good to spend the day out of the house doing something other than fucking and sucking—which I do enjoy, don't get me wrong. Still, the fact that Jasper wanted to get up early and do a road trip was a nice break from our normal Saturday routine.

After our stroll along the river, then ferry ride over to Camden, New Jersey to check out the Aquarium, we caught the ferry back to Philly, then walked over the bridge into South Street. Though long and exhausting, overall, it's been a wonderful day.

Warmdaddy's is packed as usual. We decide to eat upstairs instead of paying the extra cost to see a show. Once we're seated, the waiter hands us our menus. At first glance, I already know what I'm going to have: the Southern Neptune Seafood Salad, and for my entrée the Eastern Coast Crab Cakes with a side of smoked turkey collards. It takes Jasper a while longer before he decides on having the Southern Fried Chicken Dinner—white meat, with a side of collards and macaroni and cheese.

The waiter takes our orders, then walks off. I am surprised when Jasper asks me what's going on with the wedding. Usually he is not interested in any of the details; just how much it's going to cost. We decided to have a formal, yet small intimate wedding. Well, actually I did. Still, we both agreed to keep it very small. Twenty-to-twenty-five people at the most. However, somehow, the list has grown to close to fifty guests.

He shakes his head. "Why we need all them muhfuckas there? I thought you said this was going to be a small wedding."

"It is," I tell him. "It's still small enough for it to be intimate."

He smiles. "Yeah, aiight."

"What's that supposed to mean?"

"Yo, it's your day," he says thoughtfully, "so do it however, beautiful."

"No, it's our day," I correct him, reaching over and touching his hand. He takes mine into his and brings it up to his lips, kissing it.

There's a moment of silence between us before he asks, "Are you happy?"

Though his question catches me by surprise, I nod, smiling. "Do you even have to ask? I've waited my whole life for this. To be married, have my own family. I love a man who I *know* loves me back. How could I not be happy? I have everything I could ever want."

"You sure about that?" he asks, sounding almost skeptical.

I tread lightly. "Jasper, please, let's not ruin a potentially wonderful evening with this. Of course I'm sure."

"Oh, aiight; just checkin'."

"And if I told you I wasn't?" I ask, pushing the envelope.

He smirks. "Then I'da told your sexy-ass to get over it; too fuckin' bad. You're stuck wit' me. And that's what it is. 'Til *death* do us part, baby."

His emphasis on death makes me jittery and on edge. I shift in my seat, relieved when the waiter returns to the table with our pan of homemade cornbread.

"You know I love you, right?"

Cautiously, I nod, cutting a slice of cornbread. "I know you do. I love you, too." I bite into the buttery sweet bread, practically moaning. It's delicious.

"This, you and me," he says, cutting himself a piece as well. "Is real, baby. You do understand there's no turning back, right?" He keeps his stare locked on mine, placing the knife down. The way he's looking at me, there's a mixture of love and something else I can't quite put my finger on—suspicion, yeah, that's it—in his eyes.

He takes a bite into his bread, and smiles. "Yo, this shit is bangin'."

I agree, hoping it changes the course of this conversation. "It tastes like cake. I could eat this whole pan," I add, cutting another slice.

"No doubt. Listen," he pauses. His intense stare dashes any hopes that this discussion is. "You got anything you wanna tell me? No jokes, no games, keep it a hunnid."

I blink, shocked at the question. I am relieved when the waiter returns with my salad and Jasper's cell rings. He ignores it. I share half of it with Jasper. Jasper tells the waiter he would like to order a Chimay Grand Reserve, then looks over at me to see if I want something. As bad as I want one of their mango mojitos, I decline. Order myself a passion fruit punch instead.

While I'm eating my seafood salad, it gets quiet between us. I find myself wondering why he asked if I had something to tell him. Other than being pregnant, what else would he think I had to tell? I shake it from my head, shifting to thoughts of being a mother. I try to imagine what our baby will look like. Will he or she have Jasper's dark beautiful skin tone? Will he or she have my eyes, or Jasper's? I wonder what kind of baby Jasper was. Was he a happy, always cooing-and-smiling baby, or was he one of those fussy, whining-colicky babies?

I steal glances at Jasper and smile. In less than three months, I'll be almost five months pregnant and Jasper and I will be married. Of all the bitches he's fucked, I'm the one who's giving him a child; I'm the one he's wifing.

He looks up from his plate, catches my smile. "Why you smilin'?"

"When you asked me if I had something to tell you, I do."

He leans up in his seat, resting his elbows up on the table as if he's waiting for me to drop a bomb on him. "Oh, word?"

"It's a secret I've been keeping; actually a surprise for you," I say, grinning now from ear-to-ear. "I was going to wait a little longer to tell you, but I can't hold it in any longer."

"And what's that?"

"I'm pregnant."

His eyes widen. "You're pregnant?" he asks, clearly surprised about the news. I nod. "Stop playin' wit' me, yo. You carryin' my seed for real?"

"Yes, baby. That's why I was going to the doctor's a couple of weeks ago. I went to get tested. I'm five weeks pregnant.

His face lights up with a wide Kool-Aid smile. "Oh, shit, that's wassup, baby." He pulls me toward him, leans in and kisses me on the lips. "Yo, you just made me the happiest man alive, word up, yo." He flags the waiter over. "Yo, my man, skip the beer. Let me get a bottle of that Dom P. My wife's pregnant, yo." The waiter congratulates us, and the couple sitting in earshot next to us does the same. Jasper goes to pull out his phone to call all his people to share the news, but I quickly stop him.

"No, baby, let's wait," I say, grabbing his hand. "I want to keep this between us for now. Let's surprise everyone in a few more months."

"Oh, aiight. No doubt." He leans over and kisses me again. "I'ma be a father. I love the hell outta you, girl." When the waiter returns with the bottle of champagne, he pours it into flutes. Jasper waits for him to walk off, then raises his glass. "To us. Me, you and our beautiful baby; together forever."

Our glasses click. And for the rest of the night, Jasper talks incessantly about our life together and how nothing will come between us; how he's going to give his child everything he never had; and be what his father could never be: A dad. A tear slides down his handsome face. He quickly brushes it away. I reach over and grab his hand; kiss it. It is the first time I've ever seen my man cry.

TWENTY-EIGHT

It is after two A.M. when I slyly slip out of bed, careful not to wake up Jasper. We finished our nightly fuck session almost two hours ago, and I'm still restless. Jasper collapsed over on the side of his bed and passed out sweaty shortly after he busted his third round up in me. I can hear his heavy breathing and light snoring, letting me know he's in a deep sleep—one I fucked him into. One I should be in as well. But I am not. Instead, I have been lying in bed staring up into the darkness. I steal one last peek at Jasper as I ease out of the bedroom and saunter into the spare bedroom, quietly shutting the door behind me.

My laptop is sitting over on the cherry wood desk in sleep mode, but quickly comes to life with the touch of the mouse. I sit at the desk, closing my eyes and taking in a deep breath. It's been almost three weeks since I've shut down my Nastyfreaks4u page and close to two weeks since I've logged onto my AOL account to check my emails.

Girl, what the fuck is wrong with you? You have a fine-ass man who fucked you down lovely lying up in the other room and your trifling ass is in here on creep mode. Not to mention all the drama that nut brought you. That nigga almost turned your whole world upside down. Being the hardheaded ho that I am, I ignore my inner voice, and sign onto AOL. I wait for the screen to open. The voice alerts me I have new messages.

I open the first email. *Hello. Nice ad. Professional, happily involved white man here. 36, 5'10", 178 lbs, lean, toned body. Nice cock for your hot mouth and throat. Would love to meet. Looking for someone who is into swallowing my cock juice. I'd like to see you on your knees looking into my eyes as you feel my cock pump a hot load down your throat.*

I delete, going to the next email. *Hey Deep Throat. I'm 5'11 black 195lbs with a nice 8.5 thick, fat cock for your mouth and throat. Private, very discreet. Married with family here. Cool, laidback guy. D/D disease free here. Need the same.*

Although the email is two weeks old, I decide to send a reply, anyway. *Hello there. If you are still looking to get sucked, I'm interested in sucking your thick, fat dick. If you can, send a pic. Thanks!* Five minutes later an IM box pops up.

Ready2nutInU: Hey. What's good? Got ya email. I sent pic
Deepthroatdiva: Hey back. Don't C it in inbox, yet

When I hear, "You've got mail," I minimize the IM box, then click on the new message. The second it opens I am immediately greeted with a pic of a beautifully curved dick with a mouthwatering, juicy head. My mouth starts to drool. I reopen the IM box and type.

Deepthroatdiva: Beautiful dick! It looks like it tastes good 2
Ready2nutInU: LOL. Thx! U wanna taste it 4 urself?
Deepthroatdiva: YES!
Ready2nutInU: what u look like?
Deepthroatdiva: sexy, classy-type. U'd never know I do what I do, the way I do it
Ready2nutInU: cool. Can u send a pic?
Deepthroatdiva: No. VERY, VERY discreet here
Ready2nutInU: Cool. U married?

Deepthroatdiva: engaged. What u look like?

Ready2nutInU: brown-skin, avg type cat. Low-cut fade. Luv my dick sucked

Deepthroatdiva: Nice

Ready2nutInU: u got webcam?

Deepthroatdiva: No

Ready2nutInU: Damn. Gotta go. Wife call'n 4 me. I go to gym @ 6am. Can we meet?

I blink, try to convince myself that this is not only a bad idea; it's a dangerous one. However, I'm too caught up in the idea of sucking on his dick to see, think, clearly enough to tell this nigga no can do. Tell him that I'm engaged; that my man is in the next room; that I'm a little over two months' pregnant. I am too blinded by lust to listen to the nagging voice in my head warning me, reminding me, that Jasper is home now. Instead, I assure myself that it'll be the last time. That Jasper won't find out. I tell him yes. Tell him I go to the gym as well; that I can meet him at seven. We decide to meet at Mountainside Park. We exchange car info. I tell him how I can't wait to taste his fat dick; how I can't wait to make love to it with my mouth, lips, tongue and hands; how I love to deep throat; how I am going to suck his dick in a way his wife never has. I tell him how I am fantasizing about being on my knees and worshiping his cock and swallowing his creamy load. He tells me how hard I'm making his dick; how he can't wait to have it sucked; that his wife half-sucks it. I ask him if he's ready to bust a fat nut from some good head and a deep throat. He types: *HELL muthafuckn YEAH!*

I am so caught up in the cyber-sex play that I don't hear Jasper when he comes into the room. It isn't until he walks up on me that he startles me. "Aye, yo," he says, standing in back of me, "what you doin' in here? Who you online talkin' to this time'a night?"

I quickly click out of the screen. "Oh, hey," I say, shutting my laptop. I get up and face him. He's standing in front of me naked. "Umm, uh, I didn't hear you get up."

He studies me; narrows his eyes. "Yo, I asked you who the fuck you on the internet wit'?" I can see the veins in his neck starting to swell, which tells me if I don't give him a suitable answer within the next few seconds there's going to be major problem up in here.

I suck my teeth. "I was online with a rep from the bridal shop where I'm ordering favors for the wedding," I tell him. I let the lie continue to roll off of my tongue. "Most online stores now have agents who will ask you if you need any help."

He stares at me, clenching his jaws. "Why the fuck you online this time of night ordering shit, then?"

"Because, one, I can't get anything done during the day when I'm down at the salon. And, two, sometimes you can find cheaper deals when you shop late at night."

The vein on the side of his neck relaxes and he unclenches his jaw. "Show me the fucking website you were on then," he demands.

I suck my teeth. Flip open the laptop, then wait for the screen to come alive. I click into my web server, then pull up a bridal site. I click on a few buttons, bring up my customer account number and show him my order. "Satisfied?" I ask. I step back so he can see for himself, hoping like hell it keeps his suspicions at bay.

"Yeah, aiight. Don't let me find out some other shit, yo."

"Some other shit like what, Jasper?"

"Like you tryna fuckin' play me."

I huff. "Here we go with this shit again. I don't know why you always acting so paranoid."

"'Cause I know how bitches can be."

"You know what, I'm so sick of you saying that shit. If you feel like every bitch is on it like that, then we need to end this shit, now," I storm past him, heading back into the bedroom. "You got the wrong one if you think I'm about to keep going through this with you. We need to call off this wedding and be done with this dumb shit. You go on about your business; take care of our baby and leave me the fuck alone. I'm done."

"Yo, hold the fuck up," he snaps, grabbing me by the arm.

I yank my arm away. "Get the fuck off of me, nigga."

He blocks the doorway. "I'm not done talkin', yo."

"Well, I am. Now move the fuck out my way." The only reason I'm talking extra greasy is because I'm pregnant and he'd never hit me while I'm carrying his seed. I try to push him out of the way, but he doesn't budge. "Nigga, get the fuck out the way."

"Aye yo, what I tell you 'bout ya mouth? You 'bout to get ya whole front knocked out, word up."

I fold my arms across my chest defiantly. "Whatever. All I know is I'm sick of this shit with you."

"Well, you need to get the fuck over that," he says, eyeing me. "'Cause like I told you before, you ain't goin' nowhere, and neither am I. And now you havin' my seed, it's a wrap. You stuck wit' me, baby. So watch ya mouth or get smacked in it."

I grunt, placing my hands on my hips. "Mmmph. Well, if that's so, then know this. I've rode shit out with you your whole fucking bid. I've waited for your black ass to get home, nigga. And don't think for one fucking minute the shit was easy, because it wasn't. The next bitch woulda been done bounced on you. But I stayed. Not because I needed to, but because I wanted to. So stop coming at me all aggressive and shit. I'm yours, nigga."

He smirks, letting his eyes drop down to my hard nipples, then to my stomach. I'm not really showing yet. "Oh, you mine?"

"All yours," I tell him, stepping up into his space. The tension between us begins to lift. I press my body up against his. Grind my pelvis into him.

"Then get ya ass back in bed." He steps back to let me by. I glance over my shoulder and catch him staring back at my laptop. "I'm tellin' you, Pasha, don't have me fuck you up, yo."

TWENTY-NINE

Between the long hours at the salon, trying to tie-up last-minute wedding details—like making sure my dress will fit me by the time it's time to go down the aisle, and Jasper's constant mood swings, I don't know if I'm coming or going. Shit, I'm the one who should be on an emotional roller coaster—I'm the one knocked up! But, the way Jasper carries on, you would think he's the one three months' pregnant. The nigga's moods are too damn unpredictable for me, and it's nerve-wracking. One minute, he's yelling and cursing and screaming at me; the next minute he's telling me how much he loves me. A few days'll go by and everything will be good between us. Then without provocation, his moody ass will flip the switch and start accusing and threatening me. I'm telling you. The way he's been acting, I have to wonder if he isn't out there doing his own dirt. I mean, damn! The nigga has me walking on eggshells. I don't know what little voices he's hearing in his head, but whatever they're saying to him has him acting like a certified fool.

Since that last incident a month or so ago when Jasper walked up on me in the middle of the night while I was online, I've been keeping it real low-key. That shit was too close for comfort and I don't need any more close calls like that. I didn't even go off and meet the nigga like I had planned. And I haven't been going online looking for extra dick to suck, either. Yes, the thought crossed my mind once or twice…but, that's it. I'm not doing shit.

One, I'm pregnant; and, two, it's too damn dangerous. Jasper watches and checks every move I make. The last thing I'm interested in is having him snap the fuck out on me. I'm seriously thinking he needs to see someone to help him with whatever is going on with him. I don't know if it's nerves or what, but something isn't right. And it's starting to get on my last goddamn nerve!

Two weeks ago, he snapped to the point where I thought he was going to have a damn heart attack the way he was screaming and carrying on. "Yo, where the fuck you been at?" he snapped the minute I walked through the door. He caught me off guard, startling me. I dropped my shopping bags.

"*Excuse you!*" I said with major attitude. He had this wild, crazy look on his face, practically foaming at the mouth. Something told me he would have hit me if I wasn't pregnant.

"I asked you where the fuck you was at, yo! It's almost eight-thirty and you just walkin' up in this muthafucka when you left the shop at five. Pasha, don't have me beat ya ass, yo."

"Yeah, nigga, and when I spoke to you this afternoon, I told your black ass that I was going to the mall. So what the fuck is your problem? I'm really getting sick of this shit. Always fucking threatening me. Nigga, if you wanna beat my ass, then do it." Although I said that, I didn't really mean it. "I can't put up with this stress. It's too much for me. And it's too much for my baby."

He glanced down at the shopping bags in the middle of the floor. His tone changed. "Oh, now it's your baby. Fuck me, right?"

"Yeah, basically," I said, picking my bags up and brushing past him to go upstairs. "I think you should move out," I told him, climbing the steps.

"Say what?"

"You heard me. Pack your shit and get the fuck out. I need some time away from you."

"For what? So you can go out and fuck around on me, yo. I ain't goin' no fuckin' where. My name's on this shit, too."

I sighed. "Then don't," I told him, walking into my walk-in closet and pulling out a suitcase and overnight bag. I opened up drawers and started pulling out underwear and yanking shit off hangers, then stuffing it in the suitcases.

He snatched my travel bag. "Yo, where the fuck you think you goin', yo?"

"I can't do this with you; this constant nitpicking and badgering me. I need a break from you and your craziness."

Then he started apologizing; telling me how he worries about me when he can't get me on the phone or when I don't come home right away. "Baby, the shit stresses me. I don't want anything happening to you or our baby; feel me?" He grabbed my arm, pulled me toward him. "You're my world, Pash. You and our unborn baby are all I have in this world, yo. Without you two, I have nothing."

Needless to say, I ended up lying in his arms and falling asleep. The next day, this nigga woke up like nothing had ever happened. Then two days later, he has the audacity to tell me that when I'm not at the salon or out with Felecia or Mona planning the wedding, he wants me to check in with him every fifteen minutes. I screamed at him. "Nigga, first of all, I'm not on parole. You are. Second of all, you are out of your crazy-ass mind if you think I'm gonna be doing all that shit. I'ma grown-ass woman; what the fuck I look like checking in with you like I'm some damn child."

"Because I said so," he responded as if my statement was a question. It wasn't.

"Well, too bad. What you are asking is ridiculous. And I'm not doing it."

"Yo, you heard what I said," he calmly stated.

"Yeah, and you heard what I said. You not keeping me on a leash like I'm some goddamn poodle you tryna train. If you want a slave, then you need to go out and find you one 'cause you are not gonna be chaining me down." I snatched up my bag and keys, then made my way out the door.

Surprisingly, the last two weeks all has been calm. Honestly, a little too peaceful if you ask me. Almost like the calm before the storm. But I'm not going to complain. Jasper's curfew has been modified to eleven P.M. on weeknights, and midnight on the weekends. Although he's bitching about that, it definitely seems to have lessened the stress around here. I think the nigga was getting stir-crazy or something.

In any case, I am home, enjoying me time. Jasper has been out all day with Stax doing whatever they do. Though he's called to check in on me a few times, he seemed perfectly fine knowing I was home, lounging. Now I'm sitting here on the sofa, Sade's "Babyfather" is playing on the stereo. I rub my belly and sing. *Your daddy knows…your daddy knows…for you he is the best he can be…*

"Yo, baby," Jasper says, walking through the door, disrupting my moment. He's carrying a long white box with a big red bow wrapped around it.

Flowers, I think, smiling. "Hey," I say, reaching for the stereo remote and turning the sound down. He walks over and plants a kiss on my lips. He hands me the box. "Thank you," I say, pulling the ribbon apart, then opening the box. "This is so sweet." There's a white envelope atop a dozen Birds of Paradise. I open the envelope and pull out the card. It reads:

Pasha, baby,
I know there are times when I'm buggin' 'n shit; when you think I don't give a fuck 'bout us, or you. But, that's far from true. You are all

I think about, baby. Life with you in it is what brings me joy. You keep me smiling. Don't give up on me, baby. Or on us. One day, I'ma be the man you need me to be.

I love you, need you, and want you, baby…forever!

One love, one heart,

Ya man for life,

Jasper

Jasper is sitting across from me, watching me. I get up from my seat, walk over to him and sit in his lap, planting soft kisses all over his face, then lips. We tongue for a few seconds. Jasper's hand snakes its way up my nightgown. I part my legs; allow him to brush his fingers against my clit. I kiss him with more passion. Then, before I know it, we are both naked in the middle of the floor fucking like two wild rabbits until he carries me upstairs and finishes serving me his dick in every position imaginable.

By the time Jasper finishes blowing my back out—three rounds later—it's almost three in the morning. We both pass out, sticky and exhausted.

I glance at my watch, walking out of Bloomingdales. It's 8:51 P.M. *I can't believe I've practically shut down the damn mall, again. Two nights in a row; this shit's got to stop*, I think as my cell rings. I fish it out of my bag, pressing TALK. It's Jasper. "Hey, baby."

"Aye, yo, you still at the mall?" he asks as I walk toward the exit doors.

"I'm leaving now," I tell him.

"What time you gonna be home?"

"I'm heading there now. Why, you need something?"

"Yeah, you," he says, lowering his voice. "A muhfucka's horny as fuck, yo."

I grin. "Well, then, I guess we'll have to do something about that, won't we? Keep that dick hard for me. I'll be home shortly."

"No doubt, baby. Hurry ya sexy ass on."

"I'm on my way," I say, giggling as I walk across the street toward the parking garage. I look around and notice that there is no movement anywhere. "See you when I get there."

"No doubt, baby."

We say our goodbyes, then disconnect. I'm surprised to see how empty the parking garage is. *Then again, it's a Tuesday night,* I reason in my head, walking toward my car. *The mall didn't have many people in it tonight to begin with.* I stick my hand down into my bag for my car keys. I feel around in the bottom for them, finally pulling them out. I disarm the alarm. Open the back door and toss my bags in. Before I can shut it, I feel my hair being violently pulled and my head yanked back; then I hear the click of a gun. The sound of it being cocked as it presses against my temple. My heart stops, then starts racing a mile a minute. I drop my cell and keys.

"Bitch, if you so much as flinch, I'ma dead ya ass right here. You hear me?"

I nod, practically about to shit on myself. The only thing I am thinking at this very moment is: Not this shit again! But here I am in motherfucking white suburbia in the middle of a parking garage of an upscale mall and I have another goddamn nut standing in back of me with a gun pressed to my head. Un*fucking*believable!

"Good. Now do as I tell you and I won't haveta spill ya pretty, lil brains out all over this concrete."

The voice is deep, and unrecognizable. My mind is reeling. I have to get someone's attention before this kook does God knows what to me. I have two options. I can scream at the top of my lungs and attempt to fight him, hoping someone hears me. Or I can scream and get my brains splattered all over the place. I swear this is not how I want to die, murdered—like my mother *and* father. *Think, bitch!*

I open my mouth to scream, but he whacks me in the back of the head with the butt of his gun, causing my knees to buckle. "Don't even think it. I promise you. On e'erything I love. I *will* kill you, bitch."

"Please," I plead in a whisper, "my wallet's in my bag. I only have a few hundred dollars on me, but we can go to an ATM and get more. Whatever you do, don't hurt me."

He yanks me by the arm. "Bitch, shut the fuck up and walk." He tightens his grip on me, and starts dragging me toward a burgundy van. "You think I waited all goddamn night out in this muthafuckin' parkin' garage for ya money? Silly bitch! I don't want ya goddamn money. I want somethin' way better than that shit."

OhmyGod, this nigga is gonna rape me! Right here! In the middle of this parking garage! Where the fuck is everyone? Where the fuck is security? Think, bitch!

"What, you want some pussy? You can fuck me right here, baby. You don't have to rape me for it."

"Bitch, shut ya smutty ass up. Ain't nobody tryna rape ya trick ass. Now let's go." He yanks me by the arm. Tries to drag me with him.

For some reason I realize this is my last shot at getting away. If this nut takes me off in his vehicle, I may end up at the bottom of a river, or chopped up into tiny pieces, then tossed out somewhere. Win or lose, I have to at least try. If I have to die, then I need to go down with a fight. I start screaming at the top of my lungs and violently swinging. "HELP! SOMEBODY! PLEASE, HELP ME! THERE'S A—"

Whack! He punches me in the mouth. Blood gushes out. "Bitch, what the fuck is wrong with you, huh? I told you to keep ya motherfuckin' mouth shut, you stupid bitch." *Whack!* This time he hits me upside the head with the butt of his gun and everything around me starts to blur, but it doesn't stop me from balling up both of my hands and swinging punches at him. I stun this nigga when I hit him with an uppercut, then connect two punches to his face. I start screaming—again, to no avail. Someone else runs up and grabs me from behind. I wildly kick the nigga in front of me.

"Yo, hurry the fuck up and let's get this bitch up outta here before someone comes out," the nigga in back of me says, trying to restrain me. Then, in one swift motion, there's a blade pressed up under my throat. "I'ma tell you one time to shut the fuck up. Now shut…the fuck…up. Or I'ma slice ya muthafuckin' throat, ya heard?"

I shut my mouth, but I can feel myself starting to hyperventilate as images of my mother being found dead in the trunk of her car surface. I can't help but think how both of my parents were tragically murdered, and now…that may become my fate as well. I continue to struggle to keep them from taking me, but they overpower me. And, then, the nigga in back of me gets me in a choke hold—blocking off my airway, causing everything to fade.

When I open my eyes, it takes me a few seconds to realize where I am. I am gagged and bound, riding in the back of a vehicle. It's dark in here. I blink my eyes and try to adjust to the darkness, but then I realize that I am blindfolded as well. My head is banging and feels like it's about to explode. I am not sure how long I've been passed out, or how long we've been driving, but one thing I am certain of: I am in some deep shit!

I close my eyes, tight. Hoping someone has located my car. That Jasper, or Felecia—anyone, is calling around for me, worried.

I can't stop thinking about Jasper. About how much I love him. About how ready I am to marry him. And how I want to spend my life with him. I am not only frightened about not knowing where these nuts are taking me, or what's going to happen to me once they get me there. I am scared shitless about these mother-fuckers killing me, then tossing my body where no one will ever find me.

I'm nervous. And I can't stop wondering if I am going to be raped, first, before my body is disposed of. If they're going to torture me, or make it a swift kill. They have me riding around in the back of this van, going God knows where. I unsuccessfully struggle to break free, but give up, realizing it's a moot point. The only thing I keep thinking is: I don't want to die! Not tonight! And definitely not like this: kidnapped, gagged, blindfolded, and bound!

I frantically rack my brain, trying to figure out who is doing this to me, and why. I can't imagine whom I could have pissed off? What I might have said or done that was so fucked-up that would warrant this. The only person who comes to mind is that nut who had been harassing me. I knew not hearing from him was too good to be true. I force myself to think of happy things. Imagine being a mother. Picture myself going down the aisle. My wedding is less than a month away and here I am shackled like a slave. Then that book I read, *Sold*…no, not that one—*Stealing Candy*, comes to mind. *OhmyGod, please don't let these niggas be a part of some sex trafficking ring*, I think, letting my imagination get the best of me. *Don't let them drug me, then sell me and use me as some underground sex slave.* Suddenly, my panic intensifies, then turns to grief as my concerns and fear for my own safety shifts to that of my unborn child. *What if I lose my baby*, I think, fretfully. *Oh God, please don't let me miscarry. I beg you.*

The vehicle abruptly stops. I hear a set of voices. Then a door opens and slams shut. My heart races, knowing I've probably reached my destination; hopefully, it will not be my final destination.

The back doors swing open, and I feel two sets of hands grabbing me by the ankles, pulling me out. I attempt to fight and squirm, to no avail.

"This bitch is real feisty," one voice says.

"Yeah, I'ma have a lotta fun tamin' her hot ass," another voice adds, laughing.

"Remember, she's not to be hurt," the first nigga says. His voice is not as gruff as the first nigga's. He seems more rational.

"No doubt. I'll just rough the bitch up a bit. Treat her like the slut she is." He starts trying to manhandle me.

"C'mon, man...chill out wit' all that. Let's just get her inside," the other guy says, stopping him. "She's pregnant."

The taller nigga huffs. "Whatever, nigga. Grab the bitch's legs and let's get this shit over with."

THIRTY

"I can't wait to tear that throat up," this ignorant motherfucker says to me as he removes the blindfold, then the tape from around my mouth. Although his face is hidden behind a black ski mask, I can tell he's smirking. He's not one of the two who kidnapped me from the mall. He's taller and thicker. And more arrogant than the nigga who said he wanted to rough me up. His voice is also much deeper; more menacing than the others. He's wearing faded blue jeans, a gray wife beater and a pair of green, white and gray AirMax 95s. "Yeah, I hear you got niggas beggin' ya ass for some of that neck, but ya stuck-up ass be on some extra shit, tryna play muhfuckas. Well, guess what, bitch? A nigga like me doesn't take 'no' for an answer. I take what the fuck I want. Now I'ma treat you like the nasty, lil' freaky, dick-teasing, cumslut you are. You wanna live, bitch?"

I nod my head, praying I'm not killed.

"Then you had better suck my dick and swallow my nut for ya life…and you better not choke, vomit, or fuck it up. You understand?" I nod again, watching him massage his crotch area. A lump forms in his jeans. I shift my gaze from his growing dick to the butt of his gun tucked down in his waistband. A silent reminder of what will happen if I don't do exactly what I'm told. "Answer me, bitch, when I fuckin' speak to you. Do you fuckin' understand?"

I nod. "Yes," I meekly respond.

"Good," he says, pulling his gun out from his waist, then holding it in his left hand. He uses his other hand to unbuckle his belt, then unzip his jeans. He lets them fall down around his knees. He's not wearing any underwear. His balls are huge and hairy. His semi-erection is thickening with each stroke of his hand. He waves his dick in my face. *OhmyGod, if I have to suck this nigga off I hope he at least washed*, I think as he approaches me. The tip of his dick is pointing straight at me, like an angry arrow waiting to pierce through my lips. I jerk my head back. I decide I'm not sucking shit! I don't like this nigga.

"You fucking piece of shit!" I snap. Yes, I'm deathly afraid of not getting out of here alive, but I'm also disgusted, and pissed, at the way this nigga is treating me, having me tied up and talking to me any ole kind of way, like I'm some rabid dog.

"Oh, you wanna front on a nigga, huh, bitch? Talkin' all slick 'n greasy," he snaps, snatching me by the neck. With one hand, he lifts me up out of the chair by the throat. "Bitch, don't you know I will snap ya muthafuckin' neck?" This nigga is literally choking the shit out of me. I feel my eyes starting to bulge out of their sockets. "You either suck my dick or you gonna die tonight, ho. You understand me?"

I nod my head with pleading eyes. Reluctantly, he loosens his grip from around my neck, sitting me back in my chair. Surprisingly, his dick is rock-hard. He brings it back up to my face, pressing the head to my lips, forcing them apart. "Bitch, open ya muthafuckin' mouth and suck that shit like you love it."

He tells me to lick it. I reluctantly do so. He tells me to kiss it. I begrudgingly do. Then he tells me to slowly open my mouth and make an 'oh' shape. I do that as well. "And I don't wanna feel no fuckin' teeth on my shit, either. Or I'ma knock every muthafuckin' tooth outta ya head. You got that?"

I nod. Under normal circumstances I would tell his ass that I suck dick, not scrape it. But I'll show him instead. He pushes his dick slowly into the center of my mouth, parting my lips wider. He fucks my mouth as if it's a pussy, every so often pulling the head of his dick out to the opening, then slowly pushing back in. I keep my eyes open and locked on his every move. Watch him intently as he grunts, making contorted facial expressions. He drops his left hand to his side, tightly squeezing the handle of his gun.

As hard as I am trying to get into it, I am struggling. Yet, there's a warped, sadistic, part of me wishing this scenario of being tied up, held hostage, and having my mouth and throat fucked was a willing act on my part. Not forced. Not under threat.

My mind is reeling, trying to figure out a way to get out of here. But my first thought is getting my hands free; or at least one of them free. Though risky—and I'm sure deadly, I entertain the thought of grabbing him by the balls, digging my nails into his skin, then forcefully twisting them until I rip the mother-fuckers off.

"Suck my balls, bitch," he orders, removing his dick from my mouth. He slaps it up against my lips before lifting up his balls for me to put in my mouth.

I grin, slowly licking them. Then I open wide and let him drop them down into my mouth. I suck and swallow them. Get him moaning. I look up at him. Watch him enjoying every minute of my mouth, then bite down on them, clamp my jaws tight and chew down on his balls. He yells and screams, punching me about the face and head to get me off of him. But I am too numb by anger and hurt and fear to feel anything. This nigga wants his dick and balls wet, thinks he can disrespect me, then I am determined to give him a little extra to remember me by. I continue chewing his balls until I draw blood. He grabs me by the face, tries to pry my mouth open.

"Aaaaah, shit…fuck! Aaaaaaaah! Somebody come down here and help me get this bitch off of me!"

Someone runs down the stairs. "Yo, what the fuck?!"

"Nigga!" he yells. "Don't just stand there. Get this bitch offa my muthafuckin' balls…Aaaaaaah, fuck!"

The other nigga tries to help him pry my lips off of him. But I've become a pit bull. He's screaming at the top of his lungs. Hearing his agonizing cries only fuels me. "Yo, nigga, what the fuck did you do to her? She's not letting go, son." He squeezes my nose; tries to shut off my air, thinking that'll get me to open my mouth. But this dumb fuck doesn't know that I'm an avid swimmer; that I can hold my breath for four minutes without blinking.

"Fuck! Get this bitch offa me. Goddaaaaaaamn it! She's biting my balls off! Shoot this bitch!" I don't let go until the nigga's knees buckle and I have blood seeping out of my mouth. I spit at him, satisfied.

He grabs his bloody balls, screaming. The nigga's sweating and shaking. His partner catches him before he hits the floor. "You a dead bitch," he screams, stumbling. His boy helps him up the stairs with his pants still wrapped around his ankles. "You hear me! Dead! Aaaah, fuck! "

"Fuck you! You ball-less, bitch-ass nigga."

I yell and scream at the top of my lungs, hoping someone on the outside hears me.

THIRTY-ONE

I am not sure how many hours or days go by before I hear someone else unlocking the basement door, then flipping on the light. I have to blink a few times to adjust my eyes. I see a pair of Timberland clad feet, followed by long, muscular legs coming down the stairs. He's in a pair of Duke Basketball shorts and has on a white wife beater. Like everyone else, his face is masked. He's carrying a tray of food. I'm not sure what is on the tray, but whatever it is, it smells good. Like curry. My stomach growls as he gets closer to me and the aroma assaults my nose. I am weak to the point that I actually feel sick.

He sets the food on the pool table, then grabs a wooden dinner tray and sets it up in front of me. He removes the tape from my mouth. There's something about him that's different from the others. He seems calmer. And hopefully, he has a heart.

"Listen, I brought you something to eat and drink. You hungry?" I nod. Attempt to speak, but the back of my throat feels like it has been swallowing sandpaper. He grabs the drink from off the tray, then kneels down in front of me. "Here, drink." He holds the straw up to my lips. I take long, deep sips, allowing the cold, sweet elixir to soothe and moisten my throat. It's an Arnold Palmer—a mixture of sweet tea and lemonade, one of my favorite drinks.

"Thank you," I am finally able to say in a whisper.

"I hope you like curried chicken and rice and peas," he says, scooping up a forkful, then bringing it up to my lips. My mouth waters. Again, I nod. I open my mouth and let him feed me. I stare at him; try to see his eyes, but he won't make eye contact with me. He shifts them, almost nervously. *Maybe he has a conscience*, I think. There is something strangely familiar about him.

I chew, then swallow. "Please," I beg in a whisper, "let me go. I promise I won't tell anyone. I just want to go home." I feel myself starting to get choked up. Tears well up in my eyes. "Please…"

"Listen, that's not gonna happen," he tells me, dashing any hopes that he might have an ounce of empathy for me, maybe even become an ally. "But if you wanna get outta here alive, then you gotta do what they tell you, understand me?" I nod. A single tear rolls down my cheek, then another.

"Don't let them do this to me."

He shifts his eyes again. "No one wants to hurt you," he offers.

"Then what do they want with me? To rape me? Fuck me all night, what?"

He hangs his head. "To teach you a lesson."

"A lesson? What kind of lesson can I learn from being tied up like some dog?" He lowers his voice, glances over his shoulder to make sure no one's around. "Look, I shouldn't be tellin' you this, ma. This shit's almost over. All you gotta do is handle ya business and it's gonna be over. We gonna let you go as long as you do what you're told, feel me?"

I nod. "Why you telling me all this?"

He stares at me. "I have my reasons," he tells me. "Eat it up." He scoops up another forkful of food, then shovels it into my mouth. He alternates between feeding me and giving me sips of my drink. Although he isn't willing to help me get out of here or to give me any more information, I appreciate him not manhandling me like the others. I appreciate him saying as much as he has.

When I am finished eating, he tells me that he is going to untie me and let me use the bathroom, take a shower, then put on clean clothes. My mind immediately begins to race, plotting my escape. But, again, my hopes are quickly shot to pieces when he tells me that the bathroom door will be open. That there are no windows in the bathroom, or exit doors with the exception of the one that is chained up so if I have any ideas of trying to escape to forget it. He tells me that there are other niggas upstairs so it wouldn't be in my best interest to try, or do, anything slick.

"I'm your safest bet," he adds, standing up and removing the tray table from in front of me. "But I'm warning you. Don't take my kindness for weakness. We understand each other?"

I nod. "Do I have to suck your dick, too?" I ask.

He shakes his head, walking toward the steps. "Nah, I'm good. I'll be back to help you get cleaned up." The way he walks, his body build, is familiar to me. I stare at him. *I know this man...I know this man*, I think, watching him climb the stairs and disappear behind the door—to freedom, *but where?*

THIRTY-TWO

It is night out. There is no light coming in through the small window over in the corner. Calm One has been the only one coming down to check on me, uncuffing me, taking me to the bathroom, and allowing me to stretch. He hasn't said much more than what he's said to me earlier. I guess he knows he said more than he should have. Still, he can barely keep his eyes off my body. He glances at his watch, then looks over at the door. He whispers, "Yo, ma. It's 'bout to go down. Keep ya head, aiight? This shit's almost over."

I nod, knowingly. The next minute, the door opens and a bunch of loud, rowdy niggas come stomping down the stairs. The moment of reckoning has come. *The grand finale*, I think, swallowing back my nerves. I count—one, two, three, four, five, six of them. They all have on ski masks. And different color basketball shorts. Easy access, I suppose. They start talking shit, cat-calling and what-not. I can tell they've been drinking.

"Gottttdaaaaamn, this bitch is fiiiyah."

"Word is bond; she sexy as fuck!"

"Daaaamn, she's the bitch suckin' niggas outta they minds?"

"Wooo-ooooh, she got my dick hard already."

"Yo, she bit the shit outta L. Tried to take that nigga's balls off, yo."

They laugh. "Yeah, I heard she had that nigga cryin' like a lil bitch. She try that shit on my joint and I'ma take her pretty head off."

"Word up," they all agree.

"Yo, uncuff that bitch," the nigga wearing red shorts says to Calm One. "I'm ready to get this party started. He has a blunt dangling from his mouth. "I wanna see what all the hype is about this ho. She got muhfuckas talkin' like she's the new Superhead or some shit."

Calm One walks behind me, squats down, then whispers, "Remember what I told you." He uncuffs me, then walks over to the other side of the room.

Red Shorts walks over to me, grabs me by the face and puffs on his blunt. He squeezes my face. "Yo, ma, you pretty as fuck. But I will beat you the fuck up if you scrape, cut, or bite my shit, ya dig?" I nod. "That's what it is. Now let's see ya work."

I look around the room, scan the niggas gawking at me, then catch Calm One's eyes. He nods his head on the sly. Funny thing, I've always prided myself on being a phenomenal head giver; on knowing how to take care of a man's dick—to not only suck it, but to make love to it. To slob it because I love it; because I adore it. There's something about slobbering all over a dick, twirling my tongue all over it—its slit slick with sweet precum, gliding my lips and mouth up and down its length, engulfing it—that has always made my pussy wet, but not this time. And not under these conditions. I never imagined I'd have to do what I enjoy in order to save my own damn life. Still, if these motherfuckers want a five-star show, then damn it…that's what they'll get.

The only thing on my mind as I reach out and touch the front of Red Shorts' shorts is getting out of here alive, and getting home. I slowly rub his dick until it starts to grow. Then I reach for his waist and pull his shorts and boxers down. His dick is discolored. It's light brown with a reddish tip, and curved. I take it in my hand. Kiss it, lick it, then take him in my mouth. I bob my head slowly at first, then pick up speed, making popping sounds with my mouth.

"Aaah, shit..."

"How that shit feel, man?" I hear someone ask.

Red Shorts dips at the knees. "Nigga, what you think? Good, muhfucka."

Someone laughs.

"Aaaaah, fuck, baby...goddamn...shit, baby...aaaaah, shit. Oh, fuck... oh fuck...I'm cumming...aaaah..."

I pull out and jerk him off, letting his nut hit me in the face. Niggas start clowning his ass for busting off so quick. "Yo, fuck all ya'll muhfuckas. I haven't busted a nut in three days. You let this bitch suck you and let's see how long you hold out."

"Fifty says I can make this bitch's jaws lock," the nigga wearing yellow shorts says. He pulls out a fifty dollar bill, slapping it on the pool table. Red Shorts bets him.

"Yeah, aiight," Red Shorts says. "Make it lock, muhfucka."

Yellow shorts steps up to me. I look up at him. "Damn, this bitch is sexy," he says, pulling his shorts down. His dick is *real* short and fat. I keep a straight face, slipping him in my mouth. It doesn't take much effort to swallow him. But the nigga proves me wrong. His dick is a *grow*er, not a *show*er. It starts off small, but grows into a long, thick dick. I slurp and gargle and slob him down until his knees start to buckle. Niggas in back of him are cheering him on. Hooting and hollering. But in the end, he loses. The nigga starts shooting his seeds all over the place. Everyone laughs. "Yeah, muhfucka," Red Shorts says, sparking another blunt. "Just what I thought, nigga. That bitch's neck game is da truth."

The rest of the night these niggas take turns getting swabbed. Finally they decide they want to get creative and have me crawling around on the floor. Shouting out orders like: "Get on ya fuckin' knees." When I don't move quick enough someone comes at me yelling, "I said get on ya gotdaamn knees, bitch!"

Someone else yells, "I'ma fuck that throat real good. Crawl, bitch."

Then someone else demands, "Look at this dick, bitch! Look at how hard you got it. I'ma face-fuck the shit outta you. Open your motherfucking mouth. Say, 'Aaaaah', bitch!"

"Where the fuck you think you going, bitch? You're going the wrong way. Crawl ya ass over here …"

"Nah, fuck that," another nigga says. "Bring ya ass over here. My dick needs to get wet, too…"

"You surrounded by a buncha dicks, bitch…suck 'em all…there you go…suck on all them fuckin' cocks ," another nigga shouts.

"Open wide, bitch…Say aaaah."

"Aaaah, shiiiiiiiiit. This is one deep-throat suckin' bitch, yo…"

"Lick my fuckin' balls, bitch . Yeah, teabag them shits ."

This shit goes on for what feels like forever. There's a long glob of spit hanging from my chin. Cum dangles from my lashes, drips from my nose, is smeared all over my face. My knees are starting to burn; beginning to ache and bleed from crawling on the concrete. I'm gasping for air; gagging. Gulping in air.

Every last one of these masked niggas have made me feel cheap and dirty. But I suck them and make their knees buckle and their bodies shake, holding back my tears. I want to get out of here. Every so often I turn my eyes over toward Calm One. He watches me quietly, reassures me with his eyes that this shit's almost over.

I continue sucking, continue slurping, continue teabagging until they all can barely stand. Calm One finally walks over and puts an end to the show. He tells them all it's a wrap. Tells them they need to get me out of here. He helps me up off my knees. Walks me back over to the chair, then handcuffs me. Everyone stands around bragging, gloating, and clowning those who nutted faster than the others. Then they all follow Calm One upstairs. It isn't until the door closes that I keel over and throw my guts up.

When the door opens again, someone shuts the light off. It closes. And I am sitting here in pitch darkness. There are no sounds. No one is stirring around upstairs. I think I hear steps creaking. But I am not certain. I can't say anything. Then out of nowhere there's a dark shadow swiftly up on me. I can't make out who it is. Everything is black. He is wearing all dark colors and a mask. A gloved hand quickly goes around my throat and, at any moment this nigga—whoever he is—will either beat me unconscious or kill me. The latter seems to be his intention.

THIRTY-THREE

I awake in excruciating pain. There's a vicious throbbing in my head. I try to open my eyes to take in my surroundings. But… my left eye feels heavy as if someone has placed a weight on top of it from being punched in it. My right eyelid flutters. I attempt to open it against the bright white lights, but it is too goddamn painful. I can hear a machine beeping next to me.

Slowly, reality finally sinks in…He didn't kill me. He left me for dead. But I am alive! Somehow, I am in the hospital. I am not sure if I should be thankful that those crazy motherfuckers didn't murder me like they threatened, taunted, they would. Or if I should be pissed the fuck off that they didn't.

My lips burn and feel cracked and sore. I attempt to swallow, but my throat is raw and dry. There's a tube in my right arm. *Probably an IV tube*, I think, wincing at the thought of having been blindfolded and beaten and choked and forced to do sexually degrading things to a room full of unknown niggas who took turns having their way with me—fucking my throat, nutting in my mouth, my face, while slapping me around. *OhmyGod, I hope none of them niggas gave me an STD, or infected me with HIV or Hepatitis.* How the hell will I ever be able to look at Jasper? What do I tell him? That I was kidnapped? Raped? That I sucked a bunch of dicks and turned a few niggas out? What can I possibly tell him?

Someone comes into the room and starts fumbling with the

tube in my arm, checking my fluids. A nurse, I believe. As she's leaving from my bedside, someone else enters the room. *Jasper*, I say in my head. Before he ever opens his mouth, I know it's him. I can feel his presence; smell his scent.

"Is she okay? Has she awakened yet?" I hear him ask.

"She's stirred some," the female voice says. "But she hasn't actually opened her eyes. Her vitals are good, so that's an excellent sign."

I try to speak, but my jaw is wired. My lips are dry. My body is weak and sore. I groan, wanting to lick my chapped lips.

"Hey, baby," he says. I mumble words inaudible to him, forcing my one eye open. Jasper's face comes into view as he takes my hand into his. He smiles at me. "Don't try to speak, baby. You had me worried as fuck, yo."

I scan the room the best I can with one eye. See the nurse walking back into the room. He tells her I'm awake. "I'm going to get the doctor to come in and take a look at her," she replies, turning around.

"Aiight, cool," Jasper says.

"How long have I been here?" I ask, straining. It hurts to talk; it burns when I swallow. Four days, he tells me. Tells me an early morning jogger found me lying in the park, bloody and unconscious, and dialed 9-1-1.

"Why would someone wanna do this, yo? You know how fucked up I've been over this?"

"I don't know," I whisper, turning my head from him. How the fuck do I tell him that I literally sucked a looney nigga out of his crazy-ass mind? How do I tell him that I was bored and horny and got caught up posting ads for oral sex? That I've become a full-fledged cock and cum whore?

"Damn, baby. You had a muhfucka so fuckin' worried 'bout ya

sexy ass. Word is bond! You had a nigga stressin' hard, yo." He squeezes my hand, then brings it up to his full lips and kisses it.

Jasper becomes quiet, staring off into the distance. I watch him out of my one good eye, wondering what's going through his mind. He looks tired, worried. And my heart aches, knowing that I'm the cause of his troubles. I squeeze his hand, bringing his attention back to me. When he turns to look at me, I notice tears gliding down his face.

"What's wrong, baby?" I hear myself asking in my head, feeling myself becoming overwhelmed with care and concern and guilt and love for him. "Talk to me."

He shakes his head as if he can hear me. "I'm so fuckin' glad you aiight, feel me? This shit...not knowin' where you were had ya man fucked up, for real, yo ." His voice trails off as he's wiping his tears. "I've never cried over no fuckin' chick before, yo. That's how fucked up this shit has been for me."

I am staring at him, hurting for him, for me. Wishing I could have stayed off my knees, kept the dicks out of my throat, and waited for Jasper to come home to me, like I promised him I would. Seeing him cry is killing me.

"I love you so fucking much, yo," he tells me. He lets his tears fall unchecked. "Seeing you like this hurts me."

I hear one of my attackers' voices in my head. *You stuck up, dicksucking bitch. I'ma gag you on my cock for a while. Then when I'm done with that, I'm gonna flip you over and mercilessly fuck you in that fat, juicy ass of yours until I bust my nut in you. Then I'ma give you a piss enema deep in ya ass. After that, we should toss ya smutty ass out so you can face the world knowing you've been completely degraded and humiliated. And if you ever open ya fuckin' mouth to tell anyone, I'm gonna hunt you down and slice your muthafuckin' throat.*

I feel myself choking back tears. I squeeze Jasper's hand, my

only way of comforting him. *I hope I didn't lose the baby*, I think,
shutting my eyes. *I will never be able to forgive myself if my reckless-
ness caused something to happen to my baby.* Instinctively, he touches
my stomach as if he senses my burning need to know. "I'm all
fucked-up inside, baby. I'm tellin' you, yo. This shit had a muhfucka on edge." He lets out a sigh. "I'm so fuckin' relieved you
and the baby are aiight. That's all that matters; feel me, yo? If I
woulda lost you and my seed, I'da lost it for real, yo. We con-
nected, baby. You hear me?" I nod. "For life." His eyes lock onto
mine. There's pain and hurt mixed with love in them. I stare
back at him, unblinking. My heart aches for the pain I've caused
him. Tears are streaming down my face. I close my eye, again.
Slowly turn my head from him. *To teach you a lesson... To teach you
a lesson...To teach you a lesson...*The words replay in my head, over
and over. *To teach you a lesson...To teach you a lesson...To teach you
a lesson...*I swallow, hard. Slowly, I turn my head back toward Jasper.
He's talking to two detectives, a white male and black female. I
overhear him telling them to come back in a few days; that I need
my rest. Another voice blares in my head, causing a pounding
headache to surface. *Yo, nigga, what the fuck you doin'? She's pregnant... I told you, muhfucka, nothin' happens to her or her baby...*

She's pregnant. She's pregnant. She's pregnant. Those words echo
in my head as I repeat them over and over and over, again. How
did he know I was pregnant? The only person who knew was...I
blink back tears. *OhmyGod, it can't be.* I glance at Jasper. Watch
him wipe tears from his face. I stare at him as he walks over to
me. He shares a slight smile. Pain shoots through my head. I let
out a loud groan, which causes Jasper to press the button for the
nurse. *Don't have me fuck you up, yo...If I find out you playin' me,
yo...I'ma fuck you up...I'ma fuck you up...I'ma fuck you up...*I blink,
blink again...*she's pregnant...to teach you a lesson...*

He sees it in my eyes—fear. The nurse rushes in. I hear him tell her that I'm in pain. I grunt louder. "Helllllllp...me..."

The nurse rubs my hand. "I know, sweetie; you're in a lot of pain."

I grunt louder. "Helllllllp...meeeee..."

"I know, sweetie. I'm going to see about getting you something for the pain." I shake my head, grunt again. "Nnoooooooooo... helllllllllllp...me." She continues to fumble with my IV. Tells me everything's going to be okay. She doesn't understand my grunting. Jasper does.

"Yo, is she aiight?" I hear Jasper ask. "Is the baby okay?"

"Her vitals seem good. But I'm going to have the doctor come in and have a look at her," I hear the nurse tell him.

"I'm worried about her and my baby."

"Don't worry. Your fiancé and baby will be fine. Let me go get the doctor."

I grunt again. Make loud, agonizing growling sounds as she walks out of the room.

*I'ma fuck you up...let me find out you playin' me, yo...I'ma fuck you up...to teach you a lesson...She's pregnant...*Everything around me is blurry, but I think I see Jasper smirking. Or is he smiling. He leans in, kisses me on the forehead, then softly on the lips. "I know what you're thinkin', baby..." I hear him say.

My head is pounding. The tears burn my eyes. I blink them away. I feel like someone is crushing my chest. I struggle to breathe. Fight for air. I'm starting to hyperventilate. *OhmyGod! OhmyGod! OhmyGod!*

Jasper strokes my face. "It's over wit', baby...all that shit you was doin'..." He pauses, lets his words hover over me. Then he leans into my ear and whispers, "I warned you, Pasha. Told you don't fuckin' play me, yo."

ABOUT THE AUTHOR

Cairo is the author of *Daddy Long Stroke*, *The Manhandler* and *The Kat Trap*. He resides in New Jersey, where he is working on his next literary creation, *Kitty-Kitty, Bang-Bang*. His travels to Egypt are what inspired his pen name. You can email him at: cairo2u@verizon.net. Or visit him at www.booksbycairo.com, www.myspace.com/cairo2u, www.facebook.com/CairoBlack, or www.blackplanet.com/cairo2u

IF YOU ENJOYED "DEEP THROAT DIVA,"
CHECK OUT

KITTY-KITTY, BANG-BANG

COMING FALL 2011 FROM STREBOR BOOKS

CHAPTER ONE

> *Fly, exotic bitch wit' the long lashes and slanted eyes...smooth, buttery thighs...fat ass...soft lips...got niggas 'n they bitches tryna get up in these hips...got 'em turnin' tricks...beggin' to lick the clit...while I'm ridin' down on a nigga's dick...got muhfuckas lined up to get glazed wit' my cream...niggas tossin' 'n turnin'... can't get me outta they dreams...Ice on my neck, wrists and hands...Hermès Birkin bag draped on my arm...diamond stilettos on my feet...don't be misled...I'm from the hood, baby...shit ain't sweet...do me wrong...end up dead...*

'Scuse me, bitches! Can I have ya attention, please? In case some of you hatin'-ass tricks and hoes forgot who I am, let me reintroduce myself. I'm that cinnamon-colored beauty with that sexy swagger and straight-up bangin' body that keeps the bitches rollin' they eyes—and niggas recklessly eyeballin' me, undressin' and tryna mentally fuck me. I'm that chick rockin' all the fly wears and pushin' the hot-ass whip that all the other bitches wanna be like. I'm the chick bitches still wanna hate, but love to grin up in her face, always wantin' to be up in her space 'cause I'm e'erything they'll never be. Rich, fly and mutha-fuckin' F-I-N-E! Not braggin'; just keepin' shit real. Bitch, *whaaaat?*

Call me shallow, call me superficial; call me whatever the fuck floats ya boat, but know this: you'll never call a bitch broke, busted, or beat down. So keep hatin'. Keep poppin' shit. Keep pickin' ya face up. 'Cause a bitch like me feeds you dust. So, poof!

Annnnnnnywho, for my bitches and niggahs who I fucks wit', I was on hiatus for a hot minute. I had'a step outta the game to get my mind right. 'Cause on some real shit, after how shit went down in Atlantic City it had a bitch's dome all jacked. Oh, trust. I heard how some'a them corny-ass broads were tryna come at my neck for puttin' a bullet in Grant's bucket. Predictable, they say? Uh, what the fuck them birds thought I was gonna do? Let the nigga walk after he done popped up in the room and saw I done bodied his brotha? Bitch, puhleeze. You must be smokin' that shit if you thought I was gonna let that nigga get a free pass. Yeah, he had that bomb-ass dick. And yeah, the nigga's head game was sick. He knew how'ta tongue-fuck this pussy 'til a bitch shook. But, fuck what ya heard. Good dick, slam-min' tongue, or not. My number one rule is: No witnesses, no evi-dence. Period! So say what the fuck you want. I'ma paid bitch, not a dumb one.

Still, I'ma keep it raw wit'cha. For a hot minute, my soul ached. It ripped a bitch's heart to have'ta lay that fine, sexy nigga down. And yeah...I dropped a few tears. But there was no other option. Well, none that was gonna work for me. Prison, not! Him puttin' lead in me, not! Me stressin', wonderin' if the nigga's gonna be on some revenge-type shit, not! So, he had to go. And for a bitch like me, it was for the best.

Like I told ya'll from the dip, I fucked for sport. But I murdered for business. *Yes*, you heard me. I said *fucked* and *murdered* as in past tense. Well, for now, that is. It's been almost two years since a bitch rode down on sum dick, then took the nigga's head off. Shit, a bitch ain't had no dick since...neva mind. I ain't in the mood to get into it right now.

Annnnnywaaaayz, when I was bodyin' muhfuckas, there was no time for compassion or sympathy. And there was definitely no time for muthafuckin' regret. Unfortunately, Grant got caught up bein' at the wrong place at the wrong time, and got got. The shit wasn't personal. I couldn't let it be. It was 'bout clockin' that paper 'cause a bitch was gettin' paid by the body. Not gettin' clanked up. So fuck all that ying-yang ya'll been poppin'. I had'a do what I had'a do. And sheddin' a buncha tears 'bout sum shit I couldn't change wasn't gonna bring the nigga back. He was dead. And a bitch had'a keep pressin'. So, yes, I put back on my wig, slipped my chrome back into my bag and slid outta the hotel room, chokin' back tears. When I got back to my rental and had to make that call to Cash that was one'a the hardest things I had'a do. I remember, takin' a deep breath, tryna steady my voice as I told him, "I know why the caged bird sings."

"That's what it is," he said to me as he always did each time I called him to let him know a mission was completed. Then after I told him that there was another body in the room, I had'a tell him that a bitch needed a break. I knew if I didn't bounce I was gonna end up snappin' or doin' sum other reckless shit. Like I told ya'll before I knew that shit was in my blood—killin'. Lookin' into a nigga's eyes, splatterin' his fuckin' brains while ridin' down on his dick did sumthin' to a bitch. Made my pussy hot, made it pop. The thrill of the kill turned me on. And it overshadowed the risks. But that shit down in Atlantic City cost me sumthin'. It cost me what was startin' to feel like love—well, at least the idea of it—and the chance to finally be free.

However, a bitch had'a get the fuck over it. Heartache and cryin' over a nigga ain't what I do. My name ain't Juanita, okay? Uh, duh, the neglectful bitch—yes, you heard me right. I said *bitch!*—who dropped me outta her hairy pussy for those of you who can't remember the script. I saw enough of that shit growin' up watchin' her dumb ass go nutty over the dick. I swore I would never, *ever* be her. And I mean that.

Speakin' of that bird, I haven't seen or spoken to her ass since that night she came to my spot with her face all banged the fuck up by that young nigga she was fuckin'. Then she had the fuckin' audacity to bring her sister Rosa wit' her ass. And that bitch came poppin' outta bushes tryna bring it, callin' me out to fight her like the ghetto-ass bird she is. Get real. I'm done wit' all of 'em. As far as I'm concerned I ain't got no family. And I made that very clear when I pulled my chrome out on 'em. And, hell muthafuckin' yeah, don't get it twisted. I woulda put a bullet in both of them bitches. E'erything Juanita stands for makes me fuckin' sick. She's a weak bitch in my eyes. And I don't respect her. Nor do I have any love for her. But the crazy thing is I don't hate her ass either. I don't feel shit for her. I guess 'cause I learned to finally accept who she was, and is—neglectful, selfish, and straight pathetic. Which is why I had no problem lookin' her dead in her busted-up eyes and tellin' her flat out that I wanted nuthin' else to do wit' her, then slammin' my door in her raggedy-ass face. I meant that shit on e'erything I love. And that ain't much, trust.

My cell phone rings, snappin' me outta my thoughts. I grab it off the nightstand, peepin' the digits.

"Bitch," Chanel snaps in my ear the minute I answer. "What took ya ass so long to answer?"

"Slut," I snap back, "the last time I checked I wasn't suckin' ya clit so pump ya raggedy brakes 'fore you get ya fronts knocked."

She laughs. "Trick, puhleeze. Ya ass 'posed pick up on da first ring. You know what it is, boo. Don't have ma-ma spank that ass." She laughs harder. *Oh, I see this ho is in rare form this mornin'*, I think as I try 'n hold back a yawn.

"Yeah, I know you better fall back wit' all that *boo* 'n *ma-ma* shit. I done warned ya ass 'bout that lesbo shit. It's too early in the fuckin' mornin' for that clit-lickin' bullshit." She continues laughin'. This bitch is my girl 'n all, but I swear sometimes she be on some real extra shit. Not that I give a fuck if she's poppin' tits 'n clits in her mouth, 'cause she's gonna be my girl, regardless. But a bitch like me is only takin' a dick that's attached to a real nigga in the back of her throat and deep in her fat pussy. "Hahaha, hell, bitch. I can't stand nuthin' yo' cum-guzzlin' ass stand for."

"Yeah, right," she says, crackin' up. "That's what ya mouth says."

"*Whaaat*eva. Why the fuck is you callin' me, tramp?"

"Fuck all that you talkin'," she says, chucklin'. "Oh, before I forget, guess who I ran into the other night and was askin' 'bout you?"

"Who?"

"Patrice. And as usual ya aunt was dipped in some ill shit."

I roll my eyes. Yeah, I'll give it to her ass, though. The ho definitely knows how'ta throw it on. But, she still ain't as bad as me. And she damn sure ain't servin' me. *I bet her ass is still livin' up in da projects wit' Nana, triflin' bitch!* "Mmmph, where you see that roach at?" She tells me she ran into her at the Ledisi concert at BB King Blues Club and Grill in Times Square. "Well, I don't know why the fuck she was tryna check for me."

"She wanted to know what you were up to, then started talkin' 'bout how you done got all brand new on e'eryone, changin' ya numbers 'n shit."

"Yup, fuck all'a them hoes. And I hope you didn't tell that bitch shit, either."

"Oh, she was tryna fish me, but trust…you already know. I got you. I kept it real cute."

"Good. They all dead to me."

"I hear you, girl. But, damn…that's kinda harsh."

"Harsh my ass. It is what it is."

"Kat, you know I usually keep my mouth shut, but this craziness between ya'll has been goin' on for too long. That's still ya family, girl. Don't you think it's time ya'll try 'n peace shit up?"

"Yeah, when that bitch's in a box and I spit on her grave. Then it's peace. Until then, that bitch is invisible to me."

"Well, alrighty then. Movin' right along. The reeeeal reason I was callin' ya ass is to find out when you bringin' ya dusty-ass back to the East Coast. There's this bangin'-ass party comin' up the end of next month and you need to have ya ass here for it."

"Umm, Sweetie, you know I ain't beat to be 'round a buncha played-out, dick-thirsty Wal-mart bitches."

"Trick, don't clown me. You know I wouldn't be callin' ya ass for no low-budget showdowns. This is all top-of-da-line dick and dollas, boo."

"Hmmph. Who's givin' it?" I ask, tryna decide if I wanna blaze. I glance at the clock. 8:45 A.M. I get outta bed and walk over to my armoire and open it. I pull out a bag of purple haze. Open it, then take a deep whiff, closin' my eyes. *Yeah, this that good shit right here, but I ain't feelin' it.* I reseal the bag, then toss it back in the drawer, pullin' out the chocolate thai. *Yeah, this is what'a bitch needs to jumpstart the mornin'.*

"Remember that baller nigga Thug Gee from Newark who gave that party at Studio 9 before the shit shut down?"

"Yeah," I state, pullin' out my Dutches. I lay my stash and cigars on the nightstand, then go into the bathroom. I sit on the toilet. How could I ever forget that party? That's the night I met Grant. The night I dropped down low, popped my hips, and pressed my juicy ass up against his cock and grinded into him 'til his shit bricked up. The night I knew I'd end up fuckin' him. It's the same night e'ery bitch on the floor wish they coulda been me.

"Well, he's throwin' another one in Manhattan at Eden..." Mmmph. She's talkin' 'bout that spot over on Eight Ave between Forty-sixth and Forty-seventh streets. It used to be the China Club back in the day. Anyway, it has a lil' rooftop area for peeps to sit 'n chill and get they drink on wit'out all that loud music beatin' 'em in the head when they tired of bein' hemmed up inside. And the music's real cute. But from what I remember, the two times I went there, the drinks weren't hittin' on shit and they had more bitches than niggas up in there. And most of 'em wasn't even dimes. And the few that did look like sumthin' they weren't no high-end bitches. And the truth is, I ain't have no business up in there wit' 'em.

"If I decide to come through you need to make sure ya ass gotta back-up plan for us in case that shit is busted."

"Oh, trust. Word has it it's gonna be fiiiyah. You know that nigga only rolls wit' them baller niggas."

I roll my eyes, wipin' my snatch, then flushin' the toilet. This thirsty bitch stays tryna find her next trick. "Umm, what's good wit' Divine?" I ask sarcastically, checkin' to see if the nigga's still dickin' her. I'm at the sink washin' my hands, admirin' my reflection in the mirror. *Hmmph, even wit' ya hair tossed all over ya head, and sleep in ya eyes you still a hot, buttery bitch!*

She sucks her teeth. "He's just dandy. Thank you, very much."

I step back into my bedroom, sittin' on the side of the bed while I split open a Dutch and pack it wit' my mornin' get right. "I'm glad to hear that. I've always liked that nigga. Is he still rabbit-fuckin' you, or has his stroke game improved?"

Now, typically askin' a bitch 'bout her man's dick game is a no-no, but since she's always put it out there in the past that his dick game was mad whack; that he be fuckin' her mad fast and whatnot, then nuttin' off in minutes—then it's a fair question.

"Girl, he finally got that shit together. Took him two years to learn how'ta slow it down and not be so damn eager to nut. I mean, damn. I know I got that bomb pussy, but still."

I suck my teeth. "Ho, please. Ain't nobody tryna hear 'bout how ill ya snatch work is. I asked you 'bout Divine handlin' his. I'm glad he finally got that situation together, though. I'd hate for him to get fucked over 'cause he ain't fuckin' you right, even though the nigga's been damn good to you."

"Sweetie, don't think I don't know what you doin'. Fuck you."

I laugh, tightly rollin' my blunt. I spark it, takin' a toke. "Ho, I got nuthin' but love for ya silly ass. But that nigga Divine needs to straight dip on ya ass 'cause you ain't ever gonna 'preciate what you got."

"Bitch, how you sound? That shit ain't true. I know what I got."

"Oh, really? And what's that?"

"I gotta nigga in my bed," she snapped servin' me up a dish of 'tude. "What'a 'bout you?"

I ig the 'tude and keep pressin'. "Ho, yeah, you might gotta nigga. But ya ass is still scrapin' the barrel tryna find ya next catch. I'm paid, bitch. I don't *need* a nigga. And a bitch ain't trickin' no niggas to make shit pop. *That's* what about me."

"Bitch, what-da-fuck-eva. You still need some dick in ya life."

I sigh, blowin' weed smoke up at the ceilin'. I swear. Hoes like her make me sick. They ain't neva satisfied wit' what the fuck they have. Always lookin' to chase down the next nigga wit' the biggest dick, or thickest knot. I don't know how the fuck that nigga don't know what time it is wit' her ass. Mmmph. A hot, fuckin' mess!

"Oh, sweetie, don't go there. How 'bout you not worry 'bout what I need, okay?"

"*You* need to get ya mind right, Chanel. Do sumthin' wit' ya'self."

"And like I said, you need to get ya back knocked. But you don't hear me comin' at ya neck all sideways 'n shit."

"Bitch, I ain't comin' at ya neck. I'm tryna get you to see you too damn fly to be birdin' ya'self out. You gotta good man. Get ya'self a hobby."

"Newsflash, boo: I gotta hobby. Checkin' niggas 'n runnin' they pockets. So instead of puttin' so much energy into my situation how 'bout you focus on ya own shit."

I let out a disgusted grunt. See. You can't tell a bitch like her nuthin'. She's too damn hardheaded. A Miss Know It All bitch gotta learn the hard way. Then again, maybe she won't. She's been fuckin' wit' Divine's ass for two years and ridin' down on a few other nigga's dicks whenever she feels like gettin' her creep on, and his ass ain't peeped it yet. Either she done fucked him blind. Or the nigga just don't give a fuck 'cause he out there doin' him, too. Nah, that ain't his style. That nigga's big on Chanel's retarded ass. Like I said, this bitch gotta good-ass man who grinds hard e'ery day; a muhfucka who'd give her anything she wants, but she'd rather be out tryna trick another muhfucka up off'a his paper. Go figure. The last time I got at this ho 'bout doin' sumthin' wit' her life—you know, goin' to school or gettin' her ass a job, she flat out told me, "Hustlin' these niggas is a job. And a bitch like me is gonna always hustle a nigga off his paper." So since then, I keep my dick sucka shut. Well, most of the time.

"Mmmph, do you, boo-boo. But, trust. When that nigga finally peeps ya game, you do know he's gonna knock ya whole grill out, right?"

She sucks her teeth. "Bitch, I ain't call ya ass for no Oprah special. All I wanna know is when you bringin' ya stankan' ass home. That's it. And for the record, there ain't shit for Divine to peep. All I'm doin' is lookin'. There's no harm in that."

I laugh. "Okay, answer me this: when's the last time you popped another nigga's dick in ya mouth?"

"No comment."

I keep laughin'. "Unh-hunh; just what I thought. What you get outta it? A new Louis bag and some jewels?"

"No."

"A few stacks?"

"Nope. An iPad."

What the fuck?! This bitch givin' up throat and she ain't get no paper. No ice. No wears; just a six-hunnid-dollar electronic gadget. No extras wit' it? OhmyGod, this bitch's fuckin' 'n suckin' for peanuts! Shit, she might as well fucked the nigga for free if you ask me. 'Cause six hunnid ain't shit, especially when you fuckin' over a muhfucka whose gonna snap and do a Chris Brown on ya ass if he ever finds out. The last time this ho gave up some charity pussy was when she fucked Cash's cousin Coal. And even then I looked at her ass like she still had the nigga's dick snot hangin' from her lips.

I pull the phone from my ear, starin' at it, then put it back to my ear. *"An iPad?* Are you fuckin' serious? Let me get this shit straight. You mean to tell me you tryna fuck up ya situation by fuckin' 'round wit' a muhfucka for some bullshit-ass gadget? Shit, Divine woulda bought ya ass that."

"Whaaateva," she snaps, tryna front like she's heated.

"Hmmph. Ya nasty ho-ass is still my girl. But don't say I didn't warn ya trick ass."

"Bitch, you make me sick. I don't know why I waste my time even fuckin' wit ya ugly ass."

"Oh, get ova it," I say, crackin' up. She gets quiet. *I musta hit a nerve.* "Oh, so now you wanna be on mute? Let me find out you on some sensitive shit. I'ma fuck you up myself."

She sucks her teeth. "Kat, lick my ass. Ain't nobody on mute nuthin'. I was doin' sumthin'."

I take another pull off a my blunt. "Oh, aiight. 'Cause I was about to say."

"Puhleeze. The only think you need to be sayin' is when you gettin' here so we can shut shit down. I ain't got all day to be fuckin' wit' ya snotty ass."

"Trick, I just saw ya ugly ass two months ago when you came out here. I ain't fuckin' wit' you like that," I tease. Although I wasn't plannin' on goin' back home 'til the summer, it's been a minute since a bitch popped these hips so I might make a special appearance. "When's this shit?"

She tells me it's the last weekend in April. Then says I should probably stay 'til after Memorial Day weekend so we can party in Miami.
"Ho, don't be tryna plan my time."

"Oh whaaateva. It ain't like you punchin' a clock where you at.
Besides, ya ass misses these east coast niggas, and you know it."

"Yeah, but I don't miss ya ugly, yellow ass," I say, takin' another pull.
"Look, hit me up later. You fuckin' up my high. You know a bitch
don't like to make plans 'til after I done sparked a fatty."

"Ooooh, save me some."

"Bitch, take ya fiend ass somewhere and go suck a dick."

"Fuck you, wit' ya monkey ass."

I choke on weed smoke. "Ho, drink bleach. You smell like you been
lickin' the back of a garbage truck." We bust out laughin' poppin'
mad shit back 'n forth 'til we finally hang up. I walk over to the glass
doors and open them, walkin' out onto the balcony. I take in the
bangin'-ass view of Mt. Tam and the San Francisco Bay. Breathe in
the crisp air. *Not bad for a bitch from da hood*, I think, takin' two deep
pulls off a my blunt. Never in a million years would I think I would
be someplace like here. Quiet. No drama. No stress. No bullshit-ass
niggas and family. I could get use to this. But, Chanel's right. I miss
the east coast. I miss the hustle 'n bustle of the city. I miss the swagger
of the streets. I miss home. I take two last tokes of my blunt, tap out
what's left, then toss it over the railin'.

For some reason, talkin' to Chanel's ass got me thinkin' 'bout summer-
time in New York. How that shit be live 'n poppin' wit' mad niggas
and bitches gettin' they shine on, flossin' and flexin'; stereos blastin'
the hot beats; muhfuckas gettin' they smoke on; hoes stuntin' on da
dick; young cats poppin' off, bringin' heat to the streets. Whew, a
bitch's pussy is startin' to overheat just thinkin' 'bout it. Yeah, Cali is
cute. This quietness and scenery is real special. But it's time for a bitch
to step back on the east coast scene 'n shake shit up a bit, then dip.

I walk back into the master bedroom, pullin' off my wife beater,
then removin' my panties. I lift open my Louis trunk, searchin' for the
perfect toy to take the edge off. Sumthin' that's gonna stretch this
pussy out. Sumthin' aggressive; sumthin' raw. I pull out the Slugger—a
ten-inch, thick, jet-black dildo. *Oh, yes, I'ma ride the shit outta you*, I

think, pullin' out its harness. I walk over to my closet and drag out my stool, strap the harness over the seat, then attach Slugger. I position the stool in front of the wall mirror. I wanna watch myself gettin' off. A bitch don't even need any Wet 'cause my juicy pussy is already leakin' wit' anticipation. I'ma ride this shit like I'm ridin' the streets of New York, fast 'n furious and full of power. I hit the remote for the stereo.

As soon as Jay-Z's "Empire State of Mind" comes on, I climb up on top of the stool, lower my hips down onto the head of my rubber companion, then slather Slugger wit' all of my creamy juices. I match my rhythm to the beat of the music. Imagine I'm on the top floor of the Empire State buildin' fuckin' a nigga named New York. A nigga whose as mean and as gritty and grimy, and as rough as its streets. *"…These streets will make you feel brand new…the lights will inspire you…let's hear it for New York, New York, New York…"*

"Oooooh, yes, New York…fuck me…aaaah…mmmm…beat this pussy up, nigga…" I buck my hips, slam my hips down onto Slugger; take it balls deep, rock back 'n forth. Scream out, "Newwwwwww York!" Then, just as I'm nuttin', a bitch falls off'a the muthafuckin' stool, bangin' her dome. I bust out laughin' as my juices spurt outta me. "Bitch, you done bust ya ass tryna get that nut. What'a mess."

I get up, wipe the cream runnin' down the inside of my thigh wit' my hand, then lick my fingas. *Pussy cream this damn good should be bottled and sold on the streets*," I think, climbin' my ass back into bed. I pull the goose comforter up over me, closin' my eyes wit' thoughts of New York, where paper is made and bitches are paid. The big city of delicious dick and muthafuckin' sweet dreams.